LAURA NAVARRE

GEMINI QUEEN

I summon the lightning.
I claim my power.
The warlocks of Icarus Academy claim me.

I start my night as a cat burglar in Singapore and I end up queen of the witching world. Too bad this rags-to-riches fairytale's a gig I never applied for and won't accept. My witchcraft is wild and lethal, so I've renounced my power. I'm a fish out of water at Icarus Academy.

But these four sexy warlocks who rule the school just won't take no for an answer.

They want me to claim my power. They want me to summon the lightning. And they want to claim me as their consort.

Because the witching world is dying, and I'm their last chance. But there's a queen killer on the hunt. Unless I figure out how to claim my power before the killer claims my head, there's a global extinction event looming.

With my name written all over it.

Gemini Queen is a dark witch academy why choose paranormal romance that features teacher-student forbidden love, steamy group interactions, possessive males, sexy shifters, first-time M/M, bi awakening, and a powerful heroine who doesn't have to choose.

Chapter One

Zara

I rappel down the ventilation shaft at midnight. Because midnight's when the shift change goes down for the forty-eight guards in the two-hundred story Tai-Sun Tower in downtown Singapore. And I need every slim edge I can possibly exploit. Because this job's about to become the boldest snatch I've ever pulled off.

And Wang Tai-Sun's not the kind of guy you want catching you when you screw his shit up.

The cable hisses in the winch like a rattlesnake as I plummet sixteen stories straight down the shaft in 26.53 seconds. Just like I timed it in the mock-up. Icy air whistles past and burns my face, but every inch of my body is alive and tingling with nerves under my catsuit.

The cable plays out. The harness snaps tight around my torso with a jerk.

My bank account might be running on fumes. But my first-rate gear's worth every cent.

Suspended in pitch black over one hundred eighty-four stories of nothing but air, sweating freely under my catsuit, I switch on the headlamp strapped over my silk beanie, then fish out the Phillips screwdriver from my utility belt.

Exactly 64.3 seconds later, according to the glowing digits racing across the face of my dive watch, I've got the grate popped and I'm slipping through the chute like a moray eel wriggling through my favorite Red Sea reef.

I'm 4.2 seconds off my personal best due to a rusted screw that sticks, but that's an acceptable margin of error for me. We allowed for that when Cleo and Xiao set the timer.

I've got a twenty-three minute cushion before they detonate the bomb.

If this job goes the way I want, I'll be sitting pretty in my latest safe house in Sharm el-Sheikh on the Red Sea coast in Egypt for at least six months before I need to plan the next heist. I'll shore dive every day right from my own little crescent beach. Read smut every night in my own little hammock. And pretend my own dad isn't offering to pay a cool two mill to whoever brings him my head in a bag.

Dad upped the bounty six months ago, the day I turned twenty, on the fifth anniversary of what I like to call my liberation from the family firm.

Another ninety-one seconds and I'm through the ventilation chute and stripping down to my unmentionables in the posh ladies' room on the vacant office floor. Wang Tai-Sun lost his tenant on this level a week ago. He hasn't landed another one yet to pay his extortionate monthly rent, but the power's still on.

I peel out of my knapsack and catsuit, zip myself into the strapless black leather dress that encases my curves like latex and barely skims my thighs, snap my favorite spiked cuff around my wrist for luck, and tug on my platform boots.

Then I pull off my beanie, stuff everything into my pack, and stow my shit out of sight in the empty cabinet under the sink.

Now all I need to do is shake out the crazy mane of teal hair that was all squashed under my cap, check my makeup in the mirror, correct a smudge from the drama queen mascara that makes my turquoise eyes pop like Betty Boop's, and grab the tiny clutch that holds my burner phone and the stolen keycard I need to unlock the elevator.

My stiletto's in my boot. And that's all the backup I typically need—other than Cleo and Xiao in the van—because my hands were registered as lethal weapons in the police station back in Vegas when I turned fourteen.

There are other powers at my disposal. But I promised myself a lifetime ago I'll never, ever use them.

I'm a good liar. It's a family tradition.

But that's one promise I'll kill to keep.

The elevator's empty, all Hollywood lights and mirrors, but there's a security cam winking red at me from the corner. I play it all casual for my viewing audience, puckering up my lips to swipe on a fresh coat of pink, leaning in to blot by planting a kiss on the glass. But my nerves are vibrating like guitar strings. Under the slide of curls swinging halfway to my ass, the back of my neck feels hot and tight.

If Wang catches me with my hand in his cookie jar, he'll send me back to my dad in pieces. Cash in on that cool two mill. Though, really, for a Hong Kong triad boss like Wang, Mick Gemini's bounty for his fugitive daughter's hide has to look like pocket change.

I shoot to the rooftop penthouse in forty-nine seconds flat. I'm a solid three secs ahead of sked when the elevator doors hum open.

For a blink, I swear to God, even I stand there gawking like a Las Vegas tourist fresh from the turnip truck thinking *Sweet Jesus, Wang, what a spread.* Because nothing says posh fucking party like a Singapore billionaire getting his fucking rocks off on New Year's fucking Eve.

There goes my potty mouth again. I know, I know. Someone should wash my mouth out with soap, etc.

Grinning for the camera, I sashay onto the rooftop pool deck with plenty of sway in my booty. When you're scamming, confidence is king. And a little sexy never hurts either. Not that it stops the hired muscle that ambles up to check my invite. High-end suit, snake eyes, with the Wang noose tattoo inked around his neck.

I flash Snake Eyes the encrypted invite on my burner phone. "Cleo Ferrari. I'm on your list."

Which sounds way better than saying *Hey, I'm Zara Gemini, the casino czar's daughter. You mess with me and I'll blow your ass all the way across the pool deck into the floating bar.*

Except I don't do that shit anymore. You know, because of that whole "renouncing my powers" thing?

I'm consistent as fuck about that.

My chic best friend/business partner/occasional girl toy has the connections to land the invites. (Yeah, I'm bi. It's the 2020s. Get over it.) I have the gear and the training to bag the target. And Xiao, who's hot as fuck and hung like you wouldn't believe, handles the tech.

When he isn't handling my body. Something else he's way too good at.

Did I mention I'm bi *and* poly?

All of which means my encrypted invite passes the once-over for Snake Eyes, Cleo's name shows up on his whitelist, and the bomb will go off in eighteen minutes just like Xiao and I planned.

"You're all clear." Snake Eyes is a pro, so he doesn't leer at my hotness in my short skirt. "Enjoy the party, Ms. Ferrari."

Hell to the yeah.

I swank my way through the well-heeled masses decked out in tuxes and glitter to the rotating bar and grab a flute of bubbly for camouflage. Time to take a hefty swallow for courage. Tiny bubbles fizz up my nose and creamy foam slides down my throat, because it's top shelf Dom. The cheerful souls splashing in the turquoise pool are mostly drunk and naked. It's a Wang party, so they'll all be fucking by dawn.

Except the bomb will go off at twelve forty. Oops.

The band's rocking out on stage and couples are getting down on the dance floor, complete with disco lighting, fog machine and crystal ball, because Singapore. There's a roped-off VIP level with models snorting coke, because Wang.

And there's a private office with a wall safe and a Fabergé egg with a microchip that's gonna get nicked tonight, because me.

And whoa, over there by the caviar bar, prowling through the scene like it's a jungle and he's an apex predator and we're all raw meat, has to be the single most impressive physical specimen of manhood in all of Southeast Asia.

I'm talking six foot plus of long legs and lean hips wrapped in butter-soft leather, a silky white shirt clinging to a chest you want to lick and biceps you want to sink your teeth in, and a luscious mane of hair like ink spilling halfway to his ass. Add a face like Adam Driver, eyes like Russian amber, and a prowl like a hunting panther?

It's a Wang party, so he's probably some kind of Chinese mafia. He's all golden skin and feral hunger and custom ink licking from his open collar like black flames.

And if he fucks like he walks, he'll set my panties on fire.

Not that I'll be testing that theory anytime soon, to my complete fucking regret. Not with Xiao's bomb going off in just under seventeen ticks. I need that egg to pay the bills and that microchip to stay under the radar.

Since my dad upped the bounty, every two-bit cleaner on the planet's gunning for my head.

So I'm a look-but-don't-touch kinda girl tonight, just sipping Wang's champagne and grooving to the tunes, while Adam works the room like he's casing it himself. He's carrying a whiskey, but he's not drinking. He's getting eye-fucked by every girl at the party and a healthy smattering of the guys, but he's not flirting. He's standing right next to a chaise sporting two girls and a guy peeling out of their party clothes and tonguing each other and pretty much about to have a hot-and-heavy three-way right there on the pool deck, but he's not watching.

What he is doing is keeping an eye on everyone who comes and goes from the lift.

And keeping track of all the exits.

He lights me up for a lot more reasons than that sleek skin I want to drag my tongue over and that silky hair I want to drag my fingers through. My Spidey senses are tingling like I just stuck a fork in an electric socket. And my hair keeps wanting to float around my shoulders in this psychic charge I'm generating.

I wonder if he's here for the egg and the intel. I wonder if I'm gonna need to fight him for it or if he's got those intense topaz eyes of his fixed on some other prize.

I wonder if Wang's gonna get nicked twice tonight.

I mosey over to the glass-walled barricade that guards the two-hundred story drop from the top of the Tai-Sun Tower and work to get my head back in the game. My so-called gift almost slipped the leash back there, thanks to Adam and that vibe he's throwing off. Which, with my ironclad control, definitely isn't typical. What I can't figure out is how the guy affects me like this from all the way across the pool.

And since I don't know, I'm definitely keeping my distance.

The ends of my hair finally stop floating, but my fingers just keep tingling. Facing away from a rooftop full of eyes, I rub my fingertips together. Tiny violet sparks sputter and snap from the friction.

Not good, showgirl. You better get your psychic Gemini shit together. And I mean now.

I sneak another peek at my dive watch. Fourteen ticks to showtime. Which means I still have time to admire the view. The entire megacity hums and pulses with energy, the hiss of traffic punctuated by the blare of car horns under the band's epileptic beat. The sleek shapes and garish lights of downtown Singapore shoot skyward like rockets. Windows blossom red and gold and green with reflected New Year's fireworks, exploding over the night-black sea.

All the signs point to an auspicious year.

If I can just manage to live long enough to enjoy it.

Chapter Two
Ronin

The literal second she strolls onto the scene of Wang Tai-Sun's charming wee orgy, I recognize Zara Gemini. Strutting from the lift like the spoiled bitch owns the whole bloody building.

While the unsuspecting reason for tonight's festivities cons her way past Wang's top-notch security and beelines for the booze like the party bitch I've boned up on in her file, I order another Macallan and check out my target.

Despite the teal hair and glitter nail polish and platform boots that ought to spell *Trailer Trash* with capital T's, this alley cat manages somehow to project old Hollywood. She's got big eyes and lush lips and soft curves under that swanky leather dress that hugs her tiny waist. She's got a California tan and streamlined legs and a saucy sway to an ass that's practically begging to be spanked.

Long story short? She's a bit like a street-punk version of a vintage pinup girl like Rita Hayworth. She's Scarlett Johannson in a wig.

And that Gemini bitch is crackling with so much psychic power her mane is floating around her shoulders and lightning practically shoots from her fingers.

"Do correct me if I've missed something. Because I know how much you enjoy that sort of thing." I chisel every word from the ice of my hatred for all things Gemini and drop my commentary into the ear of the chap standing quietly by my side. "Thought you said she rejected her heritage. Suppressed her gifts. Somehow, Lucius, Zara Gemini doesn't appear to be particularly suppressed to me."

We're not really on a first name basis, he and I, but I'll be damned if I'm going to call the bloke *Master Aries* outside Academy grounds.

"I never said she wasn't gifted," Lucius murmurs, in that voice of his like gray silk, so soft I lean close to hear. "She possesses all the raw potential of her Gemini DNA, spliced with the volatility of her Scorpio recessives. I said she wasn't *trained*, Mr. Pendragon. An oversight I fully intend to remedy."

As a survivor of Lucius Aries' rather draconian instructional methods myself, I can personally attest the Gemini witch is destined for an unpleasant education. Too bloody bad, because it can't be unpleasant enough to suit me. If not for this rogue American upstart and her precious Gemini pedigree, my twin sister would be alive and thriving today at the Icarus Academy.

What happened to Gwen is purely the Geminis' fault.

That prick Damien might have passed beyond my vengeance. But his sweet sister Zara's right the fuck in front of me.

I watch the Gemini girl sip her champagne and sway to the tunes. The way her thighs flex and her hips swivel should be a felony offense. And there's no doubt she fancies the attention. But there's a vigilance lurking in that sultry face that tells me she's going to make her play. Her turquoise eyes are practically glowing with all that Gemini power.

"What if she doesn't survive your training?" I fire the question at my headmaster like a crossbow bolt.

Because surely a bloke can hope.

And, well, I can't deny a certain wicked part of me does enjoy yanking the wolf's tail.

I'll admit I'm wondering how far Lucius Aries will let me take this delicious defiance.

"Then she won't be the first, will she?" Lucius says briskly. But I know he's far less indifferent to the grim consequences of a vacant Gemini seat than he pretends. "In that case, we'll look for a Gemini recessive with enough power to claim her place. Meanwhile, you and Vasili can continue your reign of terror over the student body unimpeded."

His dry tone draws my eye. Which I've been trying my damnedest not to allow all night. At the Academy, I can just manage to ignore the savagery that lures me under his quietly contained exterior and those whiskey-colored eyes that look like a wolf's about to leap for my throat and, gods, that mouth I'd kill to kiss despite all the viciously cutting things he says with it. He's my fucking teacher and it's his job to enforce every fucking rule.

Including his own personal rule that forbids teacher-student hookups.

And enforcing every rule at the Icarus Academy is one duty Lucius Aries discharges with positive relish.

Tonight, dark hair untied and loose around his shoulders, his scholarly tweed replaced with a black leather jacket and a russet silk shirt I want to unbutton with my teeth, I can barely stand to look at him.

Still, I manage to parrot my lines. "I hate Vasili Romanov of House Scorpio. Nearly as much as I hate Neo Mercury of House Capricorn. Yet here I fucking am, bringing Neo his fucking mate since he isn't ruthless enough to bring her in himself."

Lucius tilts his head, those tousled curls thick and soft as a wolf's pelt whispering against his broad shoulders. "Am I going to have a problem with you tonight, Mr. Pendragon?"

The beast is rising in his eyes, pupils swelling to give just a glimpse of the monster that lurks inside. I'm not House Aries, so there's no genetic link, but as my headmaster, he's the alpha in our *domus* at Icarus.

And he knows how to enforce his dominance.

"No. I know what I need to do." Sullenly I claim my whiskey and walk away before I lunge for his fucking throat.

Time to get moving. Time to undertake the odious little chore Lucius dragged me across six bloody time zones to discharge. Time to make someone's life a living hell.

Across the way, Zara Gemini's just noticed me. And I don't want her knowing I noticed her first.

Until it's far too late for her to escape.

Chapter Three

Zara

I splay my fingers wide against the glass barricade between me and the two-hundred story drop to dispel the psychic charge that builds in my hands whenever I feel threatened.

Finally, the breeze up here cools down the dangerous tingle in my palms.

I pull in a slow breath of humid ocean air that smells like salt and ozone, then push the air back out to ground myself. Just a little mindfulness to settle my pre-performance jitters. I count my breaths until my heartbeat slows and my pulse steadies. When I finally swing around to rejoin the party, Adam's nowhere to be found.

Which is a little worrisome. That guy's up to something.

I mean it. He's serious trouble.

But it's time to get my own butt in gear and cause a little trouble myself.

Keeping it casual, I circle the rotating bar and maneuver through the gyrating couples getting down on the deck and sashay into the glass-walled penthouse. All the doors are wide open, to hell with the A/C, and the skunky smell of weed floats out. Inside the smoky rec room, two girls in couture cocktail gowns are getting stoned on the leather couch and two guys are making out in the corner.

I give that guy-on-guy action a double take because, hey, who wouldn't? The blond surfer type against the wall has his pants open. While the shirtless hunk with a bird of prey inked across his muscled shoulders is sliding to his knees and basically getting ready to suck his friend off right there.

Too bad that security guy who's built like a goddamn linebacker isn't joining the fun. The hired muscle's doing his job guarding the private wing where Wang keeps his office and the safe. I amble past—he's too alert and way too sober for my comfort—and stroll over to the open wing that leads to the poker den, an impressive array of total immersion video games, and the john.

The bedlam of flashing lights and howling sirens and revving engines pouring from the game room packs enough sensory overload to give anyone a migraine. Except for a girl raised in a Vegas casino like I was. But the acrid smoke coiling from the muted mutter of the poker den's thick enough to make my eyes water. I duck into a private bathroom—Wang has nine of them according to Cleo's schematic, which I've memorized—and lock the door.

Thank Christ the air's fresher in here, sweet with floral notes from some chick's designer perfume. I suck in a grateful sniff and tap out a quick text to Xiao on my burner phone.

Situation normal up here. I'm hot to trot. How's it looking on the street?

My partner sends back a thumbs-up emoji and that's it.

Honestly, I'm a little disappointed. I wouldn't have minded a little sexting to distract me from my jumpy nerves. Usually, Xiao's more than down for that kind of distraction. Later, after I've shimmied out of the Tai-Sun Tower the same way I shimmied in, once we're on board the getaway boat and motoring for Kuala Lumpur, he'll have my catsuit unzipped and my legs flung over his shoulders and his talented tongue circling my clit until I beg for mercy.

Because Xiao loves making me beg.

And that's the only way I'll do it.

I take care of a little business with the self-cleaning Japanese toilet tucked discreetly behind a screen—even my bladder's nervous tonight—and check my phone again. I'm hoping for a selfie of Xiao's impressive cock, which he's been known to provide in the past, but bummer. Still no joy.

Now it's only ten ticks to showtime.

I tuck my phone in my clutch and check the stiletto in my boot. If I need to use my blade, it'll be when the bomb goes off. And by now I realize I'm like ten separate kinds of jittery.

I don't have precognition. Sure, I've got some of the right DNA for that, but the Geminis are genetic mutts with chromosomes from all four arcane races, and we don't have that kind of gift.

Still, when I get jumpy, it usually means something major's about to go sideways.

I take a sec to case the joint for anything I might have left behind. In the dim red mood lighting Wang's got going on in here, the slab of black granite under the mirror's wide enough to hold the glass bowl sink and a fucking foursome, but I'm all alone. There's a ventilation shaft above the toilet, and my lipstick tube hides a baby Phillips in case the bomb collapses the stairwell and I need to shimmy out that way.

I've always got a Plan B.

There's no reason this won't work. There isn't. And I'm used to performing under pressure. I suck in a bracing breath, grip my clutch, summon my resting bitch face, and unlock the door.

Except when I swing it open to sashay out, someone else sashays in. And suddenly I'm not alone in here anymore. Because my Adam Driver doppelgänger, who's a good foot-plus taller than I am close up, is plenty big enough to stop me slipping past.

He stalks right into the john like he goddamn owns it, those tiger eyes of his locked onto me like tractor beams.

Up close, he's just as pretty and twice as savage, lean and feral under silk and leather, black flames in ink wicking up from his open collar, all high cheekbones and miles of blue-black hair and a fuck-me mouth I'm suddenly imagining wrapped around Xiao's cock while I straddle the new guy's hips and take him deep inside.

He reaches back and locks the door, all without breaking my stare or saying a single effing word. The heavy door muffles the dance party out on deck and enfolds this dim room in a cave-like silence. His dark sexy smell wraps around me, cedar and ambergris with a hint of bergamot. Those aggressive cat-eyes of his slide down my half-naked body like a jaguar scoping out his next snack.

For some damn reason, he looks hostile as hell.

A shiver of warning coasts down my spine and the ends of my hair start floating.

Shit, showgirl.

Suddenly, in Wang's air-conditioned john, it's getting hot as fuck.

Why, oh, why do I have to be on the clock tonight? Literally any other night, I'd be *so* down with getting locked in a room with this guy. Even if he is glaring at me like I just pissed in his cornflakes.

But Xiao's bomb goes off in less than ten ticks. And I really need to be in the safe zone when it blows.

"Help you with something?" I drawl, giving out my best attitude. "Because the Japanese toilet's pretty self-explanatory. I'm confident you'll get the hang of it without a private tutorial, Adam."

Chapter Four

Ronin

While I stalk the Gemini bitch on her casual recon through the billionaire's penthouse to the ladies' loo, I'm already planning a brutal takedown.

According to her admittedly skimpy file, Mick Gemini's little princess holds a black belt in *tae kwon do*. Considering that I've just been flown halfway round the world very much against my will to collect Neo Mercury's fated mate like a valet collecting his lord's blooming laundry, I won't mind at all working the edge off my aggression with a little close combat.

After all, that's what I do.

Warrior skills are encoded in my Valyrian DNA, I train with the world's best blades, and I'm rated the top fighter at Icarus. Which is precisely why Lucius pressed me into service for this onerous chore. Neo fucking Mercury may earn top marks on the Dean's List and have some sort of freakish off-the-charts IQ, but the Capricorn scion isn't bloody good enough at combat to bring in his own bloody mate.

I lurk about the game room and keep my eye on the loo while the Gemini witch does whatever it is girls do in there. And the wait doesn't do much to sweeten my temper.

In fact, it's all I can manage not to blow the door off its hinges and haul her ass out.

Which explains why, the moment she appears, I'm stalking straight into the loo to confront her.

I'm literally spoiling for a fight.

She wisely backs away and stays out of reach while I shoot the deadbolt behind me and watch her eyes go all wide and wary. Close up, they're a vivid turquoise, almost that deep purple blue you'd call periwinkle. And she's surprisingly tiny. Even in those platform boots she's sporting, the crown of her lightning-blue head doesn't reach my chin.

Annoyingly, despite the David-and-Goliath disparity in our sizes, she doesn't look nearly daunted enough at finding herself locked in the loo with a pissed off Leo who's about to make her regret she was ever born.

I'm willing to blooming bet she's armed. Though that fetching little frock she's wearing isn't roomy enough to hold much more than her suntanned showgirl curves. The leather cups her breasts like a bustier and skims her thighs like a lover's kiss.

But, considering the dangerous mood I'm in, Zara fucking Gemini doesn't look nearly wary enough.

A miscalculation she confirms the moment she opens her fucking mouth.

"Help you with something?" she drawls, cocking her sassy hip. "Because the Japanese toilet's pretty self-explanatory. I'm confident you'll get the hang of it without a private tutorial, Adam."

"Sorry, love. Afraid you've got the wrong bloke." Now that I've got her cornered, I can afford to play a little.

Surely Lucius won't begrudge me a spot of fun before I take her out.

Hearing my accent, she tilts her head. A little line appears between her brows—which she's also dyed teal—and I watch the thoughts flicker across her face. She might look like Marilyn Monroe and dress like a punk-rock pinup girl, but it occurs to me she's no bubblehead. She'd never have survived the wrath of Daddy Gemini and eluded his vengeance as long as she has if she weren't damn good at the game.

An unexpected tingle of anticipation shoots down my spine like an electric charge. I despise every Gemini who's ever lived. But there's no reason at all I can't enjoy my bit of sport with this one.

Before I make her suffer for all the Gemini sins.

"You're a long way from home, laddie." Her voice is low and smoky. I watch her plump pink lips shape the words and my dick sits up and takes notice.

"No more than you, love." In a breath, my tactics shift. I've been looking forward to the physical release of combat. Now it appears I might prefer a different sort of physical release entirely with Neo Mercury's fated mate. Because why the fuck not?

I stalk a single step forward. "I've been watching you."

She edges a cautious step back and eyes me under a fringe of meter-long lashes. "Ditto."

Well, aren't I the lucky one?

Admittedly, I like to play with my food.

Her astute gaze drifts over me and licks along my skin. "But I'm not all you've been watching tonight. Am I?"

Oh, top marks. She's right on the money. Because Lucius and I are far from the only carnivores who've caught her scent. This little bird doesn't know it, but she has a fox in her henhouse, and Daddy's boys are coming. I've been watching for trouble all night, but I'm not particularly easy to read, and I'm a bit surprised she's noticed.

My, you're going to be such fun to break, love.

I barely catch myself poised on the edge of a smile.

"Clever girl." I ease a step closer. Now I've got her backed against the sink, and clearly she doesn't care for it.

She places her clutch on the counter to free her hands up and eases her booted legs a little wider. *Finally* she's starting to see me as a proper threat. Her eyes swirl and pulse with violet light as her gift rises.

Warmth builds in my chest and my palms heat. That's the manifestation of my own gift, the fire gift, surging to meet her challenge. From a distance, through the bond he uses like a leash to hold me in check, I feel Lucius stir and his beast rumble a warning. My scalp prickles with the thrill of his displeasure.

I do enjoy jerking my teacher's chain.

Nearly as much as he enjoys punishing me for it.

"That's close enough, Adam." The Gemini girl's smoky voice hums and throbs with power.

"Oh, not nearly. Not for what I've got in mind," I growl, because I'm *so* not enjoying hearing her call me some other dick's name. "And, for your information, it's Ronin."

"Hey, if the shoe fits." Suddenly she's smirking at whatever the hell she's thinking.

For some reason, I need to hear the sound of *my* name on her Hollywood lips. The fact that she won't bloody say it pisses me right off.

And then, to my utter outrage, she glances at her watch.

"Oh, I do beg your pardon. Am I boring you?" My voice is silky with menace, but she doesn't know me well enough yet to be afraid.

She still looks far too fucking smug to tolerate. "Don't be offended. It's just that I'm a busy girl. I've got a pretty full dance card tonight. It isn't that you're boring me… Adam."

And I'm so blasted annoyed she's still calling me by some other bloke's name that it takes me a tick to recall that of course she's waiting those last few minutes for her blooming bomb to blow.

I flick a narrow glance at her watch myself. Another eight minutes to the boom. That's exactly how much time in this bathroom Neo fucking Mercury's fated mate and I have to kill.

And damn if I don't know exactly how I intend to use it.

"I told you," I growl. "I'm Ronin. And I'd really fancy hearing you say it. In fact, I'll settle for hearing you moan it."

Then I move all the way into Zara Gemini's personal space and plant one hand on either side of the counter to trap her.

Chapter Five

Zara

I'm letting this sexy Brit named Ronin get way the hell too close.

He's way too aggressive and he's way too hostile and he's definitely way too hot. And he moves like a trained fighter, all lethal confidence and feral grace. Every instinct in my whole body is humming a warning so loud I can barely hear him talk. He makes all that power I've renounced stir and rise until every hair on my body stands straight up and every inch of my skin tingles.

He doesn't strike me as a Mick Gemini hit man, because Adam here's way too dominant and way too cocky to kowtow to a jumped-up casino czar with a God complex like my weaselly dad.

Still, I want to unleash the full force of my Gemini curse and hurl the threat of him straight through the goddamn wall. Almost as much as I want to hop onto the counter and unzip his pants and let him sink that thick shaft shoved up against his leathers so deep inside me I can taste him in my throat.

"Well, shit, Adam," I hear myself breathe, low and throaty, like he's already fucking me raw. "You almost make me sorry to disappoint."

Because, you know, the bomb.

"Who says I'm disappointed?" he growls deep in his chest. "You're already wet for me. I can smell it."

Okay, guilty as charged on that one. My pussy's been pumping and slick with need since this feral tiger cornered me in here, with black flames licking up his neck and golden heat pooling in his eyes and the dark musk of danger rising from his skin.

He's looming over me, less than a foot away, fencing me in between his arms, but still not touching. Except for a single long swath of blue-black hair that spills over one shoulder to brush my bare arm.

Suddenly that silky tickle is all I feel.

His scent of amber and bergamot is thick enough to taste. Our eyes are locked together like two cobras poised to strike.

And I've already seen he's got knives in his boots just like I do that I'm pretty fucking sure he's lethal with. He's pissed as hell and he's too damn hostile and there's definitely something wrong about him being here.

Yet my unruly gaze drops to his fuck-me mouth and suddenly I don't give a shit about anything except feeling him kissing and sucking and biting his way up my thighs.

"Fuck, Adam," I rasp. "Don't read too much into this. But you've got literally five minutes to make me come."

"Game on," he snarls. "And it's fucking *Ronin*."

Right before he dives in and I push up and our mouths crash together.

Because, yeah, fucking Ronin is one program I can definitely get on board with. We'll just have to make it snappy.

He tastes like sin and whiskey and he kisses me like he's going to crawl down my throat and gut me. He kisses me like he hates me. Even though he doesn't even know me.

I grip two fistfuls of his silky shirt and rip it open. So I can get my hands on all that tawny skin that burns my palms like I'm handling a hot skillet. He's *really* hot, like unnaturally hot, and there's something vital here I need to register. But he's shoving his tongue in my mouth and biting my lips until they sting and gripping my thighs to hoist me hard on the counter and I need to brace an arm behind me just to stay upright.

Because I'm not going flat on my back under this psycho.

He's as likely to rip my throat out as fuck me.

He shoves my thighs wide and I rip his pants open and drag down his zipper and, *fuck*, he's going commando. I can't see a thing with him kissing me like this, which is really too bad. Because my hand wraps around what feels like a literal mile of cock, all thick and hot and ropy in my fist, a slick tendril of precum already drooling from his slit. I give him a few rough strokes to make him good and ready.

And he moans long and low into my mouth like I just goddamn knifed him.

Then my pumping hand bumps up against the smooth metal ring that pierces the head of his dick. And now it's my turn to moan.

Confession time. I have a major weakness for a pierced cock. That weakness has gotten me in trouble before.

But I still can't see shit because, really, I can't stop kissing him long enough to look.

His rough palms slide up my thighs and shove aside my skirt and drag down my panties. His hands feel like he bathes in battery acid. But, honestly, who gives a shit if he's rough. My thighs are slick with craving and my pussy aches with need.

"Hurry," I moan against his mouth, reluctantly giving up his cock long enough to wrestle his pants down around his hips.

"Trying," he mutters, biting my lower lip until I taste the salt and metal of my own blood. Then he thrusts two fingers deep inside me. Fireworks explode against my closed lids. I keen with pleasure and he snarls with satisfaction.

Hate fuck.

There's definitely something to be said for it.

Somehow I'm flat on my back across the cool granite slab, right where I know it's not safe to be, but screw being cautious and screw being safe. Skirt pushed around my hips, panties wrapped around one ankle, I'm writhing and clawing at the granite and him. His fingers pump into me, slick and hot with my own juices, the wet slide of flesh on flesh audible in the heated air.

He gives my strapless bodice a savage yank that nearly rips it open and my tits spill out, giving my own twin piercings some airplay, silver rings glinting in the dim red light.

"Oh, fucking hell," my Brit groans, diving in to tongue my nipples and work my rings like an effing maestro while his fingers keep pumping me.

He's all sharp teeth and ruthless lips, clamping down on my nipples and suckling me so hard I feel every pull burrow through my insides to tug at my clit. My pussy's milking his fingers in rhythmic pulses I can't control and I'm fucking losing it for him right there on Wang's bathroom sink, rocking my hips against his hand, and God, God, God, I'm perched *right*… on the edge…

When his thumb works the nub of my clit, my climax crashes over me and pretty much destroys me. Crying out, I ride his hand like a rodeo bull, my core clenching hard around him, a fresh gush of my own pussy juice drenching us both.

"Jesus, Ronin," I gasp. Seeing literal stars.

Hearing his savage grunt of triumph as I finally give him the climax he's demanding and the name he's jonesing to hear me say.

Well, fuck if he hasn't earned it.

This guy might have the temper of a rutting bull and the personality of a cranky rhino, but sweet Jesus, can he finger fuck.

In fact, he's still doing it, pumping me relentlessly through the aftershocks with one hand, breaking out a condom with the other. The sharp crinkle of plastic snaps my eyes open. He's fumbling the condom from his pocket and ripping the wrapper open with his teeth.

My climax recedes and my head clears. He's still looming over me, all that raven hair spilling over one shoulder and sticking to my sweaty tits, his gaze nailed on my face from a foot away like he doesn't want to miss a trick.

And, cheese on toast, his *eyes*. Those Russian amber eyes of his are literally glowing with golden fire.

He's gifted. He's fucking gifted the way I'm gifted. Only, not the way I'm gifted. I'm an air sign. And judging by that massive dragon tattoo roaring inky flames across his chest and the unnatural heat rising from his skin, this guy's a fire sign.

And no high and mighty fire lord would ever serve a casino weasel like Mick Gemini.

Nope.

This sexy Brit who's just finger fucked me into a sex coma? He's an Icarus boy.

Which means that goddamn Academy whose mandatory education I've been eluding for the past five years just freaking found me.

Chapter Six

Ronin

The instant Zara Gemini's orgasm tapers off and her brain switches on, I feel the electric charge of alarm shoot through every synapse of her sexy body like a bolt of lightning.

Because she's under me, she's inside me, we're connected, we're one. Her taste of fizzy champagne and power's singing on my tongue. Her scent of vintage roses and vanilla's swimming in my head. My hand's buried so deep in her wet silky heat as she pulses around my fingers I can practically feel her heartbeat.

Her eyes flicker over the flames spilling from my dragon across my chest and shoulders. Then her gaze locks on mine like a magnet. Her hair floats around her shoulders and her irises glow purple with power.

And if I don't bloody get inside her before she hurls me through the wall, my dick's going to explode.

"You're one of them," she says, husky with shock and breathless with pleasure. "You're a warlock."

"And you're a witch," I rasp, unrolling the magnum down my aching shaft. "I'm going to fuck you blind, Zara Gemini."

"It's Cleo Ferrari," she says, smooth as cream, without missing a single bloody beat. So smooth I'm actually thrown by it. Because *that's* how good she is. "Afraid you've got the wrong girl, Adam. And you and me? Our time's up."

Oh *hell* no. Not a single flaming chance. She's the Gemini scion all right. And according to those digits flashing on her own dive watch, we've got a solid four minutes before her blooming bomb goes off.

Which is more time than I need to bring us both off.

I ease my dripping fingers from her cunt and rub my aching cock over all that slick heat. Against my shaft she's like a split peach, all dewy and pink and glistening. If we'd only a little more time, I'd drop to my knees and tongue her until she screams.

As it stands, we've barely enough time for a bit of heavy petting.

When I rub my tip against her clit, rather regretting the latex between us, her mouth falls open and her head falls back and she arches into the contact we're both begging for with a throaty moan.

I tilt my head with a mocking grin. "That you telling me to stop then?"

"I'm not going back there." Her eyes lock on mine like guided missiles. Grim with purpose and fucking deadly.

I can't resist toying with her. "Back where, precisely?"

"To Icarus," she hisses. "I'm not some fucking broodmare for your gene bank."

You're the Gemini scion, I want to tell her. *You're the last purebred female of the Twelve Houses we've got. You should be going to Vasili. That's assuming he'd even bloody deign to take you into his extremely exclusive bed. He's got five hundred years of imperial Russian blood running like ice water in his veins and he's almost pure Scorpio.*

Instead you're going to Neo fucking Mercury.

The very thought makes me savage. Just like it has from the bloody start. Savage enough that I bare my teeth and snarl at her like a feral cat. Even as I rock my cock into that soaking, satiny crevasse between her thighs.

"Not here to knock you up." Fuck, but I want to hear her scream my name again. "Want me to stop then, love?"

She bares her teeth and snarls right back. "I want you to stop *talking*. I want you to fuck me. And I want you to make it quick. Think you can do that for me, Adam?"

Bollocks, I could almost like this girl.

If only she weren't a Gemini bitch.

Especially when she coils up to wrap her luscious body around me, shoves my hand aside to line up my cock, locks her legs around my hips, and seats me deep inside her.

She's so fucking tight I almost lose my load on the first pump.

"Fuck," I gasp.

Under those vivid brows, her eyes flash pure mischief. "Am I too much for you, Adam?"

"I'll show you what *too much* looks like." I grip the lush swell of her ass in both hands hard enough to leave bruises. "Going to make you come for me so hard you black out."

"Promises, promises." The vixen leans in to bite my lower lip sharp enough to make me curse, then tongues it all better. "Do it then. Make me come. I dare you."

Tasting blood in my mouth, I ease her off my cock and slam back into her. Pleasure coils at the base of my spine and clenches my balls in a vise. My size plus my Prince Albert's a lot for some girls to take but, gods, not this one. Her nails rake down my spine and her teeth sink into my shoulder and she shags me like she's killing me.

But fuck if I won't die smiling.

Without warning, my teacher's gray voice unspools through my brain in a ribbon of ice.

Time to go, Mr. Pendragon.

That ultimatum pours over me like a bucket of cold water thrown over my head. It's absolute rubbish. And I'm having none of it. Because I'm buried balls deep in Zara Gemini and I'm going to lose my shit and destroy this whole bloody city if I'm not allowed to come.

"Piss off," I growl under my breath, knowing Lucius can hear me through the bond.

Zara huffs out a chuckle into my neck. "So sweet."

"Not you." I grip her wild mane in my fist and silence her with a savage kiss. Our tongues thrust and parry for dominance like dueling blades.

And somehow I love that she gives me utterly no quarter.

Mick Gemini's cleaners are here. Lucius sounds entirely unamused, and I know he'll make me bleed for this little moment of rebellion until I beg. *They don't know where she is quite yet, but they're definitely on the hunt. Their carefully planned trap is snapping shut. Secure the girl and get out.*

Just one more bloody minute, I bargain through the bond, though it's literally all I can manage to form the thought. Zara's writhing in my arms, chasing her climax as hard as I'm chasing mine, our sweat-slick bodies slamming together, my cock pistoning into her cunt with the audible suction of sex in a ruthless rhythm that's driving us both right over the edge.

I won't ask again, Mr. Pendragon. The phantom heat of my teacher's hands locks around my hips, searing through our bond, though physically he's nowhere near. If I don't behave, he's completely ready to drag me off her by brute psychic force.

He's done this sort of thing before when I refuse to heed his orders. Though never when I'm fucking, for gods' sake.

But even though he's wrathful, even though I'm fighting him, even though I know he's half a penthouse floor away, the feel of Lucius Aries' powerful hands on my body when I'm about six pumps away from coming suddenly turns out to be rather more than I've bargained for.

Because in that moment of searing intimacy, while I'm fucking like blazes with my pants slid halfway down my hips, it's like he's touching me for real.

Touching me the way I've always fantasized and hoped and dreamed he would. Touching me the way a man touches his lover. Touching me with hunger and need instead of restraint and indifference. All at once, it's like I'm here in this room with both of them. Lucius *and* Zara. And all my teacher needs to do is bend me over and spread me and ream me the way I'm bloody begging for.

And he'll be fucking both of us.

Of course he has this filthy fantasy from my head in a heartbeat, thanks to that wretched mentor-student hold he has on me. I can almost hear his slow inhale.

Very well, Mr. Pendragon, he rasps in my ear, sounding a wee bit ragged himself. *I'm afraid you'll oblige me to undertake more severe measures.*

Phantom lips nuzzle my skin and every hair on my body stands straight up. The shadowy scrape of phantom fangs grazes my shoulder and my entire body breaks out in goosebumps. And even though I know it's just a disciplinary bite he's threatening me with, the alpha bite that compels complete submission from his pack… even though I know it's an abject submission I'll hate and not the mating bite I'm craving… this is the closest to sexual foreplay that sadist who calls himself my teacher and I have ever strayed.

And the Gemini witch is staring straight into my eyes like she knows he's in my head. Most girls close their eyes right about now, but this one? She just won't look away. Her face is fractured and her eyes are raw and she stares straight through me like she's seeing into my soul.

Damn you, Ronin, Lucius breathes against my skin. *I swear you're going to regret this.*

I don't doubt it. But I'm still not going to stop.

"Punish me later," I groan through clenched teeth.

Oh, I fully intend to. And I hardly require your permission.

And with his promise in my head and his hands at my waist and his teeth at my throat, with Zara arching and writhing and crying out her climax, my buttocks clench and my cock spasms and I catapult with a shout into the most soul-shattering orgasm of my entire blooming life.

In fact, I come so hard I'm still blind and reeling when the bomb goes off.

Chapter Seven

Zara

The force of the explosion blows the bathroom door off its hinges into the opposite wall. The mirror behind me shatters and glass tinkles down around us like lethal confetti. The blast throws Ronin forward and hurls our joined bodies across the granite counter.

Operating on sheer survival instinct, I wrap my body around him to anchor both of us.

Instead of pushing me away to fend for myself like I halfway expect, he grips me tight, pushing my face into his chest as broken glass rains over us.

"Shit," I gasp into his sweaty skin. Resisting the urge even now to drag my tongue down his tattooed body. "This is *not* where I'm supposed to be right now."

"Oh, did I distract you?" His smug tone annoys me to no end, and my moment of gratitude vaporizes in a nuclear flash. But he's already coiling to his feet, somehow having enough presence of mind to keep a grip on the condom—which I appreciate despite my annoyance—as he pulls out.

"Safe to say you took longer than five minutes," I grumble, snapping my thighs together and pushing up to sit.

His sly grin makes my pulse trip. "You told me to make you come. You'll have to admit I didn't disappoint."

Why does the guy have to be such a total dickwad, yet still so crazy hot?

I'm tempted to say something along those lines out loud—minus the crazy hot part. But I've got bigger problems right now than Ronin's ego. Right outside our hideaway, there's a mounting chorus of yells and screams. The acrid smell of smoke hits my nose and burns my throat. A blip later, the ululating whoop of the fire alarm joins the party, and the strobe starts flashing.

And that's my cue to brush off the glass, adding the sting of a few minor nicks to all that sensory overload I'm fighting to process, and drag my extremely well-fucked body off the counter. Glass crunches under my boots, and damn if my knees aren't wobbly from that monumental shagging that just completely distracted me from the whole point of my being here. Plus there's all sorts of debris on the floor, and my panties have gone MIA.

I guess now we'll both be going commando.

Trying to ignore the breeze down below, I tug my dress over my hips and push my hair out of my eyes and hunt around for my clutch. Meanwhile, that Brit who's just fucked me senseless is dealing with the condom and zipping himself into his pants and pulling his torn shirt over his shoulders, all with total efficiency.

For a guy who just got blown off his feet by a bomb, I can't help noticing, he's looking suspiciously unfazed.

But that would make sense, wouldn't it, if he's an Icarus boy? Because there's no way he's here, tonight, with me, by accident.

Finally spotting my clutch on the floor, I scoop it up and motor for the exit. "Well, tootles! It's been funsies—"

"Just where d'you think you're going?" Whatever else he is, this guy's Flash freaking Gordon on his feet. Because he's blocking my exit in a heartbeat, hair still tangled around his shoulders, shirt still open around his chest.

Mocking and dangerous as fuck all.

Adrenaline spurts through me and gets my Irish up. I level him with a warning look. "Nowhere you can stop me from getting. Don't even think that bomb was the only rabbit I've got up my nonexistent sleeve, Adam."

Anger pulses in his eyes like twin suns. But he reacts the way I figure he will. Shifting an arrogant hip to lean against the doorframe and folding his arms across his chest in silent challenge.

I can practically hear that liquid purr of his roll through my head. *How do you fancy you've going to dislodge me, then?*

And I *so* don't have time for these head games.

Behind him the hallway's packed with panicked and disheveled people, jostling and shouting and cursing over the siren, basically stampeding from the poker den for the emergency stairs out back. It's like the running of the bulls in Pamplona out there. In fact, I'd almost feel guilty over all that panic if Wang's friends weren't Russian *bratva*, Hong Kong triads, and assorted other bottom feeders who'd cheerfully pimp their own kids for a buck.

Anyway, this mass panic's going down precisely according to plan. Which I'd normally claim credit for, with professional pride.

Except this is exactly the moment I'm supposed to be slipping into Wang's unguarded office and ghosting off with that egg. Not to mention the damn microchip that finally spells freedom from my father and that hit he's put out for my head.

Right now, according to my dive watch, I'm an epic ninety seconds behind schedule for my Fabergé snatch-and-grab.

And I'm never late on the job.

Ronin's amber eyes lock on mine. And I swear to Christ it's like he lifts the thought right out of my head.

"Don't you blooming get it?" he exclaims. "There. Is. No. Chip. No miracle reimage of Mick Gemini's hard drive with the overrides and the codewords for his entire security apparatus for sale on the black market under the search term 'casino heist,' just sitting in Wang's wall safe on New Year's Eve camouflaged in a Fabergé egg waiting for you and your little *ménage* to pinch. This whole thing's a bloody setup."

The bottom drops from my stomach and my face goes numb. I literally feel like hurling. Because Cleo did the intel for this job—that's her specialty—and she's freaking convinced it's legit.

But something about the way Ronin's talking? That tells me he's convinced it's not.

And if he isn't lying...if this really is a setup…

The staccato bark of machine gun fire makes me jump a good two feet. The *rat-a-tat-tat* of violence is exploding from the pool deck. Or maybe from Wang's office. And it's getting a whole lot closer.

"Cheese on toast," I whisper. If this is a setup, those are Gemini hit men.

And they're coming for me.

"It's about bloody time," Ronin mutters, and it's like he just read my mind again. I don't know much about the heritage I've renounced, which is a deliberate choice on my part. I can't be tempted if I don't know what I'm missing, right? But I do know there are warlocks that can do that—read minds—and maybe he's one of them.

"Which means you need to come. With. Me." He bites off the words, every syllable crackling with impatience when I hesitate. "With *us*."

Well, shit, now there's an *us*? Sure, there was that one weird moment, when he was riding me and I was losing my mind in about fifty different ways, when I pretty much hallucinated this tall shadowy figure with Renaissance hair looming over Ronin's shoulder and fucking biting him in the dim light. A shadow with glowing crimson eyes and freaking *fangs*. But I totally know we're alone in here, so I ignored my own instincts.

Pretty sure I won't be repeating *that* mistake.

Another sputter of machine gun fire pummels the air, mixed with the crash of shattering glass and a smatter of screams. Now my heart's pumping fight-or-flight adrenaline through every synapse and the endorphins are making me twitchy.

And I'm not the only one. Ronin's watching my face, intent and alert as a crouching tiger. If he had a tail, it would be lashing.

But the bastard's still blocking my escape. And he's not here to rescue me from my own idiocy out of the kindness of his Christian heart, is he? Because I'm pretty sure he's not even Christian.

Nope. He's here to take me to Icarus.

And I'm sure as shit not going.

"Oh, that's brilliant." His topaz eyes narrow to slits. Maybe he *is* reading my mind. "Zara. I'm telling you. We've a way *out*."

Yeah, no. Like I'll be trusting some Academy freak to save my hide? Even if my heart does give that stupid little flutter every time he says my name.

My name which I never actually told him.

I make up my mind and stride across that sea of broken glass. Straight toward him.

Danger hardens in his face and light pools in his eyes. Liquid fire springs up around his hands and drips from his fingers—confirming every single suspicion I'm harboring about his shady affiliation, thank you very much. Even before he cocks his arm.

And *throws*.

So much for settling our differences peacefully.

I duck the literal fucking fireball he's just hurled at my chest. It scorches past overhead, dripping gobs of molten fire I somehow manage to avoid as I drop and spin. My booted leg sweeps around to knock his feet out from under him.

Except he isn't there to take the hit. He coils and leaps with a jungle cat's deadly grace that launches him straight over my head. Which means as I finish my spin and shoot to my feet, that bastard's right behind me.

His freaky fireball must've hit the sink, judging by the hiss of steam and the jets of vapor. But I can't exactly look because his arms clamp around my waist, pinning my elbows to my sides like he thinks that'll contain me, locking my back tight against his deadly body.

"Bloody hell, will you *listen*?" His edged voice lashes my ear like a whip. "We can sort out our little differences later."

This whole hug-me hold he's got me in? It's unsettling enough to make me pause for a sec instead of executing my tried-and-true, bend-and-twist, put-you-on-your-ass maneuver. Thankfully, the fire's stopped leaking from his fingers. Maybe he needs to, you know, recharge or something before he fires off an encore? Maybe it doesn't work when we're touching.

Or maybe this walking weapon of mass destruction is trying to show restraint.

Which seems unlikely, since he hasn't exactly been Mr. Hold It Back so far.

For literally the first time ever, I'm actively regretting my choice of willful ignorance about that family heritage I renounced years ago. Even though I made that choice when Gemini witchcraft killed my mom.

"That fireball would have flambéed me, you asshole," I snap.

"It's a knockout spell, you nitwit," he grates. "A simple common magic. Will you stop being such a fucking freshman for thirty seconds and think? If I wanted you dead, I'd have ripped out your throat while we fucked, wouldn't I?"

His voice thickens to a snarl. "And don't think for a tick I wasn't tempted. Now *move*."

The coiled tension in his body tells me he's more than ready to hurl me headlong into that mob scene in the corridor. Speaking for myself, considering he's just called me the one thing I'll *never* be—a freaking freshman at the Icarus Academy—I'm about to reconsider my own remarkable restraint and apply my boot to his balls.

That's when another, lesser explosion rips through the penthouse and makes us both stagger.

Just like last time, we grab hold of each other and barely manage to stay upright.

That'll be the booby trap in Wang's office, which my dad's casino goons apparently weren't smart enough to disarm. Over the rise and fall of the alarm and the rapid *chuk-chuk-chuk* of gunfire, guys are barking orders in Cantonese. That'll be Wang's boys cleaning house.

I'm good at calculating the odds, and the math's just shifted in a way that isn't in my favor.

"Fuck it," I mutter, tight with frustration. "You claim you've got some way to get us through this kill zone and clear of this mess in one piece?"

After all, I can always ditch him later.

Elation zings like an electric charge through his tensile body, all pressed tight to mine. We're still so close I can feel it, like somehow he's under my skin.

"Is the Pope blooming Catholic?" He finally lets me go (a big relief, of course) and prowls past me to the door. "Just try to keep pace and don't dawdle."

I palm my stiletto from my boot and give serious thought to sinking it in his back. Instead I let him slide through the doorway and keep close enough on his heels that he can feel me breathing down his sexy neck.

The hallway crowd's petered out, smoke coiling thick in the air, the floor littered with crumpled bodies I carefully don't examine, the strobe still flickering and the siren still wailing. And most of the action sounds like it's coming from a good old-fashioned gunfight—between Wang's army and my dad's casino rats, apparently—going down in the rec room.

Ronin palms his knives from his boots and slinks down the hall, keeping close to the wall, silent as spilled ink in his silk and leather, leading me away from the kill zone toward the game room. The panicky bells and clatter of the video slot machines and some drag racing VR game clutter up the air.

He's gliding into the game room when a lounge lizard with a Beretta— one of my dad's hard-bitten casino rats, natch—bulldozes into view.

"Hey, Marilyn Manson, hold up—"

Ronin blurs into ninja mode, and I swear he's a thing of beauty. He's a swirl of hair, a whisper of leather, a flash of steel, a hint of death.

Twin blades slice the air.

Then a glittering rain of blood sprays across the video slot machine and Ronin's ghosting past the game before that casino rat's body hits the floor. Gurgling. With the rat's throat slit open. Which is pretty horrible.

Okay, so I'm a little impressed.

Even though I could've taken out my own trash.

I kick the fallen Beretta out of play—guns are my dad's thing, so I've renounced them too. Then I pivot to clear my six before I follow Ronin past the drag racing console and the *Top Gun* fighter sim to the unmarked door tucked behind the popcorn machine. I'm actually starving, so I pause long enough to scoop out a warm buttery fistful and cram it in my mouth, moaning with pleasure at the salty goodness, before I follow the psycho through the door and up the narrow utility stairs. A single blue-white bulb gutters overhead as we climb, our soles silent on the metal steps.

Up is the wrong way, really, with my winch and harness stowed sixteen floors down and nothing but Wang's private helipad above, according to Cleo's schematic. But the utility stairs don't offer *down* as an option, and I do have Escape Plan C lined up on the roof.

It's just that I hoped I'd never have to use it. My gut feels a little squirmy at the prospect, but that's the job sometimes.

The business I'm in is called staying alive, and I'm pretty damn good at doing it.

Meanwhile Ronin's moving at a good clip, but I keep up, licking butter from my lips as I dig out my burner phone and whip off a few words to let Xiao know I'm coming down the hard way.

This time I don't even get a thumbs-up emoji.

Helluva time to go dark on me, babe. Cuz I sure could use the backup once I hit the street. I've got Wang's boys, my dad's casino rats, and now this freak from the Academy to shake off—

We're about to hit the top of the stairs when the rattle of machine gun fire punches through the closed door above. Over the sound of that little welcome party, I'm hearing the businesslike *thokka-thokka-thokka* of chopper blades.

Ronin crouches beside the door and looks back with a savage grin. That golden fire is rising in his eyes and dripping from his fingers. The ends of my hair shift and float around my shoulders—my own power rising in response to his and straining at the leash.

Take it easy, showgirl. Leave the pyrotechnics to Adam.

All that Gemini power's so close to the surface it feels ready to burst through my skin. He's doing it somehow, he's setting me off. Being close to him like this. But I'm in control, and I won't break my vow.

I won't take out half a city block and eighty-seven innocents. There won't be a repeat of what went down in Vegas the night my mom lost it.

"Hear those rotors?" Ronin says, and I dip my chin in a tight nod. "That's our getaway vehicle, yeah? Stick close enough and he'll cover us both."

Before I can ask who *he* is, that psycho's reaching for the knob. I grab it myself before Pyro here blows our freaking cover.

"Jesus, Ronin. How about giving *him* a heads-up before we pop into view and turn into target practice?"

"Oh, he knows we're here," Ronin murmurs, heat rising from his skin to warm the stairwell like he's a goddamn furnace. "You'll find there isn't much he doesn't know. Ready to meet your future?"

Yeah, that'll be a hard no. But he'll figure that out soon enough. I step back from the door and flourish my stiletto in an elaborate invitation to lead the way.

Because I'm sure as fuck not going out there first.

The freak bares his teeth in a grin and launches through the door with hands blazing and twin jets of fire spraying from his fingers like gasoline from a firehose. This pyrophoric display gives me a whole new appreciation for the restraint he apparently did show when he lobbed that knockout fireball at me in the john.

As he runs, he sprays the helipad with fire in all directions. The rattle of gunfire sputters out as men scatter screaming. That's one wicked effing gift he's packing. Too bad adding Ronin the human flamethrower to my growing list of enemies isn't my preferred way to end this disaster of a night.

But it's not like he's given me much choice.

There's a Sikorsky hovering two feet above the helipad with its side door wide open. There's a man crouched in the door frame, hanging half out of the thing shouting something at Ronin, long coat and Renaissance hair billowing around him in the breeze. There's Ronin flowing into a run like a charging leopard and loping across the tarmac for the chopper. Finally, there's me pelting along behind, hair streaming in my wake, tracking a good dozen bad guys around my perimeter as I haul tail. To my eye, Wang's boys look a lot less motivated than Dad's casino rats once they get a gander at me.

Their fucking target.

Because there's nothing like a head of wild teal hair hanging halfway to her ass to paint a big fat bullseye on a Gemini girl's back.

Since I calculated it when we planned the run, I know there's an 8.3 foot gap between the helipad and the roof of Tai-Sun Tower Two, the twin of the one I'm on. Tower Two's a high-end hotel with standard security and an underground garage where Cleo and Xiao parked the van.

All I need to do is get over there.

I'm halfway to the chopper and the updraft's whipping my hair like Medusa snakes around my shoulders when I angle my path away from Ronin to avoid the hovering bird dead ahead and make for the 8.3 foot gap right beyond.

I punch through the fear that's screaming at me to stop and give it as much gas as I've got.

In training, I can clear a nine-foot gap. Most of the time. But typically I'm not wearing a leather dress and platform boots and no freaking panties when I do it.

You're wearing your lucky cuff, showgirl. You can clear it. Besides, it's this or the Icarus Academy.

And you know that's not happening.

Without warning, an authoritarian whiplash of a voice snaps through the air. It curls around my charging body and just about yanks my feet out from under me.

"ZARINA SELENE GEMINI."

That mouthful happens to be my full legal name, and whoever's barking it is using Compulsion—a type of common magic—to full effect. That magic tugs at me like a seatbelt in a sharp brake. Thank Christ whoever's doing the Compelling isn't magically bonded with me, which means I can shrug it off and keep running.

Albeit with real indignation. That better not be Ronin trying to Compel my ass on the basis of one five-minute fuck.

I've just about cleared the chopper when a blur of movement snares my eye. I whip my head sideways in time to see Ronin with his fluid grace scramble aboard the bird, but the guy in the coat's long gone.

What I've got bearing down on me instead is… a goddamn timber wolf.

Never mind how completely crazy that sounds.

I swear to God it's the biggest effing wolf I've ever seen in my life, all gray and shaggy and slavering like it's rabid. And I don't know what the hell it's doing on Wang's roof. But I do know it's way the hell faster than me.

In the split second I've got to think, I decide I've got a better chance with the jump than the wolf.

I dig down deep and find that extra burst of speed. But I'm still a good ten feet from the jump when the wolf slams into the side of my legs like a freaking freight train and takes me right out.

There's this endless instant of sheer screaming chaos—actually, I'm the one screaming—when I'm flying through the air and fighting to get hold of what feels like five hundred pounds of snarling, slavering, writhing wolf that's also trying to get hold of me. Then I'm hitting the ground hard, tumbling across the tarmac, all tangled up with the wolf, scraping patches of skin off my naked knees and ass and elbows and still fighting somehow to bring my knife into play and get the beast off me.

Until my head hits the tarmac with a nuclear burst of light.

Then my whole world goes dark.

Chapter Eight

Lucius

Zarina Selene Gemini is exceedingly fortunate to be alive.

As are we all. If Ronin and I had failed to bring the last purebred female scion of the Twelve Houses back to the Academy alive, we'd have sealed the fate of the four races.

It's for precisely this reason that I take particular care in disinfecting and bandaging the various contusions and abrasions caused by the Gemini heir's unfortunate encounter with the tarmac on the roof of the Tai-Sun Tower.

Of course, it's entirely self-inflicted damage, since I clearly commanded her to stop. Just as clearly, she disobeyed.

In this world—my world, our world, the witching world—defiance and disobedience lead to punishment.

At least Zarina assists her cause now by remaining obligingly unconscious. With her wild head of blue-green curls, she's like an enchanted mermaid curled up on the oxblood leather sofa in the mahogany opulence of the in-flight library, one slim hand tucked under her cheek as she slumbers. I'll confess to imposing a magically induced sleep, one of my litany of common magics, on this fiery fugitive the moment I ascertained she hadn't suffered a head injury during that criminally reckless escape attempt.

I do wonder how she'll cope with her new reality when she wakes.

Now, with the three of us securely ensconced abroad the well-provisioned slate-and-silver luxury of the Academy's private jet, engines humming softly in the night and the near disaster of Singapore hours in our rearview mirror, the Gemini girl's somnolent state allows me the latitude to attend her myriad injuries at my leisure. Once aloft, I ordered Ronin to undress her, then left him to it to give the girl some privacy, since apparently there isn't much of Zarina Gemini he hasn't already seen and handled.

Rather thoroughly.

Besides, intimate contact with my new student's naked body won't earn me any points for academic decorum with the Dean.

Now, peeled out of that trashy dress, buttoned into one of my starched Oxford shirts and the turquoise lace panties Ronin produced from his pocket, with her colorful curls brushed out and her music video makeup sponged away, there's simply no denying her beauty.

With her mile-long lashes lowered and her plush lips parted in sleep, she looks to be barely sixteen, though I know her to be on the far side of twenty. In truth, she's barely six months shy of her twenty-first birthday—which is profoundly fortunate for all of us.

Once a scion reaches their majority at age twenty-one, they can no longer be legally compelled to attend the Icarus Academy. That's one of the witching world's many irrevocable laws. That law means I have precisely six months to train her rogue magic and tame her rebellious spirit and persuade her stubborn heart to follow the narrow path fated for her from birth.

The very path she's rejected with determination and ingenuity for five notorious years.

As though she can sense my thoughts, which is entirely possible given her arcane pedigree, the girl murmurs and throws a restless arm overhead in her sleep. I spot an unattended graze on her palm, that small hand innocent and defenseless as a child's despite the glitter polish I'll ensure she removes before class commences.

Fortified with pungent antiseptic and healing plaster, I take my time with her, respecting the fragility of that soft skin and petite frame under her Malibu tan, cleaning and bandaging this last tiny injury with meticulous care. She's precious to us, uniquely and unbelievably precious, her survival essential to our own.

To my heightened senses, the vintage scent of roses and vanilla rises from her skin and hair to perfume the air like incense. My wolf stirs under my human skin with a growl. He's frisking to scent her all over until she's redolent with the musk of fur and predator.

Until she smells like me.

I'm the only member of the Protean race currently resident among the Icarus faculty—this means I'm the only shifter, with our race the closest to extinct—though I'm not the only faculty who scents. It's genetic instinct from our primitive past, this drive to mark and claim my students for their own protection. But there are strictly prescribed limits to the degree of teacher-student contact I'll permit. Maintaining a decorous distance between myself and my students, given the power disparity between us, is a self-imposed rule to which I rigorously adhere. Thus, I'm constantly at war with my wolf, who'd like to scent my entire student cohort until they reek.

Admittedly, in Zarina Gemini's case, that predatory impulse of mine is rather more... complicated.

Not for the first time, I'm cognizant of the fact that I'm more than the faculty's only resident shifter. I'm also the only purebred male of any race currently resident at Icarus. The others are all hybrids to varying degrees, their DNA part human—part earthbound—reducing the recurrence of the arcane recessives that make any witch or warlock so lethal.

If I'd been a student instead of a teacher, Zarina Selene Gemini with her purebred pedigree would have been my fated mate.

Instead, it's my duty to deliver this fiery rebel to Neo Mercury, perennial First Boy on the Dean's List, the mannerly scion of the Capricorn clan, the teacher's pet of my own cohort, and genetically the closest analog to a purebred male in the entire student body. In truth, Neo's genetic pedigree is barely superior to Vasili Romanov's, the other almost-purebred among the Academy's male scions.

But no voting witch or warlock on the ruling Senate is willing to trust a volatile treasure like Zarina Gemini to an ungovernable reprobate like Vasili. Neo won that vote without half trying.

Despite my policy of principled neutrality toward all the students in my cohort, I can't deny a certain sense of satisfaction at the outcome. Neo's the ideal scion, the model student, the right choice. He'll willingly be governed by me in this, as he is in all matters.

My relationship with Vasili?

Well, that dynamic too is rather complicated.

Frowning at the thought of the Scorpio heir, I lower a blanket carefully over Zarina's properly cleaned and bandaged body, dim the cabin light for her comfort, and pour myself a snifter of Hungarian *palinka*.

I'm fully aware I'm going to need it before I discipline Ronin Pendragon.

At present, the hard-to-handle Leo is showering in the plane's luxurious head. With the plane in the pilot's capable hands, I'm free to settle in behind the library's substantial leather-bound desk, with Zarina's sleeping body comfortably under my surveillance and my snifter of *palinka* ensconced at my elbow. I unbutton my tweed coat, unsnap my briefcase, switch on the desk lamp, and begin briskly grading my cohort's History of Witchcraft essays.

As always, Neo's assignment was submitted early, so it's right on top. Flawlessly constructed, thoroughly researched, impeccably argued, his copperplate script earnestly advances the dominant hypothesis that the witching world's four arcane races are genetic mutations of *Homo sapiens*. And it's certainly true that the four arcane races—the Mogadon, the Valyrians, the Kryll, and the Proteans—have been successfully passing undetected among the earthbound humans for millennia. Neo's essay honors every convention, cites every source, and ticks every box in my rubric.

I award the Academy's star pupil the full marks he deserves and jot down with my fountain pen a few more obscure sources he can research for extra credit. This is the sort of learning opportunity Neo invariably seizes. The Capricorn heir is intellectually ravenous, and he's nothing if not a meticulous scholar. In fact, he'd be an entirely satisfactory ward in every respect if not for one unfortunate tendency.

His scorched-earth campaign of aggression with Vasili Romanov.

Despite all my efforts to mediate between the two, their armed *détente* threatens daily to ignite into open warfare. Which makes daily life for my cohort more than a bit tempestuous.

Refocusing on my work, I whisk through the rest of my grading with dispatch. Ronin's been excused this assignment while we planned the Singapore job, which counts as field work in his curriculum.

Vasili's paper arrived three days late, but at least this time he's turned one in. The troublesome Scorpio heir, as is typical, takes the countervailing argument on the origin of the arcane races. Citing unorthodox sources unearthed from Old Cyrillic libraries in Moscow and Kiev, Vasili's impassioned prose slashes fiercely across the parchment in defense of the alien hypothesis. To wit, he ascribes the genetic traits of the four arcane races to alien DNA, crossbred with earthbound human DNA during terrestrial visits by these hypothetical aliens in the time of the Roman Empire.

Vasili's clearly turned in a first draft, but the Scorpio scion is blisteringly intelligent and a fearless writer. His provocative phrasing leaves Neo's wooden prose eating his dust—a comparison which holds true in the classroom and beyond. It's one of the primary irritants in their volatile dynamic.

Of course, Vasili's assignment coasted under my office door at Icarus quite late. I deduct points for tardiness, but award him a solid pass.

"You must be grading Vasili," Ronin murmurs, propping an irreverent hip against my desk. The warm dark spice of ambergris twines through my senses. While my mind's been lost in thoughts of Vasili and ancient Rome, the Leo heir has finally emerged from his epic shower.

My gaze wanders from his leather-clad hips up his naked torso, all that golden skin etched with ink and glittering with moisture, damp hair spilling over one sinewy shoulder to caress the flaming dragon tattoo coiled across his chest. Our gazes clash, and one corner of his wicked mouth curls as though he knows precisely how vexing I find his inappropriate attire.

"Why do you say that?" I resist the urge to impose instant punishment for the wardrobe infraction—at times, he enjoys my correction so much it hardly seems like punishment, so with him I have to choose my battles—and sip my *palinka*. The fruity golden burn coats my suddenly dry throat.

"Because of the way you're scowling." Ronin's eyes linger on mine with a degree of intimacy I distrust. Of all the students in my cohort, he's the one who keeps me up nights worrying. "You'd like to fail him, wouldn't you, Lucius? But he's just too bloody brilliant, which means you can't."

"An astute observation, Mr. Pendragon." Briskly I gather my papers in a pile. "And you'll address me as Master Aries on Academy grounds."

Ronin's deft hand alights gently on the pile. The edge of his smallest finger barely brushes mine. "We're not on Academy grounds just yet. We're still hours from landing."

Caught in the midst of rising, I go completely still. Every single nerve in my body is suddenly riveted on that tiny frisson of contact. My wolf is violently alert. He's wanted Ronin Pendragon pinned beneath us, face down and writhing with pleasure, since the moment the Leo heir sauntered onto Academy grounds two years ago. And my wolf doesn't give a single flaming damn that Ronin's my student and therefore sacrosanct.

As long as he's a student under my charge, there's only one reason for touching Ronin Pendragon that's permitted under my own unbending rules.

Discipline.

Even the mere thought of disciplining my wayward student for his ill-considered antics in Singapore, the way I've prudently decided I must, makes my wolf rise up on his haunches and howl.

My gaze shifts from the sight of our hands, barely touching on the pile of essays I've just graded, to Zarina Gemini on the couch. She's still deeply sleeping, her vivid hair already tangling, brow puckered and soft lips parted as though even her dreams are turbulent. She's stretched an arm overhead as if reaching for the antique katana mounted on the wall. Even as I watch, one slim supple leg escapes her blanket to dangle over the couch, glittery toes grazing the floor.

I suffer a sudden, thoroughly inappropriate impulse to grasp her pretty foot and lick her all the way up. Of course, it's an impulse I firmly contain.

Bad wolf.

Between these rogue students who tempt my beast so relentlessly and this rogue wolf who refuses so utterly to grasp my scruples and constraints, I'm not feeling nearly as much self-control as I'd like.

Well, for this too, the antidote is discipline.

My gaze arrows back to Ronin, who's watching me with an open invitation burning in his molten eyes that shoots straight to my groin and squeezes. It's an invitation I need to decline with conviction.

I withdraw from his touch and straighten with a snap. "Back against the wall, Mr. Pendragon."

My student blinks and his mouth falls open. Apparently this isn't the response he's anticipated, though it's certainly the one he's asked for. "What's that, now?"

I allow myself a small humorless smile as I lock the essays away. "I believe I promised you certain consequences for defying me in Singapore, did I not? Back against the wall, and don't backtalk."

Ronin too rises, and it's a positive relief no longer having him sprawled so provocatively over my desk.

This remains the case even when his feral face shifts from arousal to anger.

"You're actually going to bite me?" His gaze swerves hard to Zarina's sleeping form. "Right bloody now? In front of the Gemini bitch?"

"It's a disciplinary bite, solely for corrective purposes." I feel the need to clarify this, both for him and for my wolf, who's demanding a mating bite in no uncertain terms. "You defied my orders, Mr. Pendragon, and your defiance could easily have gotten both of you killed."

"But it didn't! I pushed my fucking feelings aside and protected her." Ronin's agitated eyes stay fixed on her delicate frame, still and defenseless in sleep. "I bloody well know what she means for all of us, don't I? I wouldn't let anyone else hurt her."

Which leaves open the distinct possibility that Ronin might hurt her himself.

I'm well aware that he blames the Geminis for that tragic business years ago with Gwendolyn Pendragon. Fate may have deprived Ronin of the opportunity he craved to wreak his vengeance on Damien, but that selfsame fate has just delivered Damien's sister into Ronin's ruthless grasp.

Moving with careful precision, I remove my tweed coat and fold it over my chair. "You could easily have failed Ms. Gemini—and thus failed us all. To prevent a recurrence, I intend to administer a disciplinary bite to reinforce your obedience to my will."

"In front of her?" he demands, indignant.

"If she happens to wake while I'm disciplining you, I trust she'll find the experience instructive."

"Look." His tone turns close to desperate. "Don't, okay? Just… don't. I'll hate it."

You didn't exactly hate my phantom bite in the Tai-Sun Tower, did you, Ronin? No more than I hated it myself.

That's something I'll never say to him, because truly, I shouldn't have done it. I took unforgivable advantage of my authority to intrude upon an exquisitely intimate moment between two of my students. And the mere remembrance of that psychic echo, of feeling what Ronin felt the instant he lost himself inside her, is making me uncomfortably close to losing a thing or two myself.

He's straying perilously near to balking outright at my edict, and I know it's not only the prospect of Zarina Gemini watching him submit that he's resisting. A disciplinary bite gives a shifter a degree of control over his thrall that's nearly unbreakable. It's a power that's all too easily abused.

In order to submit, he'll truly need to trust me.

Keeping my steps slow and my wolf leashed, I circle the desk and approach him with care. "It's unfortunate you've forced my hand, Ronin. But I won't betray my duty to you as your teacher. I'll never hurt you or humiliate you. It's meant to keep you safe." Despite my resolve, my voice softens. "I'll always keep you safe."

And even though I know I shouldn't, I let my hand drift up to brush his cheek. Under my touch he's banked fire, skin like rough velvet after his shave, ribbons of hair like damp silk sliding against my fingers.

His eyes close and he leans into my touch. His head turns until his lips find my palm. My wolf whines softly, craving him.

"I mean it, Lucius," he says low, lips soft against my skin. "I'll hate it."

Somehow we've strayed onto dangerously prohibited terrain, and it's my duty to set us both straight. I detach from his touch and step back. For no reason at all, my heart is racing. I clear my throat and summon the requisite firmness.

"That's the entire point of discipline. And it's Master Aries. Now put your back to the wall, Mr. Pendragon." I make the point of adding, for everyone's clarity, "It's for your own good."

The imp all but rolls his eyes, but he contents himself with a snort that's eloquent with scorn. "Yeah, keep telling yourself that, mate."

He prowls to the wood-paneled wall behind my desk, inflaming my wolf with every slow sway of his hips and every soft swish of his hair. For a heartbeat, I think the young demon's going to brace his hands on the wall and bend for me, which is a dangerously sexual provocation to a shifter.

Instead, Ronin turns with a sigh and plants his back to the wall.

Keeping my wolf tightly chained, I step forward to confront my erring student. "Palms against the wall as well, please."

Arms loose at his sides, Ronin presses his palms to the wood. But devilry lurks in his gaze. "I thought you did it from behind."

"This isn't a mating bite, Mr. Pendragon." My wolf is in violent disagreement, but I ignore him. I brace my hands against the wall on either side of Ronin's dark head to ensure there's no hint of inappropriate contact between us. His scent of cedar and ambergris wraps around my shaft and squeezes.

God help me, my wolf wants me to fuck him raw.

"No touching." I remind us all of the rules, my voice thick and growly as my wolf fights to surface.

Ronin huffs out a breath and counters, "No biting."

My fangs punch through the roof of my mouth.

"I make the rules, Mr. Pendragon." And there's absolutely no force in the universe that's strong enough to stop me from diving in to bury my fangs in his shoulder.

The salty heat of his blood explodes on my tongue and a deep groan rumbles from my chest. A cry tears from his throat and his hands clamp around my waist, fighting by instinct to thrust me away. I growl a warning against his skin and lock my jaws around him, my bite designed by nature to subdue and compel.

His fist clenches in my hair and rips it loose from the neat tail I tie it back in when I'm working. His other arm winds around me and drags our hips together. The rigid blade of his arousal, sheathed in skin-tight leather, drives into my groin and knifes through every single barrier I've imposed between us.

"Hands on the wall," I mutter gruffly against his skin, mouth full of his blood, senses swimming with his scent, manhood ablaze with his need.

"No." Ronin rocks into me with a shameless moan. "Gods, Lucius, touch me."

My wolf is desperate for him, barely placated by the need to lap the bloody wound we just tore in his flesh to clean it and stop the bleeding. I drag my tongue over the puncture marks to administer the healing agent in my saliva, because we shifters have a gene that encodes for that.

Tending him like this is deeply satisfying, on an instinctive level, both for my wolf and for myself.

The fact that our hips are locked together and I'm rocking into Ronin like I'm making love to him instead of correcting him, while he arches into me and writhes under my bite, is all something I'm striving to manage. At this particular moment, he needs this—he needs the reassurance and the connection of contact—and the fact that I'm nuzzling his torn skin to comfort him between long slow licks is something *I* need.

It's all I can do to keep my own hands stapled to the wall and off the scorching heat of his naked torso.

Christ, I should have made him put more clothes on before I started all this.

But the unforgivable truth is, he's been teasing me all night, and I've been so damn eager to get my mouth on his body that I didn't want to wait. Right now, it isn't even about discipline. Or at least, it may be about discipline, but it's also about something more. It's about the fact that he's nineteen and I'm pushing thirty and if I can't control this forbidden need smoldering like an electrical fire between us, I'm a shameful failure and a shocking disgrace as a teacher.

That admission is enough to pry my mouth off him, to turn me toward him, my lips dripping with his blood.

"Ronin, I'm sorry." My fangs distort my speech, but I'm still too stirred up to retract them. "Dear God, I'm so sorry—"

"Shut up." His head turns toward me, our mouths an inch apart, and it's all I can manage not to close the distance.

"Ronin…" I whisper, our breaths mingling. My eyes close tight in a bid for restraint that I'm fairly certain I'm losing.

"Lucius," he pants against my mouth. "Please don't stop. I want this. I want *you*. D'you have any blooming idea how much I want you?"

His tongue slicks across my lower lip, still dripping with his blood, and laps at my massive fangs. My wolf goes wild for him, tearing at my skin. My body quakes with a surge of primal need—

"I'm not actually sure I want to stop the two of you, because that's hella hot to watch."

The words wrap around me, but it's not Ronin saying them. That husky female voice behind me indubitably belongs to Zarina Gemini.

My eyes snap open and I freeze where I stand, hands braced against the wall, Ronin's body wrapped tight around me, a heartbeat before I would have committed the irrevocable violation of kissing my student senseless. This student I've barely avoided violating opens his eyes and our gazes lock. His tawny orbs cloud with desire and regret.

"Some other life?" Zarina's tone hardens. "I might even be up for joining. But what I really want right now is pretty basic."

I turn my head away from Ronin, his blood still running down my chin, to find the Gemini heir on her feet in my Oxford shirt, hair wild around her shoulders, barefoot and naked from the panties down, sleek legs a mile long and braced for combat, capable hands wrapped around the hilt of that katana.

Over the deadly blade, her turquoise eyes rivet me, fearless and lethal. "Okay, Fangs, let's hear it. Where in the freaking hell am I?"

Chapter Nine

Zara

I'm 99.8 percent sure I've never fought my way out of a position this humiliating in my entire life.

I'm standing here barefoot in microscopic lace panties and some guy's starched shirt, the soft hum of jet engines vibrating though my soles, with my throat dry and my head pounding and an antique katana I pulled down from the wall for defense.

And, hello, did I mention I'm on a freaking *airplane*? An airplane I never agreed to board? An airplane posh enough to be some English lord's library? I'm surrounded by dark-paneled wood and antique books, smelling like leather and brandy and fresh-spilled blood.

That gory bite on Ronin's shoulder looks ouchy, and it's still oozing a trickle of blood over his inked-up skin. But his eyes are glowing like magma, the way they did when the two of us got busy. I'm guessing that happens whenever he's turned on. Because when I clawed my way to the surface of the effed-up quicksand of my dreams, Ronin was literally climbing the other guy's body like a ladder and pretty much dry-humping him.

While the other guy in this scenario, the one who's dressed like an Oxford don in pressed shirt and silk tie and houndstooth pants, is basically standing there staring at me like a vampire with fangs a mile long, Ronin's blood still running down his chin, and glowing red eyes like Gary Oldman in *Bram Stoker's Dracula*.

Shit. I never knew vampires were even a thing—

Ronin clears his throat and pushes away from the wall. "For fuck's sake. He isn't a vampire. He's a fucking shifter."

Reading my mind again. Yep, that's definitely part of his repertoire of warlock superpowers.

"Bloody hell," he mutters, stalking past me with a glare. "Didn't they teach you anything growing up at the casino, love?"

"They taught me that power turns men into monsters and there's a reason they burned witches at the stake." I refuse to be embarrassed by my ignorance. I don't need to impress either one of them. It's not like I'm here by choice. Hell, maybe if they decide I'm hopeless enough, I won't have to fight my way out of the Icarus Academy by force.

Since it's pretty obvi that's where these two circus freaks think they're taking me.

The vampire… oh, pardon me, *shifter*… removes a monogrammed handkerchief (of all things) from the tweed coat folded over the chair and pats gently at his gory mouth. By the time he folds the handkerchief and tucks it away, his fangs have retracted and his eyes are lightening from that awful glaring red to kind of an aged whiskey. He smooths both hands over the chestnut curls tumbled around his face and ties everything back neatly in a civilized tail at his nape. Then he claims the brandy snifter on the desk and takes a few genteel sips.

This whole time, he's watching me.

And I'm sure as shit watching him. Because now I realize he's the wolf who took me out on Wang's penthouse roof. I've never actually seen a purebred shifter before, because they're practically extinct.

But judging by the power dynamic I'm picking up between him and Ronin, it's Fangs over there who's running this show.

This guy's easy on the eyes in an elegant *Downton Abbey* kind of way, tall and pale and kind of prowly under all that houndstooth, with a sleek goatee framing that mouth Ronin seems to like kissing and sharp slanting cheekbones you could cut yourself touching. With those wolfish eyes and that exotic bone structure and those tousled curls tied sternly in place, he's like a pen-and-ink sketch of Vlad the Impaler.

I don't like the quiet confidence squaring his big shoulders and I don't like the predatory instinct firing those sherry-colored eyes.

The thing is, I'm used to being the alpha in the room.

And, clearly, so is he.

"Cat got your tongue?" I say snidely, once the silence gets to be too much. I'm starting to suspect this katana I'm still gripping might be overkill, but I'm not feeling anywhere near secure enough to lower it. "One of you better start talking and fast. Where the hell are we?"

Ronin's rummaging through the beveled glass liquor cabinet with his back to me. He doesn't bother answering or even turning around.

Which leaves it to Fangs, who glances at the old-fashioned leather watch strapped to his wrist and finally fucking talks. "By now, we'll have entered Italian airspace. I anticipate we'll be landing on the island within the hour."

His accent's thick enough to cut with a knife, all guttural consonants and sibilant S's and lavishly liquid R's. And even though I pretty much knew where we're headed, I feel sick to my stomach to hear my worst fears confirmed.

Panic scrabbles at my brain like a rat in a cage.

It's all I can manage to stay on my feet, blade slanted before me, and not launch into some desperate attempt to cut my way out through the fuselage.

"I appreciate that you're inevitably feeling a bit unbalanced, Zarina." Fangs has the kind of tenor that slides against your skin like a silk sheet, crisp with that East European edge.

"It's Zara, if you want me to answer." Even to myself, I sound sulky. But after the night I just had, I'm gonna cut myself some slack. "Zarina sounds like some prima donna ballerina with a narcissist complex. That's never been me."

"It's a queen's name, and it's your heritage. You should claim it with pride." Something I can't read ripples under the surface of that silky voice with its sharp edges. "It's regrettable that our first encounter couldn't have occurred under less fraught and… shall we say… exotic circumstances."

"I, uh, didn't mind the exotic part all that much." I sneak a look at Ronin, who's pouring a snifter of that fruity-smelling brandy for himself even though he's still totally shirtless, and catch the hint of a grin lurking in the corner of his fuck-me mouth.

Before he catches me watching him and scowls.

Yeah, there's a naughty Zara part of me that wouldn't have minded seeing where the two of them took that seriously scorching hookup I just interrupted. Watching those two go at it, I was a little bit tempted to slide a hand under my miraculously reappearing panties and finger myself into a toe-curling orgasm.

To be honest, I'm still slick and achy from the visual.

But I need to get my shit together before we reach the freak academy. Although the exact location of the Icarus Academy is bespelled, it's common lore in the witching world that it's a private island with formidable protections off the Amalfi Coast in the Med.

I say it's common knowledge because the witchy bastards pretty much blew their cover when they screwed up that fire spell and blew the top off Mt. Vesuvius back in Roman times.

I can be thankful my mom never had that kind of power, you know, given the way she lost it? Eighty-seven lives snuffed out in a blink—including Mom— is enough of a body count. My dad's fixers covered it up by calling it a rogue lightning strike that triggered a gas explosion.

In fact, it was a mass murder.

A horror-show slaughter.

And Mom wasn't the only one to blame.

Guilt twists my tummy in knots and regret makes my chest clench. God, I'd do anything to go back and change what went down that night.

But I don't like the way Fangs is watching me. Like he's reading secrets in my face I never want anyone to see.

"I know who he is." I jerk my chin at Ronin, who bares his teeth at me like he'd like to rip my throat out. "Who the fuck are you?"

"But of course, where are my manners?" Fangs shrugs deftly into the tweed coat and buttons it around his taut waist, which somehow makes him no less savage but even more intimidating. "I'm Lucius Aries, headmaster of Villa Augustus, one of three residential colleges at the Icarus Academy. You'll be joining my cohort. You're starting mid-year, which isn't optimal academically, to state it mildly. But, clearly, it can't be helped. I intend to assign a proper tutor to bring you up to snuff—"

"Don't bother. I won't be sticking around long enough to need one."

The shifter's face tightens at the interruption, but he lets it slide. This time. "I'm afraid your education is no longer a matter of personal preference, Zarina. You're the last purebred female of breeding age the four races possess—"

"Yeah, no, we're not having this convo." I extend the katana and point it at him for emphasis. Just to make sure I've got his full attention. "You already have a purebred Aquarius girl at the Academy with witchcraft and a functional uterus to do your *breeding*. I know because she's the next queen, not to mention the fated mate of my dickwad brother. Which also means you already have a Gemini ass sitting in the chair in your freak Academy classroom, Fangs. That seat belongs to Damien. And he's welcome to it."

"Bollocks," Ronin snarls. "She doesn't know a bloody thing, Lucius. How in blazes d'you fancy this brilliant plan of yours is supposed to work?"

Lucius plants both hands on his desk, leans forward, and spaces his words well apart for emphasis. "We'll. Instruct. Her. And I'll appreciate your leaving the particulars of that instruction to me, Mr. Pendragon."

"Knock yourself out, mate." Now Ronin's digging through a knapsack while he growls at me like a grumpy tiger, a sluggish trickle of blood still dripping down his arm. He yanks out a tee shirt and looks like he's about to drag it over his damn head.

"Cheese on toast, what's wrong with you? Can't you see you're still bleeding?" I lower the katana to the couch, since I don't seem to be in immediate danger. There's an open first aid kit right there, probably the same one someone clearly used to patch up my own bumps and bruises, so I grab a roll of gauze and surgical tape and head in Ronin's direction. "You gotta tape that bite up, buddy—"

He hasn't even moved, as far as I can tell. But suddenly Lucius Aries is looming over me like he's twelve feet tall, with red-tinged eyes and lips peeled back from snarling fangs.

"Mine," he growls, low and freaky in his chest, in a voice that sounds barely human.

"Jesus, man. Take it easy." I back away fast, measuring the distance between my foot and his head just in case.

Over his shoulder, Ronin stares between us, looking as startled as I am.

"Possessive much?" With a snort, I toss the supplies to Ronin, who's quick enough to catch them. "Patch up your boyfriend then. He's bleeding all over the library."

For some damn reason, Lucius Aries finally looks disturbed. He frowns, and the red tinge recedes from his eyes.

"The relationship is hardly personal. He's my student," the shifter says firmly, and now Ronin's glaring at his teacher. "I've just disciplined him. He simply requires aftercare, from my wolf and from me."

"Is that what you call it?" I scoff. If that's what *discipline* looks like at the Icarus Academy, he's just given me one more reason to steer clear of the place. "Well, have at it, Fangs."

I'm actually more interested in finding pants than talking about how discipline works at the freak academy. I'm eyeing Ronin's backpack and wondering what he's got in there that could fit me when Lucius turns toward him.

"My wolf has had more than enough excitement for one night on your account," the shifter says to him. "But I happen to agree with Zarina. That bite requires tending before wound fever sets in."

"Forget it," Ronin mutters, clearly sullen at being reduced to the role of misbehaving student, and I don't really blame him. Lucius was totally making out with him. "I've got it."

Ronin's fumbling around one-handed with the tape and gauze, and Lucius clearly wants to help, while Ronin just as clearly wants none of it. It's painful to watch the two of them—the shifter yearning to take care of him but reluctant to press, maybe a little guilty for making such a mess, with Ronin in his outraged pride snarling and warning him off.

"Oh hell," I say finally in disgust. "I'll patch you up, okay? And in exchange, Fangs can rein in his possessive side for five minutes and find me some damn pants."

Ronin still looks balky, but Lucius pivots toward me with obvious relief. "Thank you, Zarina. I've arranged a suitcase packed with everything you'll need in the coming days. I'll just fetch it while you tend to Ronin."

"Just pants," I say firmly, because I'm opposed to the idea that I'll be hanging around long enough to need a whole damn suitcase. "And don't call me Zarina."

"I'm not particularly partial to Fangs myself," he says mildly. "I'm addressed by the students as Master Aries. Feel free to do the same."

I don't bother telling Master Aries I'm not about to become one of his fucking students. Instead I leave him to his little delusions and his suitcase-fetching and corner Ronin by the desk, which has a nice broad surface to work from, plus the lamp.

Out from under his teacher's unsparing eye, the patient looks grimly resigned to my doctoring.

And now that I've got Adam here backed up to the desk with my hands on his still shirtless body, applying a disinfecting ointment with gingerly fingers to that nasty-looking bite, I'm noticing how that black dragon tattoo winds all the way around his lean sinewy torso, wings wrapping around his ribs, forked tail twining over one supple shoulder.

I'm noticing that his dark spicy scent carries the musky essence of wolf, and I'm feeling insanely turned on at the thought of Lucius going all alpha shifter and scenting him.

I'm noticing that his leather pants are zipped but the button on top is open, and I'm thinking how easy it would be to ease that zipper down and wrap my hand around that thick pierced shaft that fucked me into oblivion a few hours ago and pump him into the orgasm I just interrupted.

"You do realize by now that I can read your mind, don't you, love?" he says, low and husky. And my hands freeze in the middle of sanitizing all that hot velvety skin because, shit, I do keep forgetting he's that kind of warlock.

"I'm Valyrian," he says curtly, like he begrudges every word. "Telepathy's one of our racial traits. Not to mention the fucking Geminis hold the bloodlines of all four arcane races because you're so fucking special. How can you possibly not know your own gifts?"

"Because I've got a hate-hate relationship with my witchcraft, Adam." I busy myself measuring out the gauze so I don't respond to his aggression in kind. "My dad and my brother are warlocks and they're both complete shits. And I didn't like what being a witch did to my mom even before that witchcraft…" I clear my throat "…killed her."

Under my hands, he ripples with sudden tension. His voice lashes through me like a whip. "Belladonna Gemini was congenitally unstable, a hopeless addict to wielding power she couldn't control, and she was mad as a fucking hatter. The witching world should have locked her up years ago and thrown away the key. Instead, her precious pure blood gave her a free pass. Now innocent people are dead. Because Geminis specialize in murdering innocents, don't they?"

I flinch under the hatred that blasts from his tone and scours my skin. Because, yeah, my mom was psycho and she was deadly, so how can I even argue?

I'm as deadly as she was.

I concentrate on folding the gauze into a thick pad because if I touch him now, he'll feel my fingers tremble.

I also focus on keeping my face hidden and my tone level. "And you wonder why I turned my back on the so-called family gift that's actually more like a curse? You wonder why I choose to be the stupid ignorant moron you keep calling me, when you know what the alternative looks like?"

"All I wonder," he says, low and savage, "is why in blazes anyone at Icarus thinks you'll end up any different—"

"Ronin!" The snap of Lucius' voice behind me makes us both jump. "That's quite enough from you, Mr. Pendragon." Then he dials down the menace. "I'll finish up with him for you if you like, Ms. Gemini."

What I'd like is to walk straight out the door and leave these two to clear the air between them and clean up the mess their fucked-up dynamic has made of Ronin's shoulder. But I'm stronger than that, and I want them to know it.

"It's okay, Master Aries." I'll give him that one if he'll stop calling me Zarina. "He isn't saying anything I haven't heard before."

Or anything I don't deserve to hear.

"All the same, he'll keep a civil tongue in his head." The warning in his teacher's tone is clear.

Now Ronin holds his silence, even though he sneers.

I situate the gauze pad carefully over the nasty bite and start taping it in place. Wondering why the hell all that hatred Ronin clearly feels toward me seems so goddamn personal.

Lucius hovers at my shoulder, watching me work, and he's close enough now to make me nervous. He's way taller than I am, like pretty much everyone when you're barely five foot two, and his warm breath teases my hair. He smells like wolf and brandy, and he too seems to run hot. I can feel all that body heat licking at my back like a fever.

Making me suddenly way too aware that I'm standing there wearing nothing but panties and a shirt that's probably his.

My nervous fingers slip off the tape, and Lucius leans into me and holds the gauze in place. He's wearing honest-to-God shirt cuffs pinning his sleeves, embossed with a ram's horns worked in gold and jet, which makes me realize this guy's more than a shifter stray.

The Oxford don comes from money.

Now we're both touching Ronin, I'm basically standing between his leather-sheathed thighs, and my unwilling patient's breath sounds a little ragged. In fact, it's so quiet I can hear the shifter pull in a long slow inhale against my hair. Right before he rubs his face gently into the side of my neck.

I'm so startled I drop the tape roll completely. Ronin's hands close around my waist to steady me, while Lucius deftly catches the tape.

"Don't be alarmed, Zarina," the shifter breathes in my ear, with that thick Transylvanian accent he's rocking. "It's only my wolf. It seems that he… likes you."

That little revelation makes goosebumps cascade down my spine and the fine hairs rise down the back of my neck.

Because I'm suddenly wondering what it would take for that wolf of his to bite *me*.

Ronin groans softly and I figure he's heard that thought too. My face lifts to find him less than a foot away, luscious lips parted, lids heavy over his golden eyes. He holds my gaze as Lucius leans into another slow inhale, his nose gently nuzzling my ear.

I clear my throat, but my voice comes out barely above a whisper. "Nice wolf."

The shifter chuckles into my hair, and I realize Ronin's still holding me, that he's holding me steady for Lucius to scent, and that I don't exactly mind. In fact, this entire experience of being trapped between the two of them is making me remember that scorching scene I just interrupted.

And making me wonder if, in all that volatile chemistry between them, there's ever room for a girl.

My hands drop to Ronin's quads, all sinew sheathed in leather, and he purrs deep in his chest like a cat. Lucius rumbles a little in response, and I know without asking that's his wolf.

My voice turns low and husky. "Does your wolf do this with everyone?"

"Quite the contrary. You're very special, Zarina." Lucius is all finished taping the gauze to Ronin's shoulder, but he doesn't back away. "He's paying homage to our future queen."

"What?" I blurt out, gripping Ronin's thighs hard enough to make him hiss. "Get a grip. You've already got a fucking queen. The Aquarius queen. The daughter of the current monarch. And the day Cybelle Aquarius mates my asshole brother, you'll have a Gemini king."

And then we'll all suffer.

"I can't take this anymore," Ronin mutters, glaring over my shoulder at the shifter. "Forget about easing her into it, mate. Either you tell her or I will."

"Tell me *what*?" I release my clench on Ronin's quads and try to turn, but his grip tightens on my waist to hold me. The shifter joins in, hands closing over Ronin's, and presses into my back like he really is the tactile beast that lurks beneath his skin.

"Zarina, listen to me," Lucius breathes in my ear. "Your brother and his fated mate are dead."

A ripple of shock darts through my brain and rivets my feet to the floor.

"*Dead?* What do you mean? Not, like, dead dead?" I latch onto the certainty this has to be either some crazy mix-up or a figure of speech. I hate the little shit who calls himself my brother and I always will, but he's way too powerful a warlock to kill.

If he wasn't, I would have killed him myself. *Thanks for the fucked-up childhood, bro.*

"Someone among the arcane races wanted them dead. There were several attempts, though neither Damien nor Cybelle took the danger seriously. Despite the Academy's formidable protections, that individual finally succeeded." The shifter's words, soft and steady in my ear, shatter all my hopes about a mix-up. "Zarina Selene Gemini, you've just become the last purebred female of breeding age in all four of the arcane races with enough powerful witchcraft to take the throne. This reality makes you the witching world's future queen. Our queen. The Gemini queen."

I can't seem to move, and I'm afraid if I try my legs might buckle. But thankfully I can still speak.

"I don't want to be queen." My words come out in a whisper, but I amp up the volume to make my meaning crystal effing clear. "I don't want it! I've *never* wanted it."

"I'm afraid your wishes in this particular matter are no longer relevant," Lucius informs me gently. "If the witching world is to survive, if we're to reverse our magical decline and bolster our dwindling numbers for the next generation, you're the only option we have left. At the Icarus Academy, you'll become the powerful witch and queen our world requires to flourish rather than merely endure. You'll hone your power, embrace your heritage, and claim your mate."

The blood's pounding behind my eyes and roaring in my ears. My hair lifts all the way off my shoulders and swirls around my head like I'm underwater.

"I just told you, I don't want to be queen. And I definitely don't want a fucking mate! Didn't you get that memo?" And now I'm shouting, all that power I hate and fear echoing in my voice like bronze bells tolling. "I rejected the one they wanted me to take. Just walked away and vanished in the wind and not one of you could find me for five whole years. First chance I get, I'll do the same damn thing all over again."

Ronin's staring at me like he's never seen anything like me, and I'm staring back, but the guy's such a cipher I can't tell whether he's feeling sympathy or disgust. Or maybe he's just startled by the lightning voice—that's what they call it, that voice I'm using without having any ability to control it, because a Gemini can call lightning with that voice. Or else he's freaked by the eerie violet glow that's leaking through my clenched fists.

If I were any less furious, I'd be pretty alarmed myself. I'm an air sign, I'm on a damn airplane, and my power is rising. If I'm not careful, I'll crash this plane. Right now, that feels like it could be a real option.

Either way, Ronin leaves it to Lucius to lower the boom.

"I fear that won't be permitted," the shifter says with finality. "We'll teach you. We'll protect you. We'll worship you. But we're your destiny, Zarina Gemini, and it's a destiny we'll never allow you to escape."

My heart turns to stone in my chest. The bottom drops from my stomach with a sickening pitch.

Every unpalatable truth he's telling me seeps through my skin like acid, burning as it eats through me, dissolving my life and my freedom. That hot purple glow creeps up my arms. A sudden wind blows a stack of papers off the desk and sends them whirling through the air. My whole body starts tingling like I just jacked into a live socket.

That's the exact feeling of the world I've spent a whole quarter of my lifetime building…

Crumbling to rubble under my feet.

Chapter Ten

Vasili

By the time Lucius and Ronin land on the island airstrip and arrive at Villa Augustus with the Gemini queen, it's nearly dawn.

And I've just finished plotting how I'm going to make this new queen suffer the way I did the last.

Despite the abysmal hour, my entire cohort's still awake, scattered around the central living space in our *domus*. Frost rimes the sliding doors that open on the peristyle garden and the turquoise gleam of the heated swimming pool beyond. A brisk fire crackles in the round central hearth to ward off the winter chill.

Racetrack and Dez are cuddled up on the Renaissance sofa with its high back and scrolling arms, poring over the same textbook, painting each other's toenails and cramming for their Genetics of Witchcraft midterm. Neo's claimed the big desk in the study nook—no shocker there—and surrounded his obnoxious self as usual with piles of books and reams of paper. There he slaves away at some tiresome research project for another paper he's invariably going to ace.

I'm sprawled on the VIP leather settee before the fire, taking full advantage of my status as the alpha in this *domus* to dominate the space and sharpening my knives.

Literally.

The Aquarius queen lived her short but hateful life in daily terror of the brace of knives I wear in hidden and not-so-hidden sheaths strapped to my body.

I fully intend that the Gemini queen do the same.

The tramp of footsteps in the atrium brings Neo to his feet like the rustic fool he is, betraying the hold the fugitive queen has over his stupid heart before she's even arrived. He's wearing his entire soul on his offensively gorgeous face, eyes green as poison wide and shining with anticipation behind his stylish dark-rimmed glasses, his sculpted visage all flushed and eager, that ridiculously buff body all but humming with excitement under the merlot cashmere sweater with the Academy crest stretched across his chest.

That shade of red ought to look absurd against the mane of violently magenta hair that grazes his broad shoulders. It positively ought to hurt my eyes to look at him.

The fact that it doesn't, that he manages somehow to pull off these hideous colors, is one more offense I hold against him.

Above the fire's hiss and snap and now the sound of Neo Mercury panting like a German Shepherd in heat, I pick out Ronin's distinctive tread, prowling like a panther through the atrium, even though typically you never hear the man coming until he's right on top of you. Lucius' measured stride is easier to discern. His wolf erroneously considers himself the alpha of our little pack, and he wants you to hear him coming.

But I don't hear *her*.

The fucking queen.

I wonder if it's possible she eluded their clever bait-and-switch in Singapore. I wonder if her little *ménage* couldn't be prevailed upon to betray her for a minor fortune after all. I wonder if the prospect of Zara Gemini roaming blithely at large while the arcane races dwindle into extinction will really be the tragedy the notables of the witching world are making it out to be.

I'm still wondering about that, in particular, when Ronin stalks through the door with Zara Gemini's diminutive form dangling limply from his arms.

Neo blurts a startled noise and rushes out from behind the desk.

Dez blinks her big innocent eyes at the spectacle and exclaims, "Crikey! What happened to her?"

Even Racetrack, who's hardly more enthusiastic about the new queen's arrival than I am, sits up and looks perplexed.

"Nothing's happened to her," Lucius reassures the room at large, following Ronin with his perennial briefcase gripped in one hand and a trendy piece of ladies' luggage in the other. "Our new queen became somewhat… agitated during our final approach. I deemed it prudent to administer a sleep spell to calm her."

Lucius excels at the common magics all witches and warlocks of any race can perform, so I'm unsurprised. But if one of Icarus Island's typically bumpy landings through our protective wards was enough to agitate the little queen, an hour spent under the same roof as Ronin and me should terrify the poor thing witless.

That's assuming she isn't already. I bare my teeth in a malicious grin.

Truly, I can barely wait to get started.

Neo's already galloped across the living room like a rutting stallion to hover anxiously over the new queen. But now he's too timid to touch. Nervously he adjusts his glasses and peers into her sleeping face.

"Not that I'd ever question your methods, Master Aries," he says humbly, because that's the role he likes to play, "but was this really necessary? She'll have an awful shock waking up in a strange bed without any idea how she's gotten here."

Not nearly as much of a shock as I'm about to give her.

I don't bother shielding the thought.

And Dez, who has Valyrian blood and is therefore a strong telepath, picks it right up and shoots me a worried look. Ronin too must be receiving, since he's too strong a telepath himself to miss my public broadcast. But he hasn't even looked at me since he turned up with the fucking queen in his arms.

I find his neglect annoying, because he's been gone for three interminable days and now that he's back, I'm not in the mood to be neglected. I'm in the mood to be placated. I'm in the mood to be pleased.

And no one knows how to please me better than Ronin.

"Given the unpredictable nature of her powers and her lack of formal training, I deemed it advisable." Lucius hands her suitcase to Neo, which is an excellent use for all those muscles. "Why don't you unpack her things and light a fire in her room for her, Mr. Mercury? She'll appreciate the comfort when she wakes."

I snicker and uncoil to my feet, sliding the knife I've been sharpening into the hidden sheath strapped to my inner arm as I saunter over. "That's not at all the sort of fire our Mr. Mercury's longing to ignite for his fated mate. Is it, lover boy?"

He shoots me a murderous look around a sweep of magenta hair. But he knows better than to backtalk, or I'll make him suffer. He may be First Boy on the Dean's List, but I'm the undisputed alpha on this island. Even if I occasionally share my top dog status with Lucius Aries when he lets his wolf out to play.

Lucius too spares me a narrow look. "Mind the fire, Mr. Mercury. And you, Mr. Romanov, will kindly mind your tongue. It's been a tiring journey for all of us."

For him, the admonition's a mild one. But it still makes me want to slash one of my knives across his jugular.

Preferably *after* I shove him face down over Neo's desk and give his professorial hole the ruthlessly thorough reaming we all fantasize about getting or giving (or both) with our aloof History of Witchcraft teacher. It's all fairly standard and tedious, of course—that whole fuck-the-prof fantasy—and the fact that he's headmaster of our residential college and lives under the same roof is the sole reason it's him we all fixate on. Still, it's a complete disgrace that all of us (except Racetrack and Dez, who are exclusively into each other) can't seem to stop having it.

"Oh, I don't know, darling," I murmur, eying Ronin under my lids. "There are plenty of people right here at this Academy who positively enjoy my tongue."

Ronin makes an impatient sound and shifts the witch's weight in his arms, but he still won't fucking look at me. He's absolutely ignoring me, and he has to know what that's doing to me. I want to clamp my hand around the back of his neck and shove my tongue down his throat and kiss him until he moans.

Instead, since that's my purest desire at the moment (and since no one else on the entire island knows we're lovers) I follow the cardinal rule of my existence and conceal the impulse.

I glance down carelessly at the new arrival. "Let's have a look at our new queen."

She's so tiny she's practically swimming in a pair of pressed linen pajama pants and one of Lucius' starched shirts, a soft white blanket tucked around her. This new queen's hair is a minor sensation, a wild tangle of blue-green curls sprinkled with melting snow, draped over Ronin's arm and spilling halfway to the floor. Her dreaming face reminds me of a young Marilyn Monroe, all long lashes and lush lips and vivid teal brows.

But she can't possibly be as innocent as she looks.

Not with all that Gemini DNA.

As I study our poisonous would-be sovereign, she hooks a sleeping hand, sporting glitter nail polish and a studded leather cuff, into Ronin's lapel. That much of her appearance is what I'm expecting, because she's a rebel and a hellraiser, if you want to believe what's in her file. And her sweet roses-and-vanilla perfume is entwined with a truckload of Ronin's ambergris spice and, more subtly, the musk of Lucius and his wolf.

My nostrils flare and my eyes narrow.

Moving too quickly for anyone to counter, I swoop in, grab the girl's hand, drag her wrist to my nose, and take a good sniff. I'm Mogadon, with Mogadon senses and Mogadon pheromones. We're a scenting race ourselves, and it's plain as print to me that both Lucius and Ronin have been all over the Gemini queen.

In fact, unless I'm entirely wrong—which happens virtually never, I assure you—Lucius has also been all over Ronin.

My accusatory gaze locks on my teacher, who's calmly unwinding the cashmere scarf around his throat and watching me with a warning in his eyes which, naturally, I ignore.

"What the fuck happened between the three of you in Singapore?" I snarl.

"Not now, Mr. Romanov," Lucius says with finality, handing his scarf and trench coat to Dez, who's hovering like a helpful genie at his shoulder. "Ronin, might I prevail upon you to take Ms. Gemini to her room?"

Finally Ronin meets my gaze, and the sheer devilry that lurks in his face makes me suck in my breath. "Whatever you say, Lucius."

Now they're on a first-name basis? I want to fillet my History of

Witchcraft teacher. I want to fucking castrate him. I want to *flambé* his balls and consume them with crumpets for my afternoon tea.

Instead, as usual, I do exactly the opposite of what I want. I bare my teeth at the wolf in a silken smile.

"Oh, allow me," I purr. Before either of them can protest, I shift the Gemini queen's insubstantial weight into my arms and claim the so-called privilege of carrying the brat for myself.

It's rather a foreign experience for me, holding a girl in my arms. As anyone at this Academy will readily tell you, I vastly prefer sharing that sort of intimacy with a man. At twenty-two, I'm the oldest student here. I won't be forced to leave until I turn twenty-three. Anyone older than that on the island is merely the hired help.

In other words, the faculty.

And I can count on the fingers of one hand, with manicured digits to spare, the number of times in my life I've even toyed with the notion of dabbling in a hetero hookup. Mainly at my wretched parents' insistence. To their bitter regret, those dutiful experiments on my part were, well, disappointing.

Of course, that outcome arrived as no particular surprise to me.

Because the handful of girls in my dating history didn't exactly… shall we say… light a fire in my loins (nor did I seem to appeal to them, if I'm being honest), I'm not expecting this girl in my arms to hum like wind and lightning.

Even lost in a bespelled sleep, this little queen's literally crackling with power. Sparks practically leap from my body wherever we touch. And even I have to admit it's not merely her purebred blood or her royal status that's responsible for all this amperage. I tussled with Cybelle Aquarius a few times before her untimely demise, with that Grade A bitch giving as good as she got and nearly clawing my eyes out.

And the other queen never felt anything like this.

Power dances over Zara Gemini's suntanned skin and floats in her mermaid hair and sparkles from her painted fingertips. Even completely untutored, this little bitch has more witchcraft sparking in her baby finger than Cybelle Aquarius possessed in her entire lethal body.

My startled gaze shoots up to find the whole cohort—except for Neo, who's off playing houseboy in the new queen's suite—eyeing me with open suspicion.

"Well, well," Racetrack drawls, gray eyes glinting with sly malice under the blond bristle of her boyish hair. "Looks like your pet theory about the royals having their power bred out of them isn't working out so good, Vasili. You ready to bend the knee to our new queen after all?"

I'd drop the damn queen on the floor and tear out Racetrack's throat if it wouldn't get me expelled.

Here in front of Lucius, I need to rein in my witchy temper. Especially since my infamous anti-monarchist sentiments make me the prime suspect in the last royals' still-unsolved murders.

Besides, darling, going after Racetrack would be an entirely wasted effort. Racetrack is a Prynne, and the Prynnes are American upstarts, just like the Geminis. Racetrack's been Team Gemini, despite her formulaic protestations, since before Damien went down. Still, she's no fanatic.

Typically, like any Taurus, our Racetrack's a pragmatic sort, granting me just enough deference to leave her and Dez (mostly) unmolested.

"I wouldn't bother worrying about me, Abigail." I menace Racetrack with an icy smile and taunt her with the Christian name she despises. "Purgatory begins for our little queen the moment her precious eyes open. And she's already so weak and her powers so undisciplined she can't even fly into Icarus without being tranquilized by Lucius. By the time this week is over, she'll be licking my boots. Just like the rest of you. And don't even think about helping her."

I shove Zara Gemini's unresisting body roughly into Ronin's startled arms, earning a scowl from him that worsens my temper, and stalk toward the stairs to my bedroom.

Purgatory is a figurative term for a freshman's first days at Icarus. Plenty of new students wash out and are expelled, their powers stripped by arcane ritual. But given the nature of those powers, this potent introduction to an Academy education does produce the occasional colorful fatality.

All rather Darwinian, of course, by design. If a witch or warlock can't control their powers, they're a danger to all four races.

A danger we've grown too few and far too weak to tolerate.

By the time I've finished demonstrating to our precious queen and the entire witching world how little she deserves our devotion... assuming she survives Purgatory at all, a fate my actions may well determine...

She'll wish she was never born.

Chapter Eleven
Zara

I'm snuggled up tight in Xiao's sleeping arms.

From somewhere, pearly light leaks through a window against my closed lids. From somewhere else, a cold wisp of air tickles my cheek. But overall I'm toasty warm. This is mostly due to having Xiao wrapped completely around the back of me as we spoon under a pile of powder-soft blankets, his knees pressed into the back of mine, his brawny arm wrapped around my waist, his soft breath fanning my neck as he snores.

Even though, typically, Xiao's not one to snore.

The only problem I have with this whole comfy setup is neither one of us is sleeping in the nude. I'm gonna have to shimmy out of these PJs I'm wearing and peel him out of what feels like a sweater and a whole damn wardrobe before we can fuck.

"Xiao?" I mumble, arching into his touch, hearing his breath hitch in my ear. "Need you to tongue me awake, baby."

"Mmmmm." Warm lips find the side of my neck and nuzzle my pulse. Shivers race over my skin and a soft moan spills out of me. My reaction apparently gives Xiao all the encouragement he needs to start popping open my shirt buttons.

When his big hand finds my breast, rubbing rhythmic circles against a combat-hardened palm until my nipple sits up and takes notice with a tingle, I breathe out another moan and arch into him. The hardening jut of his cock against my ass coaxes me into a sleepy grin. I undulate against him until I wring out of him a guttural groan.

"Sweet heaven, Zara," he whispers against my skin. "I've waited so long to feel you like this."

That's sweet of him to say, because it's been like two days at the max since I straddled him in the sauna and fucked him to a noisy climax. I rub the crack of my ass into his massive cock in a silent promise of things to come. I like a little back-door action and Xiao typically doesn't.

But maybe this morning I can talk him into it.

To pay me back for my teasing, his clever fingers work my nipple into a pinch hard enough to curl my toes. I grab his hand and drag it under my PJs to find the slick heat building between my thighs.

Which makes us both moan. Especially when his patient finger takes its gold old time circling my sweet spot, which is aching for the contact, before he eases the digit inside me. I clench around him with a gasp. He sinks his teeth gently into my neck around another husky groan.

I honestly don't know why we're not both already naked. But what I do know is this uncharacteristic restraint on Xiao's part is going to catapult me through the roof when I climax.

"Xiao," I whimper. "Don't tease me, baby. I need your tongue."

"Um, Zara?" he breathes in my ear. "Believe me, I'm incredibly happy to oblige. But who the heck's Xiao?"

That gets my eyes open in a hurry. I snatch his startled hand out from under my jammies and scramble around in a gasp, dragging half the blankets with me since my shirt is gaping. Then I just stare into the sleepy face of the complete fucking stranger blinking at me from our shared pillow in the light of a snowy morning pouring through tall leaded glass doors at the foot of an equally unfamiliar bed.

I'm one hundred percent confident I've never seen the guy who's currently sharing this bed in my life.

And you don't forget a head of shoulder-length magenta hair tumbled around a clean-cut face like a young Clark Kent's, flushed and smoldering with arousal, with a kissable mouth and a sculpted chin and burning leaf-green eyes all bleary from sleep.

"Sweet Jesus! Who the hell are you?" I burst out, sitting straight up with the blankets clutched to my chest, dragging a hand through my hopelessly tangled hair, and wondering what the heck happened to that katana I used to have. "And what are you doing in my bed?"

"It's our bed. I mean, it will be." The guy still seems to be struggling to wake up, his voice all raspy with sleep. He pushes a hand through his mop of hair and scrubs his face. "I mean, it's your bed now, but I'm moving my shit in with you today."

Maybe there's something wrong with my hearing.

Or maybe there's something wrong with his head.

I space the words out so he'll be sure to understand. "Who. Are. You."

"Um." He too sits up, blankets pooling around a taut waist, showcasing a wide chest and impressive shoulders and iron biceps under the clinging cashmere of a merlot sweater with a big fat Academy logo embroidered on the breast. Just the sight of that sweater in my bed offends me. "I'm Neo… Neo Mercury. I'm your fated mate."

"Oh, hell to the no. *That* you are definitely not, buddy," I say as firmly as possible, trying to make sense of this entire bizarre encounter.

Now that I'm fully awake myself and not chasing a morning quickie, all the disturbing details from last night come flooding back like a runaway locomotive, its horn blasting an alarm as the cars clatter through my brain. The last thing I recall is standing in that library with Ronin and Lucius, struggling to wrap my head around the murder of my brother and the Aquarius queen and my own unwanted ascent, and feeling my power rise.

Then… nothing.

Until this.

Waking up in an absolutely massive medieval bed under a blue velvet canopy in a completely strange room with stone walls and a crackling fire and arched windows with frosted panes and snow piled on the flagstones. I'm still wearing Lucius' shirt, though now it's half unbuttoned thanks to this guy next to me, and I'm also sporting a pair of linen pajama pants.

At least there's that.

Because I've apparently just spent the night with this guy who's claiming to be my fated mate.

He's more than claiming, actually, because I do recognize the name. This guy Neo's supposedly in my natal horoscope, and I'm supposedly in his, according to the crazy claims my dad was spouting the night of my mom's funeral.

Right before I took off running and didn't stop till I hit Jakarta.

The Mercurys are old New England money, descended from one of the first New World witching families that sailed over with the Pilgrims on the *Mayflower*. They're solid citizens in the witching world, celebrity politicians, sort of the Kennedys of the arcane races. Mercury Senior is president *pro tem* of the Arcane Senate that makes the laws—that's an elected role, and he's so popular he just keeps on winning it—and Mercury Junior here is supposed to follow in his footsteps. The reigning queen is Messalina Aquarius, Cybelle's mom, who functions as head of the Senate pretty much for life. Which is pretty much a ceremonial role these days, but that totally depends on the queen. For decades now or maybe centuries, the queens have been weak. But the Mercurys are staunch royalists. Their support and their money prop up the whole system.

That's about as much intel on my fated mate as I let my dad impart. Along with a totally unnecessary reminder that fated mates in the witching world are legally engaged with a bunch of rights and privileges, though the law does require both parties' consent to formally tie the knot.

That's as far as my dad got before I slammed my bedroom door in his face.

"You're not my mate," I repeat now for good measure.

Because anything this important is worth saying twice.

"I am, though." My bedmate stretches that big body of his right next to me, claiming impossible amounts of real estate even in this supersized bed, then pulls his slept-in sweater over his head with one hand. "I'm your fated mate, babe, and you're mine."

Underneath that Academy sweater, he's wearing… well, pretty much nothing. And this Neo Mercury is just one seriously cut and buff and chiseled force of manhood.

Even though I have zero intention of letting him anywhere near me (you know, at least until we get this whole fated mate misunderstanding sorted out, and probably not even then) it doesn't mean I can't appreciate that Chris Evans Captain America body he's totally rocking, all massive shoulders and six-pack abs and luscious biceps I want to sink my teeth in. He's got a redhead's fair skin and a trail of fiery hair that arrows down under the waist of his wrinkled chinos. And, even as my gaze follows the temptation of that happy trail like Gretel following breadcrumbs through the forest, he stretches and yawns again.

Then he lazily unbuttons his pants and starts working on his zipper.

"Hold it right there, buddy," I almost yelp, clutching the blankets to my chest like an outraged virgin. I'm tempted to jump right out of bed. But despite the fire, it's almost cold enough to see my breath in this stone vault they're housing me in, and my pajamas are paper-thin.

I may be a world-class badass, but I'm a wimp when it comes to the cold.

Neo glances up in surprise, red brows hitching above his vivid eyes. His gaze moves over my face just like mine moves over his, slowly taking in the wild tumble of hair around my shoulders and my undoubtedly sleep-creased features. His eyes drop to my mouth and I swipe my tongue across my lips, suddenly thinking about things like night breath and mouthwash that are totally irrelevant to this situation.

Neo's full mouth curls up in a slow grin. Gently his big hand rises to cup my startled face, thumb tracing softly along my lower lip.

And damn if that careful touch doesn't light me up inside like New Year's Eve fireworks.

Disturbed by this, like any reasonable person would be, I cover his hand with mine and ease it away from my face.

His hands are twice the size of mine, palms rough like he does masonry or construction, nails blunt and buffed like a rich kid's. I cradle his warm hand between my cold ones and hold it in my lap so it doesn't stray anywhere else it shouldn't.

"Listen, Neo," I say carefully, and he gifts me with another slow smile, like just hearing me say his name makes his whole damn morning. "I'm gonna assume either Lucius or Ronin hit me with a sleep spell when the power lit me up last night. And I'm gonna take a wild guess that this is the Academy and therefore I'm on an island in the Med. How am I doing so far?"

"Brilliantly," he says happily. "And they claimed you didn't know anything."

My ignorance is starting to feel like a problem given where I am and that everyone here apparently knows about it, but first I've got a score to settle. "Was it Lucius or Ronin that knocked me out?"

"It was Master Aries who bespelled you." Neo's fingers insinuate their way between mine and give a squeeze. "Don't be mad at him, babe. He didn't want you upset when you got here."

Which officially means I'm going to murder Lucius Aries. He probably had Ronin carry me in like some medieval damsel in distress in front of the whole damn school, which would have told every soul in this Academy that I'm too weak to protect myself. And there's already someone on this island who's strong enough and smart enough to murder royals and get away with it.

This morning, every piranha on this island must be smelling blood in the water.

I groan and drop his hand to cover my face with both of mine.

"Don't worry, Zara." He has a deep rumbly voice, low and earnest, and his hand's still warm when it burrows under the blankets and cups my knee. "You're in Villa Augustus, with Master Aries' cohort. There are six of us students in this *domus*, including you, plus Master Aries who's our headmaster for the residential college. He reports up to the Dean. Because we share your roof, we're the seed of your royal court. Although it's your right to take others too, as many as you choose."

Yeah, no. I don't want the few courtiers I've already apparently got.

And I'm getting the hell off this island on the very next boat.

"Boats don't come here," Neo says with a frown. Great. Apparently he's reading my mind too. "They can't get past the wards. We're mostly self-sufficient. But what we do need is supplied by air."

Then I'll hijack a fucking plane. Even though I don't know how to fly one.

"And the reason I can read your mind is because we're fated mates," he adds helpfully. "Otherwise I couldn't, because I'm not Valyrian. The Mercurys are almost pure Kryll."

Of course they are. Of all the four races, the Kryll are the politicians and the merchants. They're good at managing money and they're brilliant at swaying hearts and minds. And we don't seem to be getting anywhere fast on resolving this whole fated mate business.

Anyway, if we really are fated mates, shouldn't I be able to read his mind too?

"You will, Zara," he says, low and earnest, "once you fully accept our union."

Which I've already told him will never happen.

We both sigh in unison.

Neo's solid hand is wrapped around my knee, warming me even with my pajamas between us. He smells sharp and fresh, like hand-milled soap, with notes of sage and juniper. I peek at him through my fingers to find another of those slow smiles breaking over his face like it makes him so goddamn happy just to look at me he's ready to burst into song.

Those smiles of his are messing with my head.

I sigh and lower my hands, then do up a couple of shirt buttons and flop down again on the mattress, wondering what on earth I'm going to do next.

Like that's the sign he's been waiting for, Neo draws the nest of blankets slowly down my legs. Then he slides both warm hands from my ankles to my knees with equal leisure.

I prop one arm behind my head and eye him suspiciously. "What are you doing?"

He eases my knees apart and crawls between them to face me. "Touching you."

His voice is a velvety growl and he gives me an upward look that smolders with green fire. He holds my gaze and rests one hand on my thigh, a touch that makes me tingle, while he drags down his zipper to give me a peek at the black briefs he's wearing underneath.

Stretched over an absolutely jaw-dropping bulge of impressive proportions.

That's a preview of coming attractions right there, if I want to let it go that far. Which I really can't, since it's hardly going to help clear up this whole fated mate confusion.

"Um, Neo." I clear my throat. "Why are you taking your clothes off?"

The look he gives me is pure seduction. "You wanted me to tongue you awake, didn't you?"

Holy shit, I did ask him for that. At least twice. But that was when I thought he was Xiao. Still, the way my nipples pucker and my clit swells and moisture slicks between my thighs tells me my body's fully onboard with the original plan.

Even with this new wingman.

I unfold one finger in careful illustration. "One, I thought you were someone else." I unfold a second finger. "And two, you don't have to take your pants off for that."

Neo's lazy grin does things to my heart I'm not ready for. "I'm an incurable optimist."

It takes my caffeine-deprived brain about six seconds to work through that. When I finally manage, I'm not sure whether to laugh or scream.

"We're not having sex here," I say out loud for both our benefits, even if he can read my mind. "The fact that I'm here at all is a fairly significant crisis, okay?"

"Okay." He absorbs this with furrowed brow.

Finally, I think we're getting somewhere. Then I notice there's a wing of magenta hair falling over his eyes. And it's all I can manage not to stroke it back. So maybe we're not getting to that new place fast enough, because my body's still stuck in the old place.

His hands sear a path up my thighs inch by scorching inch, which I tell myself I'm permitting mainly because I'm still wearing my jammies.

And not because there's a part of me that doesn't want him to stop.

Maybe he's still reading my mind, because another sleepy grin curls the corner of his mouth. "Somewhere else then?"

He has the kind of smile you want to kiss, but I have to resist that impulse. "What do you mean?"

"You said we're not having sex *here*. How about the *thermae*? That's the Roman bath downstairs. We'll have it all to ourselves, since everyone's already left for class, but you and I were excused this morning, and frankly I can't think of a better use for the time—"

"No, no, no, for cripes' sake!" I can't help laughing at his one-track mind. "We're not having sex anywhere right now."

"Which leaves open the possibility we could be having it later," he points out hopefully. "I guess I can live with later… but only if we've ruled out now as an option?"

Looking up at me under that wing of vivid hair, he slides one finger into his mouth and envelopes it with his full lips in a long slow suck. It's the finger he just had inside me. And I feel the slow hot pull of his mouth like it's wrapped directly around my clit.

"Later might be an option," I admit in a throaty voice. Shit. That isn't even what I meant to say. "But we're not mated. I need you to hear that."

"You're very confusing to me," he admits with a frown. But at least he stops sucking the taste of me off his skin and obligingly climbs off me. Which I tell myself is totally a good thing. "What you say is different than what you think."

"I think that's pretty much the way it works for everyone." I seize the moment to scramble out of bed before either one of us gets any other ideas about what else we can be doing in here.

My scramble turns into more of a jump, because it turns out this bed's on a platform a good two feet off the floor, which is probably meant to help with the drafts in this ancient building. In fact, there's an actual rolling stair backed up to the bed that I missed noticing in my haste. I stick the landing, but the icy floor makes me yelp.

Neo jumps out too—also not using the stair—and trots over to bring me a pair of royal blue slippers embroidered with the Academy logo. These slippers are the real deal, all lined with soft white fur, so I ignore the Academy marketing and get my feet into all that cushy warmth pronto.

He also produces a matching robe, likewise lined with white fur and sporting the logo I'm starting to suspect I'll see everywhere on this island. But it's warm and I'm cold, so this isn't the hill I'm gonna die on. I belt it around my waist and head for the open door that hopefully leads to the john.

"Yeah, it's a half-john," Neo says, though thankfully he isn't following. "All the suites have them."

I pause at the bathroom door and glance back. "Do you mind not doing that right now? Reading my mind? Because it's kind of freaking me out."

"Sorry. I'm not used to it either." Neo looks adorably contrite as he zips up his pants and wrestles the sweater back over his head.

Which worries me.

Not that he's getting dressed, but that he looks so cute while he's doing it. This is one guy I *really* don't need to be crushing on, because it would totally confuse this whole fated mate situation even worse than it already is.

I duck into the john and close the door to do my business. There's a toilet in here and a sink, both pretty modern and impeccably clean. And I'm relieved to find electricity is an actual thing on this island, even though the painted frieze around the ceiling and the tile floor that looks like a Roman mosaic seem to be about a million years old. Still, the setup reinforces what Neo said about there being a full Roman bath downstairs.

Though I do wonder if it's unisex.

And if all of us are supposed to be sharing it?

Not that I'm planning on sticking around the freak academy long enough to find out.

I find all the usuals behind the mirrored cabinet above the sink, which is lavishly stocked. That bonanza gives me what I need to brush and floss and wash my face and work a hairbrush through the tangled mess of my hair. Natural curls are supposed to be what every little girl wants for Christmas, but I'm here to tell you they're a total bitch to manage without exactly the right product.

While I'm doing my thing, I notice the various bumps and bruises from my encounter with the tarmac on Wang's penthouse roof are already half healed. I've got a splash of shifter blood along with all the rest, but that's pretty much all it's ever been good for. The Geminis heal up fast.

Which is useful, given the whole Gemini lifestyle.

I admittedly take my time with the once-over in here, because I'm thinking it would probably be good if Neo Mercury isn't still sitting there in my bedroom when I come out. But there's only so much you can do in a half-bath, and I'm not really the trouble-avoiding type.

When I emerge all clean and minty, Neo's big body is sprawled across my bed, thankfully dressed, with cute dark-rimmed glasses seated on his nose and his serious face buried in an antique-looking book titled *Laws of the Witching World*.

Firmly I resist the impulse to sashay over there and straddle his hips, because he really does look kind of adorable with his glasses and his book. Instead I make myself behave (for once) and look around for clothes.

Now that I'm awake, I've gotta admit these are pretty sweet digs they've stashed me in, stucco walls painted all the way around with Roman frescoes of frisky gods and lusty mortals frolicking in pastoral scenes, and kind of a broody minotaur mosaic scowling on the floor. But there's no sign of any—

"Try the armoire," Neo says, without lifting his eyes from his book.

"Um, thanks, but do you mind not doing that? Reading my mind, I mean. Reading the book is fine."

I head for the armoire, which looks big enough to take me straight to Narnia, and I'm already worried about what I'm going to find in there. Presumably *not* Tumnus the Faun and the passage to Narnia, but rather the contents of whatever was in that suitcase Lucius was toting around last night.

"Ugh, sorry," Neo repeats. "Look, don't be annoyed, okay? I'm not really used to reading minds, because I'm not Valyrian. Dez and Ronin are, so they can both project, but Dez is pretty shy and she hardly ever does that with me. And Ronin hates my guts, so anything he projects at me is usually pretty unpleasant."

Curiosity prickles through me. I pause with my hand on the armoire. "Why does Ronin hate your guts?"

"Honestly?" He hesitates long enough that I turn to look. He's laid the open book across his chest to watch me with sober eyes. "It's because I'm mated to you, loyal to you, and Ronin hates all things Gemini."

"Yeah," I mutter. "I kinda picked up on that last night. Don't suppose you have any idea why?"

I mean, I pretty much hate all things Gemini myself, but at least I have a reason. Far as I can tell, Ronin just walked into my life on Wang's rooftop already hating my guts.

"Oh, sure." Neo sighs. "It's because of Gwen."

I gesture impatiently for him to keep going, as I'm obviously hoping for a little more than a one-syllable name to work with.

He obliges with another sigh. "Gwendolyn Pendragon is… was… Ronin's twin sister. She died during freshman year. Ronin blames your brother for killing her."

Whatever awful Gemini secret I expected to hear him divulge, this one is a million times worse. I feel sick to my stomach. Sure, Damien was a monster and he made my childhood suck, so I know he's capable—*was* capable—of putting any girl through a living hell.

But it's a whole new level of trauma to learn your own brother's also apparently capable of murder.

Even if you always suspected he could be.

"He didn't murder her, *per se*." Neo sits up and adjusts his glasses with a frown, and for once I'm thankful he's reading my mind. At least it saves time. "He seduced her, stole her virginity, then told the whole school and made fun of her after. He was powerful here, the future king and all, so a lot of kids followed his lead and bullied her. With Cybelle leading the charge. Because Gwen was gorgeous—you know, like Ronin—and Cybelle was actually jealous."

"That bastard." I know what Damien could do, but I'm still vengeful as fuck on Gwen's behalf. Poor Gwen… and poor Ronin. "Wish I could say I'm surprised, but that sort of conduct was pretty standard for Damien. There's a reason I'm not grieving his death."

"Yeah." Neo grimaces. "Despite his popularity, not many of us did grieve when he and Cybelle died in that fire. When the investigator said it was suspicious, no one was all that surprised."

Fire. So that's how my brother finally bought it.

It's a bad way to go, arson is a brutal way to kill, and I feel cold and queasy. I'm extra cold and queasy knowing someone burned two royals to a crisp and got away with it.

Because, you know, I'm apparently the next royal.

And maybe the next target.

I clear my throat and focus on Neo. "Tell me more about what happened with Gwen. Couldn't Ronin defend her?"

"He definitely tried. When the bullying started, Ronin went all out to defend her. But he was new here himself, still coming into his power. He beat the living crap out of Damien and scared the shit out of Cybelle and almost got expelled himself. But it just made the bullying worse. Until…"

He hesitates, but for once this mind-reading thing works in reverse, because the outcome pops into my mind like he's just whispered it in my ear.

"Oh God," I breathe, hugging myself. "Until Gwen killed herself. And Ronin's hated every Gemini on the planet ever since."

"Pretty much." Neo sinks back to the pillow. "That was two years ago now, but he's fanatical. He hates Damien, you, and me by extension. Honestly, I can't even blame the guy."

"Yeah," I sigh. "Me neither. Thanks for telling me."

My heart aches for Gwen and it aches for Ronin. No freaking wonder he hates me. If our positions were reversed, I'd hate me too.

I can't help thinking that, what with Damien and Cybelle's still-unsolved murder, plus the fact that Ronin's a Leo who summons fire, that fucked-up history puts Ronin Pendragon's name at the top of the suspect list.

Not that it stopped Ronin from fucking me, and I *really* hope Neo isn't reading my mind now. Actually, it would be kind of handy to know how to stop the mental spillage and block out that sort of involuntary eavesdropping. If it takes me a day or two to hijack that plane, maybe I can focus on learning that while I'm here.

Just so the time isn't totally wasted.

Pondering that plan, I turn back around and investigate the armoire.

It smells like camphor and it's surprisingly full, but there's not a lot of variety given the sheer volume of shit hanging in there. There's a whole row of red-and-black plaid skirts and blue-and-white plaid skirts and green-and-gold plaid skirts and, well, you get the picture. There's a rack of crisp white blouses with pearl buttons and stiff collars. There's a half-dozen tailored wool blazers in cherry and black and burgundy with the ever-present Academy logo stitched in gold on the breast.

And there's a whole row of drawers down the side, filled with cashmere sweaters and pants and more pressed pajamas like the ones I'm wearing, along with a few actual white nightgowns, a drawer full of cable-knit knee socks, and the requisite undies. There's even a row of strappy mary jane pumps and snow boots and a pair of black-and-white saddle shoes (I swear I'm not making this up) lined up neatly on the bottom.

In other words, there's not one bloody damn thing I would normally even consider putting on my body.

Jesus. Would it have killed Lucius to throw in a pair of jeans and a tee shirt?

I turn around, ready to grumble, but I already realize it's a wasted effort. Lucius isn't here, and there's nowhere else in this room where some alternate universe of wardrobe options can secretly be lurking. There's the bed, the armoire, a vanity, a cushy window seat that looks like a reading nook, and a big desk with a well-stocked bookcase.

There really is no other option.

I'm going to have to put on something from this armoire.

"Wear the burgundy," Neo says calmly to my indignant face. "That's the color we wear on Wednesdays."

"Fine," I grumble, "but I'm not putting on the skirt." Because the color of my blazer is also not the hill I'm going to die on, but that skirt just might be. "I'll wear the pants, I guess."

Neo sits up and looks concerned. "Hey, I get that you're a rebel and you don't really want to be here, but I honestly wouldn't advise it. You and I are excused from study hall this morning, but we're due in class in an hour, and you have to wear the uniform. Otherwise it's a decorum referral and detention with Master Zerxes—he's the headmaster of Villa Tiberius—and you really don't want to risk it."

"They can't put me in detention when I'm not even a student." I fold my arms across my chest and sound belligerent, even to myself. "Anyway, why would detention with, uh, Master Zerxes be a risk?"

"Because Damien and Cybelle were both students in Zerxes' *domus*. Which means Zerxes and his entire cohort were members of Cybelle's court. That makes them loyal to the Aquarius queen. And they really hated losing their courtier status when you were assigned here instead of their *domus*, the way Zerxes wanted. That makes them our enemies."

Well, that's just peachy. I haven't even ventured out of my room yet, and I already have a whole houseful of enemies. It's starting to sound like I need to pay *really* close attention to whatever Neo's willing to tell me.

And he really must be listening about not reading my mind, because he seems to think I need more persuading.

He leans forward and props his elbows on his knees. "Trust me, Zara. You don't want to tangle with Master Zerxes, and definitely not alone. At least not until you get a handle on your power."

"No, I get that." Resigned, I dive into the armoire and start pulling out the requisite items, all of them clearly new, expensively made, and tailored to fit my size exactly. I drag everything behind an antique dressing screen that's painted with a pretty forest scene and start stripping down. "Are you telling me every single person in Villa Tiberius is my enemy? Even though I'm supposed to be their queen?"

"Pretty much," Neo admits.

"How many enemies is that exactly?"

"Nine students plus Master Zerxes in that house. They're a bigger house than we are. We're actually the smallest of the three."

"Just my luck," I mutter.

"It's because we're the most exclusive. Master Aries is super picky about who he lets in." Physically Neo's keeping his distance, but I can feel his gaze on the screen, because of course he knows I'm getting naked back here. "Queen Messalina... you know, Cybelle's mom... is still technically young enough to maybe have another kid. She's, like, in her forties? It's just she wasn't planning on it, because Cybelle was a total bitch but a weak witch—kinda like her mom—and Messalina didn't want Cybelle to have a rival. Now everyone in Villa Tiberius is hoping if you're out of the picture, maybe we'll get another Aquarius queen."

"That does sound like the best solution for everyone." Hearing this, I feel a little more hopeful. By this point, I've worked my way into the prim white silk panties and white lace bra and I'm buttoning up the crisp linen blouse. The well-made garments caress my skin, but I feel naked without my leather.

I'm still wearing my lucky cuff and my dive watch, at least, and I damn well plan to keep those.

"The Senate's already confirmed you as the next queen," Neo informs me, "and it's not a title that can be revoked. The abdication process takes decades, and that's by design. That means for another Aquarius queen to ascend right now, you'd have to be dead."

My hope plummets back to my heels. Grumpily, I pull on the burgundy-and-gold plaid skirt and button it. It's short and pleated and comes to mid-thigh. "Well, uh, what about the third house? Do they hate me too?"

"Villa Hadrian," he supplies. "Twelve students in that one, plus Mistress Agrippina, the headmistress. There are only twenty-seven students in the whole Academy right now, but in terms of status and test scores, the cohort from Villa Hadrian's at the bottom of the heap. Some of them barely have any witchcraft, just common magics, so they can't go toe to toe with the big dogs. They'll play it safe and wait to see who comes out on top."

"Which means we've got unarmed civilians in the bleacher seats when the shooting starts," I acknowledge with a sigh. "Can I trust them at least not to stab me in the back?"

"For now." He sounds cautious. "They'll mostly pay lip service to the Senate and show you the requisite deference as the current queen-in-waiting." He pauses. "Assuming you survive Purgatory. Until then, it's hunting season, and you're fair game."

"Purgatory?" I poke my head out from behind the screen. "I really hope you're speaking metaphorically."

"Yeah, you wish. That's what we call the first days here for freshmen." He's returned to lying flat on my bed, but he's still watching me, all those vivid magenta waves streaming across my pillow in an extremely distracting way. "There's no other way to say this. You'll probably be, uh, hazed."

"Hazed?" I sound as indignant as I feel. "How exactly is that necessary? Usually the whole point of hazing is to get you to drop out. I already don't want to be here. Just show me the way off this rock and it's *sayonara*."

"It's not that simple, Zara. You're already enrolled, and the wards around the island won't let any student pass without the Dean's consent. So you can't just back out."

I process this breaking headline with concern, because it could definitely have a bearing on my whole hijacking plan. "Tell me more about this Purgatory business."

He draws up one knee and props a brawny arm behind his head. "The whole purpose is to winnow out the weak and help the strong hone their power. Most freshmen start the school year together, and the hazing process encourages us to form alliances with the other plebes. But since you're starting mid-term…"

"I'm doing this alone," I finish for him, with a sigh. Because of course I am. "And all those new alliances are already formed."

"But you have *us*," Neo says firmly. "Your cohort at Villa Augustus. We're your courtiers and your allies. At least, Racetrack and Dez and I are, and they're even going to work on Ronin. He'd be a good ally to have if he can ever admit you're not responsible for what happened to Gwen. Vasili, though… he's a lost cause."

Judging by his tone, that doesn't sound good. So of course I have to ask. "Vasili's one of the students in this house?"

"As far as he's concerned, Vasili's the only student in this house," he says dryly, "and the only student on this whole island who matters. And of course his underlings buy into it. He's the Scorpio scion, pretty close to purebred Mogadon, with a little shifter. He's a really strong warlock, with a penchant for knives and some unusual gifts that don't usually come out in our recessives these days. Plus he's the oldest student, so he wields a lot of power."

"Sounds like a fun guy." Mentally I add another problem to my growing list.

"Most of the students are terrified of him." Neo's tone ratchets tight. "And of course he actively exploits that. In fact, the way he acts, he pretty much guarantees it. The only students Vasili doesn't completely terrorize are Ronin and me."

"So if I can get Ronin on my side, maybe the two of you can help me keep Vasili in line?" I button myself into the burgundy blazer and sit in the window seat to work on my stockings.

"Maybe." Neo hesitates. "It's worth a shot, I guess."

I shoot him a sharp look. "What aren't you telling me?"

He rakes a hand through his hair with a grimace. "Everyone knows Ronin and Vasili are mortal enemies. But they've been known to work together at times to take out a common rival. Even Damien was wary of those two together."

"Sounds lovely," I say, glumly unrolling the stockings. They're longer than I thought, more thigh-highs than knee-highs—which makes sense given it's winter, I guess. Once I finish rolling up the first one, there's only an inch of exposed thigh between the bottom of my skirt and the top of my stocking.

Neo's stopped talking completely and rolled onto his side, head propped on fist, to fully appreciate the stocking effect. The intense look on his face makes me abruptly remember that exactly ten minutes and twenty seconds ago, according to my dive watch, I was clenched around his finger and chasing a climax he still hasn't given me, but which he's clearly more than capable of delivering.

Holding his gaze, I prop my bare foot on the cushion beside me and unroll the second stocking, inch by inch, up the length of my leg. As I smooth the fabric leisurely over my knee, he watches in utter and complete absorption.

Suddenly his big body uncoils and he surges to his feet. He tosses his glasses on the desk and stalks toward me like some magenta-maned lion on the

African savanna. In that moment, he's so damn predatory he might as well be crawling toward me.

I freeze like a hunted impala with my knee bent and my pulse spiking and my foot propped on the cushion, plaid skirt pooling between my thighs. That arrangement leaves a good four inches of naked skin between the hem of my skirt and the top of my stocking.

There are roughly nine hundred and twelve reasons why teasing Neo Mercury is a really bad idea, and I know every one of them.

But I can't seem to make myself stop.

He drops to a crouch between my splayed knees. His hands close over my knees and ease them wide open.

And suddenly I'm face to face and eye to eye with this strange guy I've been recklessly teasing, and my pulse is jumping and my skin is hot.

"Zara," he breathes, eyes green as kryptonite locking onto mine. He's like my own personal kryptonite, this dude, because I don't want to confuse things between us any worse than they're already confused. Yet I can't seem to stop what's happening between us, and I can't seem to want him to stop either. "You have no idea how long I've waited for you, do you?"

"I'm guessing… five years?" I whisper.

He dips his chin in a nod without ever breaking my gaze. "And the only reason I didn't just peel your panties off with my teeth and fuck you with my tongue until you came apart in our bed—the *only* reason—is because you told me to stop."

"I did," I whisper, licking my dry lips, not even feeling capable of tackling that whole "our bed" assertion, which ties directly to the whole fated mate assertion I also need to tackle. I feel so incredibly exposed with my thighs splayed wide in this short skirt and silk panties, the tips of his calloused fingers barely grazing my skin above my stockings.

His eyes flicker to find my mouth and his lids drop. He leans in close enough to feel the heat of his breath, until his face is all I see. My eyes drift closed, my hands resting on my bunched-up skirt.

And all I seem capable of wondering is what he'd do if I pushed my skirt up and gave him a real show.

"Tell me to stop, babe," he says hoarsely, his breath fanning my lips, "or else I'm not going to."

"I'm not mating you," I manage to say, which seems like the most salient point.

"That's not telling me to stop." His nose bumps gently against mine and he nudges my chin with his.

I suck in a breath and take the plunge. "Then don't stop—"

His warm mouth closes gently over mine and steals every single word in my vocab. He smells like sage and he tastes like spearmint. He must've had a mint or something while I was in the john. Between parted lips, our tongues meet in a tentative touch. He groans and I whimper.

I'm braced to be devoured, but he seems content to nibble, all slow careful sweeps of his mouth over mine, his entire body still except for these long languid sips of lips meeting lips and tongue finding tongue, touching just briefly each time before we pull away. In fact, he's a lot more careful than I expect, though his breath is shallow and quick and I can feel his hands tremble.

That's how bad he wants me.

He wants me so bad I'm making his hands tremble.

He's honestly making me crazy—his restraint, his need, his oh-so-careful pace—even when I rest my hands on his waist to encourage him.

God, I want more of his hands and his tongue on my body. I don't care right now if it's going to cause problems later. My hips are tilting on the seat to give him access, little rocking thrusts to encourage him. I'm actually squirming with eagerness to get more of his hands and his mouth on me.

Too impatient and worked up now to wait, I grip his waist and drag him close. A deeper groan rumbles from his chest and he finally gives me that ravenous open-mouthed kiss I'm craving, lips crushing mine, tongue plunging deep, drinking down all the little pants and whimpers I can't seem to swallow.

That climax I was chasing this morning hasn't gone very far. It's hovering between us like a promise. Actual sex feels way too complicated given everything else that's hovering between us. But with him able to read my mind, I'm really wondering if maybe…

"You want to come for me, babe?" he mumbles into my mouth.

Now I'm really starting to see the upside to this whole fated mate concept.

He huffs out a husky chuckle and eases those rough palms of his up my thighs. The second his fingers find the edge of my panties, my head falls back. Under that little strip of silk, I'm hot and aching and slick with hunger. He mouths his way down my neck as his thumbs skate up the damp silk of my panties.

When one thumb hits the swollen nub of my clit through the silk, a sound rips out of me that I don't even recognize as mine.

Turns out that's the way I sound moaning his name.

He nuzzles deep in my neck, breathing hard against my skin, and I claw at his back through his sweater. He's kneading my slit with his cupped palm and working my clit through the silk, finding the pace and the pressure I need, and I'm drenched and rocking into him and crying out for more.

And he hasn't even gotten under my panties when that climax I've been craving all morning rolls through me like an avalanche and shatters me. My high cry of release mingles with his long low groan, like what he's doing is killing both of us.

"Oh God, babe," he breathes out against my skin, my pulse slamming against his kiss. His whole body is trembling in my arms. "That was so totally worth waiting for."

I'm still seeing stars, and now I want him to see them too. I want to take care of him the same way he just took care of me. I want to make him feel so good.

"You do," he whispers. "You will. That's worth waiting for too."

He keeps saying that, and it crosses my mind to wonder if he's *really* been waiting, like, literally? Like if he's actually been celibate while waiting for me to figure my shit out and come to my senses.

"Oh, Zara." His head lifts and my eyes open and he cradles my head in his hands. "What do you think *fated mates* means?"

My mouth falls open. "Neo, you… you can't honestly be saying…"

The deep gong of a bell makes the air tremble. It's like a church bell or something echoing through the walls. But given what's going down right now between us, the bell doesn't really register, even when it keeps on tolling at a measured pace.

"Damn," Neo whispers. He leans his forehead against mine. "That's the lunch bell. We'll have to finish this later."

"The *lunch bell*? You have got to be kidding me." I look deep into his rueful eyes, roughly three inches from mine. "Look, I need you to tell me you haven't literally been waiting for—"

"Babe, we really have to go." He lets me go and pushes firmly to his feet.

Which, at my current altitude, gives me a VIP seat for all that heat he's packing under his pants. I'm seriously tempted to forgo this awkward convo right now in favor of just dragging down his zipper and wrapping my lips around his shaft.

Not to mention bringing to an explosive end what could possibly be a major sex famine.

Color floods into his face to rival the merlot hue of his sweater. "I can tell you're going to be a bad influence on me, Zara Gemini. But I'm going to get you to class on time if it kills me."

"Okay, okay, we'll go," I huff, smoothing out my skirt and scrambling up. "But you better believe we're gonna finish this later. We're just getting started here, buddy."

That makes him smile. "Whatever you say, babe."

And he looks so purely happy, even though I'm the only one who came, that it makes my heart all floaty and my tummy all fluttery.

I pull my mind out of the gutter and duck over to the vanity for a quick peek in the glass. I'm all flushed and dewy with that post-orgasmic glow and my hair is absolutely everywhere. I pilfer the vanity and find a black scrunchie to pull my teal waves into a loose side ponytail. There's a ton of makeup too, all top-end brands, whole rows of oval palettes in rose and beige and violet that work with my complexion, though I really prefer the cobalt eyeliner and bubble-gum pink lipstick I usually wear.

I'm in a rush, so I end up settling for a few swipes of inky mascara and a nude lipstick that doesn't clash with the burgundy blazer.

Neo appears in the mirror, which he pretty much fills with his big buff body, and props a hip against the wall to watch while I apply a second coat. That emerald heat is still smoldering in his eyes, but I have to focus now on getting more of the information I need rather than the toe-curling climax my body is still recovering from.

I blot my lipstick and spritz on a little perfume from the bottle on the vanity. It's the same roses-and-vanilla fragrance I normally wear, and I wonder who's responsible for the gesture.

It makes me feel a little better to think at least someone at Icarus isn't out for my head.

"Don't forget your coat and boots," he says. "We eat lunch and have classes at the church with the other students, and that's where we're due right now. I've already packed the books and supplies you'll need in your backpack. We'll stop at my room on the way down."

He's super thoughtful and I appreciate it, especially since the prospect of a nasty hazing by all those students who hate me has my tummy tied in knots. I concentrate on finding my leather boots and woolen peacoat and bundling myself into them. I don't feel anywhere near ready to meet the rest of the student body, but I am hungry, and I need to get the lay of the land to figure out my escape plan.

As if I needed any more motivation.

Honestly, I won't be here long enough for anyone to haze me.

"I gotta tell you, Neo," I say to get him talking again, "this Academy doesn't sound like a very friendly place."

He rakes back his hair. "Friendly isn't how it works at the Academy. We're not here to make friends. We're here to learn to control our power before our power controls us. This entire setup was designed centuries ago with that end in mind."

"You ever get to leave?" I ask casually.

"Not until we graduate, not easily—and never without the Dean's consent." He frowns. "Which means we're like scorpions in a bottle. Tensions run high and survival's uncertain. If you shake the bottle too hard? We'll destroy each other."

I can't think of anything to say to that. For a sec, we're both silent.

His gaze locks on mine. He pulls in a breath and finishes, "That's what they're afraid you'll do here, Zara, with your unpredictable and undisciplined Gemini power. They're afraid you'll shake the bottle and destroy us."

Chapter Twelve
Zara

By the time Neo swaps out his slept-in clothes for his uniform and hurries me out of Villa Augustus (which I've still barely seen) into the street, my tummy's churning with nerves at the threat of the promised hazing.

Not to mention the threat of that pyromaniacal queen killer who's still at large.

It's safe to say I'm on high alert.

But right off the bat, there's no one else around. And we haven't been walking long through these silent streets, under a dusting of snowflakes whirling down from dove-gray skies, before I feel like I'm literally dreaming.

Last night when we landed, I was totally out of it thanks to Lucius and his whole non-con sleep spell—for which I owe him major payback. So as Neo and I rush through the flagstone streets, I'm seeing the Academy and this whole island for the first time.

And this place where I don't want to be is way more extensive than a building or even a walled compound.

It's a whole freaking village.

The entire thing's built on a harrowingly steep hill that plunges straight down to a frigid gray bay, which means the streets are narrow and winding and mostly stairs. Lots and lots of stairs. They zig and they zag and they twist and they tack, which obviously means there are no cars or buses or even a bicycle or a scooter anywhere in sight.

Apparently, at this Academy, you walk and you climb.

The buildings are mostly stone and stucco with terra-cotta roofs, painted in fantastic shades of cobalt and green and crimson all faded and scoured from the sun and the wind and the salt whose briny tang lingers under the metallic smell of snow. And most of these buildings, it's pretty obvi, are empty.

I mean it. These streets are so quiet you can hear the wind whistle and the waves crash against the rocks way below.

In fact, it's so quiet you can practically hear the snow fall. Fat flakes spiral from a pewter sky and accumulate in drifts against all those closed doors.

It's quickly becoming clear there's a lot more Academy than there are students to fill it.

Like… a lot.

"It never used to be this way." Neo sounds apologetic as we tromp down another interminable set of stairs in our boots, coats buttoned tight and heads bent against the icy wind raking from the sea. Climbing back up is gonna be a real bitch. "According to the history books, these buildings were bursting at the seams back in the day. We had twelve whole houses, hundreds of faculty and support staff, and a line of students waiting to get in. Nowadays, with the races dwindling, there aren't enough students to fill more than three. Throw in the faculty and the custodial staff, and there are maybe forty arcanes total on this whole island."

And out of those forty, apparently only seven live in our *domus*. That's if you include me in the tally.

Which you definitely shouldn't.

Because I'm not staying.

And I'm not going to feel guilty about leaving. The four races were failing long before I came along. Queen or no queen, even the arcane races with their freakish and terrifying powers can't escape the inevitable march to extinction. That's just the way evolution works.

We round a corner and a fresh gust of wind slams into us, making my face sting and my ears ache.

"What's up with this weather anyway?" I shiver and burrow deeper into my coat. "This climate isn't like any island in the Med I've ever seen."

"It's the wards." Gently he reaches to brush snow from my hair. He can't seem to stop touching me, and he always smiles when he does it. "The protective wards around the island. The same witchcraft that protects this place from discovery also messes with the weather. Which means our summers run hot and our winters run cold. This time of year, we're more like the North Atlantic than the Med."

"One more reason to love the place," I mutter. There's a damn good reason my safe houses always hug the equator, because I'm a total wimp about the cold. Speaking of which, I'm going to lose those digs I just lined up in Sharm on the Red Sea coast if I don't get off this rock in time to pay the rent.

The thought of finding myself homeless as well as hunted plunges me into a whole new funk. Now I'm more than anxious about the looming fun and frolic.

I'm tempted to get borderline depressed.

We don't see another soul except a flock of gulls winging past and a stray cat slinking through the streets till we get down near the water. And that too comes as a shock, because there isn't actually a beach or a seawall. The steep village streets plunge straight down into the sea. You can literally stand at the bottom step and see more white stairs burrowing down through the water below you, exactly six steps down, before it gets too dark in the gray depths under these overcast skies to see the bottom.

Cold or no cold, I'd honestly love to dive it. I'd just need a proper cold-water dry suit.

And that makes me wonder if there's another way off this island that's more subtle and simple than hijacking a plane. I wonder how deep those protective wards penetrate. I definitely need to suss out how far we are from the nearest land. If I can find my burner phone, maybe I can get a fix on my GPS.

"Another sign that the witching world's failing," Neo says, sounding sober, hunkering on his heels to peer into the depths. "Above and beyond the fact that our queens are so weak, which affects the whole witching world. It isn't just the sea that's rising. It's the island that's sinking. You can appreciate why we're all so fixated on the succession. We don't get many new enrollees these days."

"Yeah, about that." Frowning, I turn away from all that cold but intriguing-looking water and hoist my backpack higher on my shoulder.

Neo wants to carry it for me, but he has his own big heavy pack to schlep (it looks like he's toting a whole library in there) and I don't want to project any more weakness to my fellow students than I already have. So I shoulder my own weight and follow him toward a broad cobblestone piazza with a frozen fountain.

"I can't figure out who enrolled me in the first place," I continue. "My dad wants me dead, not educated. I'm a threat to his authority. And with Damien gone, I don't have any other relatives who could have signed me up."

"Well, Zara, you have me." For some reason, he sounds wary. "We're engaged under arcane law. Being your fated mate gives me the authority to enroll you."

And that's exactly why I didn't want a fated mate in the first place.

I stop in my tracks and glare. "Neo Mercury, please tell me you are not the whack job I have to thank for this unimaginable shitshow I'm about to wade into."

He's obliged to stop too, since I'm not budging from this spot till he answers. Back at the villa, he looked ten different kinds of sexy in that tailored burgundy blazer and watered silk tie and ass-hugging skinny pants that are apparently the male uniform on Wednesdays. Never mind about all that sexy being currently buttoned into a stark black woolen coat that makes his magenta hair and green eyes really pop. He's the most striking object in my visual range without even trying.

But I'm not interested in how sexy he looks right now. Seriously, I'm not.

I'm interested in what he's going to say to dig himself out of that ten-foot hole he just fell into.

Obviously picking up on my agitation, the guy frowns and looks honestly perplexed. "I did it to help you out, babe. Sooner or later, your scumbag father and his hit men were going to get lucky. You're safe from all that here."

"Safe?" The word explodes from my mouth in a puff of white vapor. "My brother and the last queen just freaking *died* here, Neo. You've literally landed me in Purgatory. And how dare you make that choice for me?"

That last point's the one I really want him to address, but he shoves a hand through his hair and tackles the first one instead.

"You're going to get through this. You've got me and your other courtiers to help. You're going to learn how to harness your power and wield your witchcraft and wear the crown you were *born to wear*, Zara Gemini." He grips my shoulders in his gloved hands and squeezes. "You'll be the strong queen and the powerful witch we need to halt our decline and help the races flourish. And the next Gemini scion will come from *us*."

I twist free from all that crazy and plant my hands on my hips. "Don't you dare even think about making decisions like that for me. I told you before, we're not freaking mates!"

His eyes narrow to smoldering green slits. "We are, though, Zara."

He makes me so mad I want to swing my backpack at his stubborn head. "No, we're not! And I'm not even going to address the topic of the next Gemini scion." Frustration churns my gut and stings my eyes with useless tears. "Has it ever occurred to you the four races would be better off without the Gemini scion they've currently got? The power of a pure witch bloodline like mine is obviously way too dangerous. The night my mom died proved that point *eighty-seven times*. How many more have to die before you people believe it?"

"What do you mean, 'you people?'" For the first time since he woke up in my bed this morning, Neo isn't smiling. In fact, he's starting to look downright pissed. *Bring it on, buddy, because I'm literally spoiling for a fight.*

"You arcanes." I shrug. "You four races."

In this open piazza, the wind's really whipping our clothes and tearing at our hair. I tug over my ears my woolen beret with the Academy logo (of course) blazoned on it and figure we maybe should have waited to get inside before having the inevitable meltdown. None of my relationships tend to last all that long, and they all end messy, so this is par for the course.

Neo scowls and pushes the hair out of his face. "For your information, you're an arcane too, Zara. You're one of us. Our problems are your problems."

"That's where you're wrong, buddy." A violent gust of wind pushes the beret right off my head, and I barely snatch it with the tips of my fingers before it goes flying. "Look, you mind if we finish our breakup fight inside? I thought you didn't want to be late for class."

Now Neo looks like I've slapped him. His brow furrows and his mouth falls open. Then he pulls in a breath and his tone softens. "Babe, this isn't a breakup fight. I'm running out of ways to say this, but let me try once more. We're *fated mates*. There's no mistake in our natal charts and no loophole in arcane law. You know our bond's for life."

Clearly, we're not getting anywhere. He's just not hearing me. This breakup fight's literally going in circles.

I huff out a breath and spin toward the monstrosity of a building with spires and gargoyles and flying buttresses that looks like a Gothic cathedral looming over the piazza. The first human life forms I've seen on this island other than Neo are trudging into it, toting backpacks and wearing uniforms, so clearly that's where we're headed. I march across the square toward it. Neo keeps pace and doesn't try to stop me.

Anyway, why should he? I'm going where he wants.

Which definitely isn't a pattern of behavior he should get used to.

My ponytail snares on my backpack and he tries to help, but I shrug free and solve the problem myself, hardening my heart against the wounded puppy look that clouds his gorgeous eyes.

After all, I need to stand on my own two feet here if I'm going to survive however long it takes to find a way through the wards off this island.

And I *am* definitely going to survive.

As we approach the iron-studded wood of the heavy double doors, my tummy knots with nerves and my heart starts hammering. My instinct's to hang back, conduct a little recon, and scope out the sitch before I go charging in.

But there's no do-over for a first impression. And this one really matters.

I march ahead of Neo, tug open the heavy door, wrestle against the wind that wants to tear it from my grasp, and stride inside like I own the whole damn building.

This isn't the hushed and echoing sanctuary you'd expect. All the pews and statues and even the altar have been ripped out to create a vast exposed space. Under stained glass windows that cast shifting kaleidoscopes of light, contemporary couches and ottomans cluster around braziers crackling with fires that blaze with heat and light. A row of secretive-looking study carrels with high curving partitions and shaded reading lamps huddles against a wall. The space under the skylight up front is an actual dining room, complete with a long wooden table and a double row of benches.

Overall, this area too is a whole lot bigger than the size of the population warrants. But at least there are finally students.

Plenty of them.

Curled up chatting on the couches, huddled over piles of books in the carrels, and parked at the dining table scarfing down steaming bowls of food.

And somehow, even though I didn't intend to make a particularly noisy entrance, every single one of those students is staring at me like I've just blown a freaking trumpet to announce my arrival.

My skin prickles and goosebumps crawl down my arms.

This is Purgatory, there's no benevolent God in sight, I'm fresh meat, and somewhere in this room there's a queen killer who wants to make me bleed.

Or burn.

I find myself looking for Ronin, even though there's no actual reason to believe he's on my side since, one, he hates Geminis and, two, he was fairly instrumental in kidnapping my ass to bring me here. But at least he'd be a familiar face.

Unfortunately (or fortunately?) Ronin's nowhere in sight.

But something is pulling at me, a steady current like a vortex that's sucking my gaze to the massive circular couch parked under the windows. It's a primo placement with good light in this dim and drafty hangout, tucked right up next to the biggest brazier, and the real estate is definitely taken. A bunch of students are scattered there.

But there's only one worth noticing.

And boy does he know it.

He's sprawled across the center seat, arms spread across the back of the couch to claim the whole space and keep anyone else from getting too close, legs planted well apart on the floor. Another guy's sitting on the rug between his feet and sort of leaning against the first guy's leg, cheek resting against his knee.

And the guy on the couch is crazy beautiful. Like the most beautiful human I've ever laid eyes on.

Maybe the most beautiful on the planet.

He's an icy blond, with longish hair tousled and moussed in shaggy layers, so gilded it's almost silver, razor-cut to graze his sharp jaw. His oblong eyes are a blue so pale they look like frost, rimmed in smoky black to make them pop. He's sexy pretty, with exotic features that are almost delicate and a cruel mouth slicked with a swipe of clear gloss. Add a wickedly tall, whippet-thin body, effortlessly on trend in the severe blazer and trousers of Academy gear, a tie tugged loose at his elegant throat, and combat boots with thick purple soles. Under pale cuffs, diamonds sparkle on his long fingers.

This guy's gorgeous enough and androgynous enough to give David Bowie's Goblin King in the movie *Labyrinth* a real run for his money.

He's staring straight at me. And the glitter in his glacial gaze is pure malice.

Neo closes the door behind us with a whomp that seals out the frigid wind and makes me flinch. The Goblin King absorbs my reaction and his eyes harden. I feel like looking away from him would be a mistake, but this staring contest is getting super awkward.

"Come on, Zara," Neo says softly in my ear, and the Goblin King's knife-sharp gaze swerves to skewer him. If anything, those deadly eyes turn even more contemptuous. "Let's get unbundled and get you some lunch."

This suggestion finally gives me the face-saving cover I need to turn away from the Goblin King.

But I can feel those cruel eyes drilling holes in my back all the way to the coat rack.

With all these fires going, it's reasonably temperate in here despite the vast space and high ceiling. We take refuge near a coat rack and a row of boots dripping with melted snow. This lets me concentrate on getting out of my peacoat and swapping out my boots for the mary janes in my backpack and basically not throwing up on the floor from nerves.

Thankfully, the convo's picking up again behind me, all scattered hisses and the occasional riff of malicious laughter. I'm careful not to look directly toward the circular couch, but I keep it in my peripheral vision.

"Who's the Goblin King?" I mutter.

Neo snorts a grim chuckle. "That's Vasili Romanov. He should've greeted you, because he's Villa Augustus and technically a member of your court."

"I'm just as glad he didn't," I say.

"He disrespected you with his silence. Ideally, you should address it."

Yeah, no. I don't feel ready to address the Goblin King before I've even had my morning coffee.

Instead, I focus on buckling on my mary janes and mourning the loss of the platform boots I had in Singapore. Not to mention the stiletto I packed inside them. In those boots, I can kick major ass.

In these pumps and this freaking skirt, I can't even kick a soccer ball.

Behind us the whispers are picking up steam. Despite our recent fight and the fact that we're in the middle of breaking up, I'm incredibly grateful for Neo's comforting presence beside me, getting out of his coat too. That feeling of comfort evaporates when I pick up the hurried *tap-tap-tap* of feet coming up fast on the flagstones behind me.

I crouch and pivot, ready to defend myself with my lethally trained fists.

But the attack I'm expecting doesn't materialize. A pretty girl with olive eyes and sorrel skin, buttoned neatly into the requisite uniform topped off with an anxious expression, rushes right past me to corner Neo. "Crikey, cobber, where you been? Master Aries has been looking for you all over."

And even though I've got a score to settle with Lucius Aries for his snatch-and-grab and another one for knocking me out and spoiling my grand entrance, I can't help feeling a little bit relieved to know he's somewhere close.

Which is fucked up. Neither Lucius nor Ronin are my friends in this situation. They're the whole reason I'm here.

Neo glances at me and hesitates. "Uh, thanks, Dez. Do you know if he needs to see me right away?"

"Yeah, he's in his office. But no worries." The girl, who's apparently named Dez, also glances my way and offers a tentative smile. "I'll make sure Zara gets fed and finds her first class, yeah?"

Neo still seems reluctant to go, and frankly I'm sorry to see the back of him. But he can't always be with me. I have to face down the lions on my own, and it's better to do it my way and on my terms. So I assume a power pose, hands on hips and legs spread, and don't bother to lower my voice the way these two just did.

"You go right ahead wherever, Neo. I got this." My voice echoes through the nave, and I can feel heads turn.

"All right, babe." He hovers awkwardly for a sec, and it's awkward for me too, because he probably wants to kiss me goodbye or something, but I'm determined not to show weakness.

So I make it easy for both of us by waving a casual goodbye and giving him my back. It's a dismissal I sense he's not crazy about, and he's probably going to say something about it later.

But, hello, we're in the middle of breaking up, remember?

Finally he gets the message and goes.

There's a staircase plunging right down into the floor, and that's the one he takes. It looks like the crypt in a vampire movie, and seeing it swallow him gives me the creeps, but I deliberately don't linger on it.

Instead, I focus all my attention on the girl. Neo's friend.

She's staring at me from five-and-a-half feet away like she's expecting me to summon lightning and blow the place up before I've had my sandwich or something. That's the Gemini reputation preceding me right there.

So I dredge up a smile and stick out my hand. "Hey, I'm Zara. You're Dez?"

"Desdemona, yeah. But everyone calls me Dez." She has a definite Down-Under accent and a super sweet smile that animates her whole face, so it's easy to warm to her, especially since Neo told me Dez is a member of my court.

Not that I have a court, since I'm not doing the whole queen thing. But the point is, he seems to think I can trust her.

"You can," she says casually, over our handshake. "Trust me, I mean."

Which officially makes the Down-Under girl named Dez one more Icarus witch who can read my mind. Which is just peachy.

Instead of being offended by my runaway train of thought like I halfway expect, Dez shoots me a wry grin. "You'll get used to it, yeah? Living with telepaths."

"I highly doubt it." Feeling disgruntled, I hoist my backpack into an empty niche in the cupboard. "Just answer me this. Do you even want to be in this so-called court I'm supposed to have?"

"Why wouldn't I?" She gives me a funny look. "Being a member of the queen's court's a major deal. Gives us all social status, not only here, but across the whole witching world. Yeah, you'll pick up other courtiers eventually, but we're the first, just because we share your roof, and that makes us yours for life. We all lucked out when Master Aries landed you for Villa Augustus."

"Huh." It blows my mind to think anyone feels lucky to have landed me, with my fucked-up history and all my Gemini baggage, as a housemate. Especially for life. "Honestly? I know the queen's supposed to have a court, but I don't even know what that means."

Not to mention the biggie: I don't actually know what it means to be queen.

Dez flashes one of her sweet smiles. "No worries, cobber. The profs will explain the queen's role and all that bit. As for what it means for me to be in your court? That's up to you and me to figure out."

"I honestly don't have a clue." Feeling awkward, I give a little shrug. "For now? Maybe we can just be, you know, friends?"

"Works for me." Easy with that whole concept in a way I envy, my new courtier hitches one shoulder in a graceful shrug. "You hungry at all? You should definitely eat now if you are, because we've only got about twenty ticks till the afternoon bell."

"Safe to say I can eat," I agree, because I actually think the last bite of anything I put in my body was that popcorn at Wang's party, which feels like a lifetime ago. My stomach was growling all the way down the hill, but now that I'm trapped in here with these pit vipers, my appetite has taken a nosedive.

Still, who knows when they'll feed us again? I need to keep my strength up if I'm going to suss out a way off this rock.

"Lead on." I wave her before me with a friendly smile. "Anything in particular on the menu you'd recommend—?"

"Desdemona Killara Maali." An imperial male voice, edged with a hint of accent, snaps through the church like a bullwhip and shreds my skin. That voice vibrates and echoes with Compulsion like a gong.

Dez jerks around to face it like she's a puppet and that voice has her strings in a fist.

I already know who owns that voice even before I too pivot to face him, my heart pounding in my ears like orc drums in a Tolkien film.

Vasili Romanov hasn't moved a finger from where I first saw him, though the guy who was sitting between his feet like a dog has vamoosed. Yet somehow, effortlessly, Vasili's relaxed pose commands every eye in the church.

"What did I tell you about helping the little queen?" he says softly, those pale eyes narrowed on Dez. He's definitely got a little bit of an accent, probably

Russian, adding an edge to a tenor so smooth and rich it's like caramel. He has the kind of voice that makes you want to drag your tongue down his throat.

If only he weren't so terrifying.

"A girl's gotta eat, Vasili." I can tell Dez is trying to keep her cool. Though judging by her unnaturally rigid pose, she's gripped tight in that Compulsion spell and can't move a muscle.

I can also tell she's scared of him. And that pisses me right off.

If there's one thing I detest, it's a goddamn bully.

"The little queen eats," Vasili says, spacing each word with surgical precision. "If and when I say she eats. The little queen sleeps. If and when I say she sleeps. And the little queen *breathes*. If and when I say she breathes. Precisely the way you do, Desdemona."

Dez sucks in an audible breath that stops like someone's turned off a spigot. Color floods into her face. Her mouth opens wide and veins bulge in her slender neck. But I can tell she's not getting any air.

That son of a bitch just choked off her air supply.

I look around in real alarm, pretty sure there should be a teacher or a hall monitor or somebody in authority to address this situation. But I'm only seeing students, all of them riveted on this awful scene just like I am. And not one of them is taking any action to help.

Well, fuck.

Given my extreme aversion to witchcraft, I don't know how to counter a choking spell. But one sure way to break any spell is to break the concentration of the witch or warlock who's casting it.

I suck in a deep breath of my own, in case it's the last oxygen I'll be breathing myself for a while, and step directly between them. Breaking the warlock's fixed stare and absorbing that dangerous gaze myself.

"Hey, Goblin King," I challenge, in a voice that's pitched to carry. "Why don't you pick on someone your own size."

He's hard to read in the kaleidoscope light, sitting in silhouette against the stained glass windows on that massive sofa like a king on a fucking throne. But for a blink, that cold bastard almost looks like he's smiling.

Behind me Dez pulls in a voluble gasp, telling me she's free to breathe again, which was the whole point of this reckless maneuver. So I've already won one battle.

Even though I'm probably about to lose the next one.

"Well, well, well," the warlock drawls. "So our would-be sovereign has a tongue."

His oblong gaze slides over me, taking in every detail from my teal hair to my glitter polish to my Academy uniform and my undoubtedly pissed-off expression. His gaze seems to linger over the exposed leg between my short skirt and thigh-highs, which of course is the whole point of dressing a girl in this ridiculous sexualized way.

But I'm in zero mood to be ogled by this bully.

"That's right, Vasili Romanov." I want him to know I know who he is. I pop my hip out like a runway model and plant my hand on it to project plenty of badass. "Feel free to greet me properly."

That's me taking Neo's advice to respond to Vasili's disrespect and address the situation.

A soft chuckle, just the wisp of a laugh, slithers from his lips. Nice to know he's enjoying himself during our little showdown.

That makes one of us.

"Oh, you'd like to receive a proper greeting, would you?" he murmurs, one gilded brow arching over a wicked eye. "Are you quite certain?"

I wait for my lungs to constrict, but this warlock's toting plenty of nasty in his bag of tricks, and that's not how he strikes. Even though physically he doesn't move an inch, it's like he leans forward to grip my entire body in a giant fist. Atmospheric pressure condenses and solidifies around me like I'm doing a deep-sea dive. That invisible pressure closes around me like a garbage crusher and drags me toward him.

I gasp and struggle, the way anyone would, fighting like hell to break free. But there's no give at all to the vise-like pressure that encases me like hardening cement from head to heels. From the corner of my eye, I glimpse Dez darting for the stairs.

Good. At least one of us is getting away from this sociopath.

The toes of my mary janes scrape over the flagstones and I'm dragged a good twenty feet in approximately 2.4 seconds. Then I'm dropped roughly to my knees at the warlock's feet.

Stone scrapes my knees and abrades my palms. When I hit the floor, I bite my tongue over a stab of pain that makes my eyes water. At least I manage to catch myself before I fall on my face. Eyeing those purple-soled combat boots he's wearing, I'd like to scramble back before I end up taking a boot in the face. But that atmospheric pressure is still squeezing me.

I can breathe. But I definitely can't move.

Loathing him with every bone in my whole body, I lift my gaze, which is awkward to say the least, since I can't lift my head.

Finally, Vasili Romanov fucking moves. He leans forward on his couch and slides one cold finger under my chin to lift my head for me. All the fine hairs on my body rise like he's an electrostatic force. The ends of my ponytail start floating. He makes my power rise, just like Ronin does.

Which is one more reason he's dangerous.

Up close, the Goblin King is even prettier, with high cheekbones and a narrow nose and a jawline sharp enough to slice. Behind his glossed lips, his teeth are white and a tiny bit crooked, with razor-sharp incisors more prominent than the rest.

Those are actual fangs. This terrible fucking viper of a man is seriously telekinetic *and* he has fangs.

Honestly, it doesn't seem fair. He should only be allowed to be one kind of horrible monster at a time.

"*Privyet*, little queen," he whispers. His wide wondering gaze searches mine, like he's honestly curious about what he'll find. "You wished for a greeting? This is how Russians say hello. And the way you'll say hello to me is by licking my boot."

Oh, hell to the no. That's not happening.

And he better not try to manipulate my body into doing it either with those telekinetic powers that have to be due to some serious recessives. I'd rather swallow my own tongue than submit to this reptile.

"You try that stunt and I'll bite off your fucking foot," I snarl. A little surprised that he's actually letting me speak, because he has to know I'll defy him.

And if he can stop my breath, he can stop my speech.

Another little chuckle, too quiet for anyone else to hear, slides from his perfect lips. "If I want your tongue on my boot, little queen… or anywhere else for that matter… how precisely do you propose to thwart me? It's said you won't use your witchcraft. And you may be very certain indeed that no one here is going to save you."

Yeah, that's turning into kind of a problem. Not that I'm wanting someone to save me (like that ever happens), but I haven't used my witchcraft in years, and I'm not about to start using it now and risk taking the roof off this cathedral and killing everyone in it. Because one consequence of spurning any training for your power is that you can't do the fancy stuff that requires fine control when you need it. Like calling a bolt of lightning and zapping just this one bully in the ass. I'll probably electrocute myself if I try.

But I've still got my Fight Club superpowers.

I just need him to fight on my terms.

I make sure my voice is loud enough that every single student in this whole church can hear me loud and clear. "I don't need my fucking witchcraft to kick your ass, Goblin King. I can do it with my bare hands. But I guess you're too scared of fighting a girl to go toe to toe."

His eyes narrow to slits and his whole face hardens. I'm not even sure where the thing comes from, but suddenly the tip of a wickedly sharp blade is hovering half an inch from the corner of my eye.

Icy sweat trickles down my spine. Because I only have two eyes, and I'm pretty attached to having them.

"I know all about your little black belt in *tae kwon do*, Zarina Selene Gemini," he purrs. Which is another subtle threat, because knowing my full name means he could use Compulsion against me just like he did against Dez, since we're apparently housemates, which means we're bonded. "But do you know all about me?"

"Why don't you try me and find out, Romanov." And then the command comes lashing out of me that I never meant to utter. "I'm your fucking queen, and you're going to fucking worship me."

His nostrils flare wide in instant offense. His lips peel back in a sneer.

"That would be a 'no' then," he muses. "It appears you know nothing at all about me. Which is really too bad for *you*, little queen."

That blade of his is still hovering at the edge of my eye. It's sharp and slender, like a throwing knife, and he holds the weapon with a casual mastery that suggests he knows how to wield it to inflict maximum pain. I'm hoping someone at this school would take offense to him using it on me but, hell, someone just fucking killed the last queen.

And maybe it was this guy in front of me.

It takes a major effort to hold his gaze instead of fixating on that blade he's threatening me with.

But that's what I do.

I stare at Vasili Romanov like he's the only thing in the whole world that matters.

And he stares at me the exact same way, pupils swelling to shrink his irises, lips parted, hardly breathing. It's like the two of us are locked together, two scorpions in a bottle, barbed tails raised and dripping venom. It's like the world has shrunk and we've expanded to become each other's whole universe.

"Come on then, bad boy," I breathe, a flat-out challenge for his ears alone. My hair's floating and my skin's tingling and we're both breathing fast. "Let's do this. Just you and me."

"VASILI NIKOLAIEVICH ROMANOV." From somewhere behind me, the whiplash of Compulsion sparks and crackles through the fraught air. The warlock's pale gaze snaps free of mine, the blade vanishes, and suddenly I too am free. I collapse in a heap right where I'm kneeling, head sagging, bones liquid, breath spilling from my lungs like water.

My nemesis uncoils to his feet with sinuous grace like a cobra rising from a basket. "Just having a bit of sport with the new freshman, Master Aries. Surely a future queen can handle a little light hazing from the common folk."

That curl of contempt in his tone brings me right to my feet. Though I'm still a good foot shorter than the Goblin King. He slithers past me like I'm not even there, all his terrifying attention now focused on Lucius, who's standing at the head of the stairs in his professorial tweed and frowning mildly at his student like Vasili forgot to turn in his homework or something.

Frankly, having been the recipient of the *Bram Stoker's Dracula* version of Lucius in a temper, all red-eyed and fangy, I'm a little disappointed that he's not showing more of his wolf to the horrible Vasili.

Ronin is looming behind Lucius, glaring at Vasili with those molten eyes like he's going to light him on fire. That's a more satisfying reaction, though I'm pretty sure it's not on my account, since Ronin and Vasili have apparently been mortal enemies since well before I showed up.

Still, I'm definitely relieved to see him, even if I have a score to settle with him too.

And even if he's the one who killed the last queen.

Dez is here, looking flushed and jubilant, and I realize she must've run straight to Lucius once I drew Vasili's fire. Smart girl that one, and an ally worth having.

By now Vasili and Lucius are eyeball to eyeball near the stairs. The Goblin King's taller and he makes the most of it, shoving his hands in his pockets and sneering down at the shifter from an elegant slouch.

"Behave yourself, Mr. Romanov," Lucius says with disappointing mildness. "I'm disturbed by your aggression toward Ms. Maali. I want a thousand-word essay on the ethics of telekinesis on my desk by first period tomorrow."

"And I want four races that aren't facing an extinction event thanks to the complete ineptitude of our ruling royals." Vasili's voice slices like a blade through the riveted silence. "Somehow, Master Aries, I doubt either one of us is particularly likely to have his desire satisfied."

Then the holy terror saunters past his teacher without any apparent objection from Lucius, and my mouth falls open in complete indignation. Lucius just took him to task for choking Dez like he absolutely should have, but the shifter didn't say one damn word about Vasili practically taking my eye out during his attack on me.

Who's calling the shots at this Academy anyway?

Lucius stirs and glances at his watch. "On second thought, Mr. Romanov, let's make that two thousand words due at midnight. You're excused from History of Magic to facilitate a timely start. After all, I'm not entirely unreasonable."

Vasili's shoulders stiffen, but this time he doesn't mouth off, probably because now he's dealing with Ronin who's just prowled into his path, and Vasili's absolutely not giving an inch. Ronin's mouthwatering in his plum-colored Academy blazer, with inky flames licking above the pale collar against his copper skin and his black hair in a sleek tail that pours over one shoulder and makes him even more feral.

The two of them smolder at each other from barely three feet apart. Like they're either going to dismember each other where they stand…

Or burn the church down with a blistering kiss.

Seriously, my guy-guy sexual fantasies are getting out of hand. Not that I'm going to be having any fantasies starring the Goblin King unless they involve boiling him in oil while he begs me for mercy.

"Mr. Pendragon," Lucius murmurs.

Ronin shoots his teacher a sulky look. Oozing insolence from every pore, he idles out of Vasili's path.

"Your day of reckoning is rapidly approaching as well, Pendragon," the Goblin King hisses. Then, like the reptile he is, he snakes downstairs and the shadows swallow him.

When he's gone, the entire church lets out a collective breath.

"Ms. Gemini," Lucius says quietly, before I can actually unwind. "You're due in Mistress Agrippina's Genetics of Witchcraft class in less than ten minutes. Ms. Maali will show you the way. Do try not to cause any more trouble."

Which only makes me feel even more indignant. This all seems grossly unfair since, one, I didn't start the last trouble but only defended myself from it and, two, now I barely have time to eat. There's also three, the fact that I don't actually want to be here on this island at all. And Lucius Aries has no idea how much trouble I can really cause once I put my mind to it.

But he's definitely going to find out.

Chapter Thirteen
Lucius

Zarina Gemini is going to cause real trouble.

Both my wolf aspect and my teacher aspect have an excellent nose for impending mischief, particularly when it's brewing in my classroom. I'm keenly aware the Gemini girl's only been sitting in my History of Witchcraft class for ten minutes.

But she's already thoroughly distracted every student in it.

To say nothing of the teacher.

She's opted to sit apart, choosing a desk with her back to the wall and a path to the door, both instincts that seem eminently prudent for a new freshman. With her wild hair and her studded cuff and her don't-mess-with-me expression, the Gemini queen manages to look thoroughly untamed and thoroughly defiant despite having dutifully assumed that rather provocative uniform. Her fellow classmates can barely take their eyes off her, even when all she's doing is frowning and scribbling notes in her leather-bound journal.

In short, she appears to be the only student in the entire room who's paying any heed whatsoever to my strategically chosen lecture on the historical origins of the witching world's endangered species status.

I rap my knuckles on the desk in a futile bid to regain the room's attention, pivot toward the chalkboard, and take up my writing stylus.

"As we saw from last night's reading," I resume, "arcane scholars have advanced three primary theories for the four races' endangered species status. First is the Theory of Genetic Exhaustion."

I chalk the phrase on the board. Like any proper teacher, I've acquired the ability to lecture and write simultaneously, while also cultivating metaphorical eyes in the back of my head to scan my classroom for trouble.

"This theory tends to be closely associated," I continue, "with the origin myth that we arcanes are descended from alien races who visited this planet in Roman times. Exhaustion scholars suggest we've drifted too far from our alien roots, our powerful DNA too attenuated by centuries of crossbreeding with earthbound humans. Consequently, the witchcraft and related traits encoded in our arcane DNA are simply being bred out of us."

I pause and scan the room. Zarina's pencil is driving across the page while she writes furiously, colorful brows furrowed and lower lip trapped between her teeth. At least I've captured her attention.

Now if only I could capture everyone else's.

Neo Mercury, typically my star pupil, is currently a hopeless cause. He's sitting as close to his fated mate as her prickly temper will permit, a scant two rows away, and he hasn't stopped mooning at her with his broody eyes since the moment he sat down.

Fortunately, Neo's already so well established at the head of my class that he can afford the occasional distraction. Academically, no other student even challenges his star billing on the Dean's List, although the absent Vasili's certainly smart enough to make Neo sweat. Given all that raw talent paired with his blistering intellect, Vasili's test scores are invariably off the charts.

If only he'd bother turning in his homework.

Ronin Pendragon's another problem child, albeit for an entirely unique set of reasons. The Leo scion is lurking at the very back of my classroom, as far from me as physically possible without sitting in the corridor. He's been scowling at me since the bell rang, and I can see my bite is troubling him.

A fine glitter of perspiration dampens his skin, and he's sitting far too stiffly, with none of his signature lounging grace. I fancy I can almost feel the pulsing heat where I've bitten him in the burn of my own flesh.

Seeing Ronin suffer on my account, my wolf whines and scratches at my skin.

My heart plummets like a stone under the heavy weight of guilt.

Christ, I never wanted Ronin to suffer. I fully meant to tend his bite thoroughly, to provide the leisurely and dedicated aftercare that allows the genetically optimized healing agent in my saliva to cleanse the wound and speed recovery, a process that's typically reassuring for all involved after a bite. The shameful truth is, after all his provocative teasing during our travels, I was so damned desperate to get my mouth on my student's diabolically alluring body in the only way my unsparing morals would sanction that I underestimated the likelihood that Zarina would interrupt our encounter, and that Ronin in a rage wouldn't permit me to finish.

If I thought I could possibly persuade him now, I'd assign the class group work in a swift minute and drag him into the privacy of my office to give him the dedicated and sustained attention he clearly requires.

Solely for therapeutic purposes, obviously.

Regrettably, it's equally obvious by the way Ronin's glowering that he'll refuse to tolerate my attentions. Of course, I can Compel him. That's the whole purpose of a disciplinary bite. It's intended to connect us in a manner both more permanent and more intimate than a common Compulsion spell.

But, for some damned reason, I want him to come to me willingly.

Besides which, judging by the way he's been behaving since the moment I humiliated and rejected him by denying any suggestion of a personal relationship in front of Zarina, thereby relegating him firmly to the role of erring student, the prospect of Ronin Pendragon ever again coming to me willingly now seems unlikely.

Deeply troubled, I turn back to the chalkboard to conceal my frown and dutifully take up my stylus.

"The second theory to explain our endangered status is pure Darwinism, and rather fatalistic." I write *Darwinism/Fatalism* on the chalkboard. "Scholars who ascribe to this view argue that all life is finite and all species must suffer eventual extinction. If it's our turn now, we arcane races may be able to slow our extinction, but we can no longer prevent it.

"The primary flaw in this argument is that most species endure for millennia; there's typically a causation such as climate change, a planetary crisis, or the introduction of a rival species that triggers an extinction event. When asked to attribute a cause to our predicament, Darwinian scholars are simply silent."

My enhanced senses are detecting in the air the distinct whiff of trouble. I pause to scan my classroom with a minatory eye.

Most of these students hail from Villa Tiberius, and Master Zerxes' little monsters always bear watching. Vasili is off somewhere brooding over his two-thousand word essay (or so I hope), although it's equally possible he's burning down the *domus* in a fit of vengeful rage. Racetrack and Dez are sequestered in the library, where they have study hall this period.

And now Ronin too is staring at Zarina.

I'm well aware there isn't a student of any gender in my classroom he hasn't fucked, with the probable exception of Neo. Still, the Leo scion is a notorious one-and-done operator. This lothario never goes back for seconds, carelessly leaving a trail of broken hearts and devastation in his sexually omnivorous wake. Now that he's enjoyed Zarina—and he certainly *did* enjoy her, as I'm extremely well placed to attest—I've assumed she too will lose his interest.

However, that doesn't seem to be what's occurring.

He's leaning forward in his seat, face savage and eyes fiery, watching her nibble on her eraser like he's wishing it could be his dick.

That explicit visual sparks an unwelcome tightening and a spike of heat in my own trousers, coupled with a bout of happy frisking from my wolf. It's really best that I not think about the prospect of Ronin Pendragon's dick with Zarina Gemini's lips wrapped around it.

Both to keep my unruly wolf in check, and for the sake of my own decorum.

"Then there's the third theory," I announce firmly, "which is by far the most interesting."

Zarina watches me alertly, her lively gaze never straying from my face. I'm gratified to be holding her attention, since she's the consequential student whose appalling ignorance of her own heritage and history I'm most determined to remedy.

The Gemini queen may have neglected her education in a manner I consider wildly irresponsible, but judging from her success in deftly eluding capture all these years, she's far from unintelligent.

"The final theory that scholars of our races have advanced to explain the threat of extinction is the Theory of Royal Culpability." I copy out this phrase as well, feeling Zarina's gaze narrow on my back. "According to this perspective, the vitality and survival of the arcane races are directly dependent upon, and derived from, the strength of the witch who wears the crown. When a queen who commands powerful witchcraft takes the throne, welcomes an equally powerful mate… or mates… to her bed, wields her witchcraft with control and conviction, and ensures the continuation of her bloodline, the four races prosper. When the ruling queen's magic is weak or uncontrolled, the four races decline."

This is of course the theory to which the anti-monarchists ascribe, indicting our queens for the witching world's decline, with Vasili Romanov the anti-monarchists' most passionate champion. Although I'm an ardent royalist myself, it's also the theory that I find to be most credible.

I turn to find Zarina watching me with a pucker between her brows and incipient rebellion brewing in her eyes. Steadily, I sustain her stare.

If I can manage to persuade this strong-willed Gemini queen to accept a powerful warlock like Neo Mercury as her fated mate, learn to embrace her witchcraft rather than reject it, and take up her role as our sovereign, I firmly believe it's our best and only chance to avert extinction.

Assuming it's not already too late.

"Oh, hell to the no. You're not pinning this one on me." She chuffs out an angry laugh and her gaze skids away from mine, only to collide with Neo's hopeful eyes.

Her lips press tight before she gives him the cold shoulder.

Admittedly, I hoped the two of them would hit it off better than they seem to have done. Neo's an appealing sort, patient enough to woo her properly, not to mention drop-dead gorgeous, and he's been pining for his fated mate as long as I've known him. Somehow he seems to have gotten off on the wrong foot with her, no doubt obliging me to add to my duties as teacher and headmaster the unwelcome role of camp counselor.

I swallow a sigh and pace across the classroom to consult my lesson plan. As I pass Zarina's desk, a peculiar odor insinuates its way into my wolfish senses. It's an appallingly putrid stench. A briny reek rather like dead fish. I wonder if someone's left a lunch behind in one of the desks that's gone rancid.

"As we know," I resume, "among the twelve arcane families, only three purebred families remain intact. These three families, their special status denoted by their use of the surname that reflects their astrological affinity, are the Aquarius, the Aries, and the Gemini. For nearly two centuries, the arcane races have been ruled by Aquarius queens and their mates, typically chosen from the most concentrated arcane bloodlines to be extant.

"With Cybelle's passing, her mother Queen Messalina stands to be the last Aquarius queen. Messalina's advanced age and currently childless state—coupled with the notable decline of the Aquarius line's witchcraft—are the reasons the Arcane Senate has confirmed as our next sovereign not only a purebred Gemini queen, but one who has already demonstrated her formidable magical potential."

I'm looking for the spark of comprehension to animate Zarina's intelligent face. To my considerable annoyance, I realize I've now lost her attention as well. She's shifting in her seat, her pretty nose wrinkled, clearly cognizant of the same pungent odor that's already assaulted my wolfish senses.

A muscle ticking in my jaw, I stride directly to stand before Zarina and plant a hand on her desk, which is a more blatant bid for a student's attention than I'd typically resort to.

But the importance of reaching her is acute enough to drive me to it.

Brought suddenly into close proximity, she lifts her face, gaze dragging slowly up the length of my body like a physical touch, lips parted, until our eyes collide. Her turquoise orbs are glowing with power.

A sudden surge of heat rolls through me like a backdraft.

When her tongue slides over her lower lip, I realize my wolf isn't the only libido in this classroom feeling frisky.

The sight of her sultry face level with my groin, soft lips glistening, warm color rising in her cheeks, lush breasts swelling against her blazer, makes my wolf growl with his own rising need. He's wondering why on earth I don't simply crouch before her, peel her out of her panties, throw her stocking-clad legs over my shoulders, and tongue her sweet quim until she shatters under my mouth.

Abruptly, I realize I've planted both hands on her desk and I'm growling low in my throat.

My palate is tingling under the press of my fangs, which are on the edge of descending, and my eyes are surely red. She's leaning forward to meet my challenge, gaze locked on mine and burning with invitation.

As for Ronin, he's watching us both like he's ready to vault over three rows of desks and join in.

Swiftly I straighten, adjust my tie, retract my fangs, and retreat to the refuge of my chalkboard.

For the love of God, what pedagogical point was I just in the midst of making?

"It's the sovereign's most sacred duty," I resume, after an exceedingly awkward pause, "to ensure the survival of the four races. How does she do this? By learning to wield her witchcraft with control and conviction for the betterment of her people. And by taking the powerful mate or mates who are most worthy to support, cherish, love, and defend her. The mates most capable of propagating her powerful witchcraft to the next generation."

I pivot to pinpoint Zarina with my stylus. "If the queen fails in her most sacred duty, the outcome will be catastrophic. We will witness in this century the dwindling of the arcane races beyond hope of recovery, thus damning ourselves to inevitable extinction and the certain doom of the witching world."

Having now abandoned all subtlety, I trust that I've delivered my point with sufficient emphasis to impress our stubborn future queen. Unfortunately, the impact of my message is blunted by the presence of that damnable aroma which is growing steadily more potent. Judging by the prevalence of grimaces and wrinkled noses now apparent across my classroom, all the students are noticing.

I'm likewise noticing an epidemic of grins and snickers from the notorious aisle near the window those little hellions from Villa Tiberius have claimed as their turf.

My lurking suspicion crystallizes to a dreadful certainty. Alarmed, I pivot to Zarina.

That appalling odor is definitely originating from her vicinity. She's frowning, glancing under her desk, trying to pinpoint the source, while the entire class watches with ill-concealed mirth. Suddenly she drags toward her the backpack she propped against the wall when she entered.

Neo leaps to his feet, apprehension exploding across his face. "Wait, Zara, don't—"

But he's far too late. She's opened the backpack.

A veritable eruption of scaly orange-and-white bodies pours flopping and gasping onto the floor, accompanied by a stomach-heaving tsunami of stench. The miasma is so foul I barely master the urge to vomit.

Her backpack is absolutely stuffed with dead and dying fish.

And I needn't look far for the culprit. One of the rotten little monsters from Villa Tiberius is the Pisces scion, and teleportation is her special talent. While I lectured away obliviously up here, that witch has teleported the entire juvenile koi population of the schoolhouse pond into Zarina Gemini's backpack.

"Oh, for fuck's sake. Are you people for real?" Zarina takes in the unappealing mess and the snickering students in a single fulminating look, then scrambles to her feet in a flurry of plaid skirts and teal hair.

Most freshmen who are hazed this brutally are inclined to flee the scene. An occasional scrappy student will attack the presumed culprit, either with fisticuffs or witchcraft.

I'm braced for Zarina to do either.

In fact, she does neither.

Instead, she fires into action, deftly tossing the distressed young koi back into her pack. Some of the juvenile fish are too stupefied by oxygen deprivation to move, while others are flopping and flailing. Handling the suffering creatures with a gentleness I wouldn't expect under the circumstances, she transports the fish handily into the pack and rushes out the door with them.

It's my responsibility to maintain order in this classroom and I fully intend to do so. Regrettably, there's no preventing an immediate exodus as the entire class streams after its victim, with Neo at the head of the pack. Ronin brings up the rear in more of a saunter than a run. His uncharacteristic lack of haste reminds me sharply, with another pang of remorse, that he's suffering.

And that it's all my fault.

"Ronin—" I attempt.

"Don't." Roughly he pushes past me into the corridor without meeting my gaze. My wolf whines in disappointment.

Jaw clenching, I surrender to the clearly inevitable and follow.

The classrooms at Icarus Academy occupy the former cloister of this deconsecrated church. Consequently, the rooms cluster in a quadrangle around a peristyle courtyard under a thick leaded glass roof. The heated central courtyard holds the conservatory, with its overgrown tangle of tropical trees and flowering plants, as well as the mossy grotto, the tumbledown ruin of the gazebo, and the koi pond.

Zarina's kneeling on the muddy stones beside the pond, decanting each gasping fish into the water with absorbed care. Her attention to this unsavory chore is absolute, her scowl ferocious.

She grimly refuses to acknowledge the Pisces scion and her cliquish Tiberius sidekicks, all of whom are howling with demonic glee.

Solid citizen that he is, Neo hunkers down alongside and provides assistance. Zarina accepts, her gaze eloquent with gratitude, since their combined efforts are returning the distressed fish to the water faster. Ronin leans one hip against the overgrown gazebo and observes this rescue operation with inscrutable eyes.

Only once the final fish has been restored to its watery home does Zarina rinse off her own hands as best she can in the scummy water and arise, brushing briskly at the mud stains on her stockings.

Her smoldering gaze rakes her howling tormentors with blistering scorn.

"Cheese on toast!" she bursts out. "How old are you people? Twelve? You just about killed those poor fish, and for what? To try and make me feel bad about the smell? I've got news for you kiddies. If you want to make me suffer, you're gonna have to try *way* harder."

This lot will consider that a challenge issued.

Clearly I've just been handed my cue to restore order. I step forward and level my erring students with a quelling look. "Ms. Gemini, you're excused to return to your *domus* and get yourself cleaned up. Mr. Mercury, kindly collect the hall pass from my desk and render assistance."

"I'll get my own hall pass. I don't need his help." Zara powers past me, moving with purpose, determined to show this entire Academy she doesn't need any of us.

Poor Neo is left standing crestfallen with stricken eyes to weather his fated mate's rejection.

Dear God. It's all I can manage not to raise my own eyes to Heaven for patience. "The rest of you miscreants have precisely thirty seconds to return to your seats and your studies before I begin writing referrals. As I'm the instructor to whom you'll report for any conduct infractions, I trust you'll proceed with suitable dispatch."

This exigent reminder achieves the desired effect and inspires a brisk scramble among my still-snickering students.

It's well known among these brats that detention with me is one ordeal that is best avoided.

I leave Zarina to her ablutions and Neo to his disappointment and turn toward Ronin, who hasn't returned to class with the rest. My wolf wants nothing more than to rub against Ronin's legs and start scenting, but that's hardly appropriate behavior for a teacher.

"Mr. Pendragon, may I see you in my office after class?"

"No, you may not," Ronin says sulkily, and stalks past me from the courtyard.

I'm left standing alone in the conservatory, with the smell of distressed fish dissipating in the air and the ache of impossible longing swelling in my heart.

Chapter Fourteen
Vasili

I grasp my *bo* in sweating palms and attack my target with vicious intent.

The gymnasium in our *domus* shares a wall with the *caldarium* in the Roman bath. In consequence, our gym is always far too warm. Today, I'm not even wearing my *gi*, the tunic and trousers I usually don when I practice my forms. Instead, I decamped straight here from the church to work off my aggression after my unsettling run-in with that bratty little queen.

Even after an hour of brutal exertion, I'm still too unsettled and far too angry to strip down properly.

Another flash of the queen's fearless face sears through my mind like a bolt of lightning, blue-green hair floating around her shoulders like seaweed in a current, turquoise eyes incandescent with anger and glowing with power.

But the Gemini bitch, for all her unruly power, isn't nearly powerful enough to challenge me.

Still, the fact that she doesn't have the blessed good sense to fear me and submit to me, the way everyone else does in this wretched Academy, hurls fresh fuel on the smoldering fire of my rage.

Goblin King, indeed.

At the time, I was so startled by the little witch's insolence that I very nearly laughed.

Barefoot in my trousers with blazer and tie abandoned, shirt half-unbuttoned and cuffs rolled back, I launch into another spinning pass at the training target, my six-foot staff whistling through the air. I've broken my opponents' bones with the *bo* in training, (mostly) by accident, and I'm certainly not holding back now.

I whirl through the air, footfalls hissing across the mat, the muted *thud-thud-thud* of my weapon striking leather in a punishing blitzkrieg.

A finger of cold air brushes my nape, my sole warning that some fool has dared enter the gymnasium I've claimed as my exclusive province while my housemates are toiling away at their tedious classes. I spin in a rush, walls blurring around me. My *bo* comes screaming down, fired by the full force of my fury.

The sharp thunk of my staff striking Ronin's makes the walls ring.

I pause in surprise, but his staff's already sweeping around to knock my legs from under me. I vault straight up and barely avoid the takedown.

My downstroke catches his upstroke in a parry hard enough to make my bones vibrate.

"Why aren't you in class?" I pant, backing off a step in case he's had enough, having failed to ambush me with his sneak attack the way the imp clearly intended. "Never tell me Master Aries' latest lecture on our inexorable march toward extinction failed to hold your interest."

Ronin's teeth flash in a savage grin. Instead of answering, he twists into another blistering attack, his inky tail of hair flying wide. He's toed off his boots for stealth, but he's still wearing tie and blazer and the rest of his rig, which hinders his impressive range and gives me a slight edge.

I'll need it with him, because he's listed as the Academy's top-ranked fighter for a reason.

I deflect his scything blow with a grin of my own. "Very well, Pendragon, keep your sullen silence. If that's the way you'd like to play this."

We advance and retreat over the training floor, staffs connecting in a hail of staccato blows. He's a thing of violent beauty, this enemy of mine, because we *are* deadly enemies in the entire world's eyes.

By the time the witching world discovers our secret, we'll have brought our ruling royals and their entire corrupt regime to its knees.

But today I have a different axe to grind.

"Why didn't you come to my room last night?" I deflect his jabbing blow from my face—a blow that would have broken my perfect nose if it landed—and follow up with a sweeping riposte that would shatter his teeth, except he parries it. "I waited up for you."

"Missed me, did you?" He grins and ducks my savage counterblow. "Entire *domus* was in an uproar, love, what with the Gemini bitch pitching up. I'm fairly certain Lucius and his wolf didn't sleep a wink. Didn't seem prudent, me creeping round the halls with a boner for my horrible rival."

"Yes, well, your horrible rival doesn't care to be kept waiting," I purr, circling away to break his deadly rhythm. "Don't do it again, or I'll make you suffer."

"Is that a promise then?" Ronin pivots to keep me in view, which is certainly wise. I'm still pissy at him for ignoring me, and I'm dead set on taking him down. "Out of curiosity, how will you make me suffer?"

"Hmmm." I lower my *bo* and pretend to think it over. He's a bit off today, because he actually takes the bait and lowers his guard as well. With a sudden grin, I dive in and administer a brisk tap to his ribs that will surely leave a bruise. "How will it be if I don't permit you to climax for a full month?"

"Oh, I dunno, mate." The bastard actually props his staff against the floor and leans against it as he pretends to think. "Suppose I'll just have to make my long-delayed play for Neo Mercury. Believe he's the only male student on this island I haven't fucked—"

My lips peel back from my teeth in a snarl. With sudden savagery, I lunge for him.

He isn't expecting it—as I've already said, he's off today—so for once, my unpremeditated rush catches him off his formidable guard. He goes flying back, staff sailing from his hands, and lands flat on the mat with me straddling his hips.

I press my staff lengthwise against his throat to pin him.

"Neo Mercury is entirely out of bounds," I hiss, keeping enough pressure under his chin to immobilize him. "Besides, you blockhead, he's fucking *straight*."

An assertion I'm virtually certain is a lie. But never mind.

"You sure about that?" His amber eyes mock me. "Is he out of bounds because you're jealous over me? Or because you're hot to pop his cherry yourself?"

My lip curls in disdain. As if *that* would ever happen. Mercury may be built like a Greek god and hung like the proverbial stallion, because you don't share a bathhouse with someone without noticing that sort of thing. But his entire clan are sniveling royalists. Mercury harbors grandiose delusions of marrying the next queen and becoming the next king and making all of us bend the knee to him and his royal bitch.

As for myself, of course, I'm an unrepentant rabble-rouser.

Even leaving politics aside, Neo and I despise one another. We're opposites in every single way. He's only at the top of the Dean's List because I don't care enough to topple him from his pathetic pedestal.

The real problem with Ronin rubbing Neo and his presumably unpopped cherry in my face is that I'm fiercely jealous—not of Neo's affection, but of Ronin's. Mercury just so happens to be buff, built, rich, the smartest boy in school (after yours truly)… and, at the very least, bi-curious. The reason I know this is because he's been eye-fucking my boyfriend for months.

I don't want him anywhere near Ronin.

Now don't mistake me. Ronin can fuck anyone on the planet he likes— *except* Mercury—because I'll tolerate Ronin's tawdry one-and-dones to indulge him.

But he always returns to me.

"You're determined to provoke me today, aren't you, darling?" Still pinning my lover to the mat with my staff, I straddle his hips and lean over him.

The intimate contact brings my body flush with his lean sinewed torso, which delivers an instant jolt of heat to my cock. "Do you truly consider that wise?"

Ronin's lids drop over his fiery eyes and his throat ripples as he swallows. When he answers, his voice drops two octaves. "Say I do provoke the great and terrible Vasili. How are you going to punish me?"

A wicked thrill of pleasure kicks my pulse into overdrive and shoots an arc of electric current through my shaft. The air floods with the dark musk of my Mogadon mating scent.

Clearly he's in the mood to be punished and, Christ, I'm more than in the mood to oblige.

Holding the staff in place with one hand, I deftly loosen his tie with the other. He grins at me lazily, fully aware of the beast he's just woken. Having unraveled his tie and draped it loosely around my own neck, I leave my staff lying crosswise over his throat to make my expectations clear—I want him to lie still and wait for me—then wrap my fists in his shirt.

One hard clench and his buttons go flying, revealing the black dragon spewing flames across his delicious chest and that flat column of abdominal muscle I never grow tired of tonguing.

I bend and drag my tongue over the burning silk of his abs and chest in a long slow swipe.

Damn, he's hot to the touch. He tastes like salt and he smells like ambergris, but he's been long enough away that he no longer smells like me. Instead, he's redolent with a teasing hint of rose-and-vanilla sweetness.

And, more blatantly, the predatory reek of wolf.

My head snaps up to skewer him with an icy glare. "Did you fuck Lucius?"

Ronin's eyes are heavy with arousal and his dick under his trousers is rigid. My sudden demand makes him frown and lift his head. "What's that?"

"While the two of you were in Singapore," I grind out, furious with him for making me ask twice. "Did you fuck him?"

"Oh fuck," he grouses, head falling back to the mat with a sigh. "Bloody hell, not this again. Vasili, you're not allowed to get jealous over Lucius."

"I'll be the judge of that." I toss the staff aside and drag Ronin up by his open blazer to sit. "You reek of his fucking wolf." Not to mention our fucking queen. But she's a more complicated topic, one I intend to address separately and at length. "Did. You. Fuck. Him."

"He fucking bit me, all right?" Ronin shifts under me like he'd really fancy me getting off him. That's just too bad, because he's insane if he thinks I'm backing off now. He knows Lucius makes me utterly mental.

"A mating bite?" I demand, incensed.

"A disciplinary bite. It's nothing." He shrugs his shoulders with a wince. An actual fucking wince. Now I'm more than suspicious.

I'm experiencing a mounting sense of concern.

"Let me see." I push his blazer and shirt off his shoulders, ignoring his half-hearted effort to fend me off. My gaze narrows on the square of white gauze taped to his shoulder and speckled with blood.

"What the actual fuck?" I don't think I've ever been more outraged. "Ronin, he hurt you. He *hurt* you."

My damn stomach is tangled in knots and I find I can barely breathe. That fucking wolf bastard hurt my love.

I swear to Christ I'm going to tear out Lucius Aries' throat.

"Pretty sure they'll expel you from Icarus if you tear out a teacher's throat." Ronin grins suddenly, because of course he's Valyrian, and he's gotten me so worked up that I've forgotten entirely to shield my thoughts. "Does it really bother you that much?"

Well, we're certainly not embarking on *that* conversational voyage. I spend my days terrorizing the entire student body and my nights shielding my thoughts from the island's dominant telepath to ensure he never guesses the alarming intensity of my foolish feelings. Feelings which render me dangerously vulnerable if anyone ever learns the truth.

He's my greatest weakness and my deadliest secret. If anyone ever hurts him, they'll destroy me.

And there are so many in the witching world who yearn to destroy me.

"You need this wound tended and this bandage changed, and this isn't a point I intend to negotiate," I state firmly, gathering my wits to rise. "I'll fetch the first aid kit. You'll stay right here if you know what's good for you—"

"Vasili." His hands land on my waist.

And I'm such a pathetic slave to the dangerous witchcraft of Ronin Pendragon that I freeze obediently, precisely as he wishes, and wait patiently (for me) to hear him out.

"Well?" I raise my signature eyebrow and give him the Romanov look.

"I missed you too," Ronin murmurs, his gaze dropping to my mouth. "Like… a lot."

A frustrated groan claws from my throat. I dive down and he lunges up and our mouths collide in a scorching kiss.

He's feral when we kiss, all teeth and tongue and temper, so I grip his head between my hands to hold him, my tongue plunging deep in his silky heat. He meets me kiss for kiss, absolutely owning my mouth and every other part of me, fearless of the fangs I loathe and never asked for and can't retract. He's the only man who's ever kissed me without flinching.

I would have loved him for that alone.

He smells like wolf and he tastes like cloves and I need him to smell and taste like *me*. He's mine. I can hardly be blamed. It's a Mogadon trait, it's encoded in our DNA, we're born and bred to possess. The drive to scent and claim our mates is a genetic imperative.

I claw the garments from his shoulders and he tugs my sweat-soaked shirt from my trousers, then deftly slips my buttons. I let him do that much before I push him flat on his back and straddle him anew, our cocks grinding together through our pants. I swear he has me so shamefully worked up over him I'm ready to spill in my own trousers.

But that's an indulgence I won't permit. I haven't had him in four days, which feels like fucking forever, and I fully intend to spill inside *him*.

I push his arms over his head, unwind his tie from around my neck, bind his wrists together, and bind his hands to the nearby weight bench so he can't move. He lets me have my terrible way with him, a grin curling one corner of his mouth as I pin his arms overhead.

His submission always makes me hot, and today is certainly no exception. I grit my teeth and drive my cock against his. He arches into me, groaning through clenched teeth as the friction spurs us both toward the edge.

It's my job to manage our pace, because I'm the one calling the shots, which is precisely the way I like it.

I pull back, ease up, enjoying the way he struggles against his bonds and chases my mouth, letting him catch my lower lip in a long slow suck before I push him back to the mat.

"There's still the matter of your shocking misbehavior to address." I mouth my way down his throat. "You kept me waiting, didn't you, little demon? Now you'll have to pay the price."

"What did you have in mind… oh gods… *Vasili*…" His words dissolve in a long groan as I work my hand between us, drag down his zipper, and reach inside to wrap my fingers around his thick cock. I jack him slow and steady, loving the way he writhes under my touch, the smooth ring of his Prince Albert bumping my fingers.

"What's that you're saying, darling?" I flick his nipple with my tongue and graze it with my teeth and jack him off with just enough pressure that he's rising to my touch. "I can't quite hear you."

"Please," he pants, writhing under my touch. "Fuck, Vasili, please. Need you to make me come."

"That's what I like to hear. And I'll be delighted to oblige… once you've asked me properly." I pin his gaze with mine, give him a final stroke to tease him, then lean in to nuzzle his lips. "I want you to suck me off until I see stars. I'll tell you when to stop."

"They're coming home from school soon," he whispers against my mouth, a sluggish protest that's meant to be overcome.

I know exactly what he needs from me, which is how I know he's fully on board with my little torments.

With my free hand, I unbuckle my belt. "Then you'll simply have to be efficient, darling. Now I intend to fuck your face until you choke. If you ever want to breathe again, suck me."

I issue this command with less authority than I intend, because something's just brushed against my acute Mogadon senses that I don't expect. It's an elusive aroma that's utterly out of place in the *domus* gymnasium.

To wit, the stomach-churning stench of rotting fish.

Chapter Fifteen
Zara

I'm in serious danger of a major sex meltdown.

I'm standing… hiding, actually… just inside what's clearly the gym in this joint. I was looking for the bathhouse to get cleaned up, with Lucius' hall pass dangling around my neck like I'm twelve or something.

But clearly that isn't what I've just found.

I definitely wasn't prepared to stumble in on Ronin and that nightmare Vasili beating twelve kinds of shit out of each other with six-foot staffs. But the ass-kicker in me is way too intrigued to tiptoe back out. They're both badass in their fury as they wield those staffs, and there's something compelling as fuck about those two locked in combat. Vasili supercilious and sneering in all his icy perfection, Ronin primal and savage with his ink and his snarls and his swirling black hair. Together, they look amazing.

In fact, I'm literally mesmerized.

I can't look away. Much less walk away.

Anyway, I don't trust that snake, and I figure Ronin might need help. A suspicion that seems justified when Vasili charges Ronin and pins him to the mat.

Lurking behind the partition that separates the gym from the shoe cubby, I can't hear everything they're muttering, thanks to the steady whoosh and hum of the geriatric furnace wheezing away down the hall. But I've got a primo view pressed up against the partition and peeking wide-eyed around the corner. They're hissing at each other and tussling on the mat, and I'm ready to charge to Ronin's rescue.

Not that I'm on his side or anything.

But this cage match is Ronin vs. Vasili. And in that throwdown, you can bet I'm Team Ronin.

Which means I've got a front-row seat when the Goblin King leans in and drags his tongue down Ronin's chest.

Oh.

My.

Freaking.

God.

Turns out these two notorious rivals aren't actually rivals. They're lovers. They're freaking *lovers*.

And for some reason that's eluding me here, they clearly don't want anyone to know.

Then Vasili uncovers Ronin's bite and just about launches into orbit. His eyes widen and his jaw drops and there's genuine distress blazing under all that fuckery he wears like a mask on that perfect David Bowie face. He's more than jealous. More than outraged.

He's more than fucking Ronin Pendragon.

This monstrous pit viper of a warlock is actually in love with Ronin.

After what happened today, I despise Vasili Romanov for life. But, for some reason, the thought of him in love with Ronin makes me breathless. By now, literal wild horses couldn't drag me from this spot because, one, these two clearly have secrets that it's useful for me to know.

And, two, they're clearly about to fuck. And they're literally so hot I'm about to self-combust.

I don't get how Ronin can kiss the guy like he's about to crawl down his throat, given that reptile's literal fangs, but they both seem to enjoy it. When Vasili binds Ronin's wrists with his own tie, I almost burst into flames on the spot.

I'm warm and achy and I'm creaming my panties.

Abruptly the laboring furnace switches off. Vasili's muttered words zoom into focus.

"…kept me waiting, didn't you, little demon? Now you'll have to pay the price."

When the Goblin King drags down Ronin's zipper and eases out Ronin's pierced cock, I almost swallow my tongue.

By now, Ronin is moaning and begging and writhing on the mat and this is just way too good to miss. Vasili jacks him off with long slow strokes, his gaze intent on Ronin's face. I lick my lips and slide a hand inside my blazer to caress my breast, which feels full and tingly. Under the starchy fabric of my shirt and bra, my nipples furl into tight little buds, just longing to be suckled.

Suddenly Vasili's head swings up. "Merciful Christ, what is that appalling stench? Smells like rotting fish."

Horror nails my feet to the floor. Right in the middle of unbuttoning my blouse to feel myself up. My mouth pops open in alarm and I dive behind the wall with my heart pounding like a sledgehammer.

"Probably the start of another sushi dinner," Ronin murmurs. "It's Racetrack's turn to cook tonight. Girl's a one-trick pony in the kitchen, yeah?"

Vasili doesn't answer. I silently curse my koi pond hazing and wonder with a sick sense of dread what that snake will do if he finds me spying.

Ronin's tone turns petulant. "You going to finish what you started or not?"

That seems to do the trick, because whatever Vasili does next wrings out of Ronin a nice long moan. That throaty sound is so drenched with sex it makes my pussy clench.

My teeth sink into my lower lip.

I should leave, but who am I kidding?

What I really want to do is ease my fingers under my panties and get myself off. The thing is, I'm a screamer when I come, and I can't begin to imagine what Mr. Telekinetic over there will do if I'm discovered.

"Like me to finish you off?" Vasili purrs, all rough and growly and sexy as fuck.

God, yes, please. Finish him off and put us both out of our misery.

When Ronin moans his name, my fingers find my nipple through the lace of my bra. I'm so sensitive there, it's all I can manage not to moan myself.

"Then do as you're told, darling." Vasili's Russian accent licks me like a tongue. "I'm waiting to feel your naughty lips wrapped firmly around my cock."

Ronin mutters some complaint about Vasili being a bloody tease that's half-obscured by the buzz of a zipper, followed by Vasili's low riff of laughter.

Now this I gotta see. I poke my head around the corner just in time.

Vasili's lounging on his back like a Roman Caesar (or a Russian czar?) And he must have released Ronin's tie, because Ronin's crawling up his legs like a jaguar. If Ronin had a tail, it would be lashing.

Now they're both shirtless and unzipped. Vasili's like an '80s pop star at a photo shoot with his frosted hair and his smoky eyes and all that androgynous glam he's rocking. He doesn't have Ronin's overt muscle, he's slim and streamlined and sleek like a fencing foil. I'm treated to one mouthwatering eyeful of the Goblin King's spectacular cock before Ronin swoops to engulf all that rigid length in his mouth.

Ronin swallows him down to the hilt, then backs off slowly, revealing inch after inch of dick glistening with spit from plenty of tongue action, his eyes lidded but open to gauge his effect.

Vasili arches into his mouth with a gasp. Ronin grins around all that cock and really goes to work.

This is seriously so hot my brain's going to short-circuit. Under my uniform skirt I'm wet and warm and definitely bothered. I trail a hand up my bare thigh above my stocking until I find the soaked gusset of my panties. My teeth sink into my lower lip to hold back a gasp of my own.

Not that anyone would notice.

Vasili has both fists wrapped in Ronin's long hair to hold him steady while

Vasili bucks into Ronin's mouth. His thrusts are brutal and punishing, and that's a lot of cock to handle, but Ronin's deep-throating him like a porn star, arms braced on either side of Vasili's slim hips to hold himself up. They're both moaning, Ronin's humping into the mat with mounting desperation, and it looks to me like Ronin might be ready to come himself just from blowing the guy.

Teeth clamped on my lip so I don't make a sound, I work a hand under my panties. I'm soaked and slick and my clit's so swollen that first grazing contact makes me hiss. I dip my middle finger into all that pussy juice and swirl it around my clit.

God, my knees are shaking. I'm going to come like a bomb going off.

Skirt rucked up and trapped between my arm and my pelvis, hand burrowed under my panties, fingers buried in my pussy, I adjust my stance and start stroking my clit, eyes glued to the scorch fest unfolding right in front of me.

Vasili's totally lost in what Ronin's doing to him.

At first he's all dominant, totally trapping Ronin in place and fucking his mouth. But Ronin seems to know how to handle him. Like his submission seems to placate the guy. Pretty soon Vasili stops fisting Ronin's hair and fucking Ronin's mouth like he's trying to punish him and starts praising him instead, moaning phrases like *oh darling* and *such a good boy* and *so gorgeous when you take my cock*, all in a sex-drenched velvety purr that just about makes me climax.

Breathless and panting, chasing my own big O, I drink in the sight of Vasili's long curving shaft, flushed and soaked with saliva and precum, plunging in and out of Ronin's mouth. Ronin's sucking up and down the guy's dick like it's a popsicle he doesn't want to melt, and he's watching Vasili lose it under his ministrations.

My orgasm's barreling toward me like a freight train when Ronin's amber eyes veer to fix on me.

Just shy of the finish line, I freeze in guilty horror. Skirt pushed up, panties shoved aside, blouse half-unbuttoned, fingers buried in my cunt, and that freaking hall pass still hanging around my neck like a medal of honor.

You enjoying the show, love?

Ronin's warm voice scrolls through my brain. At first I think he's speaking out loud. My appalled gaze shoots to Vasili, whose own eyes are closed, brow furrowed, mouth panting with pleasure so his little pointed fangs are showing. Seen in this specific context, those wicked incisors of his are almost sexy.

Ronin's voice rolls through my head again. *He isn't Valyrian. Not a telepath. He can't hear unless I want him to hear through our bond.*

I'm still standing there with my hand between my legs. But somehow Ronin doesn't seem to mind. He's sucking Vasili off like a vacuum hose, while his tiger eyes stay fixed on me the whole freaking time.

Go ahead and finish for me, he murmurs in my head, low and husky. *I quite fancy getting both of you off.*

"Yes, fuck, yes," Vasili groans, writhing on the mat. "You're going to make me come—so hard for you, darling."

Well, shit.

My magic moment comes all on its own, my climax surging through me like an electric current, triggered by the raw pleasure that roughens Vasili Romanov's sexy growl. Ronin swallows him to the hilt and squeezes Vasili's balls and we all climax in synch, Vasili's sharp cry spiraling around Ronin's filthy groan and my own lusty moan.

Shit.

I just fucking *moaned.*

My eyes snap open to find them *both* staring at me. Ronin's licking come off his lips and grinning lazily at me, all replete with satisfaction for a job well done. Vasili sprawls flat on his back with his head turned toward me, the drowsy pleasure in his ice-colored eyes swiftly eclipsed by shock.

Then a pure and incandescent rage.

I yank my hand out of my panties and run for my life.

I burst through the gym door and take off down the hall, heading for the stairs by instinct. If that viper catches me in the basement, he'll bury my body down here or torch me in the furnace with no one ever the wiser. If I can get out of the *domus* into the village, that's my best bet. I can hide and I can run and I can fight.

A heavy framed portrait wrenches from the wall and comes spinning toward me. I manage to duck it and swerve into the stairwell.

Better step lively, love. Ronin's murmur fills my head, and it's laced with unholy amusement, because of course he hates me too. Maybe he even set this whole thing up just to fuck with me. *Afraid I can't hold him. He's a holy terror when he gets like this.*

I tear up the stairs like a velociraptor in what feels like a single fear-fueled leap and scramble into the ground-floor corridor. I'm briefly confused by the layout because I still haven't seen the whole *domus.* But there's a sound like a cyclone roaring up the stairs behind me, so I take a wild guess and sprint down the hall, slipping and sliding in my stocking feet and missing my platform boots like you wouldn't believe.

I glimpse a closed door straight ahead with windows on both sides and daylight pouring through, and I don't have my coat or boots, but fuck it. I burst through the door into a crisp cold wash of afternoon sun.

But not into the street the way I wanted, damn it.

I've just stumbled on another walled garden like the one at school, a tangle of tropical plants wrapped around crumbling Roman columns and a swimming pool, not even close to overgrown enough to hide behind, and completely enclosed by the two-story *domus*. The upstairs level's all wraparound porch, while my level's all walls and windows and, wait, a set of sliding glass doors across the way.

Unless I want to have my Vasili-Zara throwdown right here, that's pretty much my only option. I dash out from under the overhang of the second-floor veranda.

A slim dark shape drops down from above like an avenging angel. It's a jump no normal human could survive without a broken leg, but apparently this telekinetic freak can levitate his own body as well as everyone else's.

I scramble to a stop barely in time to avoid colliding with six-plus feet of Vasili Romanov, half naked and all furious.

He's zipped into his pants, but still shirtless and barefoot, and I'd really enjoy the view if I wasn't so terrified of dying in the next 6.5 seconds. The Goblin King's face is flushed and his venomous eyes are lethal.

"Going somewhere, are we, little queen?" he hisses with silken menace.

Adrenaline spurts through my system and my pulse thunders in my ears. Okay, then. Looks like we're gonna throw down right here.

Unless I can talk my way out of this before he goes all telekinetic on my ass.

"Lucius expects me back in class in like five minutes. If I don't show, he'll come looking." My nerves get the better of me, and I wave the lanyard hanging around my neck like an idiot. "I have a hall pass."

His eyes narrow in annoyance. "Darling, I don't give a fuck if you have an engraved invitation to afternoon tea with the Queen of England. I'm not a hall monitor. I mean to hear you articulate whatever it is you believe you just saw."

I know it's a bad idea to provoke him, but I can't seem to help myself. My gaze drops to his crotch.

"Um, pretty much everything." I snicker. "Thanks for the free show. I gotta say Ronin impressed me with the way he took your cock—"

That's as far as I get. He bares his fangy teeth in rage. A wall of atmospheric pressure thumps into me and hurls me back a good three feet through the air into one of those Roman pillars. The back of my head slams into stone.

For a second, I see stars.

Shit. The entire back of my body's going to be one massive bruise.

Assuming I live long enough.

When my head clears, my nemesis is less than a foot away, glaring into my face like he's about to incinerate me with his eyes. I try to get my arms up and circle away for fighting room, but I'm pinned to this pillar like a bug on display. I can breathe—for now—but I definitely can't move.

"You saw *nothing*." His voice lashes into me like a scourge, sharp enough to draw blood. "Nothing of any consequence. Ronin Pendragon is a whore who'll fuck anything that moves. Even Lucius' wolf wants a go at him. You saw an opportunistic hate fuck between me and a filthy slut who was begging for it, and you saw *not one single thing more*. Is. That. Clear."

I loathe this horrible man like a goddamn plague rat. And I'd be offended as hell on Ronin's behalf if I thought Vasili meant one tenth of what he's saying.

But he doesn't. He's in love with Ronin. And he's desperate to keep anyone from knowing.

My temples are throbbing and my ears are ringing, but somehow I manage to sustain his gorgon stare without turning into stone.

"You're afraid I'll tell. But I won't." I keep my voice level, though it isn't easy. "I'll bury what I saw and I won't tell a soul. But I want something from you in exchange for my silence."

He barks a short laugh that's cutting with contempt. "In case this minor detail has escaped your notice, little queen, you're not exactly in a position to negotiate."

But he's listening. He's actually listening.

I take heart and keep talking.

"Look, Vasili. As hard as this is to believe, we actually have something in common. You're an anti-monarchist, right? You want me gone from this Academy. You want me out of the running for the royal gig. Well, newsflash, dude. *That's what I want too*." I suck in a breath and take the plunge. "Help me get off this rock, and we both get what we want. I get my freedom, and you get an empty throne."

His head cocks and his eyes narrow. "Well, but that isn't exactly true, is it? There would still be Queen Messalina to contend with. Admittedly, she's a bit long in the tooth, but she could still conceivably spawn another Aquarius brat."

"That's out of my hands." I shrug. "You help bust me out of this prison, and that's me renouncing my power in front of the whole witching world. That means I renounce the fucking throne, and the Senate can start the abdication process. I never wanted a crown and I still don't."

He cocks his hip and taps one finger against his chin. Which distracts me, and not in a good way. With his streamlined build and his aristocratic face and his arctic coloring, he really would be beautiful if he wasn't such a shit.

"You'd actually renounce all that power?" He sounds nothing but suspicious. "Willingly?"

A combustible memory explodes in my head. The memory of what happened that night with my mom in Vegas. There's a Gemini casino on The Strip that's still in the red because there isn't enough money on the planet to sanitize the ugliness of those eighty-seven deaths. Remembering those deaths—and my own role in causing them—is like poking a bad bruise. My mind flinches away from the pain.

Yeah, no. The witching world's way better off without my ass parked on the throne. A Gemini queen's plenty capable of causing her own extinction event.

"Trust me," I say bleakly. "All I want is to disappear. And this time, I'll stay gone. Me keeping quiet about you and Ronin? That's just an added bonus."

Of course I would have done that anyway—kept their secret—not for his sake, but for Ronin's. I feel like I owe Ronin for what my brother did to his sister.

But that's something Vasili doesn't need to know.

The Goblin King's watching me with narrowed eyes, trying to spot the lie, but I'm not telling one. I just hold his stare and let him read the truth. His pale gaze drifts over me, pausing on my breathless lips, my heaving chest under my half-open shirt, my bare thighs pebbled with goosebumps under my short skirt. When his gaze returns to mine, his brow furrows. I hold his stare, my own brows lifted in challenge, the hint of a smile I can't explain tugging at my lips.

He doesn't want to believe me, but I can tell he does. It's like a silent communication passes between us.

That's right, Goblin King. I'm your fucking queen, at least until I'm off this rock. And you're going to give me what I want.

Abruptly he steps back, fingers spreading wide in a dismissive flick. That awful feeling of being pressed under a sheet of glass in a display case releases its grip. Before I can hide it, my body slumps in relief.

"Truly, I must be demented," he mutters. "But, for some inexplicable reason, I find I actually believe you."

Cautiously I step clear of the pillar toward those double doors. Now that I'm not in active terror of imminent death, the frigid cold's creeping through the flagstones to numb my stocking feet and nipping at my exposed skin. Sliding a wary glance at Vasili, I edge toward my escape route.

"Wait." He slips sideways to block me, and I scowl at him in annoyance. He's barefoot and shirtless, for fuck's sake. Doesn't he feel the cold?

"Make it snappy," I say curtly.

One silver eyebrow climbs above a glacial eye. "For someone who's planning to abdicate, you've certainly mastered the knack of a royal's imperial manners. You're an absolute brat."

"Pot, kettle." I push out an impatient huff, and for a nanosecond he almost smiles.

Encouraged by this no doubt fleeting hint that he's actually human, I chafe my arms and press one cold foot atop the other. "C'mon, it's freezing. Let's do whatever this is we're doing inside."

His hint of humanity disappears with a pop.

He looms over me like a hooded cobra and hisses, "I may have agreed to help you escape this island, but don't imagine for one moment this fleeting arrangement means I'm going to start kissing your royal ass. You're a freshman at this Academy, I'm the dominant male in this institution, and we've certain standards to uphold."

Translation? He intends to keep hazing me. Yay.

"If you wanna bully me, bad boy, you're gonna have to catch me." Despite having a pretty healthy sense of self-preservation, the prospect of fighting him gets my blood up. My fingers start tingling and my ponytail floats around my shoulders. "And don't expect me to make that easy."

A soft laugh explodes from his lips in a cloud of frosty vapor and his pale eyes flash platinum. "Consider that challenge accepted, little queen."

And for some fucked-up reason, I too chuff out a laugh.

A pucker appears between his brows like I've perplexed him. Frowning, he reaches to catch a floating tendril of my hair between two fingers. And because it's weird and I'm curious, I don't stop him. He steps in close and I tense up, ready to knee him in the balls and break his fingers if he tries anything.

But he only lifts my side ponytail and bends to take a sniff.

A low rumble of warning rises from his chest, accompanied by a sudden rush of dark spicy scent. He smells like caramel and sandalwood, with a smoky undertone of vetiver. Yeah, he's definitely Mogadon, because of the way he's scenting. Which explains some of that testosterone and aggression, because those are racial traits, even if his are off the charts. Mogadon scent when they're feeling aggression, territoriality, or arousal.

And suddenly he's rubbing his face in my ponytail and scenting *me*.

I plant my hands on my hips in a power stance, because out of the three possible options, this has to be aggression, and I want him to back the hell off. "What the fuck, Goblin King—"

"You've been with Neo Mercury." He slices me a smoking look that's hot enough to singe my skin. "Your *fated mate*. I can smell him on you."

I tilt my head and squint at him suspiciously, because that sounds like territoriality… over me… and that's *not* what I expect out of him.

"Not that it's any of your business," I point out irritably. "But I totally reject that whole fated mate concept. That's what I keep telling Neo. But he just won't listen."

Now he looks positively predatory.

I can't help noticing the cold has reddened his lips and tweaked his nipples into tight little nubs that just beg to be suckled in someone's warm mouth. I wonder if he's planning to go straight back to Ronin for that after he sends me on my way.

The image of those two together gooses my vitals with a jolt of erotic heat.

And all those Mogadon pheromones Vasili's pumping out right now definitely aren't helping. He leans in closer to rub his face in my hair, his quickened breath brushing my ear. Which is even more unsettling while I'm borderline turned on by him.

I press my thighs together under my short skirt. I really need not to be thinking about the Goblin King's nipples right now. Or imagining Ronin tonguing him. Or imagining tonguing him myself—

A shrill pure sound spirals up from somewhere in the *domus* and unravels in the icy air.

It's a girl's voice.

Screaming.

Vasili clips out a curse in Russian and pivots toward the doors. That's where the scream's coming from, and he's already running toward it with me on his heels.

We tear into the house through a sitting room with a central hearth that's probably pretty cozy at night with the fire lit, then we pound down a short flight of stairs to the atrium. By now the scream's gone silent, but that's not necessarily a good thing. There's the door to the street I was looking for earlier.

Now it's wide open to let the cold pour in.

Vasili stops dead in the threshold and, for the second time today, I barely manage to avoid running right into him. Impatiently I nudge his tall obstructive body to one side so I can see too. Somewhat to my surprise, he doesn't backhand me for presuming to touch his precious self, but gives way and shifts to one side.

Dez is standing in the street, bundled up in her coat and boots, clearly just coming home from school. Another girl's standing beside her with an arm wrapped around Dez's shoulders, trying to comfort her.

And on the doormat at my feet lies a jumbo koi a good three feet long, the fish's gullet slit open from stem to stern, bloody guts spilling out all over the flagstones and spattering the door.

Jammed down around its head is a kid's toy crown.

The sight of this majestic ocean dweller brutally butchered for no freaking reason is upsetting enough. But the sight of that crown makes me feel like I've been punched in the gut. A nauseating sense of dread sweeps through me and churns in my stomach.

Because, all too clearly, this threat is meant for me.

A spray of violet sparks sputters from my icy fingers before I can twist off the spigot. Which makes this whole fiasco a thousand times worse. Because I haven't actually sprayed sparks like that since I shut down my witchcraft after the casino explosion five years ago. Here on this island, with these hostile and unpredictable warlocks, I feel like I'm coming undone.

Which is one more very real danger I have to fear.

Somewhere in the arctic sky, I barely hear a distant mutter of thunder.

But it's there.

And where there's thunder, there's lightning.

I ball my hands into fists so hard my hands ache to extinguish the last sparks and slice a wary glance all around. But no one seems to have noticed my little pyromaniacal lapse. Dez is pulling her shit together, and her friend lets her stand on her own and swings toward me. I'm guessing this is the elusive Racetrack. She's a hard-faced girl rocking a boyish look in a military-style khaki coat over her uniform, an olive knit stocking cap pulled over short blond hair. Her gray eyes lock with mine and her mouth twists in a wry grimace.

"Looks to me like someone's way of saying welcome to Icarus, Queen Zarina," she drawls. "Anyone in the mood for sushi?"

Chapter Sixteen

Neo

I'm standing on the landing outside my fated mate's bedroom with a box of pizza balanced in my hands and my whole heart jammed up in my throat. Dinner time has come and gone. The *domus* is still redolent with the peppery bite of wasabi.

But Zara never showed up to eat.

Not even after Dez went up to knock on her door and tried to lure her out with a fresh California roll, offered with Dez's general niceness.

There's a lot going on in this *domus* right now that I don't understand. For one, something's up between Ronin and Lucius that made our always complicated atmospherics at the dinner table even more fraught than usual. Ronin isn't actually looking well. He's irritable and feverish, and I caught him pilfering aspirin from the medicine cabinet after dinner. When I mustered the courage to ask if he's okay, blushing the way I do every single time I talk to him and silently cursing my fair complexion that always makes it so obvious, he just snarled at me to mind my own business.

As for Vasili, who usually amuses himself at dinner by hurling humorous little zingers at me and smirking over his own nonexistent wit, he's spent the entire night scowling at Lucius.

Our headmaster, too, seems worried and distracted.

Racetrack and Dez disappeared right after dinner, no doubt seeking refuge from the tension. Now everyone's finally settling down for the night.

Except me.

I stare at Zara's firmly closed door and feel so anxious I can hardly breathe. Having her actually here with me in this house is like a dream. But enduring her anger, most of it clearly directed at me for enrolling her against her will, has been a nightmare.

Now I straighten my shoulders, adjust the six-pack of Italian beer wedged between my hip and my elbow, and knock gently on her door with my foot.

"Zara? It's me... Neo." I remember to add my name, because she can't be expected to recognize my voice. She doesn't appear to have spent all these years yearning for me the way I've been yearning for her. "I brought you something to eat."

"Not in the mood for sushi." Her voice filters under the door. "I'll scrounge up something from the fridge later. Don't worry about me."

As if I can stop. My heart sinks to the soles of my suede shoes, but I'm not so easily discouraged. Worrying about Zara Gemini, yearning for Zara Gemini, dreaming up ways to take care of Zara Gemini… well, that's what I do.

Besides, she needs me. She really does.

Whether she wants to admit it or not.

"You know Racetrack didn't actually bring that koi into the house," I offer. "We all take turns cooking dinner, and she always makes sushi. Culinary variety isn't her strong suit. And neither is sensitivity, unfortunately. I hope you won't hold it against her."

I hear a snort, but my fated mate says nothing, and I'm determined to respect her wishes and not go rooting around in the bond between us to read her thoughts.

So I try again, the conventional way. "I gave that koi an honorable burial at sea. It's part of the food chain now—I mean, the marine food chain, not ours in the kitchen. So you don't have to worry about dealing with it."

It still makes me frantic to think of someone threatening her, frightening her, hurting her. And it's not just anyone doing it. Somewhere on this island, there's a queen killer lurking. Of course, Zara has us—her courtiers—to protect her. Speaking for myself, I'll absolutely kill to protect her. And given what happened in Vegas, obviously Zara herself is far from helpless, even if she's not comfortable using her witchcraft.

Still, the thought of my fated mate in danger makes me want to commit murder myself.

Zara's still not talking, but I sense her listening, right on the other side of this door.

So I cross my mental fingers (since my hands are full) and play my best card. "I've got homemade pizza. It's pepperoni and mushroom. Your favorite."

Finally, the door swings open. My heart floats up somewhere around my ears, the same way it always does when I see her. Her wonderful mermaid hair's tied up in two sexy pigtails and she's standing there barefoot, wearing the yoga pants and hot pink tee shirt I left in her room earlier, now that I know how much she hates the standard uniform stocking her armoire.

Zara doesn't do standard. Everything she does is extraordinary.

Seeing her comfortable wearing the clothes I left her, even if she doesn't know it, fills me with a giddy rush of happiness.

She eyes me, looming on her doorstep with my big box of pizza. Her teal eyebrows lift toward her hairline.

Damn it. I'm standing there grinning at her like a circus freak.

"One," she announces, unfolding a finger that glitters with her wild polish. "It's weird and borderline stalkery that you know my favorite toppings, and you definitely shouldn't advertise it. Two." She unfolds a second finger. "I'm still pissed at you, though I know you meant well. And three." She adds a third finger, and I'm spiraling down into despair, but the tilt of a smile on her pretty lips arrests my descent. "I'm starving and I love pizza, so you're forgiven."

She steps back so I can come in.

Dizzy with success, it's all I can manage to slip past her into the *sanctum sanctorum* of my fated mate's boudoir without dropping her pizza. I've been entertaining gloomy visions of having to leave it on her doorstep and slink off in disgrace.

Inside it's all messy, the way I know this rebel mate of mine likes it. Against the bucolic backdrop of her painted frescoes, she has the desk lamp lit and a toasty fire burning and the curtains open while fat snowflakes swirl past her frosty windows. Half the contents of her armoire are flung over the bed and the vanity like a bomb's gone off in here. She's probably spent the whole night hunting for something she can stand to wear.

I have a nice surprise lined up for her in that department, and I'm hoping she'll like it and that I don't screw everything up again. The air is sweet with roses and vanilla, like *her*.

The fragrance of my beloved.

While she closes the door behind me, I lower the pizza carefully to the desk, unload my six pack of tall green bottles, and produce plastic plates and napkins from the sack dangling over my arm.

"Juno's Pizza," she says, reading the box. "Good to know they have pizza on this rock."

"There's a pizza kiln at Villa Hadrian. I told you we're pretty self-sufficient." I fish out the bottle opener from the pocket of my chinos and concentrate on popping the cap from a pair of longnecks. I'm really hoping she doesn't send me away. In principle, I've already eaten, but I couldn't eat much knowing she's up here alone and hungry.

Honestly, I'll be perfectly happy just sitting here watching her eat.

"Silver lining to every cloud, I guess. Cop a squat." She waves a casual hand, leaving it up to me to figure out whether she wants me parked at the desk where she studies, on the stool in front of her little vanity, or sitting on her bed.

Just the thought of her bed makes my heart thunder and my whole body heat.

I had the best wake-up of my entire life this morning in that bed, with Zara in my arms mumbling in her cute sleepy voice that she wanted to feel my tongue. God knows it would've been a new experience for me, and I probably wouldn't have been sitting on top of *that* Dean's List after my first attempt.

But I'm more than willing to put all that educational reading and DVD research I've done to good use and experiment with Zara until I learn how best to please her.

While I stand there staring at her bed with a hot blush spreading across my face, my fated mate digs into the box and loads onto her plate a couple of fat triangles dripping with melted cheese. She grabs a handful of napkins and one of the open beers and beelines for the bed.

For the sake of having something to do rather than standing there marooned in the middle of her bedroom blushing like an idiot, I help myself to a slice and a beer. She's already settled cross-legged on the bed, her plate in her lap. She takes a hearty bite and moans in a way that gives me an instant hard-on.

That's exactly the way she was moaning this morning with my hand buried in her divine pussy.

It makes me so happy to see her enjoying the food I've brought for her. Actually, the fact that she's letting me take care of her at all, even in this minor way, makes me nearly euphoric. It's all I've ever wanted. To take care of her. Having her angry at me over how she ended up here has been destroying me.

I'm still wondering where to sit. The desk is too far from the bed and too far from her to suit me. She's all the way across the room. We'd need megaphones to hear each other. The vanity is closer, so I hesitantly head that way.

"Neo," she mumbles around another mouthful of pizza. "You're a great big guy and that stool is super tiny. It'll probably break if you sit on it. Just sit over here with me."

Over here means on the bed.

Her bed.

She's inviting me into her bed.

It doesn't matter that it's fully made and we're only sitting on top of her bedspread eating pizza. It's one step closer to being with her. To being hers. To making her mine.

Happily I toe off my shoes and settle on the bed across from her, careful not to crowd too close. I balance my pizza on the bedside table. I'm still way too nervous to eat, but I take a swallow of cold fizzy beer to settle my nerves.

"This is so good," she sighs, making respectable inroads into her food, though I'll be super careful not to comment on how fast she's eating. One thing I've learned from my kid sister—my primary source of female insight—is that girls really don't like you to comment on how fast or how much they eat.

Anyway, I'll happily feed Zara the whole pie by hand if she wants. It's enough just to see her enjoy something I've brought her.

"I'm so glad you like it, Zara," I say softly.

She slews a glance up at me, probably reading my entire nonexistent sexual history in my glass face. Nervously I adjust my glasses on my nose. Her own vivid face softens.

"I love it," she says, just as softly. "It's honestly the best pizza I've ever tasted. Thank you for bringing it, Neo."

"Anytime, babe." I tilt back my bottle for another sip and watch her eyes linger on my lips, then follow my throat when I swallow. Predictably, my dick hardens in my chinos all over again.

I want her so much. I've wanted her forever.

She's still slowly chewing, but she seems mostly to have forgotten her half-eaten pizza. Her gaze is roaming over my chest and shoulders in my burgundy Academy sweater as though she likes what she's seeing, and I really hope she does. I'm hers, all hers, and I'm ready to devote my entire life to protecting her, caring for her, and bringing her pleasure.

Our eyes collide. Abruptly, her chewing stops.

She swallows and licks her lips, and my dick gets harder. Never breaking my gaze, she wipes her fingers with her napkin, then reaches for my beer. Hers is on the bedside table out of her reach, and I would gladly have gotten it for her, but I'll just as gladly give her mine. She claims my bottle without any protest from me and tilts it back for a long swallow, her lips resting on the glass where mine just were.

I'm in top shape physically, but my heart is pounding like I've just run a ten-mile marathon.

"Zara," I breathe, just to say her name.

"Yes, Neo?" She's still holding my bottle, and she can definitely have it if she wants, but I wonder if she's saying my name too because she likes hearing it.

I suck in a breath and wade in with a rush. "I'm so sorry I screwed everything up. I meant to protect you by enrolling you here, I really did, but I know you're used to making your own choices and I should have consulted you first even though you're really hard to reach and your address is always changing and you don't typically respond to e-mail or answer your phone." I come up for air and try to slow down. "It's just that I wanted you here—so much—you can't imagine how much I've wanted you here. With me."

I want to talk about how she's my fated mate and we belong together, but I learned something from our fight this morning.

I know she's not ready to acknowledge this bond we share.

Her forehead puckers and she heaves a sigh. "I gotta admit it's hard to stay mad at a guy who always seems so freaking happy to see me. But you really do need to let me make my own choices. That's the only way we can be friends."

I want to be more than friends, so much more, but friends is a place to start. Earnestly I nod and hold her gaze. "I can. I will. I'm learning, I am."

Her mouth softens in a rueful smile. "You're supposed to be the smartest guy in the school, aren't you? Top of the Dean's List? I shouldn't be too hard for you to figure out."

She's *so* much harder to wrap my head around than my Honors Science of Witchcraft class, which is by far the toughest class at Icarus. She's especially hard to understand when I'm making a concerted effort to stay out of her head like I have been all night. I actually can't understand at all why she doesn't seem to get the existential crisis the witching world is dealing with.

We're literally dying. And she acts like she doesn't even care.

That can't be true, can it?

I know I should leave it alone for now, and just be happy she's not mad at me anymore. But I'm a pretty driven guy myself, and this issue is way too urgent to ignore. So I clench my fists and the words come tumbling out.

"It's just… you heard Master Aries in class, so you have to understand. The arcane races are dying, Zara. We're going extinct. It's not only that the races are all crossbred and commingled with each other. We're also crossbred with earthbound humans. There are only three purebred witch families of the original twelve left, the others are all diluted with human DNA, and the shifters are already so far gone it might not even be possible anymore to stop their decline. You're the only purebred female with enough witchcraft to ascend, if you'll only embrace your power—"

Her face darkens while I talk. Now she crushes her napkin in her fist, leans forward to toss her plate on the nightstand, and points her longneck bottle at my chest. "No way, Neo. You're not pinning the extinction of the arcane races on me. That downward glide started way before I came along."

"I'm not saying it's your fault, of course it's not," I assure her, leaning forward, desperate to persuade her. "But don't you see? If you believe the theory, you and I together, that means we can stop it! We can save our people."

"The Theory of Royal Culpability?" She huffs out an angry laugh and swigs more of my beer, which is now her beer. "It's a load of bull and a big fat guilt trip. I don't buy it."

"It's the only theory that even comes close to explaining what's happening to us!" Frantic to make her understand, I lean forward to grip her knee. "Zara, you can save us! Just by accepting your witchcraft! You're the Gemini queen! You and your—" I barely catch the fatal word *mate* before I say it and spoil my chance with her for good. "Your consort. Or consorts."

Her head tilts to study me. Interest flickers in her face. "Yeah, I heard that in class. That I'm supposed to pick my… uh, consort… or consorts… for the good of the races. It sounded like I could pick more than one."

"You can." I scoot forward a little (you know, the better to convince her) and tighten my grip on her knee. Because she might be borderline angry, but she still hasn't moved my hand. "Babe, I'm not going to lie to you. I swear I'll never lie to you. I'll be thrilled if I can be everything you need. But I've been raised for this from an early age. It's a queen's right to choose her m—uh, her consorts. As many as she wishes."

Her gaze drops to my hand on her knee. "Does that mean you'd be willing to share?"

I swallow hard. "I would. I'll share our bed with whoever you say."

"Of any gender?"

"Yeah." Gently I tease the near-empty bottle from her hand and take the last swallow myself, because at this point I really need it. "Any gender."

"You seem to have watched me pretty close," she murmurs, "if you know my favorite pizza. You have to know I'm bi *and* poly, right?"

"I know." In fact, I more than know. The thought of her being pleased by multiple lovers is a major turn-on and a fairly significant element of my sexual fantasies. "I, uh, I don't mind."

"Are you sure?" Light as a falling snowflake, her hand lands on mine, fingertips coasting over my knuckles. "How many lovers have you been with, really?"

My gaze slams into hers. "None. I'm yours. I've been waiting for you."

Didn't we cover that terrain this morning, to my complete and total embarrassment?

"That's pretty much what I figured," she sighs. "Which means you don't really know, Neo. You might not like sharing at all. Plenty of people don't. And in particular, you might not like another guy in your bed."

Involuntarily my brain jumps to those moments in the *thermae* I usually try not to think about. Because I do share a house and a bathroom with three other guys, one of whom is the student the whole school crushes on, and one of whom is the headmaster our whole house crushes on. A certain level of familiarity with my roommates' bodies, even with Vasili who's so beautiful but hates my guts, is hard to avoid. Warmth creeps down from my hairline to toast my cheeks.

"I don't think I'd mind," I mumble, watching our joined hands so I don't have to look into her face. "I'm not a total neophyte. I read very extensively."

"Wow," she whispers, and my head jerks up. She's watching me with a soft smile teasing her lush lips and a hint of color warming her cheeks under her California tan. "You're actually bi-curious, aren't you? And you really don't have any idea how tempting you are to a girl like me, do you, Neo Mercury?"

I shake my head with a smile. If the concept of having an awkward blushing virgin in her bed is somehow tempting, I can only be grateful for the miracle.

Her fingers thread through mine and her face turns troubled.

"Honestly speaking," she breathes, "I'm pretty torn."

"About what?"

Her long Marilyn Monroe lashes fall over her eyes. "About you. On the one hand, it seems criminal to let that sex famine you're needlessly enduring on my account drag on a minute longer."

I'm all for ending my sex famine too, here, now, with her. And it's possible I'm not keeping that bond between us sealed off as tight as I'm trying to, because she chuckles like she hears me.

"On the other hand," she resumes, her colorful brows scrunching together, "I'm afraid if we go down that road, it'll only confuse the situation for you and me and everyone else. Because we're not actually mated."

We are, though. We totally are. My hand clenches around hers in protest before I can stop it and her wary face lifts.

I scoot closer to her and settle down and focus like I do before a big test. Because I've been studying what I need to say to her all day. "I know it's a foreign concept in this day and age. There's no real analog for earthbound humans, even if they do understand astrology, and even if they study their natal charts. But for arcanes like us, with seventh house significators as strong as ours—each of our charts pointing straight at each other, Zara—it's more than a tendency or a prediction. Our natal charts together form an ironclad prophecy. And a natal chart prophecy as clear as ours has status in witching world law. Legal, ethical, magical status."

I lean toward her, close enough to kiss her if I only dared, and pour every atom of conviction into what I'm saying. My voice vibrates with emotion. "I'm yours in every single way, Zara Gemini. I'm so completely yours."

Her chin firms and her mouth opens and she's going to deny it, I know she is, she's going to say we aren't mated. And I can't stand it. I can't. I'm *hers*.

I lunge forward and claim my mate with a kiss.

Despite my virginal state, I've had a few kisses, because arcanes don't get their charts officially read until they turn fifteen, and I was a precocious kid. But I've never kissed anyone like her. Her lips are so soft and her kisses are so confident. She tastes a little peppery from the pizza, which should clash with the breath mint I optimistically consumed before knocking, but it doesn't.

Underneath she's sweet, like strawberries and cream, she's so sweet.

I lean into her kiss and our noses and chins bump awkwardly, because I really don't know what I'm doing. She cradles my face between her firm hands to steady me and takes command of our kiss, her mouth searching mine, her tongue finding mine, drawing my tongue into her mouth so I can explore her too. When she sucks on my tongue with her warm silky lips, a lightning bolt of need rips through me and makes my dick ache.

I groan and push closer, as close as I can get with our legs crossed and our knees nudging, my hands finding her taut waist and a scant inch of exposed skin between her tee shirt and her yoga pants. Frustration and hunger claw through me. I need more, more of this, more of her, more.

"Babe," I groan against her mouth like I'm dying.

"It's okay, baby," she whispers against my lips.

Obviously I don't know what I'm doing, and I'm worried about going too fast, but she's at least thinking about ending my sex famine (as she puts it) and I definitely want to encourage her in that direction and not in the direction of avoiding confusion and denying our bond. So I push forward and she falls back and I climb over her and straddle her, careful not to crush her with my big clumsy body.

"You're doing great," she breathes, and I wonder if she even realizes she's reading me through our bond.

If she doesn't, I don't want to say anything that will freak her out.

Her body is tight and sleek and warm under me, so warm, so right, full breasts pressing into my chest, hands still cradling my face to hold me steady. I nuzzle into her neck and breathe in roses and vanilla—she's wearing the perfume I left for her too—and I nudge up her shirt to feel the sleek skin of her tummy and the ripple of her ribs against my bare hands.

"Neo," she breathes, arching into my touch.

My glasses are steaming and slipping down my nose, but I don't want to stop touching her long enough to deal with the issue. She chuffs out a chuckle and removes my glasses and ferries them onto the nightstand. She's definitely reading me through the bond, and it makes me so happy.

I bite gently into her neck, just to see if she likes it, which makes her moan and shiver, so it seems like she does. Her hands thread through my hair to encourage me, so I open my mouth in a sucking kiss against her neck that makes her arch into me with a gasp. I suck harder to mark her.

Jeez, just the thought of her wearing my mark on her neck makes my dick throb.

"You're so hard," she moans, shoving her hips into my boner. "God, Neo, God. If we do this…"

I don't want there to be an *if*. I growl to lodge a protest against that entire grammatical conjunction and work my hand higher under her shirt to distract her. She's not wearing a bra and, sweet Lord, her ripe breast fits so perfectly in my hand, her tight pierced nipple nestling into my palm. I remember what she liked this morning and I tease and tweak that succulent bud while she gasps and squirms beneath me.

Her hands work under my sweater to stroke my back and goosebumps break out everywhere. I pinch her nipple hard, the way she liked before, and her breathless cry of pleasure almost makes me come in my pants.

"Neo," she pants, writhing under me, "if we do this… it doesn't mean we're mated, okay?"

I stiffen with instant protest. We're already mated, no matter what she thinks.

But I'm not going to convince her just by saying so.

I raise my head to gaze into her face. She's all flushed and dewy and her lips are rosy from my kisses. I swear to God I've never seen a woman so beautiful.

"Just let me do this for you, babe," I tell her, my voice gone husky with sex. "We can decide what it means later."

I sense her resistance ripple through the strengthening bond between us.

She's thinking she should push this and make me deny that bond, while I'm equally determined to make her accept it. I kiss her again to distract her, my tongue plunging deep in her sweet mouth, and peel her shirt all the way up to expose her breasts. Now I can fill both hands with her, and she's just so gorgeous the way she pushes up to meet me and shivers when I tweak her nipples.

I could honestly do this all night.

But the way she's squirming against me, rocking into my dick through the layers of clothing between us, tells me I'm not going to last that long. And neither is she. The important thing now is to make her come, to give her pleasure.

But I think if I can do that, just making her climax is going to push me over the edge too.

"Shouldn't let this happen," she mumbles, tugging at my sweater. I pull back a little so she can drag it over my head. "But fuck if I want to stop."

This captures so perfectly my own feelings on the topic that I can't help smiling at her.

She's got me out of my sweater and her hands are roaming over my body like she's trying to memorize it, which isn't necessary because she can have me in the flesh literally any time she wants me. And lying over her like this, I can finally fill my eyes with the sight of my beloved, that hot pink shirt rucked up above absolutely the most gorgeous breasts I've ever seen including on TV. For such a tiny girl, she's really curvy, and she has the prettiest pink areolae (I know all the words, because bookworm) flushing to a deeper rose at her nipples, pierced with those tiny silver hoops.

"Babe, you're so beautiful," I whisper. "Will you let me…?"

"I think I'll cry if you don't," she murmurs, a wry grin lurking around her lips. "But, Neo, this doesn't mean anything, okay? It's just for fun."

How can she say it doesn't mean anything, when it means *everything*?

She makes my stomach knot up with anxiety and my heart pound with determination. I lean in, because she's letting me and because honestly I can't resist, and carefully nuzzle the bud of one nipple, so silky and tight against my lips, her ring cool and smooth against my tongue.

Her throaty groan thrills me and makes me even harder. I want to elicit more of those sounds from my beloved.

"Harder," she says, all husky. "You can do that pretty hard with me. Teeth, too."

I happily experiment to see what she likes, and it's true, she likes it when I bite a little and then tongue her. When I tug her nipple ring between my teeth and flick it with my tongue, her hips rock into mine in a way that's absolutely electric. I'm straddling her and she wants to spread her legs for me, so I shift to one side, and she grabs my hand and presses it to her crotch over her yoga pants. I can feel the shape of her through the fabric, the heat of her as she rocks into my palm, and I'm more than ready to get her off again the way I did this morning—

Until she closes her hand over the hard bulge under my chinos.

Then I almost climax for her right there.

"Oh yeah, babe," I breathe, thrusting into her hand. She explores my length with eager fingers and I almost lose my mind.

But I focus on what she needs, which right now seems to be for me to hold steady while she pushes into the heel of my hand against her clit. When her clever hands unbutton me and work down my zipper, my heart starts pounding so hard I'm sure she can hear it.

She gets my fly open, works her hand into the slit in my briefs and… wow… the shock of her bare fingers wraps around my dick and transports me to another dimension.

"There you are," she murmurs, low and languid. "Neo Mercury, there's a lot of you to love."

"Um." I could give her exact dimensions if she wants, because I've measured, but I can't actually speak at the moment. Her fingertips glide across the head of my dick to find that I'm already slick with precum. Like, a lot of it, because she has me pretty worked up. She smooths all that moisture down my shaft to lube me up and starts jacking me and wow, just wow, this has to be the best feeling of my whole entire life.

Having her hands on my body is so much better than doing this myself.

"You haven't seen anything yet, baby," she breathes, hearing me through the bond. "Take off your pants."

I am so completely on board with that suggestion.

I scramble up to sit and peel out of my chinos and briefs and socks in record time.

I worry she might not like what she sees. Based on what I know of her history, she tends to go for guys like Ronin, long and lean and sexy, and I'm pretty ripped from all those hours in the gym honing my strength to make myself perfect for her.

But I don't have time to feel awkward, because she sits up too and peels her shirt over her head. She's still wearing her pants, but I'm going to let her set the pace, and she's already pushing me down on my back and straddling my legs. She's an absolute goddess, her pigtails all wild and tousled around her pouting breasts, her nipple rings glinting through all that blue hair, her body all sleek and taut and tan.

Her eyes are glowing violet, because she has Valyrian blood, and what we're doing is making her power rise.

"Damn," she whispers, squeezing her eyes closed. "I don't *want* my power rising, Neo."

"It's okay, babe. You're safe with me," I promise her, my voice cracking a little. "I swear I won't let anything happen to you."

"It's not me I'm worried about." But her eyes open to find me and roam over my body, and I'm relieved to see the hunger swallow the fear in her gaze.

My dick is standing straight up for her. When she licks her lips and cups my shaft between her hands, I groan and buck into her touch. And then I can't think about anything, because she bends to encase me in the wet sucking heat of her mouth.

And my entire world goes white with pleasure.

Chapter Seventeen

Zara

I've sucked plenty of cock in my day, but I'm pretty sure I've never sucked off a virgin.

And that changes everything.

That, plus the fact that it's Neo. He's been waiting for this—for *me*—for a lifetime. He's been so good. I want to make it good for him.

I want to make it so good.

And he's so open and so responsive to every little touch that he's making it easy for me. Just circling the thick head of his supersized cock with the tip of my tongue has him fisting the blankets and bucking into my mouth. It's weird, because obviously I barely know him, but I feel so connected with him somehow.

He's effing huge, so I open wider and mouth my way down his shaft, working the silky ridge down the underside with my tongue, one hand holding him steady for my mouth, the other slipping between his corded thighs to find the heavy sac of his balls.

He cries out like I'm killing him and fucks my mouth. The salty taste of another spurt of precum explodes across my palate.

"Babe," he gasps. "Oh, babe. Let me…"

What is it, baby? I say without stopping, my mouth riding his thick cock like he's a horse and I'm Mustang Sally. *What do you need?*

"I need to come inside you," he groans. "Please let me come inside you."

I haven't one hundred percent made up my mind to that, because it hasn't escaped my notice that he hasn't actually agreed to a single one of my cautionary efforts to set boundaries around what this whole hookup means.

But he's just so… Neo.

I want to please him. I want to make him happy. And it doesn't have to be because we're mates.

My silence makes him lift his head from the pillow. "We can be safe. There's, uh, condoms in my pocket."

Of course there are, because he's a boy scout and he's always trying to take care of me. He's Mr. Prepared. I take care of me too, so I'm equipped with an IUD. I'm safe because I'm careful and I'm tested regularly, the last time in Singapore a few days ago. And he's safe because he's a virgin.

It actually shocks me to realize I'm toying with the concept of fucking him bare. Because honestly, I never do that. And if I'm wanting to discourage him from thinking we're fated mates, this is hardly the way to accomplish that either.

Still, I'm tempted. It's his first time. It's supposed to be special.

"God, I want that *so* much," he whispers.

With my lips still wrapped around him, I lift my eyes to his. His purple hair's all tumbled on my pillow and his face is flushed and his green eyes are fixed on me like I'm the only thing that matters in his whole universe. There's so much longing burning in his eyes and aching in his voice that my own eyes sting with tears.

What can I say? He's really hard to resist when he's begging.

"Okay, baby." I sit up and peel out of my yoga pants and panties.

He rises on his elbows to watch. He's a total sex god sprawled in my bed, those Captain America shoulders and chest and biceps all bulging with muscle, a well-defined six pack rippling down his abs, thick quads bracketing a good 8.5 inches of cock, all flushed purple and slick with my spit and his precum.

Just the sight of all that cock makes me wet.

I wonder if I should edge him a little more first. But I'm so hot to feel him inside me that I don't want to wait, and he doesn't seem to need more foreplay.

I swing my thigh over his to crouch over him on hands and needs, dragging my tits over his chest and rubbing my pussy against his well-lubed cock. The friction is sublime, and it makes us both moan. His hands close around my hips and knead my ass and rock me into him harder.

My face is hovering right over his, my pigtails streaming down on either side to enclose us in our own little world, and he's locked on my eyes like he'll never look away. The inner walls of my pussy are clenching, starving to feel him inside me.

Every time my clit brushes his cock, the tide of my need surges higher.

"Zara," he breathes, his shaft sliding down the soaking crevasse between my pussy lips. "Oh Zara… oh God… oh God…"

I reach between us and fit his cock to the mouth of my pussy. "Hold on tight for me, baby."

I lower myself a careful inch onto him, trying to take it slow and give him time to adjust to this whole new thing. But he's a really quick study. He thrusts hard and deep and seats himself deep inside me with a jolt that makes us both moan.

God, he's so thick. The way he's stretching me, filling every little centimeter of space inside me, I'm really close to getting off before he's even started thrusting.

"Sorry!" he gasps, anxious eyes searching my face. "Am I… did I…?"

"You're perfect," I assure him, awed and breathless. "You're so perfect."

And he is. He really is.

I'm clamped around him like the feeder valve sealing an oxygen tank in a deep dive. I feel like I'm drifting in an ocean current, buoyant in thirty feet of water, with a dazzle of sunlight on green water sparkling all around me. I sit up and grip his ribs for balance and start to undulate on top of him. He spans my hips with his hands to steady me and thrusts carefully into me, every stroke slow and deep.

His face is amazing to watch, eyes wide with wonder and blazing with passion, lips parted with concentration, face flushed with pleasure.

I'm giving him that pleasure, and in that moment he's mine.

He's all mine.

A sudden flood of vanilla musk fills my head and makes me feel all floaty.

I have Mogadon blood and Mogadon pheromones along with the rest of my genetics, but it's so diluted I hardly ever scent, and never when I'm fucking. Because sexually, Mogadon scent to claim their mates, and that's never been me.

But that's what I'm doing now. I'm scenting him to claim him.

Even though he's not my mate.

His eyes darken and his jaw locks.

"I am though, Zara," he growls, low and intense. "So claim me."

This entire concept is unacceptable, but somehow my body doesn't seem to be getting the message. My thighs lock around him and my pace kicks up, riding him hard and fast. He meets me thrust for thrust, grunting through clenched teeth, his eyes locked on mine, refusing to let me look away. The adrenaline rush of my own pheromones is making me dizzy, and it's torquing him even tighter.

With a wild cry, I lean forward to pin his shoulders, my tits swinging between us as I work us both into a frenzy. His arms lock around me and the clean-smelling tang of his sage-and-juniper soap rises from his skin to mix with my scent. His cock pistons into me like he's punishing me.

And I know it's because of what he's bound and determined to make me admit.

He makes me so furious with his complete fucking refusal to hear what I keep telling him.

But he's still going to make me come harder than I've ever come in my life.

"That's right," he grits through bared teeth, his hips snapping against mine in a relentless rhythm. "You're my queen. I'm your mate. Claim me. Make me yours."

Cries are ripping out of me with every thrust, cries of rage and denial and pleasure. Static electricity sparks in the bedding from the magical charge I'm giving off. I'm drenching him with my mating scent, rubbing my essence deeper into his skin with every thrust, and he's crying out too, raw agonized shouts that only urge me higher. I can feel his savage need for this brutal claiming, his intense satisfaction that I'm doing it, I can feel every single thing he feels blazing through this bond between us.

It's the fucking mating bond. I know it and I'm furious. I want it but I don't.

"You're my queen," he groans, slamming into me. "I'm your mate. Make me yours."

I kiss him to shut him up, a sloppy desperate kiss that's halfway to a bite. Our mouths fuse together with an electric shock—me snarling, him moaning—and the avalanche force of our shared climax roars through me and through him like our whole world is ending.

We're making insane amounts of noise and I'm vaguely aware the whole house can hear us, it actually feels like maybe the whole house is shaking, the entire bed is crackling with magical energy, and I'm betraying every single thing I've ever believed by claiming him as my mate. But this is beyond my control, beyond anyone's control.

I lost control the minute I mounted him, and maybe even the minute I met him.

His cock spasms inside me and his essence spurts into me, over and over, so much more intimate and intense because I'm fucking him bare. It feels like he never stops coming, and I'm sobbing out loud, and the whole room is shades of lilac thanks to the witchy electric glow that's pouring from my eyes.

Then he's holding me, he's kissing me, and his voice is deep inside me.

I'm yours, my queen. I'm yours. I'm so totally yours.

Which means I'm so totally fucked.

Chapter Eighteen
Lucius

I scramble through the open window of my ground-floor bedroom and land on all four paws on the bearskin pelt in front of my dying fire.

I'm panting from loping and burrowing and bounding all through the rugged slopes and forests beyond the village and howling under the waxing moon. The cold is trapped in my thick fur and the pure sweet music of my howl still burns in my lungs.

But, Christ, I needed the run. I needed my wolf.

I fling myself down on my belly and let my tongue loll while I pant. Well past midnight, it's dark and cold as Hades in my bedroom, with the window propped open and the fire burning low. Momentarily I'll be obliged to shift to attend my various human needs.

Still, I'm in no particular hurry. When I shift, all my intractable human concerns—all the troubles and pressures and dilemmas that drove me relentlessly into the night like the lash of a whip—will come clamoring to the fore.

I lower my muzzle to my paws and heave a wolfish sigh.

When I slipped out, the entire *domus* was still humming under the sexual amperage of the Gemini queen's climax. The force of her release blew out half the lights and fuses in the house, which is one more problem I'll need to address. In fact, we're all quite fortunate she didn't summon lightning.

Next time, we could very well be less fortunate.

Her untutored witchcraft is crying out for training. I'd hoped to delay until Zarina accepts her fate, and I don't mistake her apparent compliance for anything close to acceptance. Indeed, I fully expect her to test the strength of this island's protective wards with some sort of daredevil caper.

But now that she's claiming her mates and channeling her power much more quickly than I dared to hope, the gift of time to embrace her fate is a luxury we can no longer afford.

Zarina's climax may have short-circuited the house, but it was Neo's earth magic that made the island shake. He's the Capricorn scion, well-trained and well-focused, and his control is typically excellent. Clearly the potency of this long-sought consummation with his fated mate overcame my typically responsible and civic-minded student.

Now, thankfully, the house is steeped in late night silence. With my lupine senses, I can smell my queen sleeping, wrapped in dreams of lightning and her lover's arms. Dez is asleep in Racetrack's room and undoubtedly in her bed, which according to the Academy Codex is a conduct violation until they both turn twenty, although I'll allow it tonight after the day's unsettling disturbances.

But the light in Vasili's bedroom is still burning.

And I'm deeply worried about Ronin.

A disciplinary bite is a two-way tie, and this one between me and my troublesome student feels particularly potent. All night I've been suffering, like a phantom pain in my flesh, the dull throb of his untended bite and the hectic burn of his fever. He clearly needs me, but he simply won't tolerate me. Uncharacteristically, I find myself at an utter loss about how to proceed with him.

Dear God, I should never have bitten him.

If I'm being entirely honest about my motives—given his flirtation with me, my wolf's fascination with him, and the pull of this forbidden attraction for a student ten years my junior—my own conduct has scarcely been beyond reproach.

Softly I whine, swimming in guilt.

The urgent hammer of knuckles on my door drags me from my remorse and drives me to my feet. I push onto my back legs and rise, bones lengthening, tail dwindling, fur vanishing as I will my human form to take shape.

"Lucius?" Vasili's low voice is ragged with strain. He rattles the knob, but it doesn't budge. With students like mine in the house, not least the amorous Ronin, I sleep with that door securely bolted. "Damn it, will you wake the hell up?"

I thrust my legs into my trousers and hasten to the door before he wakes the whole household.

My most difficult student is pacing on the dark landing, his tall frame encased in the black silk turtleneck, high boots and riding breeches he wore to dinner, which passes as casual for Vasili. But his gilded hair is disheveled and he hasn't shaved, which for him passes as haggard.

He's taller than I am, which he milks for every molecule of advantage. His disapproving gaze skates over my naked chest and tangled hair as though he expects me to spring fashionably forth in full professorial attire from my bed at one a.m.

I carefully tamp down a spike of annoyance.

Our relationship is damnably complex, two alphas warily circling, both thoroughly accustomed to dominance. There's shifter blood in Vasili, a Protean ancestor somewhere in his Mogadon DNA. That distant legacy supplies just enough genetic fodder to give him those fangs he despises but uses so effectively to sow terror in the student body, although not enough to permit him to actually shift.

And alpha shifters of any moiety, few though we are these days, take care to give one another an exceedingly wide berth.

I'm the best headmaster for a warlock of his formidable talent, since he terrifies Agrippina and I don't trust Zerxes. Still, tolerating such prolonged proximity to a rival alpha is discomfiting at best and dangerous at worst. I allow him as much leeway as I can without ceding my place entirely as dominant alpha in this *domus*.

One of these days, Vasili's own alpha instincts will drive him to challenge me. It's bred into his DNA to challenge me. Indeed, given Ronin's current condition, Vasili may very well challenge me tonight.

I make my tone and my face carefully neutral. "What is it, Mr. Romanov?"

"It's Ronin and your fucking bite," he hisses, every syllable dripping with venom. "I can hear him through the wall. He's delirious in his bed. You need to come. Now."

Worry for my student clenches my chest and churns my gut.

Never mind that the reason Vasili can hear Ronin in his bed is probably because they're sharing it, which is likewise a conduct violation since Ronin's barely nineteen. Of course, when they're not creeping in and out of each other's beds, the pair of them put on a thoroughly convincing display of hating each other's guts.

This volatile dynamic between them is another matter to which I've deliberately turned a blind eye in order to give my subordinate alpha his space.

"Damnation," I mutter, tying my hair in a hasty tail and pulling a shirt around my shoulders. I don't bother buttoning it as I push into the chilly confines of the hall.

"You'll need a candle," Vasili says shortly. "Thanks to our fucking queen claiming her fucking mate, lights are out in the bedrooms, and the flashlights are all shorted."

"Thank you, Mr. Romanov." Striving to project an air of calm I'm far from feeling, I find the candles I keep for emergencies and light one for each of us. I'm thankful Vasili waits in the hall, giving me my space as well. We've never actually spoken about the fraught dynamic between us, but he's exceedingly perceptive, with a keen nose for danger.

He knows that, to each other, we're deadly.

Clutching our candles like two Gothic monsters in a vintage horror film, shadows leaping high on the walls beside us, we climb the stairs and stalk the darkened corridor to Ronin's room. Vasili swings the door wide and pushes in first.

But I'm right on his heels.

By the pale glow of the waxing moon pouring through the glass, I don't need to see Ronin to know his condition has taken a profound pivot for the worst. At this proximity, my body ignites with the fever that's burning in his blood, a physical fever fueled purely by relentless and overwhelming sexual need.

Merciful God, I'd thought myself prepared for this, but I was so utterly wrong.

Ronin *needs*. He's writhing in that bed, gripped in the ravenous maw of a mating rut.

Sweet saints above. I did this to him. I did this to *me*.

I bite back a moan and clutch the door and silently pray for fortitude. The knob sparks with static electricity at my touch. Hours have passed since our queen's climax, but this entire *domus* is still bleeding amperage and pulsing with sex.

The fire is dead and the room is icy. Still, in the flickering light of our candles, Ronin is twisting and muttering in a hopeless tangle of sweat-soaked sheets. He's shirtless, senseless, long hair an inky tangle pouring down his back, dragon tattoo spewing ebony flames over gleaming skin.

The gauze taped to his shoulder is black with seeping blood.

Vasili bends over his lover, the alpha's entire body rigid with distress. If I'd harbored any question about the state of affairs between these two, his desperation now would have erased all doubt.

"He's burning up," Vasili mutters, pressing a hand to Ronin's brow. "You did this to him, you wolf bastard. You and your vile bite."

His naked aggression makes my hackles rise. A subterranean rumble rolls from my chest. Careful to keep my distance from the agitated alpha, I approach the bed warily.

An empty glass stands next to a bottle of aspirin on the nightstand. I prop my candle in the glass. My body is a riot of sensation—Ronin's heat, Ronin's pain, Ronin's need. My brain is swirling in a fog.

My wolf prowls and paces in my skin. *Ours, he's ours, claim our mate.*

"Yes," I murmur, in a daze.

Vasili's still hovering anxiously over the bed, and I retain barely enough detachment to recall I can't simply nudge him aside without triggering him. My wolf doesn't care, he'll gladly fight another alpha. He'd take savage pleasure in tearing out a rival's throat. But I'm in control here.

I'm in control.

"You did well to fetch me, Mr. Romanov," I say softly. "I'll take care of him now. I know what to do. Rest assured you may safely leave him with me."

I withstand the probe of Vasili's stare, silver as mercury in the candlelight. He too senses my wolf rising.

"Go, Vasili." My voice roughens. "For the love of Christ, will you *go*."

He leans forward, eyes firing, and in that moment we're both pure alpha and bristling with fury. He bares his teeth, fangs gleaming with menace. It's a shifter impulse, an intimidation display, one I've never seen him deploy. I barely rein in my impulse to snarl back. The dark musk of Mogadon pheromones pours from his skin, aggression spiked with lust. Every pore of his body oozes pure hatred.

But I'm the dominant alpha under this roof, and I hold my ground. At last, unwillingly, his hostile gaze drops.

Yet his voice slices into me, edged and vicious as a scalpel. "Hurt him again, you mangy beast, and I'll fucking grind your bones."

I clench my jaw around a whiplash retort. I fear if I open my mouth, I'll growl like the beast he calls me.

Vasili pinches his candle into darkness and slips away until the shadows swallow him.

Thank God he's retreating, and it's best not to watch him go. My wolf wants to disembowel him, this enemy alpha who covets our mate.

But our rival is leaving, and we have to let him.

Now, at last, Ronin lies before me unguarded.

He's subsided into restless stillness, no doubt sensing my presence. I stroke a hand over his damp brow, slicking back the silken tangle of his hair, every atom of my essence focused on the feel and sight and smell of him.

Under the scent of blood and ambergris, he smells like Vasili, drenched in the caramel and sandalwood of Mogadon mating scent, a claiming that drives my wolf wild with jealousy and rage. But that dark fragrance is threaded with a haunting whiff of roses and vanilla, the unmistakable scent of my queen.

That hint of her essence steadies me. She's marked him too, this lover of hers, even if she still doesn't know it.

For our queen's sake, my wolf subsides.

My troublesome rival was right about one thing. Ronin is unconscious and delirious. But even in delirium, his hot face turns toward my touch and rubs into my palm. My wolf whines to soothe him as I peel away the blood-soaked bandage. The sight of that reddened flesh, puncture wounds still seeping, makes my wolf whine louder.

I fall to my knees beside the bed and whisper, "Ronin."

"Lucius," he breathes in his sleep.

I wrap one arm around his hot naked torso to cradle him and seal my lips to the horrible bite on his shoulder. My mouth is swimming with healing saliva, fangs descending in my desperate need, but I'm careful not to hurt him worse. I press my lips to his feverish skin and lave the weeping punctures with the enzymes and clotting agent in my saliva. With meticulous care, I tend him as I've been aching to do all day. I lick his bite absolutely clean.

Under the metallic tang of blood, he tastes like salt and sex. Beneath my trousers, my manhood is rising. Which is far from typical for a disciplinary bite. A deepening suspicion makes me suck in my breath.

Damnation.

I've suspected, but I'm beginning to be hideously certain.

I've made the most appalling error.

I've utterly betrayed my student's trust.

He moans under my touch, but it's a moan of relief. The tension of his body under my arm is melting, my care easing his pain. Aching with need and guilt, I crawl into the bed and wrap myself around him, my face buried in his shoulder, my mouth still nuzzling and licking at his bite. With a deep sigh, he rolls to his side until our bodies press together. The electric shock of his lean muscled frame sears through me and wrenches a groan from my throat.

His need is throbbing in my shaft. His need is my need. Slowly he undulates against me. Under the sheet that's dragged over him, he's rigid and aching.

For me.

And I'm keenly aware that he's naked.

He's my student, I remind my wolf desperately, chanting it like a mantra. *My student. My student. My student.*

If I do this, if I break my own inviolate rule, if I prey upon my own student, if anyone finds out, I deserve to be cast out from the Academy in disgrace. And there's no one left in the witching world to take my place. Only a handful of frightened shifters survive, each of them even less suitable for this crucial duty than I.

My people need me.

My students need me.

Ours ours ours, my wolf growls in my head. *Our mate.*

"Ronin, I'm so sorry," I mumble against his shoulder, voice thick and slurred through my fully descended fangs. "I've made a reprehensible error in judgment."

"Lucius?" His voice too is thick, but his sinewy frame twines around me, one hand fisting in my hair. "I *need* you."

"I know, my dear one. None of this is your fault." Tenderly I nuzzle into his shoulder, his neck, the underside of his jaw. Even here, he reeks of ambergris and Vasili and wolf. This is wrong, so wrong, and I never meant for this to happen, but I wanted it and my wolf wanted it and now it's far too late to resist.

Somehow I muster the words to make my act of confession. I owe him that. Let him at least comprehend what's happening.

"Ronin. This isn't a disciplinary bite. It's a mating bite. You're burning with mating fever."

"What? You… gave me… a mating bite?" He's struggling to wake up, to clear his head. Since I've cleansed the wound and stopped the bleeding, the punctures are knitting and his wound is starting to heal. I'll tend him well in the coming days, so very well, to ensure his complete recovery.

But to break this fever, there's something more his body needs from me.

I raise my head to find his feral face, haggard but curious, his amber eyes lidded and molten with need.

"I swear to you, Ronin, on the survival of my race, I never meant for this to happen. But dear God, it's happened, and it's all my fault. In order to break this fever, you must… mate."

I search his face to see if he understands me. Christ, I barely understand myself, since this is the first mating bite I've ever inflicted. Mating fever is a shifter affliction. It only affects my race… and our mates.

He's watching me, still only half lucid. Truly, I can't be certain how much of this debacle he's grasping.

I pull in a fortifying breath and forge on. It's my duty now to help him through this. "Ideally, to break the fever fully, you should… should mate… with me. Quite frequently in the coming days. But any mate who satisfies you can ease the worst of it." Now the words rush out of me, fueled by guilt. "I can… I can get Zarina."

The last thing our erratic and untrained queen needs is to take her second mate within hours of taking her first. And Ronin, in his rut, will be savage. She'll summon the lightning for certain, and then I'll have failed her too. But Ronin—he needs—

"Lucius." A sleepy grin curls the corners of his succulent mouth. His words fall slow but certain. "There is definitely a thing between me and Zara. But I don't think you're getting her away from Neo tonight."

"Vasili then," I offer desperately.

Not him! my jealous wolf snarls.

Sly humor flickers in Ronin's unholy eyes. "You know I hate Vasili Romanov. Besides, he's not the one who bit me, Lucius."

Ours! my wolf growls. *Our mate.*

My entire body tingles and my chest swells with an overwhelming sense of certainty. The bitter fruit of this night will mean the end of my career, the death of my honor, the failure of my duty. But in this singular moment, the price I may well be compelled to pay for violating my student's trust feels unavoidable, if only I can claim the mate every chromosome in my shifter DNA is howling for me to possess.

I squeeze my eyes closed. "Forgive me—"

His mouth crashes into mine and obliterates every particle of apology.

I welcome his kiss, my mate, the one I've yearned for, my fangs retracting, making myself vulnerable, letting him inside. Beneath my kiss he's burning up, all ravenous mouth and plunging tongue and the peaty tang of scotch. He must have been consuming the damnable liquor to help him cope with the pain.

Frantic with remorse, I clasp him in my arms and drag him in close, my hands fisting in his hair, my shaft aching, my hips pistoning against him with driving need.

He moans into my mouth and grapples with my trousers, dragging them clumsily down my hips. There's no room now for the languorous foreplay I long to lavish upon him, not in the grip of a mating fever. What he needs now and in the days to come is sexual intercourse, lots of it, as much of it as I can possibly provide given the press of my other duties. Vasili, too, I'll somehow bring myself to encourage in his amorous attentions, because my mate's needs supersede my own. Perhaps even Zarina, once she senses the intensity of Ronin's need, will rise to meet the moment and become the queen we all need her to be—

Ronin's hand wraps around my naked cock.

The contact wrenches a hoarse cry from my throat. My hips jolt into his grip, his wicked hand knowing exactly how to work me. I claw the sheet down to find the supple flex of gluteal muscle and clench his rump to drag him closer.

My wolf howls to mark him, but I keep my claws and teeth fiercely contained. My desperate grip finds Ronin's length, rigid and swollen with need, precum already oozing from his slit and slicking the cold heavy ring that pierces his cock.

"Lucius," he gasps into my mouth, our tongues tangling together.

"Ronin," I breathe, the name of my mate. "Ronin. Ronin."

I can't say his name enough. He's so hard for me. He's so wet for me. He's so absolutely dripping for me. Indeed, he's already so close to the edge that perhaps just my hand alone will be enough to—

"No." He drags his mouth free of mine with a growl. "I need to feel you inside me. Fuck me."

His words wrap around my sac and squeeze. My own anticipation is drenching me, slicking the wet audible friction of his fist around my shaft.

Merciful Mary, I'm so ready for him it's a marvel I don't spill in his hand.

I push him hard onto his back and crawl over him, shoving his thighs apart roughly, my mouth claiming his in a blazing kiss. He's working my length in one hand and gripping my neck with the other and writhing beneath me like he'll combust if I don't fuck him.

Admittedly, it's been quite a long time for me. Being headmaster in residence of this *domus* for the past four years has hardly lent itself to a lively sex life.

I grasp after my scattered thoughts. "If we're truly doing this—"

"Not open for debate," he pants, shoving my open shirt off my shoulders. "We are."

He's so eager for me he'd let me fuck him bare, but I can't bear to hurt him. I can never hurt him. "In that case, my dear one, there are things we require. Lubricant. Protection."

"Nightstand," he mutters, between nips at my lower lip with his sharp teeth. "But, Lucius, I'm clean. And you've been celibate."

Of course, he's Valyrian. He's reading my mind. I know how to shield my thoughts, but I'm scarcely able to manage the feat with both of us gripped in a mating frenzy.

You'll never keep me out again, he whispers in my head. *And you won't need to. We're together now.*

Hearing his faith, feeling his trust, my heart clenches in a knot.

In actual truth, I am what his body needs most.

A shifter's semen is infused with bioregulators that are engineered by nature to break a mating fever and bring one's mate relief. The lover he truly needs to be taking into his body tonight is me.

I shove to my feet at the foot of the bed, then grip his legs and drag him toward me with a snarl.

He grins and reaches for the nightstand to fumble the drawer open and toss the lube in my vicinity.

By the light of the lone candle, his skin is bronze and ink, etched with the pale glow of moonlight. His hair is a midnight banner against the tangled sheets. His eyes are pools of liquid fire. I stroke one hand down the hard plane of his abdomen, his skin burning with an inferno of fever, and trail my fingers over the straining column of his shaft, which makes him moan and writhe. I'm intrigued and a bit intimidated by the heavy ring of his piercing—this sort of adornment is new for me with a lover.

But that isn't the foreplay he needs right now.

Clearly he knows what I intend. Indeed, he's more than obliging, lying with his rump on the edge of the bed, legs bent and thighs parted. I'm so aroused myself I scarcely dare look at him, but my eyes follow my exploratory hand over the taut swell of his sac to trace the hot skin of his perineum. Framed by the luscious bulge of gluteal muscle, his hole is a puckered rose that lures me in close.

I circle his rim with a careful finger that makes him groan and shift, impatient in his need. I know he's no virgin, but I can't help wondering if he and Vasili…

"Bollocks, you're obsessed with the bloke," Ronin gasps, shoving into my finger to hurry me along. "Same way he is with you. Seriously, the two of you should be fucking."

A river of icy shock pours through me.

But it would take far more than words to halt what I'm doing.

"I wouldn't hold my breath waiting for that encounter, dear one," I say mildly, leaning in to nuzzle his thigh. Next time, perhaps I'll prepare him with my tongue.

"You want to know the truth?" He pants and writhes like a cat in heat. "I want both of you. Either of you. Both of you together. All of us with Zara—gods, that more than anything."

My mind reels under the concussive impact of these bombshell revelations. I'm honestly not certain whether I'm more disturbed by the thought of bedding my rival alpha or bedding my youthful queen. But the electric concept of bedding all three of them together—my students, God help me, every one of them forbidden—makes my wolf sit straight up and howl.

"Fuck, Lucius," Ronin groans. "I'm literally losing my mind here. Are you bloody going to fuck me or not?"

At this point, I'm so emotionally lost in this man that the likelihood I won't claim him has dwindled to zero.

My voice rumbles deep in my chest. "Rest assured I am definitely going to fuck you, my dear one."

Standing naked at the foot of his bed, with my mate spread naked and desperate before me, I squeeze out a copious quantity of lubricant and tease one slick finger around his rim. I'd definitely like to do this with my tongue, but that's a pleasure I'll reserve for later, once my mate is well sated. When I ease my finger a careful inch inside him, he's tight and hot and fluttering. I know he's going to feel like absolute heaven clamped around my shaft.

Already he's panting for *more* and *harder* and *for fuck's sake, Lucius* and in no time at all I'm two fingers deep inside him. He's gasping with pleasure and riding my hand. The instant I peg his prostate, he's going to erupt like Mt. Vesuvius, and perhaps this first time that would truly be for the best—

"Uh-uh, no way, mate," Ronin pants, rising up on his elbows to scowl at me. "We're doing this together. Or we're not bloody doing it."

A reluctant chuckle slips past my guard. "Very well, you little tyrant. I find I'm in no mood to deny you anything."

I slather a generous quantity of lubricant down my own length while my mate watches my every motion with heated eyes, hand wrapping around his own pierced length for a few leisurely strokes. I'm so incredibly hard and so hungry for him, my shaft leaking with eagerness, balls swollen and full with need. Just a few pumps of my hand would finish me off.

But my seed is for him tonight, all for him, only to bring him pleasure.

I fit my aching length to his well-prepared passage and push in with agonizing care.

He moans my name and clamps tight around me and I was right, this is absolute heaven. I'm on the thick side and I'm trying not to hurt him, but when I breach the ring of muscle that guards his passage, we both cry out in pleasure.

"Deeper, Lucius, I mean it. Give it to me, damn you," he grits through clenched teeth.

I push his thighs toward him to deepen the angle and sheathe myself fully in my mate's hot vise.

Sweet Blood of Christ, I've been craving this with him for months now—a secret truth I can no longer deny—but this is a pinnacle of delirium I never dared to imagine. I pin him to hold him still and pound into him with utter abandon, my mind empty of everything that isn't his pleasure and mine. I'm growling curses and praise and promises in my mother tongue, while he's crying out his own mindless ecstasy, so close to getting what he needs from me.

The knowledge that it's me and not my rival Vasili who's giving this to him affords me a vicious sense of triumph.

"Next time—want both of you," he grunts. "Both of you—inside me—together."

This blasphemous visual of sharing a double penetration with my troublesome rival ignites me with an erotic charge. The thrill of the utterly forbidden. My head snaps up with a shout, my balls clenching hard as my climax barrels toward me. My frenzied gaze lands on the opposite wall near the door, where a tall shadow stands in a slim shaft of moonlight.

It's Vasili.

Watching.

Dear God in Heaven, he's watching us fuck.

While I break every rule in my personal codex by fornicating with a student ten years my junior—and fornicating without a damned condom at that—my rival has been watching and listening this entire time.

Shock forks through me like a bolt of lightning.

Ronin, it's quite clear, has been fully aware Vasili never left. My mischievous mate is taking his pleasure from both his lovers.

The one who's making love to him.

And the one who's making him come just by watching.

In furious protest, my eyes lock on Vasili's platinum gaze, his irises burning with nuclear heat. Every line in his chiseled face is etched with rage. But the turgid bulge shoved up against his breeches is swollen with lust.

Truly, I can do nothing about Vasili now. My mate is going wild beneath me, clawing at the sheets while I piston into him in a savage frenzy. With a hoarse shout, my climax boils through me and pours into Ronin.

As the first jet fills him, his own orgasm explodes, spurting from his shaft to drench my chest and his in hot milky spurts. Triggered by the biochemical stimulus of my own seed, this is the copious release of the mating fever breaking. Relentlessly I fuck him through it, prolonging his climax, pumping him full of my essence, coming so hard myself the world around me goes black.

Until all I see is Vasili Romanov.

My enemy alpha.

My sexual rival.

Both of us locked together, in lust and hatred, over the sated body of the mate we'll both kill to possess.

Chapter Nineteen
Zara

Neo sleeps like I've killed him with sex.

His big warm body wraps tight around me in the complete disaster we've made of my medieval canopy bed, pillows hurled everywhere, blankets in a twist, fire burned down to embers hours ago. Silvery daylight leaks through the glass doors below my bed. According to the blinking digits on my dive watch and the academic schedule Lucius left with my orientation packet, it's definitely time to rise and shine.

It's probably time for Neo to rise and shine too.

But the truth is, I need a little space.

I need a little time to process the insanely intense sex that blasted our mating bond wide open and everything else that went down between us last night.

I need a little perspective to remember what kind of life I chose years ago and am now supposed to be living.

And I need all that without the steam of sex with this mind-blowing male I never meant to claim clouding all my reason.

Cheese on toast. It's really going to suck for both of us when I leave.

So I extricate myself from under Neo's heavy body, one careful limb at a time, and pray I won't wake him. Fortunately, he doesn't exactly seem to be a morning guy. When he stirs and mumbles, I slide my pillow—warm and reeking with my mating scent—into the cradle of his arms. Sure enough, his powerful body wraps around it. He snuggles into my pillow with a happy murmur and sinks back down to dreamland.

Which, admittedly, is super adorable.

Gently I stroke his tumbled curls away from his sleeping face. He's really a good-looking guy with that rugged jaw and those strong cheekbones and those full lips I could lose myself kissing.

Not to mention he's absolutely devoted to pleasing me. He's such a dreamboat of a man. I pretty much have to force myself out of bed into the frigid cold.

Honestly, I don't think much of the crappy furnace in this joint. These rooms seem to rely mostly on the fireplaces for warmth.

Teeth chattering, I bundle into my fur-lined Academy robe and slippers and tiptoe around piling my toiletries and the uniform I'll need for the day into my new canvas tote with its Academy logo. According to my orientation packet, the uniform for Thursday is blue, so my sapphire blazer and blue-and-white plaid skirt go in the bag, along with some cream-knit thigh-highs and the ubiquitous mary janes.

At least they're better than the damn saddle shoes.

I steal twenty-three seconds, according to my dive watch, to stir the embers with my poker and add a log to the hearth for Neo's benefit before I sneak out.

Admittedly, I feel guilty for ghosting him.

Which is exactly why I don't do relationships.

At this ungodly hour, the house is still and shadowy, and it definitely doesn't make me happy that the hallway light doesn't work when I hit the switch. Neither does the one on the stairs. This means I'm blowing fuses again.

Which means my careful control over my witchcraft is slipping.

God help this house if I summon lightning.

Frowning, I veer to avoid the distant clatter of crockery and Racetrack grumbling over something in the kitchen. The acrid scent of coffee almost derails me, but I recall from the house rules in my packet that the boys get dibs on the *thermae* starting in exactly—I check my watch—nineteen minutes.

I aim to be well clear of the place before that horrible Vasili shows up.

The basement *thermae* is a Roman bath, and it looks like an actual restored ruin. The main room's dominated by a big built-in soaking pool, lit from beneath by deep green lights. The surface steams and bubbles with water that's cloudy with minerals and smells like rotten eggs from the sulfur. A row of crumbling pillars marches down both sides under a skylight rimed with frost. As I pad through the steamy heat, my footsteps echo on the mosaic floors with their scrolling patterns.

Seems like I've got the place all to myself.

Thank fuck.

Behind a glass wall I find the perfect six-person shower, shiny rows of rain shower heads poking down from sea-green tiles. There's even a thick pile of towels in the changing room, and an actual Finnish sauna.

I may not be here by choice, but I gotta admit the whole setup is really nice, and the warmth is so much more temperate than the rest of the house. It's relaxing just standing here. Still, cognizant of the boys' imminent arrival, I strip right down in the changing room and crank up two of the rain shower heads to give myself plenty of steam. Within seconds, the whole glass wall has totally steamed over.

Now I can no longer see into—or be seen from—the big room with the soaking pool.

This is the first real shower I've had since Singapore, and it honestly feels like heaven. My bumps and bruises from that night are all but healed, thanks to that little shot of shifter DNA in the Gemini cocktail. I try to hurry through my lather-and-rinse routine with my color-treated shampoo and the deep conditioner that keeps my turquoise waves quasi-tamed. These are exactly the products I use at home, just another little reminder of how close someone at this Academy's been watching me. How the hell could I have missed that kind of scrutiny?

I can hardly believe I'm actually starting to wonder if maybe Cleo or Xiao sold me out. And if one of them might have been feeding the Academy intel on me long before that night in Singapore.

I mean, it's not like the three of us are fated mates or anything. We're pals, fuck buddies, partners in crime. Friends. Still, I really don't like to consider the possibility that one of my own *ménage* might have betrayed me.

It just hurts way too much to process.

So I won't. And I won't ask the question either. Not right now. Until and unless I learn otherwise, I'm putting that whole idea of being betrayed by Cleo or Xiao on the back burner in my brain. That's easier to do than you might think, because I've got more than enough to worry about right here.

Like the fact that I really, really shouldn't have slept with Neo.

Because this time, I'm the one who's violating a trust. I already hate myself for doing it.

Heaving a sigh, I pop open the bottle of body wash. The silky pink goop is exactly the high-end roses-and-vanilla label I love, and this hot water is melting all the tension from my strung-out body, so it's really hard to hurry.

I'm in the middle of rinsing the conditioner out of my hair when, abruptly, the nice steamy water goes cold.

In less than ten seconds, I'm standing in an arctic cascade of ice.

With a yelp, I scramble out from under the shocking spray and fiddle with the knobs, but no joy. This water is absolutely fucking frigid. I can barely stand to stick my head back under long enough to rinse out the soap.

The hot water tank in this joint must be miniscule, and I'm resentful as hell over it. Blue-lipped and shivering, I knot a thick sage towel around my torso and rush into the changing room for my clothes.

"Well, princess, it's about fucking time." Vasili Romanov's velvety drawl, edged in his Russian accent, sends fear and fury spurting through my veins. "I haven't all day to waste loitering in the *thermae* while you undertake literally the world's longest shower. Hence my excursion to the hot water tank."

My nemesis is lounging gracefully against the pale bamboo of the lockers, one hand wrapped in casual possession around a steaming mug of fragrant coffee that makes me hate him even more (if that's possible). He's dazzling as always in the tailored blue blazer and trousers of his uniform, silver tie loose in some complicated twist, colorful gemstones glittering on his fingers, frosted hair artfully tousled. His cobalt-soled combat boots add the final flourish of rock star chic.

Under his smoky liner, his eyes look a bit haggard, like maybe he hasn't slept. Well, cry me a river. I doubt he's losing sleep over the way he's bullying me.

The latest example being his complete and total sabotage of my well-earned shower.

Prick.

"Oh, I'm sorry, was I taking too long?" I ask sweetly, making an exaggerated show of consulting my dive watch. "Because this shower's still mine for the next nine minutes. It's in the house rules."

Vasili sips his coffee and arches one perfectly groomed eyebrow. "Haven't you learned *anything* from our delightful encounters? This *thermae*, like everyone and everything else at this Academy, belongs to *me*. That's in the house rules as well."

I roll my eyes and tighten my towel, because this is not the time for my hasty knot to slip. Standing here all but naked, dripping and shivering in the face of his sartorial elegance, I'm at a desperate disadvantage. Which of course is his whole intent. My only play now is to pretend I don't give a shit.

And, really, I don't.

I'm your fucking queen, Goblin King, whether you like it or not.

His pale brows rush together in a scowl, and I wonder if he hears. I don't think the old Russian families like the Romanovs have Valyrian genes, but I do. With my Gemini DNA, I can theoretically project my thoughts, but I've definitely never been trained to do it.

"Didn't exactly see that in the rules myself, but I'm sure Master Aries would be interested to hear your whole ownership theory." I reach for a fresh towel and scrub my dripping hair in the hope of stopping the icy trickle seeping down my spine. "Why are you here, Vasili? I didn't take you for the type to go full stalker in the girls' shower."

"Then apparently you're not a complete imbecile." He sneers around his coffee. "Which is fortunate, since your gender holds no physical appeal for me whatsoever."

"Yeah, I kinda figured that out at the gym." It's probably not a good idea to remind him of what I saw, and it doesn't actually prove my point. For all I know, he could be bi…?

"I'm fucking gay, all right?" he snaps. "And if you don't want me reading your precious royal mind, kindly cease blasting your every annoying thought directly into my head. Have you no modicum of telepathic control?"

Okay, so he's gay.

I'm definitely not disappointed or anything to hear it. It's not like his sexuality matters to me in the slightest.

I give my towel another firm tug and start digging around in my tote bag. I'm more than a little reluctant to produce the white lace bra with its little rosette and the white lace panties with their pretty pink bows. They're nothing I would have chosen myself, but beggars can't be choosers at this Academy.

However, the alternative means standing around in a towel in front of Vasili fucking Romanov, so I bite the bullet.

Of course he doesn't have the grace to look away. His predatory eyes track my every movement (which he's clearly doing just to be obnoxious, because gay) while I shimmy the little panties up my legs and try to get them over my girly parts without giving him too much of a show. For some reason, this entire awkward maneuver is making me way more self-conscious than the situation warrants. After all, plenty of guys have seen me naked.

And it's not like he cares. Because gay, remember?

"Are you here for an actual reason?" I demand, propping a foot on the bench so I can unroll a thigh-high up my leg. "Or should I just chalk this up to more of your general fuckery?"

"There's a reason they call it Purgatory, little queen," he purrs, seemingly delighted with my cranky temper. Even while his gaze follows the unrolling of my thigh-high like a cat stalking a string. "I'll confess, having risen so early to arrange this personal wake-up hazing especially for you, I'd appreciate a touch more gratitude."

I snort and reach for my second stocking to repeat the whole process. "Yeah, Goblin King, you're a real Mr. Magnanimous. And payback's a bitch. Appreciate *that*."

I wait for the inevitable stinging takedown, but he's still just watching, face half-hidden behind his upraised cup, eyes like mirrors glinting at me through the steam.

For absolutely no reason, his sustained attention is bringing heat to my cheeks. In fact, my whole body's getting hot. Which is pissing me right off. Because gay!

Annoyed with this entire setup, I pluck my bra from the tote, spin to give him my back, and drop the towel.

He's taking a sip when I turn, which morphs into a sudden cough.

Good.

Duran Duran back there's apparently not used to girls stripping down naked right in front of him.

Standing casually before him in my miniscule panties and thigh-highs, hair still dripping down my back, I take my time working my arms into my bra and tucking my tits into the cups and reaching behind me to clasp the garment. What with the wet tangle of my hair and my current lack of coffee and my general morning clumsiness, I'm having a hard time managing. In fact, I've got a serious case of butterfingers. I have to struggle with the clasp, which is really too bad, because it's totally going to ruin the effect—

"Need a little assistance with that?" His raspy whisper in my ear makes me yelp and lose my grip, just when I was about to maneuver the little hook into the eyelet and declare victory.

His fingers graze my back, warm and smooth. Goosebumps race down my arms and sheet across my shoulders. Deftly he hooks the catch, far more capable than a guy's hands have any right to be with a woman's bra.

Although maybe, who knows, he likes to dress up?

"I've been known to experiment," he breathes in my ear, which for no good reason makes my heart thunder. "With fashion."

Now the visual of him wearing my lacy unmentionables just about lights my brain on fire. With his slim body and his sexy-pretty face, he could definitely pull it off.

Shit, he'd probably look better in my lingerie than I do.

Somehow, I've gotta stop thinking about this, because clearly he can hear my thoughts, and I don't have the first clue how to stop projecting them.

"What's your plan?" he murmurs, low and husky.

"Um, I'm gonna ask Lucius or maybe Neo to teach me to shield my thoughts. Starting today, because this whole situation is totally intolerable." It's definitely time to put my blouse on, but for some reason I'm not moving.

"For fuck's sake, I'm not referring to your education." If I didn't know that viper better, I'd think he's struggling to contain a laugh. "I'm referring to your plan for getting off this island."

Oh, right. Because he agreed to help me do that.

I want to reach for my blouse, but he's still lurking behind me, and now he's rubbing a towel over my sopping hair with a care that makes me deeply suspicious. Any second, I expect him to bury one of those hidden knives he carries in my back.

I don't want to trust him with my plan, but he can hardly help unless I tell him. Still, definitely, the less I tell him the better.

"Neo says this island's self-sufficient," I say carefully. "Is there, like, a water sports shop?"

He huffs out a disdainful snort, the auditory equivalent of a sneer. "You won't be kayaking or stand-up paddleboarding your way out of this captivity, if that's what you're imagining. The sea around this island is freezing, and the wards make the surf far too rough."

"Just tell me." I've had more than enough of his disturbing proximity. More than enough of him in general, with his telekinesis and his fangs and all that sexy he wields like a weapon. I evade the towel and duck around him to grab my blouse.

He pivots to watch, gaze tracking my fingers as I hastily button my blouse, all without trying to seem like I'm hurrying.

When he finally answers, he sounds weirdly distracted. "There's a dive shop at the marina. It isn't much, but it's Racetrack's summer job to run the wretched place. We attract a few tourists from the witching world during summer holidays."

Then maybe I can get Racetrack to help me, if I can trust her with my plan. She's not exactly a warm-and-fuzzy, and she and I haven't exactly bonded at this point or even talked about what we want this connection between us to mean, but Neo did say she's one of my courtiers.

"So I'll ask Racetrack. I'd like to get in there," I say casually, fastening the last little pearl button at my throat. Now I'm almost decent, standing in front of him in my blouse and panties and thigh-highs. He's still studying me like I'm a puzzle he can't quite decipher, his narrowed gaze sliding slowly over my disarray.

I grab my short plaid skirt and shimmy into it while he watches the whole time.

"Never mind asking Racetrack. She holds no particular affection for royals, she doesn't give a shit about social prestige or being one of your courtiers, and she'll very likely instruct you to pound sand. In any event, what precisely do you fancy you'll accomplish in a place like that?" His eyes land on my dive watch. "Icarus is twelve kilometers from the nearest private island—an island that's uninhabited in winter, incidentally—and we're much farther than that from the mainland."

Twelve clicks. With proper gear and planning, like an inflatable float, I can handle twelve clicks of open ocean.

Even if that neighboring island is uninhabited, they'll have shelter, supplies, maybe even comms. It's the weirdest thing, but I haven't seen a computer or even a smart phone since I woke up on this island, just a few old landlines. And the burner phone I finally found in my clutch from Singapore is dead as a rock. I'm dying to plug back into cyberspace and pay my rent before I lose my safe house in Sharm.

Even if the idea of losing it feels slightly less pressing than it did yesterday.

"What do you care?" I counter. "Our deal's to get me past the wards and that's it. What happens to me after that's none of your business."

"That's entirely true… so long as you abide by your end of our little arrangement." He bristles with sudden menace. "I want a signed statement of abdication before you embark upon your suicide stunt, so the Senate can initiate the relinquishment process. Otherwise you'll go missing at sea, it will take years to have you declared legally dead, and the entire royal tyranny will keep grinding along with Messalina keeping your throne warm."

"Fine." I definitely don't mind signing a statement like that, even though I firmly crush another pang of remorse at the thought of what this betrayal is going to do to Neo. I really shouldn't have slept with him. This is all going to be so much worse for him than if I hadn't. "But I won't sign it till I've got one foot in the water. When can I hit the dive shop?"

By now I've tucked in my blouse and buttoned up my blazer. The naked Zara show's all over.

Even if it's a show that can't hold much interest for a gay guy.

"Meet me alone near the piazza fountain at midnight." Vasili reclaims his coffee and prowls for the door. "And, for your information, the person you want tutoring you to shield your thoughts isn't Lucius, and it certainly isn't Neo. The tutor you want for telepathy is Ronin."

Before I can swallow my surprise that he'd volunteer anything to help me that he isn't being forced to provide, he's vanished.

Meet the psycho anti-monarchist who's hazing me alone at midnight, huh? Not really sure I should. It's even odds he's the queen killer. He's probably planning to whack me over the head with some telekinetic hammer and hurl my senseless body into the sea.

Although, in that case, he wouldn't have the signed letter of abdication he seems to need.

I listen to the measured tread of his boots whispering like serpents against the tiles and wonder how far I can trust the Goblin King.

Then again, maybe it doesn't make much of a difference.

Because it's not like he's given me much of a choice.

Chapter Twenty

Ronin

I swear to gods I've never been so well fucked in my life.

And I've never been so sexed up in my life either.

At least now I've got some blooming clue why I feel this way, after Lucius spilled the beans and copped to the truth last night. He's clearly wretched, tortured by guilt, and wishes like fuck he'd never bitten me.

Whereas I feel the complete opposite.

If I know the guy—and it's pretty good odds I do, after lusting and obsessing over him and borderline stalking him since the day I pitched up at Icarus—he's trying his bloody damnedest to work out some way to release me from our horrible mating.

Which is the exact opposite of what I want.

I'm only keeping mum about the whole gig now for his sake. If it were me making the rules? I'd rent a fucking blimp and broadcast to the whole island that Lucius fucking Aries is my lover.

Just the thought of him in my bed… tender, repentant, growling through his fangs and intensely devoted to my pleasure… nearly makes me hard enough to spill in my trousers. Which is problematic, yeah?

And not just because I'm not wearing a stitch under my uniform.

I'm currently occupying an extremely public couch in the drafty student commons, boots propped against the fire grate, posing for the populace the way we do here.

Vasili's likewise holding court with his army of admirers under the stained glass windows across the way.

Occasionally, we scowl at each other. You know, for appearances' sake.

Technically, it's study hall in the commons for the Schedule A's, while the Schedule B's sweat through their Witching Law midterm, and the Honors track chumps like Neo are off doing fuck knows what.

But any poor schmuck who really wants to hit the books hunkers down in the library. This scene in the commons is all about social signaling and prestige.

Just another of the many realms at this Academy where Vasili reigns supreme.

From his elegant sprawl on the circular couch, his dangerous eyes find mine with a secretive smirk. These days, with him, I don't mind my thoughts much. Lowering that curtain for him is my way of feeling close to the only lover I've ever thought of as my boyfriend (since I don't keep anyone else around long enough) while we both pretend to hate each other's guts.

Now I glower at him for the benefit of our viewing audience—all the wicked little witches and junior warlocks scattered round the firepits and the carrells and the long table under the dome.

Vasili glowers right back. But one eyelid dips in a sly wink.

I'm honestly worried he's going to be pissy that I've finally landed Lucius in my bed. He's always been utterly mental about Lucius. It definitely helped that I let Vasili watch, particularly since my boyfriend fancies he stayed to protect me from his rival alpha and his rival's wolf. Not that any protection was needed. In fact, I know Vasili got off—and I know exactly how hard he got off—after watching the two of us fuck.

Still, I bloody hate that he and Lucius can't seem to sort out that crackling alpha animosity between them.

Such a load of codswallop.

Personally, I think they should fuck it out. Because I meant what I said about wanting to be double dicked by both of—

The heavy doors swing open with a bang that echoes off the vaulted ceiling.

And our new queen saunters in like she owns the whole damn school. For the first time all day, my cock stops thinking about Lucius and becomes extremely focused on her.

The Gemini bitch shrugs out of her coat and tosses it over the rack without bothering to find a hanger. She toes off her snowy boots and… whoa… bends over *really* slowly to work her feet into her mary janes. Considering the way her long legs and curvy hips are rocking that short plaid skirt and those thigh-highs, she's giving every guy in this room an instant boner. Speaking for myself, I'd need roughly ten seconds—if that much—to ease her skirt up and tease her panties down and give her the monumental shagging she's begging for.

Too bad I'd have to stand in a damn queue. Right now, every bloke on this island would pay real money to have her straddling his lap.

From the long table under the skylight where those bitches from Villa Tiberius lurk like a grumble of maggots, someone hisses, "Gemini whore! You won't live to be queen."

A vicious chorus of jeers and catcalls from the witch's little cronies parrots all that ugly.

And Zara laughs.

She fucking *laughs*.

Like she's having the time of her life getting hazed and downright threatened by every witch and warlock in the school. I'm no fan of royalty (there's actually a reason beyond sex that Vasili and I are allies) and I'm definitely no fan of Geminis, but admittedly this one gets the nod for moxie. I always fancy an underdog, so I can appreciate the girl's attitude.

Little Miss Gemini swings her knapsack over her shoulder, because she's clearly learned her lesson on leaving her things lying about after the recent koi incident.

Then she beelines straight for me.

Fuck.

"Morning, love," I murmur, letting my eyes slide slowly over every centimeter of her luscious frame.

Gemini or no, I fucking adore those Hollywood starlet curves of hers. She fills out her royal blue Academy blazer like Scarlett Johansson in an Avenger suit. I could have an actual orgasm just from the way the buttons on her blouse strain over her perfect tits. The girl's wearing the same bubble-gum pink lipstick and cobalt eyeliner she was sporting back at Wang's, and the combination of her good-girl uniform and her bad-girl makeup is lethal. She's swept her blue hair in a pert ponytail that shows off the earrings rimming her ear, and she's actually tucked a sharpened pencil behind that ear—clearly just to fuck with me.

That prep school ponytail makes me fantasize about wrapping her silky curls in my fist and kissing her lush bubble-gum lips till she moans for me.

Yeah, she's Damien's sister, but she's not Damien, is she? He's bloody well gotten his comeuppance. Burned to death by psi fire the way he and that bitch Cybelle fucking deserved. So he's not here anymore to torment. Far as I can tell, Zara and that bastard weren't even close.

For a second, doubt nibbles at the wicked edge of my resolve.

Maybe I've pursued this revenge business far enough.

Then the familiar fist of grief and rage punches me in the gut. That prick killed my fucking sister, same as if he tied the noose she swung from. I'm nowhere near ready to sing *kumbaya* and let all that go.

Just the thought of letting it go makes me murderous.

"Morning, Adam." Since my outstretched legs block her path, the Gemini bitch pulls up and plants a hand on her cocked hip. "Mind if I have a word?"

Damn, but she's got that whole queen bit down pat. Her imperious eyes give me a nudge to lower my legs like a gent and let her take a load off.

Well, she can piss off. I keep my legs where they are, because our would-be queen hasn't earned the privilege.

"Knock yourself out." I shrug.

Her teal brows scrunch together in a way that makes my dick hard. She looked exactly the same… perplexed but fascinated… spreadeagled on the sink in that Singapore penthouse the night she took my cock.

A distinctive heat creeps down my neck and spreads over my chest. The simmering heat of mating fever.

Shit.

Lucius was nowhere to be seen when my alarm sounded off this morning, because of course my skittish new lover ghosted me. But he left a lengthy list of numbered instructions on my nightstand, including the clear order to look him up—or look Vasili up—for a sex fix the instant I start getting hot.

Simply put, I'm under strict orders to break the fever and fast. Even if I have to turn to his rival alpha to do it. Lucius never said a word about exclusivity, so it's not like I need his permission.

But I fancy the fact that he cares enough for my comfort to give it.

Too bad for me Vasili's off preening for his little groupies, while Lucius is proctoring Mistress Agrippina's Schedule B's in their midterm since Aggie's under the weather. Zara hasn't gotten the memo about my mating heat. Actually, no one's gotten it except Lucius and Vasili. But I am definitely seeing an opportunity for the little witch to service me through my current predicament. That's assuming I can nudge her into a repeat of our memorable go-round in Singapore.

Zara clears her throat and glances about, to confirm no one's lurking within earshot. Then she lowers her knapsack to the floor. "I'm looking for a tutor."

"Let me put your mind at ease," I say, low and throaty. "You don't need a bloody tutor. You could teach this entire student body a few tricks."

Because I'm a rotten prick, I'm not guarding my randy thoughts.

At all.

And because she's Valyrian, odds are she can hear my every salacious thought.

Her soft lips pop open with indignation and color floods under her Malibu tan. "For cripes' sake, I'm not looking for a tutor for *that*. I'm looking for someone to teach me to, you know, shield my thoughts. For privacy. To shut down all the back-and-forth with Neo. And not broadcast my every thought to anyone with a scrap of telepathy on the whole damn island."

"Bollocks." For some reason, she's actually managed to surprise me. Not because she doesn't want to broadcast her secrets to the masses (because who would, with this lot?) I went through that whole public broadcast phase myself a few years ago when my power rose, and it's a bloody nuisance.

But I'm surprised as fuck she wants to shut out Neo after that mating we all heard last night.

In fact, I've got to check, because I'm not sure I'm following. "Come again? You want to shut down the bond with your precious fated mate?"

Her eyes narrow dangerously. "Why is that surprising? I believe I've been pretty effing clear that I reject the whole concept."

"Even though you didn't reject the actual bloke? You aware you blew out half the lights in the *domus* last night when you got your rocks off?"

She colors up with a rosy blush that makes her look more than ever like a '50s pinup girl. I want to see her bent over a vintage Chevy wearing a polka-dot dress and cherry lipstick just for me.

"Neo can be very… persuasive." She nibbles that bitable lower lip of hers and looks troubled. "He knows it doesn't mean anything. He knows I don't plan to stay. We talked it through before we started. We agreed it was just, you know, a hookup? And I'm really sorry about the lights."

"A pox on the blooming lights, love." I bark out a short laugh that's high on astonishment but low on tact. "I don't think you know the first damn thing about that bloke you just shagged."

Now the girl's definitely flustered, and she's starting to look downright pissed. "Look, forget I even asked, all right? I'll find someone else—"

"Someone else to do what?" Suddenly the bloke himself is looming at her shoulder, Neo Mercury in the flesh, popped up from God knows where, because I'm way too focused on the Gemini girl to give a shit about anything else going down in the commons.

"I missed you this morning, babe. For real." He wraps his big hands around her tiny waist and nuzzles her neck with his sexy lips.

Which is a fairly effective greeting for both of us.

Zara's angry mouth softens and her eyes go all misty and she leans into his touch with a murmur and (in my opinion) a bit of a guilty look. For my part, I've never seen Neo put the moves on anyone, because he's always been waiting for her.

Turns out watching him stake his claim now is sexy as fuck.

I've never conflated the concepts of Neo and sexy in the same sentence because Vasili hates his guts, and what with me being a telepath and Vasili's boyfriend, it's hard to see past all that hostility when we're in the same room. But this big lug's clearly got the little queen all sexed up.

And what's working for her seems now also to be working for me.

No doubt it's this mating fever fucking with my libido. An inferno of fiery heat's spreading down my torso, and my dick's shoved up against the zipper of my trousers hard enough to hurt.

"Neo," she murmurs, turning to kiss his cheek and detaching from his grip at the same time. She's going to give him a fucking complex with all those mixed signals she's sending. Hell, she's practically giving *me* one. "I'm looking for a telepathy tutor. To help me, uh, manage some of the… spillage?"

I'm interested to note she doesn't specify *whose* spillage she's so keen to manage.

Which makes me all the more certain she and Neo aren't exactly on the same page regarding their mating bond, and clearly she knows it.

"Oh, are you projecting?" Neo asks, one arm slipping comfortably around her waist like he's been doing it his whole life. And, yeah, confident Neo is sexy Neo. Who knew? "Then Ronin can definitely help. He's one of the strongest telepaths at the Academy. Along with Master Zerxes. But you definitely don't want Zerxes."

The Mercurys have zilch in the Valyrian DNA department, so Neo can only share thoughts with his fated mate and no one else (except a Valyrian like me). But he's been round the four races his whole life, so he grasps the essentials of hereditary telepathy.

Looking hopeful for her sake, he adjusts his glasses and blinks his bright green eyes at me.

I actually feel some sympathy for the chap. Maybe he's not such a bad sort, except for his sycophantic royalist tendencies and his annoying habit of polishing Teacher's apple.

The only one I want polishing Lucius' apple is me.

Though Zara can help if she likes.

"Turns out Ronin's not interested in helping." Takes me a sec to realize the girl's talking about her telepathy training, not polishing Lucius' apple. She stoops to lift her knapsack, which Neo promptly shifts to his own broad shoulder. "I'm actually just leaving."

Now she's making decisions for me instead of letting me make them for myself? That pisses me right off. Thinks she knows me, does she?

"Ronin hasn't actually answered, love." I swing my feet to the floor with a thud. "Because you haven't given Ronin the blooming chance. If you want my help, you can fucking have it—under one condition."

Surprise shifts to suspicion in her pretty face. "What condition?"

"You tell *him* why we're doing this." I cock my head toward Neo. "Because I've got to live under the same roof with the lot of you. And I'm going to need a raincoat to shield myself from the shitstorm once your fated mate here tumbles to the truth."

Neo's formidable brain may currently be parked between his legs, but he's still a sharp fellow. Faster than she's likely ready for, shock flashes across his face.

To be quickly eclipsed by hurt.

"You… you're… trying to shut down our bond?" Swimming with betrayal, his eyes swing toward her. "Babe, why would you want to do that?"

For some damn reason, I actually feel sorry for the man. I even feel a wee bit sorry for her… Zara… despite the fact this emotional train wreck is clearly her fault.

Her and her mixed messages.

She lays a gentle hand on his forearm (again with the mixed messages). "I told you from the start we're not mated. I told you I'm not staying. Remember?"

"Yes, but I thought you changed your mind when we bonded." Neo wears his whole heart in his face.

I'm really not sure why this whole daytime drama is getting to me. No doubt the heat simmering in my blood has something to do with it. But I find I can't just stand about like a rubbernecker at a traffic accident and watch the carnage.

With a curse, I shove to my feet.

In unison, their faces swivel toward me, Zara trapped and guilty, Neo hurt and increasingly pissed.

It's an interesting look on him. Makes me want to kiss it right off him.

That's definitely the mating fever talking.

"The pair of you are drawing quite the crowd," I point out, which is true. Every set of eyes in the commons is riveted on this twelve-car pileup. I ought to be selling tickets.

Vasili's actually leaning forward in his seat like he's trying to hear as well as see. VIP ticket for him then.

I angle my head and lock eyes with the girl's wary stare. "You want a telepathy tutor? I'll fucking do it. But I'm not a performing monkey. I won't put on a show for the huddled masses."

I pivot on my heel and make for the door that leads back to the cloister and the classrooms. I don't bother waiting round to see if she swallows the bait and follows me either.

If she doesn't, I'm heading straight to Lucius' office. I need a major fuck the minute his class lets out.

I pitch up in the conservatory—that's the glassed-in cloister garden—and both of them pitch up there right behind me. The walk gives everyone the chance to get their shit together. Not to mention the warm damp environs, infused with lush green smells, enfolds us like a hug.

A Villa Hadrian chap is loitering by the koi pond, but one menacing look from me sends him scampering. I head for the overgrown gazebo, whose peaked roof and lattice walls are thick with moss and vines, which makes it almost totally private.

It's actually a make-out spot, so thank fuck it's vacant. My revved-up libido couldn't take the sight of anyone fucking right now without me joining in.

The two of them crowd in with me.

Which is a bit imprudent given my state.

Neo props Zara's knapsack on the bench that rims the octagon and rakes back his wild hair. Even in the midst of his hurt and anger, struggling to understand this complicated queen, he's careful with her things.

He really is a decent sort. Probably doesn't deserve half the shit Vasili puts him through.

"He definitely doesn't," Zara says aloud, because I've already opened my mind to her. "None of this is his fault."

Neo looms, all sober and protective, at her shoulder. "What are you going to do, Ronin?"

"I'm going to teach her to shield her mind, because that's what she fucking asked for. So she can shut out anyone she doesn't want. I figure that's her call. If you've got a problem with that, mate, you shouldn't be here."

"I don't have a problem with Zara learning to protect herself," he says slowly. "Even if she's protecting herself from me. I'm going to stay and watch, but I won't interfere. I promise."

Which pretty much puts a bow on it. He's just confirmed my growing belief that he doesn't deserve this shit.

But that's his call to make.

My gaze shifts to her, marooned in the middle of the gazebo with arms clutched protectively round her middle. She's wary and a bit scared, which shows how uncomfortable she is with all those Gemini powers.

Of course, it's the lightning voice she really fears. Because it's the lightning voice she kills with.

Maybe if she's more at ease with her telepathy, her lethal recessives will seem a bit less daunting. Not that I'm losing sleep over her and her little problems. But if I say I'm going to do something, I bloody well do it.

For once, I make an actual effort not to sound like a total arse. "Come over here, then. Telepathy's easier to control when you're in physical contact."

She squares her shoulders and walks where I want, but she's hugging her elbows like a prisoner marching to the gallows. I uncross her arms, grip her hands in mine, and plant her palms firmly on my waist.

In my current state, the heat of her touch scorches through me like a prairie fire.

It's all I can manage to settle my hands on her shoulders for the exercise.

Because I'm suddenly burning to get much closer.

If this queen ever claims her formidable power, she can cast lightning with those hands that are currently resting so chastely at my waist. A lightning witch calls the lightning with her voice, but she casts it with her hands.

The way this one reportedly did in Vegas the night she fried those poor bastards.

"That was an *accident*," she whispers, her gaze searching mine like she's terrified I won't believe her. "Those men were… hurting me. Hurting my mom. I only wanted them to *stop*. I never meant to…" She swallows hard. "…kill."

Damn. She feels so bloody wretched any telepath would ache to wrap her in his arms.

But she's a Gemini, so she can just fucking suffer.

Apparently Neo feels the same pull, because he comes up behind and wraps *his* arms about her waist. She leans into his touch. For some damn reason, I've got to actively resist the impulse to shove into her space and cover her trembling lips with mine. To trap her between the two of us and eradicate all that fear by giving her something else to think about.

Like the two of us and our matching boners.

Plague take this mating fever.

I grip her shoulders and give her a little shake. Not hard enough to snap her Gemini neck, more's the pity. "Let's just focus on your telepathy, yeah? You're clearly receiving and transmitting right as rain, but you can choose not to. You need to imagine you're building a good solid wall between us."

Wide and wary, her gaze holds mine. "What kind of wall?"

"Make it a brick wall. Lay it bit by bit, and slather on plenty of mortar. The key trick's to visualize. The sun-warmed weight of the bricks in your hand. The chalky scent of the mortar in your lungs. The solid chink of the trowel as the wall rises and rises between us."

It's a fairly basic exercise that will only keep me out (if she does it right) and not Neo behind her, but I want the poor dear to have an easy win to build her trust in me. It will also build her confidence before she tries something trickier, like building a circular wall to keep everyone out. She's leaning on Neo telepathically as well as physically, though she doesn't seem to realize it.

Whatever she might be telling herself, she doesn't actually want to shut him out.

Over her shoulder, his open face lifts to mine. Which makes me realize *I'm* projecting at *him*.

Silently he lets me know he doesn't mind, a little smile stealing over his lips.

He isn't Valyrian, so he can't initiate a link—except with her. And even that much telepathy seems problematic in his case, since Zara means to block him. Still, since I'm Valyrian myself, I can project to him, and I can read him too if I like. It's just I typically wouldn't without an invite, as a matter of telepath ethics.

I leave the mental door open for him. With a little shove from my end, he can see through my mind the lively progress Zara's making on her wall. She may distrust her witchcraft, but she's a damn quick study. The turbulent current of her guilt and distress over the whole Vegas slaughter eases to a trickle and then stops.

Damn me. She's done it. She's shut me out.

And for some blooming reason, I don't like it.

I don't like it one bit.

"That's brilliant. You're doing it." I crush my bizarre antipathy for the whole notion of this queen shutting me out (which is good self-preservation on her part). Her quick grin of triumph stokes the mating fever I'm likewise trying to ignore. "I'm going to probe a bit now. Your job's to reinforce those bricks wherever you feel me pushing to keep me out."

I'm not using all my strength, but I'm making some effort, and she's mostly managing to keep me out. The more we practice doing this, the better she'll get. I offer a few words of grudging praise and some pointers to boost her confidence and hone her technique. And I'm not paying much attention to the fact that, during this whole tutorial, I'm wide open to both of them and projecting myself.

Until a furrow appears between her brows.

"Ronin," she says softly. "You're hurting."

Fuck. I knew she'd be a quick study.

She's picked up that my blasted bite is aching again, just like Lucius said it would if I kept away from him too long. And now Zara's entire wall has collapsed into rubble and she's projecting all that concern and distress straight at me.

"It's nothing." I shrug, which is a bad idea because the movement makes me wince. "Just need a spot of tending for the, uh, disciplinary bite after class. Let's try again with that wall."

It's actually time to put up a wall myself so they don't know it's a mating bite, a truth Lucius has insisted needs to stay our guilty little secret. He blasted his own rules to rubble when he fucked me, and even the fact that Vasili knows is giving Lucius fits.

Anyway, I need to protect Lucius. And, wall or no wall, both Zara and Neo are frowning at my evasion.

"You're hurt?" Behind his dark-rimmed glasses, Neo's big earnest eyes search my face. Which gives me a funny feeling in my chest.

"It's honestly not an issue," I say gruffly. "Who's teaching this lesson, anyway?"

"Let me see that bite, Ronin." Zara lets go of my waist and actually starts unbuttoning my fucking shirt.

"Now wait one bloody tick—"

"I have shifter blood, don't I? Along with all the rest?" She completely ignores my efforts to fend her off and unknots my tie with a few twists of her capable fingers. "Might as well put it to use. I can't shift or anything, but I bet I can help with this."

Well, fuck. I wanted to get us both naked, didn't I?

This aspect of her heritage might be new to her, but I can feel her certainty pulsing at me through the link. Clearly she's never tended a bite, but the damn thing is aching. If she wants to try, she can bloody well have at it.

It's not like I'll mind having her mouth on my body.

In fact, I don't mind at all.

"That's the spirit," she murmurs, with a quick upward glance brimming with turquoise heat that gives me an instant hard-on. Because, yeah, I'd want her on her back for me again even without the mating fever. Or my boundless thirst for vengeance.

"You'll have to put the bloody tie back on me then," I grouse. "I can't manage without a mirror."

"No worries. I've got you," Neo says easily, hands still resting on Zara's waist. I search the link between us for jealousy or some shit, but he truly does seem fine with what Zara's proposing.

"I *am* fine with it," he says with a smile.

She gives me a little backward push and says firmly, "Now sit."

Which is how I find myself parked on the gazebo bench with Zara perched on my thigh and my shirt and jacket open. Before I'm half ready for it, her lush Hollywood mouth grazes my half-healed bite.

The first hot lick of her tongue makes me groan in mingled pleasure and relief.

The double whammy of that slick of pleasure—intense as a blow job given my sexed-up state—and the instant easing of the pain makes me sway a bit. Neo sits alongside and grips my undamaged shoulder to give me a brace. Which is decent of him, even when I'm so turned on all this physical contact is torture. His knee brushes my thigh and he starts to shift away.

I squeeze his knee to hold him right there and say roughly, "Stay."

He sucks in a breath but does what I say.

He does what I say just beautifully.

I leave my hand on his knee and close my eyes against the sudden pulse of heat in my cock.

Looks like the bitch was right, because her care takes the edge off that ache straightaway. Beyond the physical kick, I rather fancy the emotional aspect of all this intimacy. There's something unique about this whole experience of having a queen care for me.

It might even make me want to care for her right back…

If I didn't hate her Gemini guts.

And the sleek curve of her ass parked firmly on my thigh makes me want to peel off her panties and spread her legs in her thigh-high stockings and tongue her till she creams in my mouth.

That's one thought I don't shield, and she moans against my bite, but she keeps right on working me with her tongue. I wrap an arm round her waist to drag her closer. Gods, she's fucking scenting me, that whiff of spice and sweetness potent with Mogadon mating scent. I know from my Mogadon boyfriend exactly how susceptible I am to those Mogadon pheromones, even when I'm not tortured by mating fever. Those pheromones are engineered by nature to stimulate a mate, and that's exactly what's happening.

In my current state, I'm so turned on she might as well be edging me.

"Fuck, Zara," I breathe, shifting on the bench, my legs falling open in an invite I literally can't hold back.

Her hand slides up my inner thigh to find the hot bulge under my trousers. A groan tears from my throat and I shove into her touch.

Looks like my tongue on your bite's not the only thing you need, is it, Adam? she whispers in my head.

"What are you offering?" I rasp, eyes closed against the rush of all that pleasure.

"Neo?" she murmurs, easing down my zipper one slow centimeter at a time. "Kiss Ronin for me."

My eyes pop open in instant protest.

Vasili's maniacally insistent the bloke's one hundred percent straight, and I've pretty much taken my boyfriend's word for it.

Neo's absolutely still under the death grip I've got on his knee. And he's fiery blushing all the way to the roots of his purple hair, which pretty much validates every single word Vasili's ever said on the subject.

Though, come to think of it, Neo blushes every time I talk to him.

"Forget it, mate," I say roughly. "You don't have to if you don't want to."

But for some fucking reason, I'm still gripping his knee in a silent command to stay.

Blushing absolutely crimson, he nails me with a brilliant green stare. "What if I *do* want to?"

"Look, I'm not some fucking charity case—"

He sucks in a breath and dives in to press his mouth against mine. And he bloody does it at exactly the moment Zara works her wicked little hand into my fly and wraps her fingers around my violently erect cock.

Completely fucking ambushed by the two of them, it's all I can manage not to spill right there.

"It's okay, Ronin," Zara whispers against my bite, and the feel of her soft mouth on my skin drags another moan out of me. "You need this, don't you? You took care of me. Now let us take care of you."

Fuck if I'm going to say no.

She swipes a finger around the head of my cock to collect the precum I'm pumping out for both of them and slathers it down my shaft. Neo's warm full mouth is fumbling a little against mine. Now he's pulling back with a mumbled apology.

I grab his hair in my fist and drag his mouth hard to mine.

His breath explodes against my lips in a gasp of surprise. Our tongues collide with an eagerness that just about vaporizes me in a flash of atomic heat. Zara's working my dick and I'm thrusting into her fist and I'm kissing Neo Mercury like he's oxygen and I'm suffocating.

I'm pretty sure I'm the first bloke he's ever kissed. And I'm making a right mess of it. But he breathes out a happy little murmur and rests a hand gently against my face, steadying us both for this sloppy kiss.

Shit. Between the two of them, I'm going to erupt like a volcano in about six seconds flat. Or possibly sooner. I'm going to come all over my own blasted uniform—

"No, it's okay. We've got you." Zara slides to her knees between my spread thighs and wraps her perfect mouth around my cock.

A strangled cry claws from my throat.

Neo swallows my desperate noises, his big hands pinning me to the gazebo wall. He's learning the feel of my mouth and I'm learning his. His glasses are sliding down his nose and he tastes like mint and innocence, but he's so hungry for me it's a revelation. Like, seriously, how could I possibly have missed that he's crushing on me?

But he's following her silent lead. He's very good indeed at following orders, this lad is.

And right now she's determined to make me come undone.

My circuits are frying with sexual overload. Smoke must be rising from my skin. Thank fuck Zara skips the foreplay and goes straight for the main event, her head bobbing up and down my dick with a determination I silently bless her for. I wrap her sweet schoolgirl ponytail in my fist like I've been dying to do all day so I can set the pace and I buck into the hot wet suck of her mouth. My piercing bumps against her tongue and she moans around my cock and Neo moans too and sucks on my tongue in exactly the same rhythm.

I can't seem to swallow the sharp urgent cries climbing from my throat. Which would definitely be a problem, from a discretion perspective, if our mouths weren't fused together so hard you'd need a crowbar to pry us apart.

Gods, I need *more* of them, both of them. Between them, they've got me pinned down and writhing and I'm so… bloody… *close…*

I'm trying my damnedest not to choke the girl with my cock. But when she takes me in deep, throat rippling around me as she swallows me down, I'm done for.

Especially when her deadly hand cups my balls and squeezes.

I arch off the bench and come with a shout that would take the roof off the gazebo if not for Neo's muffling mouth. The mating fever intensifies the whole experience, just like it did last night. Then, both Lucius and I came buckets, and now it feels again like I'll never stop spurting. I empty my load down Zara's throat for what seems like forever.

Finally I collapse on the bench with a gasp. Right before the damn church bell starts tolling for class.

"Sweet gods," I pant, loosening my clench on Zara's ponytail and Neo's hair and patting clumsily at both of them.

Zara lifts her head and licks her lips and grins smugly up at me. She's left smudges of bubble-gum pink lipstick all over my cock (not that I'm complaining). Neo's smiling too, all flushed and rumpled with his well-kissed mouth and his steamed-up glasses. He pushes a hand through his tumbled curls, which has no discernable taming effect whatsoever, and climbs to his feet.

Shit. Vasili's going to murder me for snogging Neo Mercury.

My boyfriend's far too observant and far too connected to me not to have noticed, and he's going to be jealous as fuck. But at this juncture, with my mating heat broken and endorphins flooding my system, I can't bring myself to give a single combustible damn.

The little Gemini zips me up and scrambles to her feet. Her nose wrinkles at me, but she's still smiling. "Honestly, Ronin, don't you even *own* underwear?"

"Never seen the point, love," I murmur, still working to catch my breath. Quite possibly, I'll skip my next class. I actually need to recover.

Yet for some reason, I hear myself asking, "Know where you need to go?"

"Genetics class," Neo answers for her, shouldering her knapsack. "I'll get her there on my way to Honors Earth Magic with the Dean."

Because, yeah, the bloke's that gifted. He bloody takes Honors track with the bloody Dean, who isn't exactly the nurturing type and typically doesn't teach.

"I know where to go," Zara points out with a frown, fixing her lipstick and tightening her ponytail with a determined twist.

Neo and I exchange a quick look. Turns out we're both thinking if he goes with, odds are she won't be hazed on the way.

Or worse.

Catching the byplay, she huffs out a breath and repeats firmly, "I know where to go, and I know how to take care of myself. Don't worry about me, okay?"

Yeah, like that's about to happen. Her fated mate not worrying. Or even me not worrying, for that matter.

Somehow, after what just went down between us, she's got *me* fucking worrying.

And she's not waiting about for permission, is she? The witch slips her knapsack off Neo's shoulder and takes off before he can formulate a word of protest.

Brow furrowing, Neo ducks out after her.

Left abruptly to my own devices, I press my wobbly legs into service and struggle upright, fumbling to fasten my shirt buttons.

Fuck, that was one *intense* orgasm—

Suddenly Neo rushes back in.

"Your tie," he murmurs, diving in to knot it neatly at my throat. "I promised."

He's blushing again and avoiding my gaze again. Still shy then.

And he's sweet as fuck.

"Hey, Red," I say softly, and wait until his kryptonite-green eyes lift to mine. "Next time it's your turn, yeah?"

"Okay," he says breathlessly, blush deepening exponentially. "But only, you know, if Zara doesn't mind."

"Mind?" I chuckle. "She's into both of us, isn't she? She'll be right in the bloody thick of it."

Of course, that's assuming she survives that long.

She's fresh meat, there's a queen killer out there, and given that slaughtered koi incident, he's quite likely on the hunt for her head.

Chapter Twenty-One
Zara

Master Zerxes is giving me the creeps.

In my regular schedule which Lucius put together, I somehow manage to avoid having the scary-as-fuck headmaster of Villa Tiberius as a prof. And I'm guessing Lucius really had to work at that, because it's a small Academy. But Mistress Agrippina's just gone down hard with a bad case of food poisoning, so Master Zerxes is subbing for my Genetics of Witchcraft class.

And he's certainly memorable.

He's lecturing in a rolling British baritone that purrs and growls and rumbles and effortlessly commands attention, which I guess is his job as a teacher. And I definitely don't like the guy, but he's sort of fascinating to watch.

He's tall and menacing with broad shoulders and a powerful frame under his black robe slashed with sangoire—that's the color of blood, which I've figured out is his house color—and the garment flows around him like liquid shadow. He's definitely got dramatic flair, and his sweeping gestures make those sangoire slashes appear and vanish like some invisible monster is raking him with unseen claws and he's magically healing himself.

Which is an unsettling effect.

Not to mention he's sleek and prowly like a snow leopard as he stalks around the lectern. He's basically a witching world version of Severus Snape, with glacial blue eyes and a fall of silver hair twisted into a long braid at his nape. And that menacing purr he's rocking? It's pure Alan Rickman.

Fifteen years ago—even ten—this guy would've been gorgeous with his strong bones and his ruthless mouth. He's honestly not too shabby on the eyes even now. My substitute prof's half Mogadon and half Valyrian—insights I gleaned from Racetrack over the breakfast table while I rewired the toaster I short-circuited last night. (With Gemini witchcraft, you gotta learn to do that sort of thing.)

In Bucephalus Zerxes, that genetic legacy is purely lethal.

He pretty much has the predatory instincts of a Mogadon and the telepathic precision of a Valyrian. I've been watching him eviscerate my classmates for every tiny lapse in attention or decorum the whole damn period.

Yet Mr. Menacing up there seems perfectly happy to ignore the stinging hail of spitballs those assholes in the back row have been lobbing at my head ever since the bell. A few have hit the back of my neck, which is totally disgusting as well as annoying, and I'm seriously worried there might be some stuck in my ponytail.

But I refuse to give my tormentors the satisfaction of looking.

Or reacting.

In any way.

What.

So.

Ever.

This is kids' stuff. I'm fucking twenty. Of course Vasili's back there too, and I wouldn't put it past him to be directing the whole assault. He's definitely not doing squat to stop it.

Long story short? I'm steadily adding to the tally of scores I intend to settle at this Academy.

Zerxes is going on my hit list too. This guy could definitely do a better job keeping order in his classroom. The entire student body seems to be terrified of him, and clearly for good reason.

Like he can hear my thoughts… which, you know, he can… my substitute prof pivots toward me in a cloud of ink and sangoire and extends his long pointer straight at me.

"Let us turn our attention," he drawls with sepulchral doom, "to recessives."

My stomach squirms and I shift in my seat.

Because the lightning voice is a recessive trait.

"The strongest magical gifts in the witching world," Zerxes breathes, "derive from recessive genetic traits, which the four arcane races have endeavored to strengthen over the centuries through meticulous genealogical records and selective breeding. Our future queen is a case. In. Point."

With deadly softness, he pads toward me. "Twelve vast families, named in antiquity for the twelve signs of the zodiac, comprise the four races. Among those twelve families, only three have managed to minimize the genetic pollution of earthbound human DNA in their magical lineage, and therefore to concentrate those recessives in their formidable offspring. Those three elite families are of course the Aquarius, the Aries, and… the Gemini."

Prowling past my desk, he pivots and pounces. "Tell us about the lightning voice, Ms. Gemini."

I swallow hard, because telling this roomful of jerks who hate my guts about the lethal genetic legacy that killed my mom and eighty-seven innocent people is the last thing I feel like doing. As in, the very last. Unfortunately, I don't think Severus here has any intention of letting me wiggle off the hook.

Fortunately, because it's Genetics class, I can hide behind the science.

This doesn't need to get personal.

I clear my throat and square my shoulders. "I have the lightning gene because both my parents carried it. So did my brother Damien. But it's sex-linked to the X chromosome. And since it's recessive, you need an XX to express the trait. Guys are an XY in the chromosome department, so it's dormant in Gemini males."

My mom was born Gemini, she's like my dad's third cousin or something. But I have zero intention of mentioning my mom in front of this apex predator. Not to mention those cackling jackals in the back row. This whole room knows the lightning voice killed my mom.

If I'm not careful, someday it'll do the same to me.

"Correct." Zerxes stalks back and forth before my desk, stabbing his steel-tipped pointer at the flagstones for emphasis. "The lightning voice is a recessive trait that only expresses in Gemini females. Your sons will carry the gene, but they won't express it. Only your daughters can inherit the full force of your mighty gifts, and only if you mate a purebred arcane… or *arcanes*, plural… with powerful witchcraft bred into their DNA.

"The wielding of this potent witchcraft carries both symbolic and magical import; every time a queen casts a spell, she strengthens the entire witching world. Therefore, this exercise of your witchcraft—*and* your attendant mating—are in fact sacred duties and the most essential functions to be undertaken by you, as our queen, for the preservation of our power. And the survival. Of the entire. Witching. World."

Which pretty much puts my substitute prof firmly in the monarchist camp. That makes sense, I guess, since both the dead queen and my shitty brother were in Zerxes' cohort at Villa Tiberius.

The prof looms over my desk to pin me with his intensely blue eyes. "As our future queen, these sacred obligations are among the many reasons why your choice of mate is so momentous."

Yeah, we're not talking about my choice of mate. But I'm pretty much on my own here in terms of fending him off. Neo's off somewhere taking Honors Science of Witchcraft with the Dean. Vasili's been lurking in the back all period, but of course he's no help. He's probably enjoying the fuck out of this entire ordeal. I've already noticed he and Zerxes—the two alphas in the room—seem to give each other plenty of space.

That's kinda the way it works here, and in the witching world generally. We've all so crossbred there's plenty of alpha shifter splashed around the gene pool. I've even got a dollop myself.

When alpha shifters meet, either they fight or they fuck. If that's not what they want, they tend to give each other a pretty wide berth.

I'm guessing Ronin's got a little alpha too, though not enough to shift. But I've seen him submit to Lucius and Vasili, so he seems like more of a switch than a pure alpha. He's actually supposed to be sitting in this class with me, but he hasn't shown since Neo and I blew his mind and his load in the gazebo…

Master Zerxes hums in the back of his throat. With a spurt of horror, I realize I'm projecting. With his Valyrian gifts, my prof's hearing every word.

Heat rushes into my face.

Hastily I concentrate on building the wall between us like Ronin taught me. The prof gives a sharp inhale and leans over my desk, and I know he's sensing my resistance to his psychic intrusion.

And that he doesn't much like it.

"Your perception is remarkably astute," he murmurs, so soft they must barely be able to hear him in the back. Yet the whole room's riveted, you could hear a flea sneeze in here, with my classmates straining to catch every word that passes between us.

My queen. You're everything they've ever called you and more.

That's him. His voice.

I want him out of my head. I pour all my energy into visualizing the wall the way Ronin taught me, and I add extra mortar and extra bricks to keep him out.

With a short huff that resonates with displeasure, the bastard resumes his liquid prowl around my desk.

"Let us consider the case of our First Boy, Mr. Mercury," he says, low and lethal. After every sentence, he taps his pointer on the floor. "Head of the Dean's List." Tap. "One of the most purebred arcanes currently resident at this Academy." Tap. "His arcane pedigree barely attenuated to any discernible degree by his earthbound human DNA." *Tap.* "Your. Fated. Mate."

"He isn't," I blurt out. Which probably isn't wise, but I feel a driving need to contradict him. For some reason it feels instinctive, this need to challenge him, and I'm burning to put this prick in his place. "I don't care what's in our natal charts. I'm not claiming a fucking mate."

"Why, my future queen, how not?" Zerxes sweeps his arms wide, long sleeves trailing, and addresses his astonishment to the entire class. "This entire Academy felt the earthquake that rocked this island only last night, and the Med is hardly a seismic zone, is it? The ability to make the earth tremble is distinctly a Capricorn trait. To wit, your fated mate is the Capricorn scion, and the only Capricorn on this island strong enough to accomplish such a feat. By this token, you do seem to be in a claiming sort of mood, Ms. Gemini."

I've had way more than enough of being threatened and bullied by him and every goddamn asshole at this Academy. I push my chair back with a noisy scrape, fold my arms over my chest, and glare a warning straight at him. "Actually, I'm in a none-of-your-damn-business sort of mood, Master Zerxes."

I use his title for politeness, when what I really want to say is *you asshole*.

And I don't give a fuck if he hears me. In fact, I open a portal in the brick wall I've built between us and fire the phrase like a cannon straight into his fucking head.

A soft breath puffs past his parted lips. I probably just gave him a migraine with that telepathic fusillade, but it sounds to me like a gasp of pleasure.

The air turns thick with a potent onslaught of Mogadon pheromones.

Right now the psycho's either feeling aggressive or aroused, and I'm hoping like fuck it's the former. He leans over my desk like the carnivore he is. I practically expect to see gobbets of blood and shredded flesh dripping from his jaws. It's all I can manage to hold my ground and not lean back in my chair.

"Detention," he breathes in a whisper, a mere scrap of sound. "Tonight. After moonrise. With me."

Oh fuck no. Not tonight. And *definitely* not with him.

But, admittedly, I'm not exactly sure what my options are. If I'm a no-show for our little date, what exactly can he do to me? Is it possible they'll actually expel me for disobedience? And isn't that what I want? I don't know why the idea of expulsion hasn't occurred to me before.

Or why I'm not feeling more enthusiastic about the concept now.

I'm still working through my complex emotions about expulsion and whether that should be my new strategy when Zerxes stalks back to his lectern.

"Four arcane races," he announces, sweeping his pointer across the incomprehensible jumble of genetic code spilling across the old-fashioned chalkboard. No prof in this Academy seems to use a laptop, and I haven't actually seen a computer or a smart phone since I got here. I'm betting the magical wards on this island seriously mess with the electronics.

"Ms. Prynne," he raps out without turning. "Grace us with your insights. What genetic traits are expressed by Mogadon DNA?"

Racetrack, whom I've already learned hates being called Ms. Prynne or, God help us all, Abigail (which is apparently her real name) pops her gum and doesn't bother answering. She's parked two rows over, so I've got an unobstructed view of her sulky profile.

Zerxes sighs and raises his gaze heavenward for patience. "Ms. *Prynne*. Unless you're particularly eager to join Ms. Gemini in her impending detention, I'd strongly advise you to answer the question."

"Riiiiight." Slowly Racetrack tips back her chair and swings her booted feet to the desk with a thunk. She's wearing knee-high combat boots, which is definitely not part of the girls' uni, but no one seems inclined to make an issue out of it.

"So." She pops her gum. "Mogadon traits. Pheromones. Mating scent. Aggressive. Territorial. Witchcraft manifests as telekinesis, teleportation, levitation—basically, physical manipulation of matter. Most Mogadon only have one of those tricks in their bag of laughs. Because of all the human DNA."

"Very good, Ms. Prynne. That wasn't so difficult, even for you," Zerxes purrs. His pointer drops to another line of genetic code. "Next, we have the Valyrian race, with its own distinctive traits. Ms. Maali?"

Dez is Valyrian, so it's no surprise he'd call on her. She poises her sharpened pencil above the neat lines of text in her notebook and answers promptly. "Gifts of the mind, yeah? Telepathy, clairvoyance, clairsentience, precognition. The strongest Valyrians can summon and wield psi fire… or, er, lightning."

She adds the last with an apologetic look at me, which is unnecessary. I already know I have my Valyrian DNA to thank for the lightning voice. It's a distant cousin to the psi fire Ronin sprayed all over Wang's penthouse roof.

"Correct." Zerxes seems almost bored with her recitation, if not for the sly look he casts over his shoulder at me. "Due once again to genetic pollution with human DNA, the vast majority of this Academy's current Valyrian population—like our own Ms. Maali—is barely capable of party tricks. The few inhabitants currently capable of summoning psi fire include our absent Mr. Pendragon… and myself."

Great. Another pyromaniac warlock. In addition to belittling Dez, it almost feels like he's warning me, except I don't know why he'd bother. Since I refuse to use my power at all, I'm pretty much a magical nonentity.

"Next we arrive at the Kryll, whose genetic pedigree may best be described as the Turkish bazaar of the witching world." Zerxes slices his pointer across another line of code. "Mr. Romanov?"

"Weather magic." Vasili sounds bored to tears. "Earth magic, wind magic, rain magic, alchemy. A veritable grab bag of magical minutia. Cyclones and earthquakes if they're exceptionally lucky, although most Kryll are nowhere near that powerful. But a Kryll can only cast by channeling psi power harvested from other arcanes through a telepathic, physical, or sexual bond. A Kryll on his own is entirely useless."

Somehow I know he's talking about Neo, and that pisses me right off. Neo fucking made the earth move last night—literally as well as figuratively—in my bed. Although I didn't actually realize he must have been channeling *my* power through our mating bond (our temporary mating bond that I'm going to sever when I leave) when he did it.

Somehow the thought of leaving this insane asylum of warlocks and witches in my rear view mirror doesn't spark the urgency it should. Probably because I'm feeling guilty and therefore conflicted about hurting Neo. If I'm being totally honest, I'll even miss Ronin a tiny bit.

Not that it'll stop me from going or anything.

Frowning, I tap my pencil against my lips.

"Now, now, one mustn't allow oneself to be *too* blinded by one's own parochial squabbles and prejudices, Mr. Romanov." Zerxes smirks. And I get the distinct sense he too is thinking about Neo. "Which brings us to the final arcane race, the verminous Proteans, colloquially known to the masses as the *shifters*." The sneer in his voice is audible, and now I'm annoyed on Lucius' behalf. "Ms. Gemini?"

I blink and lower my pencil with a frown. I'm way behind in this class, just like I am in all my classes, and admittedly I haven't made much headway in the reading since I know I'm leaving.

Which means I'm going to struggle with this impromptu quiz. Still, I know a little just from watching Lucius and hearing him talk.

"Um, rarest of the four races. They're kinda on top of the endangered species list. Capable of shifting into their animal form at will." My prof seems to be waiting in mounting impatience for more, so I rummage around in my head. "The animal coexists as, like, a separate entity with the human inside the same skin. There aren't many purebred shifters left, and I'm guessing Lucius— uh, Master Aries—is probably one of the few on this whole rock who can even shift."

"Nearly correct, but not quite," the prof murmurs. "There's a bear shifter among the custodial staff. Polar bear, for your information, greatly to be avoided when he shifts. In addition, we claim a shark shifter in Villa Tiberius. A great white, to be precise. Also to be avoided."

Fuck, I didn't even know it was possible to *be* a shark shifter. Talk about feeling out of my depth. The concept of a great white shifter who answers to Bucephalus Zerxes sharking around this island definitely gives me second thoughts about my whole deep sea dive idea.

"Great. Thanks for the warning," I mutter.

Zerxes looks like he'd love to keep grilling me to expose the full extent of my ignorance to my classmates' mockery, but the deep toll of the church bell brings this whole ordeal to a blessed close. Around me students shove noisily to their feet, slamming notebooks closed, tossing books into backpacks. I pop up too, using the opportunity to give my ponytail a brisk shake in the hope of dislodging any clinging spitballs.

"Kindly recall Schedule A students have midterm examinations next week," Zerxes projects coldly above the bedlam. "I'm certain you'll all distinguish yourselves in your examinations and emerge covered with academic glory."

Yeah, me? Not so much. I'd love a hard pass on those midterms myself, but Lucius already told me they'll use the tests to gauge my level, then assign remedial learning as needed. Of course, that's only if I'm going to stay.

Which I'm not.

Grim with resolve, I swing my backpack over my shoulder and motor for the exit. Most of the students are already gone, and I'm definitely not eager to be alone with—

"Ms. Gemini." The prof's voice curls around my waist like a bullwhip. "Kindly remain behind. With. Me. We must arrange the details of your impending detention."

The detention I have no intention of serving. But no point telling him that. I'll just cross my fingers behind my back and agree to whatever I need to in order to get out of this room.

Ahead of me, Dez loiters in the doorway like she's unwilling to leave me alone with the monster.

Bless that girl for her loyalty.

"Kindly close the door on your way out, Ms. Maali." Zerxes' icy gaze veers behind me. "And take Mr. Romanov with you."

Actually, I'm surprised Vasili's stuck around. I pivot to find him right behind me, looking like a rock star in his tailored blazer with his tie loose and his collar popped, his gorgeous face hard and unreadable as one elegant hand reaches to flick a spitball (disgusting) out of my ponytail. His smoky eyes narrow on Bucephalus Zerxes like the man's a crouching menace.

"The little queen can't serve detention with you tonight," Vasili says flatly. "She's already serving detention with Master Aries."

That's a blatant lie, and I suck in my breath to hear it. Vasili's gaze flashes a wintry warning, which tells me I'm projecting again. I remember barely in time to throw up a hasty wall between me and the telepathic Zerxes.

"How interesting, and how irrelevant." The prof's voice slashes through me like a razor, and I pivot to keep the apex predator in sight. "In that case, it sounds like double detention duty for our future queen." His burning stare crawls over me and his tone thickens. "I'll take her after Lucius is finished. I do hope you don't require much sleep, Ms. Gemini."

Yeah, no. There are so many things wrong with those sentences I can't even list them. One of them being the hint of a predatory sexual undertone from my fucking middle-aged teacher lurking under those double *entendres*.

"He has the bitch all night. Rest assured she'll be quite thoroughly occupied," Vasili says coolly, like I'm not even in the room. "She's barely been at this Academy a day, yet it seems she's been quite the naughty girl."

My mouth pops open and I glare at him. Now it's apparently his turn for the double *entendres*.

"You think I'm a bitch now? Just wait till I get going," I mutter.

But I don't say it too loudly, because for whatever reason, the Goblin King appears to be momentarily on my side.

What is this, anyway? Why is he protecting me? He can't be all that eager for our midnight rendezvous, since he's only helping me because I bribed him with the promise of my silence about him and Ronin.

Zerxes looks annoyed, but Lucius is my headmaster and probably has dibs or something, because he waves a languid hand and sighs. "Oh, very well then. Tomorrow night. After dinner. My office. I'd advise you to come well-fortified, Ms. Gemini, since I've a substantial endeavor planned for your benefit—"

"She can't do tomorrow either." Vasili jams his hands in his pockets and shifts in his electric blue combat boots like this entire tedious affair is a dreadful bore. "Tomorrow night's the Janus Dance. The little queen's our newest student, and our illustrious Dean's made her attendance compulsory."

Zerxes studies him through narrowed eyes. "I'm well aware the Janus festivities were rescheduled for Lucius' benefit since he was off collecting our queen in Singapore on the actual holiday. But I'm aware of no such mandate from the Dean for our new arrival."

"Why would you be aware, darling? You're not her headmaster." Vasili lifts one shoulder in an insolent shrug. "If you doubt me, why not ask the old bird in the Dean's tower yourself? If you fancy being skinned alive for questioning the great and powerful Oz, that's entirely your affair."

With that, my horrible snake of a housemate rudely turns his back and slithers for the door. If he had a tail, it would be rattling. "Rest assured the little queen *will* be attending the dance."

"Yep, that's the plan," I agree, starting after him. Snake or no snake, right now he's my snake, and I'm going with him.

Too bad Zerxes oozes into my path, dark robes whispering around his powerful frame.

"I'm rather tempted to state that, in that case, you'll be attending the dance with me," he purrs. "I do dislike to postpone any punishment for too long."

"Sorry, but I've already got a date," I manufacture hastily, just totally making shit up at this point. This whole Janus Dance is news to me, but I'm done letting these two duke it out over me without taking a few swings myself.

"With whom, your *fated mate*?" Zerxes sneers. "It's tradition at this Academy for the strongest witch to attend formal events with the strongest warlock. If your attendance is indeed compulsory, that means you'll be attending with me."

I just stare at the old nightmare, completely fucking appalled by the entire concept. One, I don't know what gave him the idea I'm the strongest witch at this Academy. Two, what makes him the strongest warlock and not Lucius, or maybe even Vasili? And three, I mean, who makes rules like that? It definitely puts me at a real disadvantage in this argument since these guys both know them, but I don't.

"Actually, that claim of arcane supremacy on your part is entirely subjective, not to mention entirely debatable," Vasili drawls from the door. "In any event, it fails to signify."

Zerxes whirls to savage him and all but snarls. "And why would that be, Mr. Romanov? Pray enlighten me as to precisely *why* my status as the senior warlock at this Academy fails to signify."

Vasili lifts one arctic eyebrow. "Your status fails to signify because the little bitch is attending the Janus Dance with me." He levels our prof with a single sweeping glance that's bristling with aggression. "So unless you're planning to poach my date, Bucephalus, I'd sincerely advise you to step aside."

Chapter Twenty-Two
Zara

"What the actual fuck, Vasili?" I aim my demand at his slender back as my new frenemy powers down the hall. Curious students stream past on their way to next period, and I'm not too thrilled to be trotting after Vasili Romanov like one of his numerous lackeys.

But I'm too determined to ferret out his motives to let a little social awkwardness get in my way.

"Come on, I asked you a question." I take advantage of a momentary lightening in the corridor traffic to pull up alongside him. And I pitch my voice under the general chatter to make it private. "Why'd you help me back there?"

"Help *you*?" Vasili's staring straight ahead as he strides along, but I can see his jaw tick. "I wasn't helping you. I was helping *me*. And all the denizens of the witching world who don't subscribe to Bucephalus Zerxes' fanatical monarchist manifesto."

Well, this sounds more like the Vasili I know. Still, I'm feeling a little slow on the uptake. "How does it help you and the anti-monarchists if Zerxes doesn't clap me in detention?"

His pretty lip curls in a sneer. "*Detention.* That term is a barely adequate euphemism for what Bucephalus Zerxes would truly like to do to you. Everyone in this Academy knows Cybelle was sucking his cock and doing it with Damien's blessing. Zerxes was one of Messalina's suitors at this school when they were both students eons ago, but she chose another mate. Now he's determined to be one of yours."

"One of *mine*?" My gut literally curdles at the prospect. I swallow down a surge of nausea. "Um, hello. He's, like, our prof? I thought there were rules against that sort of thing. Not to mention he's freaking old enough to be my dad."

"Rules? Dear God, princess, will you please wake up and look around you?" Vasili rolls his gorgeous eyes. "This Academy is so thinly staffed it's barely functional. The Dean is nearly eighty, and she isn't exactly deeply engaged these days in the didoes of her staff or the nuances of faculty-student relations. It's a damn good thing this institution practically runs itself, with some reinforcement from Lucius and Agrippina, or let's just say we wouldn't be getting much of an education."

Vasili shoulders ahead of me and pushes through the swinging door into the student commons, and I have to put up an arm to keep from getting smacked in the face when the door swings back. This would normally annoy me enough to say something, but he's giving me good intel and I don't want to distract him.

He's making for his favorite spot, the thronelike couch under the stained glass windows he clearly owns, since I haven't seen any other ass occupy those cushions without his say-so.

His legs are a lot longer than mine and he's not encumbered by a great big backpack the way I am, because he doesn't seem to bother much with schoolbooks or supplies, but I'm way more determined.

I quicken my pace to keep up. "I still don't get why you'd give a shit if he makes a play for me at detention. You already know I'm not staying."

"I know that's what you've *said*." He slices me a narrow look that brims with hostility. "Your actions say something else entirely. You've barely been here a day, and you've already claimed your mate and practically claimed mine. Don't even think I don't know what you and that book-faced nincompoop just did with Ronin."

"Projecting again, huh?" I say glumly, my spirits taking a nosedive. "Damn. I'm working on that."

"Don't flatter yourself, darling." He smirks so insufferably I want to slap him. "If I don't want you inside my head, rest assured you won't get past my defenses. I'm telepathically linked with *him*, because that's what he likes. Which means I had a fucking front-row seat for your gazebo porn."

Well, shit. This is concerning. I didn't realize everything I share with Ronin I'm also sharing with Vasili, and I'm definitely not crazy about the concept.

But it's important that I not get distracted myself.

"Why do you care who I fuck, Vasili?" I'm determined to get it out of him. "You know I'm leaving. You're *helping* me leave."

By now he's reached the circular couch. He sprawls in it, spreads his arms across the back to keep me from claiming any of his real estate, and scowls at me. "Indeed those are the current terms of our arrangement. I trust you're fully aware that arrangement constitutes the one and only reason I'm not an active accomplice to whoever on this island is hunting for your head. Should you happen to change your mind about leaving… should you renege on your vow to abdicate… the terms of our temporary peace treaty are history. Then you'd better watch your back."

Well, at least now I know where I stand. He helped me fend off Zerxes because he thinks a powerful warlock and committed monarchist like our prof might persuade me to stay.

Maybe he even thinks I'm weak enough and dumb enough to let Zerxes seduce me into staying.

"You know something? Those assumptions you're making about me are offensive on so many levels I'd need a calculator to keep track." I glare down at him, sprawled with effortless glamor across his monster couch, and barely restrain the urge to kick him in the balls.

"Hmmm. If the shoe fits, Cinderella, *et cetera*." Seemingly indifferent to my fuming, he slips a little silver mirror and a wand of lip gloss from his pocket and starts touching up his makeup.

Despite my fury at his condescending attitude, I'm thoroughly distracted by how sexy he looks doing it. In fact, it's so distracting watching that slender wand glide over his perfect mouth, clear gloss framing those sharp little fangs of his, that it's practically mesmerizing.

I find myself wondering if he bites with those fangs when he fucks.

And how much Ronin likes it.

The deep gong of the church bell vibrates through the commons, which is my cue to vamoose to my next class.

But I'm not quite ready to let this serpent slither free.

"You do realize, Goblin King, that I'll actually have to go with you now to that fucking dance? Or Zerxes will know we lied so I could get out of detention. And he'll take it out on me."

"Oh, don't be so dramatic. We'll put in an exceedingly brief joint appearance, then go our separate ways." His glacial eyes slide over me with disdain. "I trust you'll find something appropriate to wear. I've certain appearances to uphold at this Academy."

"Hey, no worries, bad boy. I'll dress to impress." I pop my hip like a runway model while I think briefly and unhappily about the collection of schoolgirl uniforms in my wardrobe. I'll have to persuade Racetrack to loan me something. Her edgy vibe's a lot closer to mine than the soft feminine style Dez cultivates.

"Hmmm." Vasili tucks away his cosmetics and flicks an unimpressed look over my posturing form. "We'll finish this delightful discussion at our midnight rendezvous, shall we? For now, I'd advise you to hurry along. You're running late for Double Witchcraft, and Lucius doesn't like to be kept waiting."

"For someone who doesn't give a shit, you seem pretty fucking familiar with my schedule." I frown, because I do have two back-to-back Witchcraft sessions—basically a big fat independent study with Lucius—that just got added to my schedule this morning.

"Rest assured I don't give a single incendiary damn about your piddling academic schedule." Vasili bares his sexy fangs in a scowl. "I'm tracking Lucius because the two of us are taking care of something for Ronin. Now run along before you begin to annoy me, little queen."

My temper spikes to match his. "Till midnight then, asshole. And if you pull a no-show, I'm going to show up in your fucking bedroom."

He looks so horrified by that prospect I almost laugh. There's actually nothing that would induce me to show up in the snake den this pit viper calls a bedroom, but he's so freaking arrogant he believes it.

I leave him completely appalled over the nonexistent possibility of my late-night visit to his bed and head off to the belfry to find Lucius.

Chapter Twenty-Three
Lucius

There's a winter storm brewing and the wind up here in the church belfry is wicked, but my wolf enjoys the wild weather. The moon will be nearly full tonight, and it's a supermoon this month to boot, which makes both of us unusually edgy.

My wolf is itching for another long lope on the wooded slopes. I'm more than inclined to indulge him, since I desperately need to blunt the edge of my own savage appetites.

Given the fraught situation at the *domus*, that blunting of the edge can't possibly occur soon enough to pacify me.

In fact, our young queen has my household's entire male cohort on edge. There's a queen killer lurking, she refuses to claim her power and save our failing races, and I'm responsible for her education, her safety, and thus the survival of the entire witching world. Yet her power *is* rising, whether she claims it or not, along with her sexual allure. For a warlock, there's nothing more compelling—even irresistible—than an unclaimed queen.

To all of us.

Only Dez and Racetrack, exclusively committed to each other, seem anywhere close to normally functional. Zarina has even managed to unsettle the unshakable Vasili, although I'm convinced my rival alpha hasn't begun to suspect the true reason for his discomfiture.

Suffice it to say there's more than one reason the atmosphere in our house is electric.

The plain truth is that I too am far from immune to my queen's allure. The magnetic pull I feel toward her is a dangerous distraction.

For four long years, since the day I assumed the headmaster's post, I've been more a priest than a teacher. Now I'm grimly cognizant of the fact that, for better or worse, my long drought of celibacy has drawn to a close.

I'm deeply conflicted about this forbidden mating with Ronin. The mere thought of my sullen yet seductive lover tangles my heart in knots, while the sight of him steals my soul. This connection I share with him is far more complicated than sexual infatuation. My emotions are deeply implicated. Unfortunately, given my commitment to this Academy, ours is a union that can only end in one way.

Disaster.

Truly, the more Ronin turns to our queen or my rival alpha rather than myself to slake his mating heat, the easier it will be to break our bond once the fever passes.

Even if the prospect of breaking our bond makes the predator that shares my skin sit straight up and howl in anguished protest.

It's because of this difficult business with Ronin that I'm uncharacteristically forgiving of Zarina's tardiness. Ronin stopped by my office earlier and confided what she and Neo did for him. I'm astounded but delighted that the Academy's notorious Sir One and Done, with his hatred of all things Gemini, actually seems to have enjoyed his encore encounter with Zarina.

For her part, she's actually tending his bite. This unexpected hint of queenly conduct offers a rare sprig of hope that perhaps our future royal is beginning to embrace her fate.

It's her royal duty to claim her mates, the way she's already extremely close to doing with Neo. Now if only she'll claim Ronin as well…

The quick staccato tap of my errant student's shoes on the spiral stairs is too faint for the mortal ear to detect. Nonetheless, my wolf hears her coming and scrambles up to greet her with an eager bark. A whiff of our queen's sweet yet potent scent floods my senses as she climbs into view, swathed in her black peacoat with the Academy logo, face flushed from the cold and the climb, teal hair vivid against slate-colored skies.

I direct a mild glance at the old-fashioned timepiece strapped to my wrist. "You're at least ten minutes late for our lesson, Ms. Gemini."

"Sorry, Teach," she says, with an impudent upward look that makes both of us catch our breath. Ronin isn't the only one of my students my incorrigible wolf is stubbornly insistent that we claim.

Ours ours ours, my beast rumbles under my skin. *She's ours.*

"Go ahead and blame me." Zarina lowers her backpack and throws me a rueful look. "I was naughty in Genetics. Master Zerxes kept me late after class."

My wolf growls in my ear and my skin tightens in warning. It's unavoidable that Zarina would cross Zerxes' path, given Agrippina's unexpectedly severe illness and this faculty shortage that seems to become more acute with each passing year. But it's damnably unfortunate that Aggie fell ill during this delicate settling-in period in Zarina's education. I'm deeply hopeful my dependable colleague will be back on her feet tomorrow.

Still, I can scarcely hope to keep Zarina safe from Zerxes forever.

"I trust all is well with your class," I murmur blandly, careful not to betray my unease. This isn't a particularly easy feat to manage since my student is a wickedly powerful natural telepath.

She's studying me closely, perceptive eyes roaming over my face and my wind-whipped greatcoat. Heat flares under my skin and streaks along the path of her gaze.

"Fair to say we didn't exactly hit it off," she admits, sauntering up alongside me at the hip-high stone wall. Together we peer over the jumble of sloping rooftops that tumbles downhill to the steely sea. "He tried giving me late-night detention, but I managed to wiggle out of that. Then he wanted me to be his freaking date for this Janus Dance."

"Damn the man," I whisper under the whistling wind.

It's an open secret that Bucephalus and Cybelle were lovers, although their union was always tempestuous. Our late queen-in-waiting alternately toyed with Ceph and pushed him away. But his pursuit of her was relentless, and the man himself entirely untroubled by the reprehensible ethics and power disparity of a teacher sexually exploiting his student. It was a source of endless frustration that my numerous hints to the Dean about the inappropriate nature of their association invariably fell on deaf ears. Cybelle was still a minor in the witching world and therefore, at least theoretically, off limits. But beyond any doubt, Ceph was a wily devil. Thus, I never managed to secure the irrefutable evidence I needed to indict him for his indiscretions.

I'm grimly aware there aren't enough of us left on this faculty anymore for the Dean to spuriously dismiss a tenured professor. She's steadily refused to act, particularly since I've never been able to produce rock-solid proof of misconduct.

I've known Bucephalus Zerxes for years. He was my own professor at this Academy a decade ago—when *I* was the student he pursued, albeit unsuccessfully—and the secret terror of my entire class. Even then, the man was a sexual predator, offended and infuriated by my rejection. He's the primary reason for my own ironclad rule against teacher-student entanglements. Yet he's been my adamantly unapproachable colleague since my return, a dynamic I vastly prefer. Because we're both unmated faculty (until Ronin, in my case, which is temporary), there were many who assumed Ceph and I would become lovers.

That prospect still turns my stomach.

Nonetheless, the entire witching world knows Ceph Zerxes is a rabid monarchist and one of Messalina's most loyal allies.

Far fewer know of his conviction, shared only within the privacy of the Academy's wards, that a genetic infusion of his powerful DNA will be the salvation of the faltering royal bloodline.

For these reasons, I've thought myself fully prepared for Ceph to pursue Zarina.

Yet, somehow, the news manages to arrive as an unwelcome shock.

"You must inform me immediately if Master Zerxes gives you any difficulty, Ms. Gemini," I say quietly. "I'm your headmaster, which gives me some authority to intervene if he ventures beyond the pale."

"Good to know, but I'm handling him. You can believe I was a hard no on the whole Janus Dance." She seems eager to put the thought of Bucephalus Zerxes behind her, an impulse for which I can scarcely blame her. A gust of wind makes her huddle into her coat. "Fuck, that wind's biting. Why are we up here, Lucius?"

"Master Aries," I remind her lightly, scrupulous to reveal no inkling of how much it pleases me to hear my Christian name on my queen's sweet tongue. She's absolute trouble, this one, and she's my student and she's strictly off limits.

But she's compelling.

So compelling I can barely look away.

Clearly, my wolf wants her.

As for myself, I'm the Aries scion. Under any other circumstances, I'd be one of her suitors.

Her gaze veers to me, and I realize with a shock that I've neglected to shield my thoughts. Her wide eyes roam over my chest and shoulders and slide up my neck to linger on my mouth. Her tongue slicks over the soft pink bow of her lower lip.

I'm assailed with a sudden, violent impulse to lean down and claim her in a savage kiss.

Ours, my wolf growls in agreement. *Our queen. We should claim her too.*

Of course, I restrain myself. Having one student in my bed is more than enough indiscretion.

"Master Aries," she whispers, obedient in that, at least. Her knowing eyes find mine. "That's a mating bite you gave Ronin, isn't it? I can tell by the way he acts. It sexes him up when I go anywhere near it."

Damnation. This time I *was* shielding my thoughts. But my queen's a powerful witch, even more powerful than I've appreciated. Clearly, her untrained power is growing.

This revelation only makes our business in this belfry more pressing.

Notwithstanding the fact that Zarina herself is certain to resist.

"Mr. Pendragon's condition is confidential information," I say briskly. "To answer your earlier question, Ms. Gemini, we're in this belfry because it's the safest location on this campus for me to endeavor to teach you to control your lightning."

"My *lightning*?" she repeats, happily sidetracked by this diversion. Her indignant lips pop open with instant protest. "Lucius." (So much for Master Aries.) "I don't summon lightning. Remember?"

"You don't summon it voluntarily," I correct her carefully, angling to maneuver past her swiftly mounting resistance, "but it comes unbidden, does it not? Half the lights in our *domus* needed to be replaced this morning. My job is to help you control the lightning. So that it never again comes unbidden. To speak plainly, my queen, this is knowledge you require."

"Nope." She pops the P and waves a mittened hand to fend me off. "It's not. That's knowledge *you* require if I'm going to ascend. I keep telling you. I'm. Not. Ascending. Okay?"

In fact, the prospect of this queen refusing to ascend isn't at all okay.

It's intolerable.

My fists clench and my shoulders knit in bitter frustration. Our people need her on that throne. They need her there wielding her witchcraft with control and conviction. Her stubbornness is condemning us all to extinction.

But I know far better than to say so outright.

Instead I pull in a steadying breath of crisp cold air and cling tight to my patience. "Even if you never ascend, you still need to learn to control this power. You've already killed with it, Zarina—"

"Damn it! I keep telling you, it's Zara." Her voice rings over the rooftops, echoing with a resonance that makes her peacoat float and her eyes glow violet. "You won't even listen to me about *that*, much less my feelings about my so-called fate and my fucking witchcraft. God, don't you realize—?"

Her voice splinters and she shakes her head, hard and angry, blinking back a glitter of tears.

Over the wintry sea, I hear an ominous rumble of thunder.

"Do you even know what happened in Vegas?" she whispers, low and miserable. "I mean, do you *really* know?"

"I know what everyone in the witching world knows." I keep my voice level, professorial, my gaze fixed on the ocean to give her space. "I know eighty-seven people died in the Gemini Casino on the Las Vegas Strip. I know your mother was one of them. I've even seen the feed from the security camera before the grid went down. I know you and your mother both summoned lightning that night. I know you were a child and Belladonna was to blame."

She sucks in her breath and whirls toward me. Protest gathers like a storm in her turbulent face.

I raise a hand for patience and forge ahead. "I know your father used his bankroll and his mafia connections to bury the truth. According to the insurance records, his casino's destruction was a freak weather event. An act of God."

"An act of God," she repeats bitterly, swiping at her eyes with a mittened hand. "What a fucking joke. That's what my dad always calls the Gemini. He says we're gods. The truth is, we're *monsters*. Especially the women. Gemini witchcraft is too powerful to be controlled. Now you want me to summon it? My mom was psycho way before she lost it that night."

The truth of the burden this girl has been carrying trembles between us in the silence. The truth of what happened that night is a secret she's been running from her entire adult life. To free my queen's power, I must free her from her guilt.

And for that, I must exhume this buried truth.

"Your mother," I murmur. "Tell me about her. She studied here before my time."

"Mom?" Her brows draw together. She stares out to sea with a bittersweet smile. "She was more like a sister than a mom. A kid sister. Always dragging me off to some wild party or guerilla fashion show or unlicensed club where no one batted an eye to see a kid like me pounding shots with her mom."

A shadow darkens her eyes to indigo. "That's what we were doing that night at the casino. Every dealer and bartender under that roof knew who we were. If Belladonna Gemini wants to sneak her tipsy daughter into some mafia don's high-stakes poker game in a private room on a lark, who's gonna say no?"

I would.

I would have said no.

I would have protected her.

Instead, her entire clan apparently abandoned her to her unstable parent's poor judgment. Mick Gemini must have been worse than useless.

Her startled face turns toward me. Clearly, she's sensing all those fiercely protective instincts I'm struggling to contain. Somehow I contrive to unclench my fists and unlock my jaw.

"Your father," I manage to say without shouting, "should obviously have intervened."

"Oh, he tried at first, believe me. But eventually, he just gave up." Zara's lips tilt in a wobbly smile. "My mom… I loved her and all, but I mean it, she was psycho. Totally gorgeous, so she always got tons of attention. And she liked it really rough." Her voice lowers. "Like, brutal, you know? She'd go where she could find that, and I'd just do my own thing, find some game to play or whatever, while she got what she needed. And she liked… having a lot of guys at once."

She slides me a sidelong look, because of course I know Zarina—no, Zara, the name she prefers—is polyamorous. That's how Ronin and I captured our fugitive queen in the first place.

By paying her opportunistic lovers to betray her.

"Many of our queens are polyamorous," I say lightly, letting her know I pass no judgment. "From a genetic perspective, the arrangement is beneficial."

It's also damnably arousing. The thought of her and Neo getting Ronin off in the gazebo nearly set my trousers alight. That incendiary visual has been playing through my imagination on rewind since the moment Ronin confided in me—precisely as my mischievous mate knew it would.

Christ, I'm getting hard again now just thinking about it.

Fortunately, the voluminous folds of my caped greatcoat are capable of concealing a vast array of indiscretions.

I shift my stance to ease the pressure against my zipper and clear my throat. "Is this what happened that night? Did Belladonna lose control of her game?"

Zara presses her lips together and shakes her head. "She was fine at first. Just, you know, flat on her back on the poker table same as always, while they all took turns. I was behind the bar experimenting with martini recipes. Until… the don, the mafia guy who owned that game… decided he wanted me to join in."

Despite my determination to manage my own reactions in a way that keeps her talking, my chest rumbles in a growl of outrage. "You were fifteen. You should never have been in that room in the first place."

"Yeah, well…" She shrugs stiffly, but her voice sounds strangled. "Mom was busy, so I tried to joke my way out of it, but the guy wasn't taking no for an answer. Told him how old I was, but he didn't care. Then he got handsy, so I used my fists. But there were… a lotta guys in that room, you know? And he's the one calling the shots. Two or three guys, I can hold my own, but not when there's like twenty of them all sexed up."

A cold white rage blooms in my chest and my wolf claws at my skin. Dear God, in that moment I want to murder Belladonna Gemini myself.

I can barely bring myself to voice the question. "Were you… did they…?"

"Rape me?" She pivots to face me, her face hard and guarded. "No. When I started screaming, Mom finally realized what was going down. She was yelling for them to stop, but no one gave a shit. So she did what she always did whenever she couldn't get her way. She summoned the lightning."

"Merciful God," I whisper.

"Yeah, not so much." Zara hugs her waist and hunches over the wall. The cruel wind whips curly tendrils from her ponytail to lash around her face. "Mom's witchcraft was scary powerful. But her control was always shitty. Drunk and horny and pissed, she just about took the roof off that place. I realized pretty quick what was happening. That she'd lost *all* control. That people all over the casino were getting hurt. Even tourist kids just sightseeing with their parents."

Her throat moves as she swallows. "I'd never summoned lightning before, but I was coming into my power, and that's the first time I did it. I was trying to focus it on the men who were hurting us, but it was fucking bedlam in there, lights out, alarms screaming, the roof on fire, and she was fighting me, she was crazy, she wanted to kill every person in that casino. I was trying to control it but… Lucius…"

She covers her face with her mittened hands and drags in a ragged breath. "I hit *her*. The first and only time in my life I ever summoned lightning, I blasted my own mom. I blasted her to a fucking *cinder*."

This is it.

The secret truth she's been running from for five lonely years.

I want to wrap my entire body around her to shield her from the pain. I want to swear on my soul that I'll never let anyone hurt her. I want to rule at her side and make the entire witching world bow down to her in worship.

But every single thing I want with Zara Gemini is wrong.

The wind tears the black ribbon from her ponytail and sends it spiraling away in the wind. She pushes out a shaky breath, wipes her eyes with her mittens, and finishes in a whisper. "It was a mistake, all of it, I… can't even remember much after that. But when the dust settled, eighty-seven people were dead. Including her. And I'm the one to blame."

"Zara," I breathe, while my wolf whines and scratches at my skin. He wants out. He's desperate to comfort her. "My precious heart. You were just a child. Nothing that happened was your fault."

"No, but it was." She squares her shoulders and locks onto my gaze. Her hair flutters in the wind like blue-green flames. "Don't you get it? If I hadn't fought her… if I hadn't fought *them*… if I just let those guys do what they wanted—"

"No! Zara—just—no." As a scholar, words are typically my slaves, but today they utterly fail me. I know it's far from wise, but I can't help reaching for her.

Just to smooth the wild tangle of hair from her face.

I never wear gloves because my wolf won't tolerate them, he barely tolerates me wearing shoes, and ribbons of her untamed hair wrap around my fingers. I can't seem to stop myself from cradling her beautiful face between my clumsy hands and wiping away with my thumbs the silver traces of her tears.

Her skin is sleek as satin and cold as stone. Yet color and heat flood into her face under my touch.

My heart thunders, hard and fast, beating only for her.

"You can trust me, my queen," I rasp through the tightness that clenches my chest. "I swear I'll protect you. I swear I'll teach you to claim your power. And I swear I'll keep you safe."

Her thick lashes flutter against her skin and her teeth sink into her lower lip. "I want to believe you, Lucius. I do. If there's anything at all to that Royal Culpability theory, I don't want the four races to die. But… now you know what happened… what I did…"

"You were a child who suffered an appalling assault." My wolf bares his teeth in rage. "That will never happen to you again. If you hadn't killed those men, I swear on my soul I'd hunt them down and kill them myself."

Her mittened hand rises to land on my chest.

Even through all those layers between us, her chaste touch makes me burn for her.

"You think you'd kill for me?" she whispers, her face haunted. "You don't even know me. Maybe I deserve what happened."

I trace the sweet curve of her lower lip with my thumb. The immutable truth rises straight from my heart. "I may not know all of you. But I know that I'm yours."

"My teacher?" A whimsical smile plays over her lips. "My mentor? My courtier?"

"Yes, damn it, all of that." The words tear roughly from my throat. "If that's all you want from me."

Mischief flares in her turquoise eyes. I know with a swelling sense of inevitability that I'm doomed.

I'm hers.

She owns me.

I burn to shove her against the wall and wrap her legs around my waist and rut into her until both of us see stars. I ache to pin her face-first to the wall and pound into her from behind until she sobs with pleasure. I yearn to send her home with her panties shredded and her skin reeking of wolf and my seed dripping down her thighs, leaving absolutely no doubt in anyone's mind that our queen is thoroughly mine.

My palate tingles under the press of my fangs, and I know my eyes are glowing red.

She sucks in a gasp and holds my wicked gaze.

Then, playfully, she tilts her head and muses. "I'm told I seem to be in a claiming mood. How much can I claim of you, Lucius Aries?"

My wolf and I loom over her, my innocent witch of a student, like the monster in a Gothic novel. My voice comes thick with passion. "God help me, Zara. How much more of me do you want?"

"All of you," she whispers, head tipping back, her gaze falling to my mouth.

My fangs descend on cue, always and forever hers.

"That's it," she breathes. "I want what you're giving Ronin."

From somewhere deep in the riot of madness that overwhelms all reason in my mind, a fragment of caution surfaces. "My… disciplinary bite?"

Her mittens wrap in the folds of my greatcoat and ease me close to her succulent body. "It's a mating bite. You've claimed him. You and your wolf.

Haven't you?" My conflicted silence makes her face soften. "Well, I'm your queen and his. And I think you want to claim me too. Is that what you want?"

Dear God in Heaven, there's nothing on this earth I want more.

I want her to be completely mine in every way. I want her naked and needy and writhing beneath me, crying out my name when I empty myself inside her deep in the night. I want her nestled close to sleep between Ronin and me, trusting our strength to guard her slumber. I want her ruling the arcane races and saving us all from extinction like the powerful witch I know she can be. I even want to know if she has enough shifter DNA in her heritage to shift her form if I teach her. I want her loping through the woods under the full moon with my wolf at her side, so that he too can have her.

There's so very much I want.

But now, in this moment, what I want more than I've ever wanted anything in my life is to bite her and mate her.

The deep shuddering toll of the bell, shocking in its volume, makes my bones vibrate.

Zara and I leap apart with a guilty start. She claps her mittens to her ears with a laughing wince. Thwarted in my criminal desire to obliterate this final flimsy barrier of propriety between us, I find I can release her and even back away a step—but no farther.

My wolf is maddened to be denied our prize.

I steel myself against the noise and thrust my hands deep in my greatcoat pockets. It's impossible to bite her or court her or even speak to her amid all this great racket, so I have until the last gong to collect my shattered poise and reinforce my fractured resolve. I've arranged a double period in her academic schedule for this independent study, so no one else can claim this time with her. She's mine.

Ours, my wolf mutters, doggedly insistent. *We should claim her.*

Somehow I turn away from her, this witch queen who's bespelled us both, and prowl the belfry's crowded confines to cool my blood.

We've begun to make halting progress, she and I, toward the only objectives I'll allow myself to acknowledge—her command of her power and her ascension to the throne. My own desire to claim her must be subordinate to the greater good. Our imperiled people deserve no less.

By sheer force of will, I retract my fangs. By the time the bell falls silent, I've stoked my determination and mastered my lust.

With the temptation of my queen placed safely out of sight behind me, I square my shoulders and announce crisply to the rooftops, "Very well, Ms. Gemini. Let us begin our first lesson with a simple exercise. There's plenty of ocean all around us and nothing there to be avoided. That's where I'd like you to summon the lightning."

Chapter Twenty-Four
Zara

The taste of ozone still lingers on my tongue. Even though it's been hours since my lightning lesson with Lucius in the belfry.

Our group dinner in the *domus* leaves a lot to be desired. I'm frustrated and on edge from my unsuccessful effort to blast past five years of resistance and actually summon the damn lightning that seems to be always fizzling at my fingertips.

Today, the lightning was a no-show. My witchcraft was totally uncooperative. Probably because, even if I planned to buy into this whole insane premise that somehow it's supposed to save the witching world, I'm still pretty damn conflicted about summoning it.

Story of my life.

And doesn't that just fucking figure?

Ronin's sexed up from his bite again and eyeing Lucius across the dinner table with a smoldering purpose in those tiger eyes of his that makes me hot every time I look at him. Someone's going to be fucking him tonight, and I'll love if it's Lucius.

Especially if I can figure out some way to wiggle past my headmaster's professorial ethics and get in on that male-male action.

Vasili's still pissy and possessive and pretty much impossible to deal with. When he isn't leveling long smoking looks at Ronin that nearly make the guy's clothes ignite, he's at his most abrasive. Bristling with open aggression toward Lucius, Neo, and me like he hates all our guts.

Which means Vasili is jealous.

Every word he says makes me want to punch him in the face.

Even my normally sunny-tempered Neo is distressed by "only" getting a B on his Honors Science of Witchcraft quiz, since he wasn't exactly boning up (at least not for his test, ha ha) last night in my bed. For him, a B is apparently some sort of disaster.

This prompts a caustic comment from Vasili about Neo losing his precious perch on the Dean's List that doesn't help Neo at all. Between irate looks at Vasili, Neo mutters feverishly about some alchemy experiment he has to keep an eye on in the lab at the Dean's tower tonight.

Evidently, keeping that A in Honors class is a life-or-death thing for him.

To be honest, I'm a little disappointed. Because I was sort of hoping Neo meant what he said about spending more time in my bed. Not that I want him moving in or anything because, again, I'm leaving. But I won't totally mind if, until then, he bunks down at night with me.

Then I berate myself for being selfish. The closer Neo and I get, the harder it's gonna be when I leave.

For both of us.

At least his alchemy experiment means Neo won't be a problem when I slip out at midnight to meet Vasili.

As for Lucius, he's clearly alarmed by the barely averted calamity of almost biting me in the belfry, worried to distraction about his thing with Ronin, and increasingly annoyed by Vasili and his antics.

Overall, our headmaster looks like he'd rather be spending the night in Hell than here.

Racetrack and Dez can barely wait to empty their plates of the succulent shepherd's pie and salad Ronin rustled up for dinner. (A man who cooks! Heart, be still.) They do their time on dishwasher duty and abandon the rest of us to our mercurial moods.

I do a little prep for my gig with Vasili, then try studying in my bedroom, curled up with my books on the rug near the fire. Because I'm not getting any less behind in my classes.

But it's literally impossible to concentrate.

I can't believe I actually *asked* Lucius to bite me.

True, I've felt so incredibly drawn to him since the night I woke up on that airplane to find him practically fucking Ronin against the wall, especially when he acted so tender and repentant after. I'm simultaneously grateful and disappointed that our prof didn't bite me too.

Actually, no, I'm not disappointed at all.

I'm just grateful. Really.

The last thing I need is an emotional bond with another Icarus Academy warlock.

And I still can't believe Lucius actually got me to try summoning lightning. I'm both relieved and perplexed that I couldn't.

Long story short? The sooner I get off this rock, the better.

Before I lose the old me completely and become the dangerously powerful queen they're all demanding.

It's almost midnight when I slip out of the *domus* to meet Vasili at the fountain. The cruel cold bites my cheeks and fogs my breath, but Lucius' downstairs window is wide open (no wonder the house is drafty!) I figure maybe his wolf is out, and I better be careful not to run into him.

According to the house rules, curfew starts at ten. And, like I saw with Ronin's bite, our headmaster's hardcore in the discipline department.

Not to mention the tension between the two of us is torqued pretty tight. I honestly don't know what got into me, *asking* for his fucking bite. Thank Christ he didn't do it. All we need right now is two of us in this house with mating fever.

Fuck knows I'm already sexed up. I might not be planning to stick around, but I can't deny I loved what went down with Neo and Ronin and me, and I'd love to see how far we could take that.

In my current revved-up state, even thoroughly gay Vasili's a sexual distraction.

At least until that snake opens his mouth and ruins all that sexy by talking.

I hurry down endless flights of stairs, zigging and zagging toward the sea, boots crunching softly through a crust of freshly fallen snow. At first, a few fat flakes float in the intermittent glow of the old-fashioned streetlights (the few that still work). By the time I reach the big piazza in front of the church, the air's thick with whirling flakes.

I'm about to venture out of the narrow street into the open when the furtive crunch of a footstep sounds in the snow behind me.

My heart leaps into my throat and lodges there like a peach pit.

Adrenaline spurting, I spin toward the noise. Suddenly I'm super aware there's a queen killer on the loose. And I'm deeply missing that stiletto I lost on Wang's penthouse roof.

But the shadowy zigzag stairs that climb behind me are empty. My solitary footsteps dimple the snowy drifts.

Still, the back of my neck is crawling. Suddenly I'm not so crazy about breaking cover and popping into the open with a big *ta-dah!* for whoever's fucking with me.

But I'm even less crazy about lurking in this alley.

I put on my game face and saunter into the piazza like the queen I am. Right away my chest unlocks and that closed-in feeling recedes.

Whatever was bugging me was definitely in that alley.

I huff out a frosty breath and beeline to the fountain, all encrusted with icicles that glitter like crystal daggers in the light of a far-off streetlamp. There's no sign of that snake Vasili, and I swear to God, he better not have stood me up—

With silent grace, a slim dark shape drops from the snow-filled skies and lands gently on the cobblestones in front of me. I leap back and squeak in surprise like a fucking mouse. Then I make out Vasili's smug smirk and curse myself for giving him the satisfaction.

"Cheese on toast, can you really fucking *fly*?" I grouse. "On top of all your other charming traits?"

Because I was kind of hoping I hallucinated him flying in the courtyard yesterday after his secret Ronin sex-fest when he chased me through the *domus*.

"Weren't you listening in Genetics class?" His amused voice slithers through the falling snow. "Levitation is a Mogadon gift."

"Yeah, but you're only supposed to have *one*," I point out irritably, brushing snow from my peacoat with my mitten. "You're already telekinetic."

"I'm a very powerful warlock," he says lightly. "There's a reason I'm the Scorpio scion, destined to rule my clan. Best to bear that in mind if you ever cross me, princess."

Yeah, just go ahead and give me a warning I don't effing need, you pit viper. And the fact that he stands there looking like a glam '80s rock star while he's doing it just annoys me more.

He's given the regulation Academy peacoat a hard pass in favor of a black slim-cut coat that whispers around his boots and a ribbed standing collar that frames his silver hair. Faux military medals glitter on his chest and some sort of pale fur nestles against his long throat. Plenty of room in all those layers for him to hide his knives. He's like a cross between a runway model and a fairytale prince.

He's the Goblin King. He's lethal in so many ways I can't even count.

I hate him and I want him.

He watches me watching him and his head tilts like he's trying to figure me out. And the silence is getting awkward, so I shove my hands in my pockets and say curtly, "That was you back there in the alley playing games with me, wasn't it? I want you to knock it off."

"In the alley?" His silver brows draw together. "No. But we do have shifters on this island, and the moon is nearly full. So we really shouldn't dawdle in the open. Do you want inside the dive shop or not?"

It's all there in his voice, every word edged with challenge. He thinks I'm all hat and no horse, that I'm not really serious about this whole *Escape from Alcatraz* caper.

That's only because he's never seen me on a heist.

"I want," I say flatly.

Which, for some reason, makes his pale eyes flash like lightning. He glides toward me through the snow. I have to make a conscious effort to stand my ground.

"Tell me, little queen, precisely how badly do you want?" he breathes. "Badly enough to trust me?"

My heart's slamming against my breastbone like it wants to get out. I dredge up my tough-girl voice, but I need to work at it. "Yeah, Goblin King, and that's pretty bad. But don't even think about trying anything, or I'll put you on your glamorous ass."

He huffs out a little chuckle and I give him a warning glare, but my entire body is tingling. By now, he's standing way too close for my peace of mind. I can actually smell him, the potent scent of sandalwood and Ronin's ambergris, spiked with a kick of caramel.

He's scenting.

For some reason.

But it's him coming into my space, not me threatening him in his.

"Someday, Zara Gemini, you and that mouth of yours," he murmurs, his dangerous gaze dropping to my offending mouth, "are going to land you in real trouble."

"Yeah, that's what they tell me." The cold kiss of a snowflake lands on my upper lip. I lick it off and watch his lips part over his sexy little fangs.

I swallow hard and whisper, "Dive shop."

"Indeed." With reptilian speed, he swoops in, wraps an arm around my waist, and sweeps me up against his tall slim frame. "I do hope you're not afraid of heights."

"Hey—" My feet leave the ground and my protest unravels in a short scream. "Fuck! *Vasili*—"

His laughter unfurls like a silk scarf in the snowy air.

We're fucking airborne, the piazza falling away under my dangling feet with stomach-dropping speed. I clutch the Goblin King's sinewy frame with every limb I've got and wrap my whole body around him. If I had a tail, I'd have that wrapped around him too.

Icy wind laced with snow buffets my face and whips under my fluttering coat. Which makes me really glad I'm wearing leggings and a cable-knit sweater underneath instead of that freaking uniform. The disorienting sight of slanting rooftops whizzing past makes me yelp—another noise I'm not proud of.

This guy seems to specialize in getting them out of me.

I need to throttle back on all this sensory overload and get a grip, so I bury my face in his neck. His dark fragrance wraps around me and seeps through my brain and invades every pore in my body. I pull in a long slow breath of him and his pheromones. I know my body's hard-wired to respond the way it does to the biochemicals in his scent.

But I'm still thankful when my terrified pulse ratchets down a notch.

Yeah, we're fucking flying, but he isn't dropping me or even toying with me the way I expect. His arms, wrapped around my waist, hold me clasped against him nice and steady. Under my clutching limbs, he's all streamlined slimness and silky heat.

My lips part against the sleek column of his neck and my shaky exhale rushes past his skin. His head angles down and he rubs his chin against my hair.

Now he's scenting *me*. And there isn't one damn thing I can do about it.

"Vasili." I whisper the weakest protest in history into his neck, lips moving against his skin.

His throat vibrates in a hum, almost an actual purr, against my lips.

I barely resist the sudden temptation to drag my tongue down his neck. Just to see if he tastes as good as he smells.

Of course, if I pull something like that, he'll probably drop me.

"Well." He clears his throat. "Zara?"

Shit. That sounds like amusement in his voice. I hope like fuck I wasn't just projecting. "Yeah?"

"We've arrived. You can let go now."

Shit.

My head pops up with a gasp. Turns out we are indeed stationary on the flat roof of a low building next to the ocean's black expanse. Through thick curtains of falling snow, pale curls of foam appear and vanish with a whisper all down the crescent beach. Around us on the roof, there's a clutter of patio furniture heaped with virgin snow. A skylight yawns at our feet.

And I'm wrapped around Vasili Romanov like the heroine in a bodice ripper romance. Which is totally fucking mortifying.

Even though, for some reason, he hasn't let go of me either.

Probably enjoying his temporary advantage over me way too much to end it. Because, one, I was more freaked out than any self-respecting professional cat burglar should be during that whole Superman-Lois Lane ascent. Two, I was turned on as fuck by the whole experience. And three, the Goblin King fucking knows it.

I hop down to the roof and scramble out of his arms with as much casual as I can muster. Which, admittedly, isn't all that much. I concentrate on brushing the snow off myself so I don't have to see his smug smirk.

"Thanks for the ride." I glance around the cluttered roof, which looks like Party Central in the summer. "Dive shop, huh?"

"Hmmmm." He flips up his high collar and drapes his tall frame elegantly over the crescent loop of a swinging hammock. "I wasn't able to winkle the key from Racetrack without tipping her off to our secret accord. But I've done my bit and gotten you here. Now it's your turn to deliver... if you can."

Skepticism lurks in his voice.

If he expects a little thing like a locked skylight to stop me, he really doesn't know me very well.

"Good thing I came prepared." I saunter over to the skylight and fish out of my pocket the Phillips screwdriver I pinched from the tool chest in the furnace room. I've got a flathead tucked away too, because I like to have options, but I can already see the Phillips is what I need.

Even though I really miss my actual gear, last seen stowed under a sink on Wang's vacant penthouse floor, which I'll probably never see again.

Swallowing a sigh, I pull out a mini-flashlight, switch it on, grip it between my teeth for light, then hunker down and get to work.

First I case the setup for security cams or alarms, but I'm not seeing any. The little hatch is locked from the inside (of course), but this dive shop isn't exactly Fort Knox. I've got the skylight unbolted and swung aside in—I glance at my dive watch—just under three minutes.

Which isn't too shabby considering I just did the whole job with shit for gear in heavily falling snow. With Vasili freaking Romanov idly swinging in a hammock and watching me the whole time.

"Impressive," he murmurs, inspecting the toe of one gleaming boot and not even looking at me. "Not just a pretty face, are we?"

Does he even notice a pretty face if it doesn't come with a cock as part of the package? Yeah, probably just a figure of speech. "Toss me that clothesline, will you, Goblin King?"

One eyebrow climbs with his trademark disdain. But he idles out of his hammock and slinks over to bring me what I need, which is the rope from the clothesline that probably holds dive gear and bathing suits to drip dry in the summer sun. I loop one end around a fixture and knot it tight.

"You're not planning to come in with me, are you?" I meet his curious stare, since he's still looming. "Because I can definitely handle things from here. And I'll find my own way back."

That comes out more belligerent than I planned, but he's making me nervous with his lurking.

"So gracious." He sneers like the comic book villain he is. "Yes, I'm coming in. It's not as though you're capable of keeping me out. Color me curious about your diabolical plan for getting off this island and past the wards without the Dean's consent, since no other student has ever managed the feat."

"Well, shit, you just made it interesting." I swing a casual leg over the skylight sill. "Bet you can't make it down here my way, can you, bad boy?"

Then I trot out my Catwoman superpowers, clamp the flashlight between my teeth, and slither down the rope into the darkened interior. It feels good to use my muscles for something I'm trained to do, and maybe I'm showing off a little, making the whole descent a little slinkier than it needs to be.

I land lightly on the ground floor, reposition my flashlight, perch my hands on my hips, and shoot a challenging look up at my nemesis.

Vasili's silhouetted in the skylight against a canvas of falling snow, his face invisible against the dark curl of the collar rearing like a cobra hood behind his head.

"You think I can't manage a little rope play?" he calls down to me.

And something about the way he says it heats my skin like I've been dipped in oil and tossed in the deep fryer.

"That's right, Goblin King," I call back to him, jerking his chain for fuck knows what reason, except I like pushing him. "I don't think you can handle it."

Which, of course, only prompts him to slither over the rim like the serpent he is and uncoil down my rope with reptilian grace, like a fucking rope dancer at the Cirque de Soleil. He drops silently to my side and arches that same infuriating eyebrow.

"You were saying?" he murmurs.

What I'm thinking is, it was a major turn-on watching him wrapped around my rope. But that's definitely *not* what I'm saying.

"If you really want to impress me, wait till it's time to go back up." I force a shrug and turn away, determined to focus on the gig and not his extremely distracting presence.

I play the beam of my little flashlight over the shop.

Its familiar contents leap into view, because dive shops everywhere tend to have a certain look. Racks of dive gear looming, a row of paddleboards bracketed to the wall, a wooden kayak suspended slantwise from the ceiling.

I'd look for the light switch, but I haven't forgotten that spooky feeling of being watched in the alley, and I'm not eager to draw attention.

I mosey over to the dive gear and start thumbing through the racks, aided by the shore light that streams through the frosted windows in front. A rack of neoprene shorties for tropical dives does me no good at all, but I'm hopeful that given these wintry seas, someone might actually have invested in a decent dry suit.

That's what I'll need to swim in these waters, along with plenty of nitrox, a decent compass, and some good night gear.

There's nothing obvi out front, but there's a windowless back room which is more likely to hold specialty gear. I weave through the tight confines behind the sales counter into the back, my flashlight playing over the space.

Right away, I see what I need. A spurt of excitement zings through me and I beeline over to investigate.

Bingo.

I'm eyeing a black neoprene dry suit with hood and dive boots, vacuum-sealed at wrists and neck. It's pretty clear this is a guy's suit, but the label says size small, and I bet I can make this work. I'll just need to test the suit and do a practice dive before I entrust my life to it—

"Please *do* tell me," Vasili says suddenly from the doorway, which gives me an annoying start, "you aren't honestly contemplating the insane suicide stunt you actually appear to be contemplating. Which part of freezing water inhabited by a great white shifter who hunts close to shore due to the island wards have you failed to comprehend?"

"He can't always be in the water," I point out patiently, because I've obviously thought this through, having no desire to climb into the water with a Jaws-like antagonist myself. "He has to be in class sometimes like a regular student, doesn't he? I'll just suss out his schedule and go when he's taking a test or something. And once I'm past the wards, he won't be able to follow."

He folds his arms and lounges against the doorframe. "Perhaps I'm a bit slow to grasp the essentials, but I trust you'll indulge me. Precisely how are you planning to get past the wards yourself?"

"Well, that's where you come in, oh great and powerful warlock. You and your mad levitation skills," I drawl, rummaging through the dry suit. I'll quickly pop in and out of the water with it tonight just to check for any immediate problems. "I was originally gonna put you in a powerboat or maybe a kayak if I thought you could handle it, but now you can just fly out there. Because I've got a little theory about those wards, which you're gonna help me test. And you'll do it without bitching in order to finally get rid of me."

"Oh, for fuck's sake. I'm not a passenger pigeon. Surely you *must* be joking—"

A tinny jingle from out front cuts him short. The distinctive sound of the bells hanging on the front door—the *locked* front door, because I did check before I came back here—designed to do their thing whenever anyone comes into the shop.

Vasili and I freeze in mid-bicker, staring at each other in the shadows.

The floor creaks under the weight of a footstep.

Instantly I switch off the flashlight. Vasili slides into the darkness of the back room at my side.

Of course it's way too late to hide, since we were just arguing at a pretty decent volume. My heart's hammering way up in my throat. I'm revisiting that creepy feeling of being watched in the alley, and the butchered koi on our front step, and the queen killer who still hasn't been caught.

I don't enjoy the feeling of being hunted.

In fact, I hate it.

Vasili presses something cool and smooth against my palm. I glance down at the pale gleam of steel and realize he's just given me one of his knives.

And despite being trapped in the windowless back room of this dive shop and hiding from someone who's hunting me and who probably killed the last queen, a warm glow spreads through my chest.

Let's split up by the door, I urge silently. Vasili doesn't answer and he's not Valyrian, but I am, and somehow I know he can hear.

I slink one way and he slips the other, putting the door between us. I'm betting no one's coming through without getting a good telekinetic whack from Vasili. And anyone who manages to get past him gets me and this pigsticker and my mixed martial arts to contend with. That might get a little messy.

A tall shadow fills the door. My breath stalls in my throat.

Vasili steps into view and his arm sweeps up, face absolutely lethal with intent.

A hand darts past the lintel and hits the light switch. The tall halogen lamp in the corner lights up with an electric hum.

"I'd suggest you hold your bloody fire, love, because I'm already seriously ticked off," our new arrival says curtly. "Bad enough the two of you light out together without me, leaving me completely fucking alone in that house to contend with this fucking heat. What in blazes d'you think you're doing in here?"

"Ronin," I gasp, lowering my knife—I mean Vasili's knife—with a scowl. "For cripes' sake, why didn't you give a shout-out? We literally could have killed you. And how did you even know where to find us?"

"Clairsentience." Ronin sweeps back his long hair with an irritable shrug. "I have a telepathic bond with him, and you're not exactly hard for me to sense either."

These warlocks and their telepathy. It honestly doesn't seem fair.

But I'm realizing more and more the advantages of training a gift like that.

"How'd you get through the front door?" I demand.

"How do you think? When I realized where Vasili was taking you, I asked Racetrack to loan me the bloody key." For some reason, Ronin sounds irate. "And if you imagine for one tick you're putting on that dive suit and taking a little dip in the ocean the night before a supermoon, you're mental."

So he's been listening in on me telepathically as well.

Great.

Vasili strolls over to an oversized futon and sprawls gracefully into it. "You might as well save your breath, darling, *do*. Our little queen's made up her precious mind to abdicate. If she wants to get herself drowned or dined upon by our resident great white in the process, at least we'll have her letter of abdication to bring down the monarchy."

If anything, Ronin looks more annoyed than he did before. He's wrapped in the leather pants he wore in Wang's penthouse and a vintage military wool coat with snowflakes melting in his sleek black hair, with a murderous gleam in his golden eyes.

He pivots to confront me with a scowl. "Oh, that's bloody brilliant, that is. You're going to kill yourself, and he's going to help you."

If he isn't careful, I'll be starting to think the thought of me killing myself actually bothers him. Notwithstanding his hatred of all things Gemini.

It's a concept that's foreign to me—someone, anyone, actually giving a single shit what happens to me—but I don't totally mind the soft gooey warmth that spreads through my chest.

It's the same way I felt when Vasili gave me his knife.

"Never mind his abominable temper," Vasili says silkily to me. "He's sexed up and it makes him pissy. Which is precisely why he's followed us all the way here in the first place, by his own admission. Aren't you, darling?" Ronin snarls at him, and Vasili's face softens. "Did we really leave you all alone at the *domus*?"

"Lucius is out running with his wolf," Ronin mutters. "Neo's at the tower minding his science experiment. That leaves Racetrack and Dez, who are hardly a fucking option, are they, mate?"

"Hmmm, you really *are* worked up. Well, now that you're here…" Vasili purrs, stretching his sexy body across the futon and opening his long coat.

Everyone in the room pretty much stops breathing.

Because that's definitely a sexual invite.

Vasili just put it right out there.

And the thought of those two doing it right here on this futon makes me wonder if maybe, this time, the Goblin King will let me watch.

I don't guard the thought—like, *at all*—and Ronin's gaze veers from Vasili to me. That predatory look in his hungry face just about lights my panties on fire.

"You'd best believe I didn't tramp all the way down here at midnight through the worst snowstorm of the season just to perform for you, love," Ronin growls. "I intend you to do far more than watch. Both of you."

Okay, now it's official. I definitely can't breathe.

Because Ronin's just said right out loud the fantasy I've been getting off on since I spied on the two of them going at it.

The fantasy that's been relegated firmly to the make-believe room in my head because Vasili hates me and I hate him and, you know, he's gay.

"Go ahead and hate him all you like," Ronin murmurs, unbuttoning his own coat and prowling toward me and completely avoiding the issue of Vasili's sexuality.

He drops the garment to the ground, which lets me fully appreciate the visual of Ronin Pendragon wrapped in a silky charcoal button-down shirt open halfway down his chest so his dragon tattoo is showing, and the sway of his hips in those sinful leather pants.

Maybe Vasili's sexuality can be dealt with later.

"I'm not saying you have to fuck him," Ronin drawls. "But I'd fancy quite a bit fucking *you*. And, while I'm at it, being fucked by *him*."

Sweet Jesus, Ronin. Talk about an offer I can't refuse.

Chapter Twenty-Five
Vasili

Ronin Pendragon knows better than anyone on this planet how to get me off like a ballistic missile, and he knows precisely how to deliver the payload. Which is why he's always known that what gets me off has never been a woman in my bed.

But my boyfriend may have just outlined one proposition involving a woman that I'm rather tempted to entertain.

With Ronin burning up with mating heat and my own body throbbing with the telepathic impact of all that raw need, I find I'm not nearly as violently opposed to the notion of this particular woman in my bed as I always fancied I would be.

It's been abundantly clear to me from the outset that Ronin's obsessed with the little Gemini. He started out hating her and blaming her for happened to Gwen. Determined to make her pay for her odious brother's unforgivable sins. Now it seems Ronin's finally beginning to appreciate the fact that it's the odious brother and not the little queen herself who's actually to blame for the tragedy of Gwen's suicide.

By now, it's also perfectly obvious that my boyfriend—the elusive fuck all his heartbroken leftovers at this Academy have dubbed Sir One and Done—is perilously close to falling for the Gemini queen.

I'm the one he returns to, so I've never felt threatened by his casual conquests.

But this girl is far more than casual.

And she's far from being a conquest.

Consequently, I'm not at all certain how I should feel about this mettlesome female.

God knows, I started out hating her for my own reasons. Reasons that are quite dear to my rotten little anti-monarchist heart. But even I'm compelled to admit this queen is nothing like Cybelle or any other prissy bitch of a royal whose existence I've terrorized.

This particular queen is actually… rather… intriguing.

She's sassy. Stubborn. Strong. Formidable. Fearless. And the way she stands up to me and provokes me at every turn ignites me to meet her challenge.

In consequence, I find that I'm actually rather… curious… to experience the electric connection that sparks between Ronin and Zara.

To experience that connection *intimately*.

My gaze shifts to her—this iconoclast of a queen who's turned the entire Academy on its ear. She's staring at me from across the room with her wild tangle of blue-green curls tumbling down her back and her big eyes glowing with ultraviolet fire. With a jolt, I sense she might actually be entertaining the notion of letting me watch while she fucks him.

And I already know exactly how much she enjoys watching *me* fuck my boyfriend's sulky mouth.

This time, I might not mind quite so much.

Unexpectedly, under the gaze of this troublesome queen, my cock tightens and swells.

"Well, love," Ronin says huskily, lids dropping over his burning stare. "You can see he isn't exactly opposed. And you're not typically the shy one when it comes to saying what you'd fancy. Would that turn you on? Watching him fuck me? While I'm fucking you?"

Her lush mouth opens and she licks her lips. "I'm, uh, supposed to test the dry suit."

"You do realize," I say, voice rasping in my throat, "he's in the water right fucking now? I'm talking about Malcolm, the great white shifter. He always swims when the moon waxes, just like Lucius runs and Bjorn—the polar bear—hunts. You'd best put that dry suit aside until tomorrow if you intend to survive your immersion, little queen."

Of course, if she does become shark bait, that's one way to solve our monarchy problem. The difficulty is, though I'm not at all certain how it's happened, somehow I seem to have decided to help our rebel queen survive.

At least to survive the night.

Perhaps it's because she's checking out my body sprawled across the futon in a way that makes my skin ignite.

"I'd be fucking him and not you," she warns, her voice low and husky.

"Ob-vi-ous-ly." I bite off the syllables with a snap. I'm annoyed that she seems to feel the need to clarify. This *obviously* isn't a conversation about the two of us fucking.

Between the three of us, the silence stretches taut.

Ronin's on fire and pulsing with a sexual heat so intense all three of us are sweating.

Slowly, without breaking my gaze, Zara reaches for the halogen lamp and twists the knob. The light in the cluttered storeroom plunges from bright gold to a deep amber.

"Okay, Adam," she breathes. "Go over there and sit on the Goblin King's lap."

Possibly, she truly is meant to rule. Because one command delivered in Zara Gemini's sex voice is more than sufficient to give me the full-blown boner I've been fighting since the moment Ronin burst in here with his incendiary proposition.

Of course it's Ronin I'm hard for.

Not her.

He shifts into motion and saunters toward me, a sultry grin curling his fuckable mouth. "You'd best believe you won't be calling some other bloke's name when I'm fucking you, love."

She doesn't even miss a beat. "I'll call you whatever I fucking please, Adam."

"Hmmm," I chuckle, appreciating the byplay between them. "It appears our queen's a film fan. She seems to prefer the villains. You're Kylo Ren and I'm the Goblin King."

"For fuck's sake," Ronin mutters. But that sexy smile is still lurking when he straddles my legs with sinuous grace and settles over my lap.

His scent and his heat envelop me. The reek of Lucius' wolf lurks like a threat under the dark musk of ambergris. Ronin's cock shoves up hard against his leathers, so succulent he's making my mouth water. My own flesh pulses with the phantom heat of his bite.

He tilts his head so all that long midnight hair pours over one shoulder and glances back at Zara. "This what you're wanting, then, love?"

"Let's just say it's a good start." She sidles a little closer to give herself a proper view and peels out of her peacoat. Underneath she's wearing leggings and a snug black sweater that clings to her Hollywood curves like a catsuit.

I can't wait to see what all those curves will look like wrapped around my boyfriend.

"Very well, little queen," I murmur, unbuttoning Ronin's silk shirt to reveal all that tawny skin I crave so relentlessly. "Ronin's bite needs tending. Why don't you amble over here and help our man out?"

Our man.

I've never shared our bed with anyone. Yet I'm startled to hear how right that phrase sounds when it's uttered in this context.

With her.

Ronin groans at my words and flexes his hips into my pelvis, letting me feel all that heat he's packing for both of us. I bite back a moan and rock into his dick. His eyes lock on mine, but he's waiting for her. He's waiting to hear what she'll say.

And she doesn't disappoint, this queen of ours. She prowls up behind him and peels the shirt I've opened for him right off his shoulders.

"Is that something you'd like, Ronin?" she breathes, eyes locked on mine. "My mouth on your body?"

"Fuck, yeah." He angles his head to give her a smoking look and reaches back to drag her in close. Now they're both straddling my lap, him lean and hard, her supple and sleek. She winds her arms around his waist and drags her tongue across the healing punctures of Lucius' bite, her upward gaze through her long lashes holding mine the whole time.

When the hot lick of her naughty tongue scorches through the bond between us, Ronin and I groan in unison. It's quite possible that sharing this encounter with two telepaths—both of them projecting—will positively kill me with pleasure.

I grip Ronin's hips and thrust my cock against his, frotting him through our layers.

"Nice," she whispers against his skin. "Now you two kiss."

I really couldn't say how we've ended up in this situation where she's calling the shots for all three of us, because typically that's my job.

But damn if I don't appreciate where she's taking us.

Ronin cups my face and leans in to explore my mouth. I open for him and savor the taste of him—the peaty burn of scotch he typically downs after dinner—and he gives me plenty of tongue, long slow licks that are for her pleasure as much as mine. I pull him closer, our tongues twining, my hands grazing our queen's commanding grip. The contact with her makes my palms tingle.

"That's so nice," she whispers, mouthing his bite, while he shivers and moans between us. Admittedly, I'm shivering a bit myself at her praise. "Can you feel what we're doing to him, bad boy?"

I carefully neglect to observe I'm not exactly immune to what we're doing myself.

"Driving me straight to bedlam, the both of you," Ronin mutters against my mouth. "And we're all wearing way too much."

His hand dips to my belt and flips open my buckle. My gaze meets Zara's in a moment of perfect accord.

"You heard the man," I whisper.

I hardly dare hope she'll heed any order I give. She gives me a long look that I can't read. Then her hands slide out from under mine to peel her sweater over her head.

Underneath she's barely wearing a thing, just a pretty white lace brassiere with a pink satin rosette stretched over her luscious breasts. They're firm and full, shoved up against all that lace and satin like they're yearning to be set free.

The jut of her tight nipples presses against the lace, along with the distinct ringed outline of twin piercings.

Have I mentioned I adore piercings in sex play?

Well, darling, consider it mentioned.

The sight of hers sends a jolt of electric energy arcing straight to my cock. Which isn't exactly a reaction I'm prepared for.

Of course, Ronin has me hot for him, a response he's diligently stoking with the filthy way he's rubbing his cock against me. Now that he's working my zipper open and I'm aching to feel his hand wrapped around my dick, it's easy to conclude my body is merely confused by all these stimuli.

Zara's eyes lock on mine like lasers as she reaches behind her to pop the clasp on her bra. The straps slip from her shoulders, but she catches the lacy scrap of fabric barely in time and holds it to her breasts.

The tease makes me catch my breath.

"Will this be okay for you?" she whispers, uncertainty flickering in her face. "I know you don't…"

I'm edgy, restless, hungry to see what her lingerie only hints at. I swallow hard and nod.

This is for Ronin, after all.

He needs her.

She swallows too, then lets the lingerie fall. At exactly the same moment, Ronin reaches into my minuscule lavender briefs and wraps his fist around my cock. A moan claws up my throat and I thrust into the familiar vise of my boyfriend's grip. But I can't seem to look away from her.

Zara.

Her dark rose nipples are swollen and erect, areolae blooming a pretty carnation pink against all that soft skin. Her perfect breasts are framed in pale triangles from the world's tiniest bikini, standing out against her Malibu tan, and I truly don't have the first damn notion why I'm so inflamed by the sight. Quite possibly it's those dainty silver rings piercing her nipples, which must make her so sensitive there to touch.

"Like what you see, don't you?" Ronin whispers in my ear, nipping my earlobe.

I moan in response, even though he hardly requires a verbal confirmation since he's in my head, he's feeling what I feel, and I'm so hard for him I'm nearly spilling in his hand.

It's him, it's what he's doing to me. And it's *her*. It's what he'll be doing to her.

"Stop thinking so bloody hard and just enjoy the show," he breathes. "It's not a bloody felony for you to enjoy this."

"This doesn't mean I'm straight," I feel the need to stipulate. Because I paid far too steep a price to admit I'm not to let my sexuality be called into question ever again.

"Gods, I fucking hope not," Ronin growls, nuzzling hard into my throat.

His need is riding him hard, but Zara clearly senses my conflict. She's holding back, that hint of vulnerability still lurking in her gaze. She glances toward her fallen sweater like she's seriously thinking about slipping back into it.

Well, we can't have that.

We're all in this together. We started this together. For some elusive reason I can't seem to articulate, we need to finish this together.

All three of us.

I release Ronin and grip Zara's hands. Tiny sparks of electricity pop and sparkle violet between us in the dim light. If what we're doing rings her bell, she'll probably blow every circuit on the block. Because she truly *is* that powerful, and the thought of setting her off like that should actually alarm me.

Instead, the notion clamps my cock in a fist of savage pleasure.

I bare my teeth in a snarl and grapple her closer. I love the way she's straddling my lap, the supple flex of her thighs wrapped around mine, the hot juncture at her core pressed against me.

"Vasili," she says on an indrawn breath, gaze pinned to my exposed fangs.

I manage to stop snarling, because of course my fucking fangs repel her.

Now her naked front is pressed against Ronin's naked back. He growls in sensual pleasure and strokes my shaft and sucks hard on my neck. The perennial worry over my fangs dissolves in a vortex of pain and pleasure.

"God, yes, mark me," I gasp into his stinging suck.

I want him savage and hurting me, which will free me to hurt him in return. When the two of us fuck, it's brutal.

Except this time, it's going to be the three of us.

I fumble to find Zara and press her palm flat over his leather against the thick bulge of his cock.

He rocks his hips into her touch and says thickly, "Going to fuck both of you so hard."

It's like the three of us are wired to a bomb and his words trigger the charge.

Suddenly she knows what to do, her deft little fingers popping the button on his pants and dragging down his zipper. Bless that girl for giving me an absolutely pornographic image of the swollen head of my boyfriend's cock shoving past his open zipper, already flushed and dripping with need, the heavy ring of his piercing simply begging for my tongue.

She works a hand inside to knead him. He fucks her fist, his breath heavy and labored in my ear. His passion pounds and rages through me. I lean in to swipe my tongue over his bite, because I too have shifter blood. And suddenly, this protective tending of him is something I too crave.

The knowledge that my mouth rests where hers was—my queen, my nemesis—sparks an erotic frisson that makes me savage.

I span the lean ripple of his ribs with my hands. Her silken arms graze mine. Static crackles and pops against my skin with every glancing contact. She's wired to blow, and he's burning up, he's hot to the touch with mating heat.

The longer he has to wait, the worse he'll have to suffer.

He drags up my shirt and I arch my back to help him, fighting free of my coat so he can peel the shirt over my head. I'm scenting like blazes and, damn, I want both of them positively reeking of my essence. I want both of them underneath me so I can control the pace of our pleasure.

"As much as I adore these leather pants of yours, darling," I purr at Ronin, "I do believe we'd both like to get you out of them."

Zara murmurs her approval and rolls to her feet, which frees him too to scramble up.

She toes off her boots and he seizes the moment to haul her into his arms and claim her in a primal kiss, one hand fisting in her hair to bend her back, the other hooking under her thigh to wrap her leg around him and rut into her. She shoves his pants lower and writhes against his cock, her sexy hips already finding the brutal rhythm they'll share when they're fucking.

I sprawl on the futon to enjoy the show, my eyes drinking them in, her sleek suntanned body wrapped around his tattooed frame, my ears soaking in their gasps and moans.

Dear God, I'm going to self-combust.

I slide a hand into my tight briefs, already drenched with my own precum, and wrap a fist around my aching cock. The pleasure's so intense my toes are curling. I slick my own fluid down my length and arch into my pumping fist, loving the audible liquid slide of flesh on flesh.

"Off," Ronin growls, dragging at her leggings. "I want to bloody see you naked when you suck my cock."

God, that's what I want to see too, our queen naked at his feet with his big dick in her mouth. A groan wrenches through me, and their heated eyes swerve to find me jacking off, thighs spread and trousers open, my bulging cock straining against my lavender briefs, appropriately embellished with a glittering rhinestone crown.

I swear the two of them look like angels, my Valyrian lovers, his eyes glowing golden and hers glowing purple, her hair floating around her shoulders like seaweed in a gentle current. My skin tingles with sexual charge, because it's perfectly clear she likes what she's seeing.

"I do like it," she breathes. "You're sexy as fuck, Vasili."

She's inside my head, my queen, we're bonding, and for some incomprehensible reason it's arousing as hell that it's I as well as Ronin who's flipping her switch. I gasp out a curse and tilt my head back and let them both watch.

"Gods, I need to be fucking you," Ronin growls. "Both of you."

The rustle of clothing snaps my head up in a hurry, because I don't want to miss a single moment of what's about to take place. Ronin's peeling her out of her leggings to expose the innocent white panties wrapped around her showgirl hips, panties that frame the streamlined legs of a runway model. I can't believe how gorgeous she is, with her Hollywood curves and her supermodel tan and her Penthouse piercings and her virginal panties.

But there's nothing virginal about the way she's dragging Ronin's pants off.

He's so hard for her, his thick cock absolutely rigid and dripping with need, his sleek skin gleaming with a fine sheen of sweat. The sight of him makes my heart hammer.

I literally can't wait to see her take his cock.

"And I can't wait to see him take yours," she breathes.

God, yes, there's no hiding anything from her. I don't even want to hide anything from her. I don't want to hide from anything that's about to happen between us.

"Come over here, darling," I murmur to Ronin. "I want you sitting on this futon and spread wide for us."

He gives me a smoking look. "I hope that means I'm about to feel both your mouths wrapped around my cock."

I grin, because my boyfriend never has a problem asking for what he wants, and tonight he's definitely going to get it. The thought of sharing his cock with Zara quickens the glide of my palm along my shaft. But I don't want to come just yet.

Somehow, I force myself to stop and stand and wait for them.

He saunters over and sits the way I want him, knees spread wide enough to expose not only his cock but his swollen sac, just begging to be tongued.

I don't want to wait, and I don't want her to wait either. Yet I hesitate, because this choreography might very well be about to create more intimacy with despicable me than our little royal has bargained for.

"Don't even," he growls, glaring at me. "I fucking need both of you. Are you not getting how totally okay she is with this setup?"

"I'm not a telepath, darlings," I whisper. "I need to hear the words."

"Vasili." Her fingers graze mine, and I welcome the tiny sparks that fly when we touch. Yet the discharge makes her grimace. "Damn! I'm trying to control that."

"Don't," I say roughly, turning my palm to meet hers, looking down into her upturned face. "Don't try to control a fucking thing. We can handle you and everything you throw at us. I just need to know what you want."

"I want you," she whispers, and my heart literally stops beating. "Kneeling next to me on the floor and sucking his cock."

Damn if the mere notion doesn't make me nearly come in my pants.

"Fortunately, that's one desire I believe I can fully accommodate." I sink to my knees between Ronin's legs.

He obligingly spreads wider to welcome both of us. From this vantage, I've a front row seat for his massive dick and swollen balls and even that sweet pucker I'll be pounding into until we all see flaming comets.

Roughly I grip his sinewed thigh to open him wider. My other hand works back under my briefs to find my own cock, which I can't seem to stop stroking.

She slides down beside me and wraps her hand around his shaft.

Ronin's panting for her, for *us*, but she's so captivating to watch as she licks up the underside of his dick and paints a glistening stripe from his balls to his tip. His fists clench and his thighs tense. She plays with his Prince Albert and circles the head of his cock with another long slow lick I can *feel*, oh God, I can feel her tongue through the bond I share with him.

"Vasili," he gasps.

"Darlings, I could watch the two of you all night." I give myself another few pumps. "But, after all, a promise *is* a promise."

I lean in to mouth his inner thigh and work my way up, tasting salt and Ronin on my tongue, my boyfriend's familiar taste. There's nothing I won't give him, nothing I won't do for him.

But I recall barely in time the imperative to guard my thoughts with two telepaths in the room, both of them linked with me and each other.

My love makes me vulnerable.

This is why it's a secret that's essential for me to hide.

Just below his groin I linger to administer my own stinging bite, marking him with savage purpose while he writhes and moans, though I'm careful not to puncture his perfect skin with my horrible fangs. Zara's working him in sweet earnest, her head bobbing up and down his shaft. I stroke the riotous tangle of her silky curls over one shoulder so I can admire her technique, which is absolutely stellar. I can feel the captivating suck of those plump lips like she's wrapped around my own cock.

By now they're both panting with lust, his cock soaked and glistening with her saliva.

My hand is slick with my own need, my pace quickening, and I'm truly going to have to work not to come too early before I even get inside him.

We're kneeling side by side, she and I. In these crowded quarters, a certain degree of intimate contact is inevitable. She's naked except for her tiny panties, and she has the softest skin, and she smells like roses and vanilla. I have the strangest urge to wrap my arms around her from behind and fill my hands with her lush breasts and torment her pierced nipples the way she's tormenting Ronin's cock.

Slowly her face turns toward me, lips damp and puffy, face flushed and lids heavy.

"Hey, Goblin King," she says, low in her throat. "I'll get him nice and ready for you. Lose the pants."

Fuck.

I don't think I've ever stripped faster in my life.

Somehow she's sensing what I need to hold myself together, which is to focus on what Ronin needs rather than all these overwhelming and unfamiliar needs of my own. These needs that my unprecedented proximity to her is bringing to the surface.

She thrusts a finger in her mouth to get it good and wet, then starts teasing his hole. And the thought of this queen on her knees prepping my boyfriend to take my cock nearly makes me explode.

Suddenly I don't want to wait another moment. And the beauty of this moment is that I don't have to.

Naked and tingling with all our need, ready to rut blindly into the damn futon, I swoop in to tongue his balls, a tease to which I know he's extremely susceptible. She's open to me too now, linked, so we're in synch. The moment I capture one of his balls between my lips and suck, she breeches him with her finger.

He cries out and nearly jackknifes off the futon.

"Fucking hell, the two of you," he gasps. "There's lube and condoms in my coat."

Of course there is, because he came here spoiling for a fuck.

Without lifting my head, I fumble blindly through his fallen coat, because she's occupied probing and stretching him.

Making him ready for me.

Still mouthing his balls, I find the lube and flip the cap and press it into her unoccupied hand. We're so close now, telepathically as well as physically, that it feels natural to slip my arm around her slim waist.

We're doing this together, after all, for him.

A ripple of tension moves through her. Then she softens into my touch.

She pauses the proceedings to lube up properly, and clearly this isn't the first ass play our queen has indulged, which comes as a lovely surprise. There's no conceivable way Cybelle would ever have slipped her royal finger in anyone's ass, even if Ronin and I had been willing to tolerate her.

Which we emphatically were not.

I mouth my way up his fat veined cock, this luscious cock I utterly adore, while my boyfriend loses his damn mind under our combined ministrations. I know the instant she penetrates him again, nice and slick this time, and I savor his long low moan as he undulates into her invasion.

He's really tight, she whispers in my head. *He's going to feel so incredible when you're buried inside him.*

I groan in heartfelt agreement.

She leans in close, tonguing his balls the way I did, then licking the base of his shaft while I play with his piercing and lap the precum from his slit.

Our faces are quite close, and I'm angling to give her as much room as possible and praying my loathsome proximity doesn't make her too uncomfortable, because with both our mouths working his cock in tandem, Ronin is truly and delectably losing it. Now we're sharing his cock between us. Her aqua eyes are all I see, riveted to mine as we share his pleasure.

Our lips are almost touching as we nuzzle his slick hard length.

But I scrupulously keep my distance from her soft sucking mouth.

I'm well aware that absolutely no one except Ronin has ever wanted an up-close-and-personal with my freakish fangs—

"Stop it," Zara whispers around his cock. "There's nothing wrong with your fangs."

"He's given himself a fucking complex," Ronin gasps, hands fisting desperately in my hair and hers. "He's absolutely mental about his blooming fangs."

"Because they're revolting," I snap. He's trying to nudge the two of us together, Zara and me, he wants us to kiss. But I'm doggedly resisting to spare her the horror show.

And, I suppose, to spare myself the inevitable rejection.

"Vasili," she says clearly, her gaze locked on mine. "Listen up, because I'm only gonna say this once. Your fangs. Are *so. Fucking. Sexy.*"

Something inside my chest splits wide open.

Something that I'm very much afraid may be my long-neglected heart.

I lunge forward on a moan and kiss her.

Chapter Twenty-Six
Zara

I can't believe I'm kissing the Goblin King.

God knows I've wanted to, pretty much from the second I first saw him terrorizing the entire student body from his tyrannical throne in the commons. I wanted him even after running the gauntlet of his reign of tyranny and barely surviving him myself. But he's been one hundred percent off limits this whole time because, one, he's anti-monarchist and I'm the new queen; two, he hates me for reason number one; and three, you know, he's gay.

But he just freaking *kissed* me.

And even though I'm shocked as fuck, it's pretty obvi that he's into what's going down between us.

He kisses like a hurricane, all wind and fury, sucking in my gasp and shoving his tongue in my mouth before I can even think about keeping him out. He kisses like he's famished and I'm the feast he'll kill to consume. He kisses like the world will freaking end if I don't kiss him back.

So I do.

I kiss him back.

I kiss him the way I'm dying to kiss him.

I kiss him to make him mine.

He kisses like an alpha, one hand cupping the back of my neck to hold me in a commanding grip. He tastes like Ronin's cock, sweetened with a trace of butterscotch from the sundae he had for dessert tonight. And the graze of his sharp little fangs against my lower lip adds a salty hint of blood to the Vasili cocktail I'm imbibing.

As for him, he's… horrified? Not because we're kissing (I hope) but mainly because those fangs he's so self-conscious over just made me bleed. We're linked now, all three of us, which means I can feel the cringing humiliation that spirals through him. He stiffens and starts to recoil.

But he won't be the first guy who's drawn blood in my bed.

And given these four scary warlocks I seem to be craving with all their scary power, he won't be the last to draw blood in my bed either.

No, don't pull away, you're sexy as fuck, I mean it, I whisper in his head. *Kiss me.*

He shudders in my arms and moans like his heart's breaking. This is his weakness. He secretly believes no one can ever possibly love him.

Well, he's wrong about that. Dead wrong. I'm his fucking queen.

He's mine to love.

I clasp his face between my hands so he can't pull back and drag my tongue over his sexy fangs. I don't give a shit if I'm bleeding. Kissing Vasili Romanov is like kissing a vampire, a completely mythical creature I've always found mesmerizing. I grew up reading J.R. Ward and Anne Rice and dreaming the vampire Lestat was real.

Beyond his fangs and my vampire fetish, he's sexy just because he's Vasili.

Ronin's fist clenches in my hair, and I know he's getting off on watching this, that he wants the two of us much closer. And this kiss might be about Vasili and what he needs, but this whole night's about pleasing Ronin and breaking his heat.

Plus, this night is for me. I want this. I want this for myself. I want this with both of them.

I rise to my knees and pull Vasili close. Until now, he's been a total gentleman—frustratingly so—about the two of us crouched naked (practically, since I'm still wearing panties) between Ronin's spread thighs. His restraint could totally be because I don't turn him on.

But I hope it isn't.

His hand comes chastely to rest on my waist, but there's nothing chaste about what I want to happen. I don't quite have the nerve to feel him up, and I think he might bolt if I do, but I'm searingly aware of his tensile length nudging my belly and the flood of caramel and vetiver that's thick in the air. He's hard and he's scenting. And when I stripped out of my sweater, he was definitely checking out my tits.

Just like I've been checking him out. And trying to do it without, you know, making him freak.

I open my eyes to sneak a peek. He has a ballet dancer's streamlined build and a serpent's supple grace. He's all sleek pale skin and hard little nipples I'd love to tongue. His shaggy silver layers are all tousled and his makeup is mostly gone, though he's still rocking a thick coat of cobalt mascara that makes his ice-colored eyes pop.

I lean in so my breasts brush his naked chest. Twin tingles race through me, from my nipples straight to my clit.

"Fuck, the two of you," Ronin mutters, fisting his own cock since we've both (temporarily) stopped blowing him. "I can't bloody hold out much longer."

This pulls Vasili and me apart, because we are one hundred percent united in our desire to get Ronin off. Also, there's a lot of turmoil and resistance churning through the Goblin King's head. His sexual identity matters to him— it matters a *lot*, it's central to how he sees himself—and what's happening right now is a truckload for him to process.

Heck, maybe he just got carried away by all those Mogadon pheromones he's pumping out and all the telepathic sex vibes he's picking up from Ronin and me.

Firmly squashing my own reluctance, because I really don't want to let Vasili go *at all*, I stand and shimmy out of my panties.

This gets both of them focused on me in a hurry.

I'm a Brazilian girl, I don't even cultivate a landing strip, so the sight of me naked doesn't leave much to the imagination. Vasili looks intrigued, eyes glittering like diamonds and riveted as he kneels at my feet and drinks in every inch of me. Without once looking away, Ronin rips open a condom and unrolls it down his shaft, his predatory gaze absolutely smoking.

Suddenly Ronin lunges, and I don't even see him coming. Fight-or-flight adrenaline spurts through me and lights up every synapse in my body.

For a heartbeat I think this setup is all one big con and here's when he evens the score for his twin's death and takes me out.

I'm dangerous to startle, and a hum gathers in my throat.

But before I can summon the lightning I swore I'd never call, he flips me flat on my back on the futon and crawls between my legs.

"That's so bloody beautiful, love," he says, low in his chest. "You standing there naked with your hair floating and your hands sparking and your cunt dripping, just waiting to be fucked. Didn't think you ought to be kept waiting."

I always knew there's a reason I like him.

Our mouths collide and his long silky hair cascades down around my face and my arms wrap around him, palms slicking down his sweating back. His cock tunnels into the soaking crevasse between my thighs and I tilt my hips to give him access. I'm so slick and ready, God, more than ready. Ready for him to thrust in deep.

And that he does, the shock of his thick rod burning as he stretches me. He grunts like an animal and a cry rips from my throat.

"Gods, yes," he groans into my mouth. "Shit, Zara, *yes.*"

"That's right," I pant. "I've got what you need, Ronin. Fuck me."

He eases back a breath, then his pelvis snaps forward. I hook my legs around his lean hips and rock into him. He grapples my arms from around his neck and pins them safely over my head, my dangerous hands that wield power I can barely control, his grip hard enough to leave bruises. He's out of his head with mating fever, pounding into me in a blind and brutal rut.

But I'm not afraid of this, he's mine, he's mine even if he doesn't know it, and his need is my need.

I meet every vicious thrust, every bit as wild and frenzied as he is, my teeth sinking into his lower lip hard enough to make him curse, the rapid slap of flesh against flesh noisy in the little room. He's hitting my sweet spot with every stroke, that Prince Albert he's rocking is literally God's gift to me in that moment, and I'm writhing and pinned under his heavy weight and just freaking loving it.

When I get my rocks off, this whole building's going to explode.

Especially when I see Vasili looming over us watching every pump while he rolls on a condom. He has an absolutely gorgeous cock, longer than Ronin's but not as thick, curving and supple like the rest of him, and my mouth is literally starving to suck the soul out of him.

But he's Ronin's boyfriend, not mine.

Damn it. I *cannot* lose track of that basic truth.

Even when what I really want is to claim them both.

Ronin clamps his mouth onto my neck and sucks hard enough to raise a bruise. I gasp under his stinging bite. Now I guess all three of us will be sporting them in various places, but I love that he wants to mark me. Vasili climbs onto the futon behind Ronin and, between thrusts, we all adjust for that. Good thing I got Ronin nice and lubed before I got so distracted kissing the shit out of Vasili, who might not even have wanted to be kissed. He even tried to recoil, didn't he? But I just wouldn't let him.

He probably only kissed me in the first place because Ronin wanted him to.

Sweet Jesus, what if I kiss-raped him?

If I did, Vasili must be totally fucking horrified.

Either way, he seems to have survived being kissed, and having a girl do the deed. He's recovered enough that he's working a few fingers into Ronin to test the fit, because Ronin buries his face in my shoulder and bites out a desperate curse.

"I prepped him already," I pant, tonguing his bite to comfort him. "Stop teasing him. He fucking needs you."

"This may come as quite the shock," Vasili mutters, eyes fixed on what he's doing, face ruthless with intent, "but I'm the master of ceremonies who's running this show."

Oh hell to the no. I know better than to give an alpha like him free rein in my bed.

But, admittedly, the sight of Vasili Romanov fisting his own cock and thrusting three fingers in Ronin Pendragon's needy hole *is* a major distraction.

Ronin's fucking me on every downstroke and fucking himself on Vasili's fingers with every recoil. The expression on his face is amazing, jaw clenched with determination, eyes blazing with need, brow furrowed with effort. Just that look on his face is almost enough to push me over the edge.

Especially with Vasili finally lining up to give Ronin the brutal reaming he clearly craves. My head pops up, because this I definitely want to see.

"Give me a moment," Vasili murmurs, but Ronin's not anywhere near ready to stop. The Goblin King's face hardens and he administers a stinging slap to Ronin's ass so hard my own ass burns in sympathy.

Ronin bites out another oath and freezes, ass in the air, just the tip of his cock still inside me. I whimper and writhe against him, perched right on the edge of my own big O.

"Now behave, darlings, *do*," Vasili purrs, gripping Ronin's hips and working his way deep inside. His lips part so his pointy little fangs are showing… and by now, I fucking *adore* those fangs… and his pupils blow wide and his face goes rigid with pleasure.

And fuck if he doesn't stare straight into my eyes the whole time.

Ronin groans and Vasili gasps and I breathe out a soft cry. These two men, the two of them together, they get to me in a way I can't even describe.

Vasili eases back and thrusts deep inside Ronin. Which thrusts Ronin deep inside me.

Now this I can get behind.

Vasili sets the pace for all three of us, and he's freaking relentless. My pussy is soaked and dripping with girl cream and Ronin's pinning me to the futon and riding me so hard I'll probably be sore for a week and Vasili, Jesus, he stares straight in my eyes the whole time he pumps like he's making love to both of us.

It's an intimate thing, watching someone's face while they fuck. I can see every flicker of pleasure and every tremor of need and every clench of hunger in his gorgeous face. And I can feel through the link how deeply he's enjoying the two of us giving Ronin everything he needs.

"Gods," Ronin moans through his clenched teeth. "The two of you. I love… love this so fucking much."

My heart rabbits around wildly, because I thought for a sec he was gonna say something else.

My climax is rushing toward me and my whole body's tingling, surging, driving toward that peak. Ronin's burning up and drenched in sweat and Vasili's pounding hard and fast into both of us and I'm crying out for both of them, the deep echo of the lightning voice edging my screams.

"Vasili," Ronin grinds out, "need you to come—all over me, love—to break this bloody heat."

Vasili locks onto my frenzied stare and bares his teeth in a brutal grin. "My… absolute… pleasure."

He pulls out, peels off the condom, gives his cock a few strokes so rough it looks like he might break it, then flings his head back and spurts ropes of creamy jizz all over Ronin's back.

That does it for Ronin, and that definitely does it for me. I'm shattered by it, by him, by the two of them together. I can feel the kick and spurt of Ronin's climax even through the layer of latex between us. My climax roars through me like an avalanche. My scream shorts the lamp out and plunges the room into darkness.

But my eyes are glowing so bright, so many purple sparks spraying from my hands which Ronin still has pinned over my head, that our three bodies are bathed in violet light.

Which is how I see Vasili lean in, drag his tongue through the river of his own seed splashed across Ronin's back, then claim me in a messy open-mouthed kiss.

God, he's so filthy and I just freaking love it.

I love it so much my cunt clenches hard around Ronin's cock and I shudder with a second climax. Ravenously I suck the musky essence of Vasili's spunk off his tongue and drive my tongue deep into my warlock's fanged mouth and claim him right back.

Too soon, he's pulling away, leaving me to lick the taste of him off my lips while he collapses across Ronin with a gasping sigh.

Ronin lies still and panting between us, his skin cool to the touch.

We just effing did it. We broke his heat.

And me? I'm a limp boneless wreck lying comatose beneath them. I'm smothered in warlock in all the best ways. Vasili's leg is grazing mine and his essence lingers in my mouth and I honestly don't know if I just made love to him or not, if he's my lover or not, if we're allies now or not.

Or if he's still my enemy.

Chapter Twenty-Seven

Neo

It's after two a.m. by the time I finish my alchemy experiment in the science lab at the Dean's Tower and hike back to the *domus* through the season's worst snowstorm, but I don't mind the time or the weather. Honors Science of Witchcraft has been kicking my butt all semester, and the Dean's a pretty relentless prof.

But that feat I managed to pull off in the lab tonight should be sufficient to put me solidly back in her good graces and back in straight A territory.

That's just where I like to be.

It might sound petty, this fixation on my grades, but it really isn't about me. I've grown up knowing the four races are dying and it's my duty to save them, first by making a suitable marriage, then by running for my father's elected seat on the Arcane Senate. Doing well at the Academy, making First Boy on the Dean's List, and building the resume and the alliances I need to be effective are all part of that plan.

Still, I have to be honest. I have to admit the fact that I've just become the first student in six years to ace that honors alchemy experiment feels pretty amazing.

I wonder if Zara will be proud of me. I can't wait to tell her.

Given the hour, I'm definitely expecting my housemates to be asleep, so I'm super careful not to make any noise creeping into the house, because we've all been under a lot of pressure since Zara got here and we all need our sleep.

Especially my fated mate.

So it's surprising to find Lucius' bedroom window still open, which means his wolf is still out, and the light in Vasili's room still burning. This makes me extra careful, peeling out of my coat and boots in the atrium before I tiptoe through the darkened living room and up the stairs. Another of my famous rows with Vasili would just upset everyone and wake the whole house.

I'm pretty zonked, but I have every intention of crashing in Zara's bed tonight, even if all we do there is sleep. I literally sneak down the darkened corridor past Vasili's closed door like I'm creeping past a monster's lair.

But what I see piled outside Zara's door makes me stop and smile.

Someone's dropped off two hard-shell suitcases covered with punk rock decals and travel stickers. The color of those cases is hard to tell in the gray moonlight leaking through the window down the hall, but it looks like hot pink.

Which is *so* Zara.

I'm the one who arranged this delivery, which must have come in on the supply plane.

She's going to be so happy when she sees what I got her.

I'm just putting my hand on the door and hoping she left it unlocked for me when the floor creaks right behind me. My heart gives a hard thump and jams up in my throat.

I'm instantly on guard for Vasili.

"Boo," someone whispers in my ear. Two warm hands settle on my waist. "Up a bit late tonight, aren't we, mate?"

My heart settles back behind my sternum where it belongs and the tension eases from my shoulders. Now my late-night fright shifts to a very different kind of tension. Ronin's hated me since Gwen died, and it's only today… yesterday?… in the gazebo that I finally did what Zara wanted me to do and what I've wanted to do myself the whole time I've known him.

That's when I finally manned up and kissed him.

It's really too soon to say if he's going to revert to form and just keep hating me.

I'm not a telepath or anything fancy. I'm just a plain old Kryll, even if I am the Capricorn scion. I'm an ordinary warlock with earth magic and a work ethic and solid study skills. So I totally have no idea what he's thinking.

"I had an alchemy experiment," I remind him, speaking softly so we don't wake Zara. His hands are still on my waist, which could either be a good sign or the start of some violent martial arts technique that's going to end with me on the floor.

"How'd we do then?" He's still whispering in my ear, his breath playing with my hair. Despite my fatigue and my caution, he's making me shiver all over.

"Lead into copper." I try not to sound too self-congratulatory, because I take a lot of heat for my grades from the other students.

But he's a telepath even if I'm not, and some of my pleasure probably leaks through.

"Not bad, Red." He murmurs this against the side of my neck, and my pulse starts pounding. Which I know he can feel, since my jugular's right under his lips. He brushes a little kiss… oh my God, an actual kiss from Ronin Pendragon, a kiss he's initiating… against my jackrabbit pulse. "Am I making you nervous, love?"

"No, um, not nervous." I lie through my teeth and clear my throat. "Is there a reason you're lurking out here in the hall?"

He can't have been waiting up for me, and I won't even let myself think it. Still, I *am* thinking it, and he chuckles under his breath because he can probably hear me thinking it. I don't have a single Valyrian chromosome in my entire DNA, so even at basic telepathic defense I'm pretty hopeless.

"Just on my way to bed from the shower." He nuzzles the side of my neck and releases me. I'm simultaneously thankful and bitterly disappointed. "I'm bunking down with our girl tonight, yeah?"

"Oh." I try not to sound too crestfallen that he's beaten me to her bed. "Well, let me at least carry these suitcases in for her." *And maybe kiss her goodnight before I go.*

He steps between me and the cases. "Why would you have to go?"

My startled gaze swings up to his. With the window behind him, I can't see a thing, which is definitely for the best, because looking at him also makes me nervous. And maybe in the dark he can't see the blush heating my face. (It's extremely inconvenient being a redhead who blushes.)

In silhouette against the moonlit night, Ronin's a tall but still extremely sexy shadow smelling like bergamot soap and, pretty strongly, like both Zara and Vasili. Zara I can totally get, because she scents a lot when she's turned on, and she's definitely into Ronin.

Vasili I can't get at all, because those two guys hate each other's guts. I wonder if maybe they've been fighting.

"Cat got your tongue then, Red?" he murmurs, humor lurking in his voice.

Belatedly I focus on his question. "I thought you said you're staying?"

"Yeah, I am." He shrugs. "Her bed's plenty big enough for all three of us."

That's a concept that pretty much renders me speechless. Just sleeping in the same bed with Zara would be more than enough to make me happy. The thought of sharing that bed with both of them—the fated mate I adore and the guy I've been crushing on since I got here—just about makes my head explode.

Not to mention my dick.

"You don't think she'd… mind?" I venture.

"Mind?" My naïveté wrings another chuckle out of Ronin. "Thought you're supposed to be top of the Dean's List? She's polyamorous, Neo, like pretty much all the queens. Think she made it pretty bloody clear in that gazebo that she's claiming both of us, yeah?"

That concept is so foreign to me (since just having one lover in my bed is a massive leap) that I stand there gaping at him like a confused freshman at orientation.

Can that possibly be true? My fated mate seems fairly resistant even to claiming me, and I'm secretly waiting for her to try sneaking off this island and ending up with six months' detention. If she's willing to claim both me and Ronin, does that mean she's thinking about staying?

That possibility fills me up with such a painful swell of hope I can't even speak.

"Go on in," he says to me kindly. "You're dead on your feet. I'll bring in the cases. Hers, are they?"

"From her hotel in Singapore," I explain. "I had them picked up when I realized how much she misses having her own things."

"You're a decent sort." Ronin bends to lift the bulky cases like they weigh nothing. "She's going to bloody adore that you did this."

"I hope so," I say happily. "I'm having everything boxed up and shipped from her old flat in Cairo too."

Ronin pauses in mid-lift, a case hanging from each hand. "You're, ah, having everything she owns shipped here, are you?"

"Yes, and I managed to break the lease on her new rental house in Sharm el-Sheikh and get her security deposit returned to her bank account. That's the advantage of being her legal fiancé in the witching world *and* a Mercury. We have access to really good lawyers."

I'm aware that I'm rambling, because Ronin still makes me nervous, and there's definitely something he isn't telling me. I force myself to stop speaking and take a deep breath.

"Do me a favor, mate," Ronin says at last. "Don't, ah, tell her about the lease or the shipment from Cairo just yet. It's late and we all need our sleep."

"Sure." Now I know there's something he isn't telling me, but I'm not going to learn whatever it is standing out here on the landing. "I'll tell her tomorrow."

"Yeah, all right," he sighs. "You do that."

Filing away my questions for later, I try the door and it swings open without a problem, which makes me hope she left it unlocked for me, even though I haven't officially moved in yet. I swing it wide so Ronin can carry in the cases, then I follow him in.

It's dark in here, just a dim red light leaking from the banked coals and pale moonlight streaming through the glass doors over her canopy bed. The air's sweet and creamy with her fragrance. Soft snores—her snores, because I learned last night that my wonderful mate does snore—emanate from the blanketed lump in the bed where my cherished one slumbers, the wild tangle of her mermaid hair flung across the pillow.

Just the sight of her gives me a fluttery feeling in my chest. My heart lifts like it's on wings.

That's the euphoric rush of pure happiness.

I close the door softly in Ronin's wake and shoot the deadbolt, because given what happened to Cybelle, we definitely can't be too careful. I check to make sure the glass doors are latched too, because Lucius left his window open, so the house really isn't secure, and someone could climb up the trellis from the garden.

By the time I'm satisfied that my cherished mate is safe, Ronin's parked her cases near the armoire, tossed a chunk of wood on the fire, and is peeling out of his shirt in front of the flames.

For me, the planet almost stops spinning.

He's just so… beautiful. His long hair's still damp and messy from his shower, and he's all supple skin and flexing muscle and that fantastic dragon roaring and spitting black flame across his chest. I can hardly believe he's willing to share Zara with me, and I'm desperately wondering if that means the two of us—Ronin and me—might also be together.

Then he peels out of his pants, and I just stop thinking.

About anything.

Dear God, he isn't even wearing briefs. He has the most sculpted ass, and that ringed piercing I glimpsed a few times in the *thermae* while I was pretending not to look at his junk is definitely a thing. He isn't hard or anything, but—oh damn—he *has* just totally caught me staring.

I'm busted.

He goes still before the fire, with no sound at all to fill this superheated silence except the crackle of the flames and Zara's cute little snores and my own heavy breathing. I yearn for something to do with my hands and my big clumsy body, but the only thing I can think of is to undress too, which will just make this entire encounter a thousand times more awkward.

"Take a breath, Red," he says, and I'm deeply thankful he sounds kind and not mocking. "Seriously, mate, no one here's going to do anything but sleep tonight. All three of us together in that bed, yeah?"

"Yeah. Okay." That statement frees me up enough to pull the Academy sweater over my head and start working on the buttons of my shirt. Which in turn lets me duck my head so my hair flops over my face. "You don't, uh, need anything? For your heat?"

"Nah, I'm good for a bit yet. But thanks for the thought."

I glance up through my hair and he spares me a slow grin that heats me all the way through. Thank goodness for the dark, because I'm pretty sure even my eyebrows are blushing. This is the curse of having a fair complexion.

"Don't mention it," I mumble.

Ronin drops his clothes on the floor and pads across to the massive bed. He climbs in, graceful as a panther as he slides under the heavy blankets, careful not to disturb Zara's sleep. He does lean over my adored one to stroke the wild hair gently away from her face. He's usually so hard and feral that I love seeing how tender he is with her right now.

Our mate.

If he really meant what he said about Zara claiming both of us, maybe that means he can help me take care of her and make her happy. That scenario makes me feel warm all over for an entirely different set of reasons. These reasons too center in my chest.

I've been into him so long, yearning for him so long, that it wouldn't take much for me to fall in love with him.

And I've always been in love with Zara.

Now that the warm spot by the fire is vacant, I could undress over there, but I'm still grateful for this darker corner near the door, so I strip down here in the chilly air and fold everything neatly over Zara's chair. I keep my briefs on, since I usually wear them to sleep anyway, and I'm way too self-conscious to take them off with the unattainable Ronin Pendragon lying there in our soon-to-be mutual bed just watching me.

He's rolled on his side toward me and propped his head on his hand, his silky hair pouring over one shoulder and pooling on the pillow, his eyes gleaming like a demon's in the firelight.

I spend a lot of time in the gym and I know physically I've got nothing to be ashamed of, but I feel too big and too awkward for Zara's pretty bedroom, like I've got too many arms and legs, under Ronin's knowing gaze. He can have anyone in the whole school he wants, even Zara, so why would he want anything to do with an awkward twenty-year-old almost-virgin like me?

In guy terms, I actually am a virgin, because no one's ever… I've never… I can't even finish that thought. If he wants Zara, though, he'll have to put up with me at least in a platonic sense, because I'm definitely not going anywhere—

"Neo," he murmurs. "Stop thinking so hard and come to bed. You'll bloody freeze to death over there thinking and worrying like that."

"Right." I steel myself and cross the icy flagstone floor. He's definitely watching me, because I can feel the heat of his stare, but I'm carefully not watching back. He's left me plenty of room, he even holds the blanket up for me.

I scramble in as quick as I can, so I don't let the warm air out from underneath.

But I'm completely aware that he's naked in this bed, and I'm almost naked, and we're here in bed together with our mate.

He could be lying on her other side, but he's chosen to stay on this side with me. Though maybe it doesn't mean anything. It's totally possible he really doesn't want a total virg—

"Fuck," Ronin sighs, and rolls toward me. He props himself up on one elbow and frowns down at me. "There's only one blooming way to stop you thinking and worrying, isn't there?"

"I'm sorry that I don't know how to stop thinking—" I begin, feeling pretty frustrated with the whole situation.

He leans over me and stops my words and my breath with a soft kiss. It's such a tender kiss, so unlike that desperate sex-charged one we shared in the gazebo, that I forget how to breathe at all.

"Listen, love," he sighs against my mouth. "Have I got your attention?"

"Yes," I whisper, my pulse racing and my lips tingling. Because how could he possibly not?

I open my eyes and gaze into his.

"When we're all three properly awake and Zara's alert enough to enjoy it," he says deliberately, "we're going to bloody deal with this apparently awkward subject of your virginity once and for all. And the way we're going to deal with it is that I'm going to thoroughly and pleasurably fuck you."

A thunderous gasp spills out, but he presses a finger to my lips to quiet me.

"I'm going to start with my fingers," he says deliberately, in a low sexy growl, "and get your tight little hole all opened up. Then I'm going to fuck you with my tongue until you're soaked and desperate." He cups my chin and his thumb strokes my lower lip. "Then and only then, when you're thoroughly prepped and begging for me, I'm going to bend you over this bed, with that pretty mouth of yours buried in Zara's sweet cunt, and you're going to take my cock balls-deep in that absolutely succulent arse."

His heated whisper wrings out of me a helpless whimper.

And he just keeps going. "I'm going to wrap my fist around your cock and fuck you long and slow, until you come absolute buckets all over my hand. Zara's going to come too under your clever tongue, just hearing those desperate little sounds you're making. And you're going to feel so bloody good clamped around my cock that I'm going to come inside you, because being your first male fuck is going to drive me so wild I won't be able to stop."

He leans in close, his warm breath mingling with mine. "When I'm quite finished, you'll no longer be a virgin, and I guarantee we'll all three of us enjoy the experience. Now how does that sound to you?"

By now he's gone so far beyond any place I've ever been before, even in my imagination, that his words make me totally dizzy. Not to mention sexed up enough to give the whole thing a green light right now.

A slow giddy grin spreads over my lips. "I think I can live with it?"

"Right. Sounds like that's all settled then." He kisses me again, just a brief press of his lips to mine, but I can feel him smiling against my mouth. "Now, love, let's all get a bit of sleep, shall we?"

Chapter Twenty-Eight
Lucius

By the time my wolf and I return from our midnight run, a thick carpet of fresh snow blankets the narrow streets. The snowfall has slowed to reveal glimpses of the massive moon hovering low over the mountainous slopes. The supermoon is tomorrow, and I can already feel its powerful pull.

But my wolf senses this winter weather isn't finished with us. Moon or no moon, this storm is going to worsen. The supply plane won't be able to fly out at all today.

We're marooned on this island.

Until the fist of winter loosens its grip on this Academy, Icarus Island is truly cut off from the outside world.

I scramble through my open window and rise to my hind legs, fur dwindling and bones lengthening as I assume my human shape. I'm aching with exertion and pleasantly weary as I close the window, stoke the fire, and pull on my shirt and trousers.

But I've been hiding from Ronin and what I've done to him all night. I've hidden from my own actions. I've relied upon Zara and Vasili to give Ronin what he needs.

Before I crawl into bed, duty as well as devotion compel me to check on my mate.

Perhaps I'd better check on my queen as well. She was so distressed in the belfry today, finally spilling out the brimful goblet of all her long-held secrets.

Yet she still fears the lightning that is both her gift and her curse.

Yes, I'll look in on Zara as well.

I'm too close to my wolf form at present to tolerate shoes or even socks. Thus, I prowl barefoot up the stairs to my students' bedrooms and steal down the hall to Ronin's.

His door is gaping wide and it's dark inside, which is unusual enough that I linger in the doorway, pulling in a deep breath of my mate's familiar bergamot-and-ambergris scent.

But another scent entirely hits my nostrils like ammonia.

That scent rips an animal growl from my throat.

It's the predatory whiff of smoke and vetiver from the other alpha who shares my roof. The sexual rival for my mate's affection.

Vasili is huddled in the dark in the window seat, his fair head sagging against the wall as he stares out at the drifting snow, an open bottle cradled between his feet.

I slice a suspicious glance toward Ronin's empty bed, which clearly hasn't been slept in tonight. Then my gaze slews back to my most troublesome student.

"Mr. Romanov?" I make my tone brisk and businesslike. "What are you doing in here alone?"

"Drinking," he says succinctly, without even doing me the courtesy of looking at me. "And brooding. And I don't recall asking for company."

My impulse is the same as it always is with him, my talented and deadly prodigy, this rival alpha in my little pack. My instinct as a shifter is to give him his space and his privacy and accede to his demand for solitude.

But I've been giving Vasili his solitude since he joined my *domus* three-plus years ago, and keeping my distance hasn't seemed to help. He doesn't even go home for summer holidays like the rest of my students, and I have the sense it's because there isn't much of a home back at the Romanov *dacha* near Moscow or the family superyacht in the Seychelles to welcome him. They never contact him here either, and I sense they don't want much to do with him, even if he is the Scorpio scion.

I struggle with my instincts for a moment, then slip into the room, because now there are two students who need me. "Where's Ronin?"

"Sleeping with the little queen and Neo fucking Mercury after we broke his heat," he says curtly. "She's claiming both of them, in case their cozy little dynamic has escaped your notice. I'll be exceedingly lucky not to lose him entirely. And if you're going to write them all up for some sort of conduct violation, don't fucking blame it on me."

Ah. Perhaps this explains why my problem child here is so utterly out of sorts. Vasili despises Neo and his royalist clan beyond reason, and he's jealous that his lover is sharing a bed with his rival.

But I suspect what's truly troubling Vasili goes far deeper than that.

Vasili raises the half-empty bottle for a swig. The dry bite of vodka sears my lupine senses.

I vastly prefer Hungarian *palinka* for a sundowner myself, yet I find myself drawn inexorably closer to my troubled ward. Moving slowly so I don't trigger his own instincts, I pad softly to the window seat. "Would you mind terribly if I join you for a nightcap, Mr. Romanov?"

This overture earns me a long look from his narrowed eyes. Against the backdrop of falling snow, his profile is delicate as a woman's, all straight nose and sharp jaw and pretty lips parted over those little fangs he tries so hard to hide.

I keep my face open and my hands still at my sides. My goal is not to trigger him.

"Well, darling, it's your funeral," he says at last, and offers me the bottle.

I seize this moment to slide into the opposite end of the window seat, prop my back against the wall, draw my knees to my chest, and accept his bottle like a peace offering. The vodka scorches my sinuses and practically cauterizes my throat going down. Gasping, I take another long swallow of liquid fire before I pass the bottle hastily back.

Damnation. My eyes are watering.

"That's a potent beverage," I rasp.

"Only the best for a Romanov," he mutters, turning back to the falling snow. He's shutting me out again, the way we're always shutting each other out.

"Mr. Romanov…" I begin, not at all certain how I mean to go on. I'm losing him as a student when he graduates this spring. In truth, I lost him long before that. I've been so careful of his shifter recessives, the same recessives that give him those fangs he loathes. I've been so scrupulous never to trigger him—or myself. We're both alphas, even if he can't shift, and nature intends one of two paths for the pair of us, neither of which I've cared to inflict upon him.

By giving him his space, I've left him alone.

Alone without a mentor for the obscure shifter legacy he hasn't a clue how to manage. Somehow, tonight, he's never seemed more alone.

And I've never felt more like a failure.

"Vasili," I say softly. His startled gaze jerks toward me. His eyes are reddened, and I find myself wondering if he might have been weeping. An unfamiliar sentiment pings in my chest and twists my heart in knots. "I very much fear that I owe you an apology."

"An apology?" His lips part in surprise. "For what?"

"For failing you as a teacher." I reclaim the bottle from his slack hand and tilt it back for another blistering swallow. This drink is a form of penance for the cardinal sin of failure. "You're the subordinate alpha in this *domus*. I've been so concerned to avoid fighting you that I've neglected my duty to teach you—"

"Who says I'm subordinate?" he sneers. The sudden spice of Mogadon aggression floods the night air. "I'm more your peer than your student."

"Mr. Romanov, you're a solid seven years my junior—"

"I'll be twenty-three this summer. That's six years," he points out. "I'll be teaching at this Academy myself next fall once the Dean accepts my application. Which, of course, she will."

I've secretly suspected as much, but I'm quietly unsettled to hear my suspicions confirmed. Dear God in Heaven, we'll never be rid of each other.

"Subordinate?" He flings the word at my head like a throwing knife. "I've more witchcraft in my little finger than you command in your entire shifter carcass. You're a mangy beast with a knack for common magics. Whereas I'm the Scorpio scion and the most powerful telekinetic on this entire island. You can't tolerate me because I threaten you."

His accusation hits home with deadly accuracy. I know he's saying these cutting things to warn me away. A day ago, even an hour ago, I'd simply have heeded his warning and gone.

But he's wretched. And he's alone.

Just as I'm alone, alone among the last purebred shifters of a dying race, and always have been.

"I've never wanted to fight you, Vasili," I murmur, low and soothing. "And, despite your dangerous anti-monarchist tendencies, I don't want to fight you now."

He studies me with a slow blink, then reclaims the bottle with a sneer. He tips it back and I watch the muscles in his long throat ripple as he swallows. He's wearing what looks like one of Ronin's silky shirts, open all the way down the front, and the top button of his ripped jeans is undone.

Unexpectedly, my wolf stirs inside me. But what we're feeling toward this other alpha is distinctly *not* aggression.

When Vasili lowers the bottle and looks up at me, his eyes shimmer like liquid mercury. For no discernible reason, my pulse is spiking.

"Despite your ridiculous royalist loyalties, I've never wanted to fight you either," he says, so quietly even my wolf can barely hear him. "I assure you, I had more than enough fighting back home."

I know he's an only child and the only Romanov here. However, to my shame, I know very little about his background beyond his disastrous transcript, his dazzling test scores, and the basic genealogy that's in his student file. Therefore, I choose my words with excruciating care. "I gather your parents are… distant. Perhaps even… estranged?"

"My parents." He snorts and turns back to the window. "They're Old Russian. Which means Russian Orthodox, which *means* they believe in a church that makes the Catholic Pope look like a damn radical. I haven't seen them or spoken to them once in the past five years. My parents disowned me the day I told them I'm gay."

I'll admit I was expecting something along these lines, but nothing quite so extreme. I lean forward in shock. "They can't disown you. You're the scion of your clan."

His voice lashes the night like a whip. "That's the only reason they don't take legal action to formalize their repudiation. I'm their only heir. Even if I am *defective*."

"You're not defective." I pull in a breath to steady myself and quietly say the rest. "Nor am I entirely certain you're gay."

There.

I've said it.

I've been watching him with Zara Gemini since the moment our queen arrived. And ever since I crawled into the close confines of this window seat with him, I've been breathing in the rose-and-vanilla sweetness of our queen's mating scent.

"What am I then? Bisexual?" He gestures wildly, bristling with frustration. "That's as bad as the other, as far as my parents are concerned. Believe me, Lucius, I couldn't be any more gay. And if somehow I'm not gay, it's only with *her*. The fucking queen. She's the only woman I've ever…"

Gently I supply the missing word. "Wanted?"

"Kissed." He groans. "Fucked, practically. I don't know whether she and I shared Ronin, or whether Ronin and I shared her. It was all three of us. All three of us together. And, yes, I fucking loved every minute of it. Loved every minute of… *her*."

"Well, Mr. Romanov, that's hardly a crime." Secretly, I'm deeply pleased. Despite the electric sexual tension that crackles between the two of them, I've scarcely dared hope our rebel queen might claim a third consort, or that Vasili would permit himself to be claimed. With Neo, Ronin, and Vasili all sharing her bed, she'll be the strongest queen-in-waiting the witching world has known in centuries.

Now if only I can persuade her to conquer her fears and summon the damned lightning.

"And you'd like it to be the three of you again?" I venture.

"Not exactly the *three* of us." Unexpectedly his ice-colored eyes lock on me. His butterscotch voice drops two octaves. "Lucius."

The dark spice of his Mogadon pheromones floods the air, potent enough to make a saint drunk. But it isn't aggression he's projecting. In fact, it hasn't been aggression all night. That dizzying biochemical cocktail suddenly flooding my senses is, indisputably, his mating scent.

Without warning, my wolf rises on his back legs and claws at my skin. He wants out, and it's not to fight.

But I don't want to hear from my wolf right now.

"Vasili," I begin, tingling with caution.

"We've been talking about Vasili all night," he purrs, absolutely silken with menace. "Vasili and Ronin. Vasili and Zara. Now let's talk about *you*, Lucius. Let's talk about Vasili and Lucius."

The sudden heat in his gaze is utterly impossible to mistake. All at once, I'm reeling under the shock of this unanticipated disaster and scrambling to find my footing before we all career into ruin.

I raise a cautionary finger to halt his words, but he's well beyond heeding.

"I've already said I never wanted to fight you." He forges ahead with vicious purpose. "And you never wanted to fight me. That's not why you've kept your distance from me and lived celibate as a damn priest for four fucking years. Nor is fighting what you want to do with me right now." One silver brow arches. "Is it?"

"Vasili, ah, Mr. Romanov," I fumble, and weather his mocking smirk. "I assure you, whatever I might or might not happen to desire in this moment is entirely irrelevant to the facts at hand. I'm a teacher at this Academy and the headmaster of this residential college. Whereas you, sir, are my student. I'm responsible for your education and your welfare—"

"You hide behind that tweed coat and briefcase and that professorial twaddle because you're afraid of what you want." He overrides my decorous protests with alarming ease. "I imagine it's easier to admit you want Ronin, isn't it, because there's no alpha shifter bullshit for you in his bed. And you can pretend all you like that what you feel for Zara is a teacher's devotion to duty. You can pretend what drives you is some sort of sacred mission to train the next royal. But you're just as afraid of what you want from her as you're afraid of what you want from me.

"I see what you want now, Lucius Aries."

I need to put real distance between us—and quickly. I should never have ignored my instincts and abolished that protective distance between us in the first place.

"Clearly," I state firmly, "you've had a bit too much to drink, Mr. Romanov. I do think it's best that we call it a night."

I rise to my feet with as much composure as I can summon and stride decisively for the door.

The thunk as he tosses the bottle aside precedes the crash of shattering glass when it rolls to the floor.

I abandon all semblance of decorum and break into a dead run.

But after my long lope through the forest, I'm far from fresh, while he's never been more determined. Still, my own desperation lends wings to my feet. I've nearly managed to reach the door when his lithe weight crashes into my back and drives me face first into the wall. His arms wrap around me from behind and his hands lock on my shirt. He tears it open, buttons flying in all directions, and drags it off my shoulders.

I'm struggling to heave him off, but it's a struggle in panting silence, because it would be disastrous for the others to find us like this, reeking of liquor and all but naked in a student's bedroom. Yet it's hardly a fair fight because he's been training for combat with Ronin, who's the highest-ranked fighter at Icarus, while I'm admittedly more a scholar than a warrior.

These factors explain why I'm still struggling to throw him off when the twin spikes of his fangs sink deep into my shoulder.

I gasp under an exquisite double stab of pain and pleasure.

Shifter instinct takes over completely. I fall absolutely still, panting and shuddering under his dominating bite. He's completely untrained in shifter ways; he was raised Mogadon, which means he doesn't have the skill to administer a disciplinary bite. In any event, a disciplinary bite isn't what he's seeking.

He's just sunk his teeth into my flesh in a goddamned mating bite.

This remains the reality although I can barely comprehend the fact that I, the dominant alpha in my swiftly dwindling race, have just accepted a mating bite from another alpha.

"Damn you, Vasili," I gasp, clawing at the wall for purchase. "This is outright disobedience. Cease this scandalous outrage. At once!"

My brain is reeling and I can scarcely even think. But what I can grasp is that he's only part shifter, so this may not be a proper bite. If only I can end this fiasco quickly, perhaps I'll suffer no untoward effect.

But my wolf, my wolf who would never accept a mating bite from another alpha, my wolf is strangely quiescent.

"Oh God, Lucius," Vasili says thickly against my shoulder. Twin trickles of hot blood spill over my skin. The languid lap of his tongue drags out a moan I can't contain. "Is this the way you do it?"

"That is most definitely the way," I gasp. "Vasili, for the love of the risen Christ…"

With every atom of my essence, I intend to order him to stop. But the inevitable effect of a mating bite is stealing insidiously through me. I'm thoroughly unnerved and thoroughly distracted. It's also the case that his wicked tongue is making my predicament a hundred times worse with every swipe. When he begins nuzzling my wound affectionately, every infernal thought in my head vaporizes into smoke.

This is classic alpha tending behavior, and he's doing it entirely by instinct.

Under my trousers my manhood is rising for him, hard and urgent, notwithstanding this untenable situation in which I find myself. My unruly wolf seems somehow to be accepting this submissive posture beneath a subordinate alpha.

A submission which, for me, is entirely without precedent.

I too am acting by instinct.

"Notwithstanding my horrible reputation, I'm not entirely a monster, you know," he whispers between kisses so tender I can't believe it's him giving them. "If you truly want me to stop doing this, darling, then tell me like you mean it."

With desperate resolve, I gather oxygen into my lungs and summon the necessary words. Then his hand slides down my abdomen to wrap over the bulge straining the crotch of my trousers. A delirious sense of anticipation spirals through me. All my breath spills out in a jagged gasp.

"I didn't think so," he murmurs against my skin, kneading my swelling shaft in a mesmerizing rhythm. "Do you like the way this feels?"

"Please, Vasili," I groan, and the naked need in my own voice appalls me. It's all I can manage not to rut into his grip. "If we do this now, there's no going back."

This line of argument ignores the fact that if he has indeed succeeded in inflicting a mating bite with his sharp baby fangs, there's already no going back. I'm already his. I'm already as good as beneath him in his bed, eager and begging for his cock.

That's something else I've never tolerated from anyone.

I'm referring to being on, well, the receiving end of another man's passion.

"Easy, pet. I'm not going to fuck you." He stops licking my bite long enough to nibble my ear with his wicked little teeth, which makes me tremble and him sigh. "At least, not tonight, not when we're both dead on our feet, and not before we've had a chance to explain all this to Ronin, and I suppose also to Zara. But I am going to make you climax for me before I send you off to sleep. I'm going to make you climax for me so hard you shout my name to the rafters and your legs buckle with pleasure and you can't stand without me holding you up. Would you like that?"

I'm hardly in any state to protest and, for better or worse, this young demon who's currently seducing me is scarcely in the mood to wait.

Deftly he opens the buttons of my trousers and draws me out. I'm rigid nearly to spilling in his hand, the head of my shaft already dripping for him. He purrs with approval and starts to work my length with his sinfully skillful fingers.

My pelvis punches forward into his fist. A low needy moan spills out of me.

"This isn't going to take very long, is it?" he whispers in my ear. "Just relax and let me take care of you."

And I discover to my utter disgrace that I've lost every particle of desire to protest.

Chapter Twenty-Nine
Zara

Something soft and silky is tickling my sleeping face.

And I know even before opening my eyes, just from the yummy aroma of bergamot soap and wolf and the mingled essence of my mating scent and Vasili's, that what's brushing my face is Ronin's hair.

His hot naked limbs are entwined with mine under an ocean of blankets in my canopy bed. This setup is even hotter because I'm half naked myself, just wearing panties and Lucius' button-down shirt, which I never returned to him and somehow like sleeping in. And, for maximum hotness, I'm half buried in the fat mattress because Neo's sprawled over both of us, also sleeping, his face mashed against the back of Ronin's shoulder.

Which is so freaking adorable I just lie there grinning, in the sappiest way, in the soft light that's leaking through the frosty glass.

Then I notice that glass is piled high with snowdrifts. Judging by the quality of the light, I forgot to set the alarm on my dive watch before I crashed.

Which means we're all three going to be massively late for Lucius' Common Magics class.

"Shit," I whisper.

"Mmmm." Ronin sighs into my neck and snuggles closer. I would never have taken this guy for a snuggler during our famous hate sex hookup in Singapore, but he totally is. And what with his fire gift and his mating heat and the low-grade fever that's apparently normal body temp for a Leo like him, he's keeping all three of us toasty.

"I honestly hate to say this," I murmur, "but we have to get up. We're super late for class."

That brings Neo's head up from Ronin's shoulder, magenta hair falling into confused eyes as he blinks at the snow-covered window.

"Delayed start… because snow," Neo mumbles. "Dean called th' landline last night."

This message relayed, my sleepy mate's head flops back down to Ronin's shoulder and his eyes drift closed.

That's a double shot of adorable right there.

Class or no class, I feel like I really ought to get up, because I do have a dry suit to test and a caper to plan. You know, my whole *Escape from Alcatraz* caper? But I have to admit it's really… nice… being snuggled up here like this with the two of them. Right now I'm actually more worried that something yummy might've gone down last night between my guys without me getting to watch than I'm worried about getting off this rock.

That alone should worry me more than anything else.

"Gotta stop thinking so bloody loud, love," Ronin mutters into my neck. "You'll wake the blooming neighbors."

By which he means, once Neo's a little more awake, he'll pick up that I'm making solid plans to vamoose. Then my wonderful mate who's so devoted to my happiness will be totally devastated, and it'll be all my fault.

Of course, Vasili warned me just yesterday that if I'm *not* still planning to abdicate and vamoose, *he'*ll start scheming to take me out.

For good.

I can't help wondering whether, after everything that went down with the three of us last night, Vasili still feels that way?

Because I don't actually know if he's my lover now or my enemy.

Then there's Lucius, my more-or-less kidnapper, who firmly insists that I stay—but *not* so we can explore this incredibly powerful connection that's growing between us. Nope, he's hellbent on keeping that whole teacher-student barrier not only rock-solid but sky-high, and making me summon lightning.

Cheese on toast, how did everything with these four warlocks get so *complicated*? And so freaking fast too?

"Bollocks." Ronin sighs. "Guess I'll just get up then."

Neither Neo nor I are on board with that plan, so we both wrap around Ronin in tandem to persuade him to stay. I figure my persuasive powers are assisted by the fact that I smell like his other mate in Lucius' shirt. Either way, Ronin settles easily into trading long slow kisses with Neo and me that make me wonder again just what I might've missed between the two of them last night.

"Nothing," Neo mumbles, leaning over Ronin to kiss me too. "I mean, you didn't miss anything. We waited for you, babe. But maybe… if you don't mind… tonight…?"

Neo's the only guy I know who blushes while he kisses, and he's doing it all the way to his hairline right now. But he sounds so hopeful that it pings my heart like a guitar string. Because of course I figured out after watching him with Ronin that my mate is toting around a fairly significant torch for this guy.

And I have to stop calling him my mate.

Especially since I'm starting to fall into the habit of thinking of them both that way.

"Safe to say I don't mind, baby." I reassure Neo with another deep kiss that he melts right into. "You know the way I roll."

"Mmmm, I love the way you roll," Neo breathes against my lips.

Then I turn on my side and prop up my head to give Ronin a stern look. "You know you have to be careful with him, right, Adam? You can't just one-and-done him and break his heart. Because I won't freaking stand for it."

"I know it's his first time with a guy. I'm going to take care of him. And you're going to join in and make sure I do." Ronin's hot amber gaze drifts over me. "Any rate, starting to feel a bit like maybe my one-and-done days are history, yeah?"

This gives me *such* a warm feeling in my chest. Yeah, this is it. That feeling I'm always chasing in a polycule but somehow never finding. The feeling that we're all here for each other, that we have each other's backs, that it's us against the whole world.

Only I'm a greedy witch because I want *us*, in this case, to mean not only Ronin and Neo and me, but also Vasili and Lucius.

Even though Vasili and Lucius are not currently on the menu. And they're definitely not on board with joining my polycule.

Especially since I haven't been planning to stay.

And therefore I don't really have a polycule.

Fortunately, since Neo still doesn't know about Vasili and Ronin being an item, and they should probably be the ones to tell him, Neo's only half awake. (He's definitely not a morning guy, this mate/not mate of mine.) Also fortunately, he's focused on what Ronin just said and not on what I just thought.

"If this is going to be an actual thing, like a real relationship, with all three of us?" Neo snuggles up happily against both of us. "Then I think we should all commit. That way we can all, you know… um… fuck each other bare? The way Zara and I do."

I'm not expecting that, like, at all. In fact, my brain seems stuck like a broken record on the word *commit*.

Because that's something else I've never had in any of my casual *ménage* or polycule setups.

Commitment.

Considering his whole one-and-done history, Ronin handles this commitment bombshell pretty well himself. His eyes go molten at the thought of fucking us bare. Then he wraps one arm around me and one around Neo and settles us both against his chest, his fingers winding in our hair.

"We'd still need to protect Zara," Ronin says slowly, and I'm shocked to realize he's actually even considering it. "Guessing you've got that squared away already though, haven't you, love?"

"IUD," I confirm, reaching across Ronin to link hands with Neo.

Okay, maybe right at this moment, I do have a polycule.

"Right. That's my girl." Ronin nods. Which just about makes me combust with happiness. "I'd still want to get tested again. I know I'm clean because I'm bloody careful, but I've quite the history, haven't I? I'd want both of you to feel totally certain and totally safe."

I relax in his arms, because I can see I don't need to worry about Ronin taking care of Neo. In fact, he wants to take care of both of us. And I totally love him… I mean *it*. This. I totally love that he's doing this.

"And it isn't just the two of you I'd be committed to, yeah?" Ronin points out, which makes my heart pound like a jackhammer. I hope now he'll tell Neo about Vasili, let him in on their big secret, which in turn would open the door to letting Vasili into *our* arrangement too… the one going on in this bed right now… if he wanted that. The Goblin King doesn't seem to play the field, he's way too aloof and abrasive, but since he's crazy in love with Ronin, I figure Vasili's already committed to whatever Ronin wants.

"Obviously I know you're mated now to Lucius—Master Aries, I mean." Neo snuggles against Ronin and brings my hand to his luscious lips to nuzzle my palm. I cup his strong jaw, all raspy with stubble. "I'm not saying he wouldn't take some getting used to. He's been my teacher since freshman year. But he is very… interesting."

That's clearly Neo's way of saying he wouldn't mind having our wolfish headmaster prowling into our bed. Which is a scenario I'm more than on board for.

Lucius himself, of course, is still hella skittish.

And then there's the fact that I'm leaving.

"Yeah, love, he is that," Ronin murmurs in response to Neo. "There's, uh, someone else too."

Now I definitely hold my breath. Vasili hovers like a ghost in the air between us, but I work on shielding my thoughts, because it really should be Ronin who tells Neo.

If he's going to.

"Really?" Neo's tousled head pops up from Ronin's shoulder. "Someone else you're committed to?"

"Deeply," Ronin says softly.

My heart gives another ping.

"Wow." Neo's brow furrows. Clearly his encyclopedic brain is scrolling through the various options. "Who?"

Ronin pulls in a breath. "Well, uh, it's actually…"

For a second there, it seems like maybe he's really going to say.

Until right outside my bedroom door, someone fucking *screams*.

There's a reason Ronin Pendragon's the top-ranked fighter at Icarus. I'm still clawing my way through ten tons of bedding and trying to force my heart out of my throat so I can breathe again by the time Ronin's rolled out of bed, unsheathed two knives from his boots, and strode to the door.

Buck naked.

Neo's on his feet too, wearing black briefs and a determined expression, standing defensively between me and the door. I've just leaped out of our love nest and armed myself with Vasili's knife, which he never reclaimed and which I liked having next to me on my nightstand while I slept, when Ronin unbolts the door and flings it wide.

Turns out it's Racetrack who gave that godawful yell, because she's still standing there looking totally freaked out. And the obvious reason she lost it is lying across my doorstep in a horrific mess of matted chestnut fur soaked and clotted with old blood.

It's a dog… no… it's a wolf.

There's a fucking dead wolf on my fucking doorstep with its carcass slit open from throat to anus and its insides spilling out.

My stomach plunges to the floor and my head starts spinning.

"No," I whisper. *"No."*

Just no. No to what I'm seeing. No to the whole concept.

But no one can hear me. Because there's no air in my lungs.

Ronin staggers and just about sinks to his knees. He grips the doorframe to hold himself up and rasps one word in a horrible voice.

"Lucius."

Chapter Thirty

Neo

It takes me less than three seconds flat to race across Zara's bedroom and get my shoulder under Ronin's arm to brace him. And Zara's literally right behind me, because my mate doesn't let anyone fight her battles.

I barely have time to think about my own feelings, because the two of them need me. But my stomach is heaving and my hands are cold and my face is numb with shock as I struggle to absorb this unbelievable horror. Really, there is no absorbing it. Memories flash through my brain way too fast to track. Memories of this wonderful and fascinating mentor who's always been rock-solid there for me.

This can't have happened to him.

Not Lucius.

Who'd ever want to hurt Lucius?

And what it's going to mean for Ronin who's mated to him? Or for Zara who, I'm pretty sure, was really close to claiming Lucius as a mate herself?

I'm still struggling to process my own shock and holding a white-faced Ronin on his feet as he sways, even though I'm not feeling overly steady on my own two feet, when the man himself comes tearing up the stairs in response to the commotion.

Lucius.

It's Lucius running toward us.

My entire body empties out and goes completely limp. I'm swamped by a sense of relief so strong it makes me lightheaded. Beside me, Zara gives a shuddering gasp, and I wrap a firm arm around her too.

It is truly Lucius in human form racing down the hall toward us, dressed in his houndstooth pants and tweed coat and respectable tie like he's already teaching Common Magics class.

Which means it's *not* Lucius in wolf form lying dead and gutted at our feet.

"Lucius," Ronin groans like he's dying. Now I've got an arm around him

and an arm around Zara, who's simultaneously clinging to me and gripping Racetrack's shoulder to give our housemate a brace.

That's what I love about Zara, I mean, one of the many things about her I love. That she can simultaneously ask for comfort and lend her own strength to someone else who needs it.

"Lucius," she breathes. "Oh my God, *Lucius*. Thank fuck."

By now, we're all in the hall enveloping Lucius, or he's enveloping us. He's wrapped up in Zara and Ronin and they're wrapped up in him. And, somehow, I'm right in the middle of it with an arm wrapped around both my mates and my forehead bowed against Lucius' shoulder. My head fills with his comforting wolfish scent. I breathe him in deep, because I need a little comfort myself.

Weirdly, he also smells like Vasili.

It's like we're all starting to smell like each other. Despite the reek of blood and violence that's also emanating from the actual dead wolf on Zara's doorstep.

Something's definitely going on in this *domus* that I don't understand, except for knowing my fated mate's right in the middle of it.

But I guess, at the most basic level, I do understand what's happening.

Our queen is claiming her mates.

That wonderful prospect gives me the strength I need to deal with our hallway crisis.

"We're going to be okay," I reassure everyone, tightening my grip on Zara and Ronin and meeting Lucius' unblinking whiskey-colored stare. "But clearly someone got in the house last night. And the first thing we need to do is make sure they're not still here."

"Oh… my fucking… God," Racetrack says. I turn to find her staring at our big practically naked tangle with a white face and eyes round as frisbees. "Are you four, like, *together*?"

Well, no one's exactly rushing to confirm it.

Or deny it.

We're rescued from the awkward silence by Vasili (of all people) who's suddenly looming behind Lucius. He takes in the scene with one narrow stare.

"I'll check the house," he says briefly, and he's gone before I can offer to help.

Not that he'd typically need help, with his knives and his telekinesis and his general badassery. Or that he's likely to accept help from me of all people, even if he does need it.

But we don't know what we're dealing with here.

All we know—all I know—is that someone's just threatened and upset my mate. Someone close enough and smart enough to get in this house without any of us knowing. Someone who's clearly just threatened Lucius too.

We all stare grimly at each other, thinking these horrible thoughts.

"Okay." Racetrack pulls herself together and scrubs a hand through the blond bristle of her hair. "I'm gonna check the basement right the fuck now. Dez is down there in the shower."

"Take Vasili with you," Lucius instructs her right away, taking charge as usual. "I'll be along myself in just a moment."

"Are you kidding? If we've got an uninvited guest down there, I don't need you or Vasili. I'll roll out the welcome wagon myself," Racetrack says with a hard look.

She's gone in an eyeblink. Literally.

Because Racetrack's Mogadon gift is teleportation.

She's also a hellraiser, just because she's Racetrack. My guess is, she's with Dez in the *thermae* already. And if anyone else is hanging around down there, my wrathful housemate's sudden appearance will probably give that person a heart attack.

"Wow," Zara breathes. "That's handy. I wonder if she's ever thought about a career in burglary?"

"Blood of Christ," Lucius mutters. "I trust the rest of you will oblige me by putting some clothes on." He leans in to nuzzle Ronin's cheek, because even I can feel Ronin's still shaken. "Especially you, dear one. You're mother-naked and it's freezing out here."

And right there in front of all of us, Ronin cups a hand around the back of Lucius' neck and pulls him into a hard claiming kiss.

Zara makes a soft noise next to me, and everything I'm picking up from my fated mate tells me she's burning to claim Lucius that exact same way.

When Ronin comes up for air, Lucius' head snaps toward her—and *whoa*—my teacher's eyes are fiery red and he's going all fangy. Not to mention he looks hot as heck doing it. He and Zara are just consuming each other with their eyes.

But it's pretty clear things between them aren't settled. I sense she's not as afraid of whoever's trying to terrorize her as she's afraid Lucius might not want her.

Like there's anyone on this planet who wouldn't want her. She's queen of the witching world. She's practically a goddess.

But she's also her own self. She's our Zara.

And the next thing she says proves it.

"Yeah, we'll all uniform up—on one condition. You don't get to freaking run off this time, Lucius." Zara disentangles from our group hug and plants her hands on her hips, looking even sexier than usual standing there barefoot in her wild hair, schoolgirl panties, and Lucius' rumpled shirt. "Because you've been doing a lot of that lately. The four of us—and probably the five of us—really need to talk."

Lucius blinks and his fangs retract.

"I happen to agree," he says mildly. "But I'd rather not conduct that long-overdue discussion in a student's bedroom with the three of you standing about half dressed. Let me secure the house, check on Racetrack whether she wants it or not, and deal with this poor beast while the rest of you make yourselves decent. We'll address this matter properly before class." He glances at his wristwatch. "Let's reconvene at the breakfast table in, shall we say, thirty minutes?"

That's Lucius' way of maintaining that professorial propriety he's so fond of. I can respect that.

Zara's definitely giving him the fish eye. But she snorts and pivots back inside to dress.

"And Mr. Pendragon?" Lucius adds. Now it's Ronin's turn to snort, and I swear my prof blushes. "Very well then. *Ronin*. After you're decent, you'd best collect Mr. Romanov as well."

Now I know Lucius has to be more unsettled than he's letting on, because everyone knows Ronin and Vasili hate each other.

Sending Ronin after him is the best way of guaranteeing Vasili won't show up at all.

"And that right there's exactly why we need to talk," Zara calls from inside her bedroom, clearly picking up my thought. "Along with about ten thousand other secrets people are keeping around here. Neo, baby, wanna help me start the fire?"

Chapter Thirty-One
Zara

I'm so pumped for our long-overdue group gab that I beat the guys downstairs. Five minutes after Lucius knocks on my door to give the all-clear, I pop out from my bedroom, looking all prep school spiffy in the cherry blazer and red-and-black plaid of the Friday uni, complete with blue pigtails, black thigh-highs, and a black beret sporting (you guessed it) the Academy logo.

By now, that poor dead wolf is long gone from my doorstep. Someone's taken care of business.

I'm putting my money on Lucius.

The visible symbol of that ugly threat may be gone, but the psychological impact isn't so easy to erase. Even though I know the house is secure, I can't shake that creepy feeling of being stalked through the streets. Under my pulled-together facade, my chest is tight and it's hard to get enough air, which I recognize as the prelude to the full-blown panic attack I won't let myself surrender to.

I can't stop wondering, if I'd been any less alert and wary last night, whether *I'd* have been what Ronin found slaughtered on our doorstep.

When I let my brain go there, it's pretty unsettling to imagine the probable queen killer operating freely in this house I've started to think of as a sanctuary. Because this incident with the wolf goes way beyond casual hazing. Someone hunted down that poor critter, slaughtered it in a really gruesome way (which can't have been easy, a wild wolf like that), schlepped it all the way here, broke into this house, and either knew enough about the layout or had enough clairsentience to know which room is mine.

That kind of determination feels like obsession.

And not the good kind.

If the guys hadn't bolted my bedroom door before they crashed, I wonder if I'd have woken up with that dead wolf in my bed.

Or if I'd have woken up.

Period.

Not to mention killing that dead wolf with fur the exact freaking shade of Lucius' hair and leaving the carcass in this *domus* is a direct threat to my teacher. Just one more reason, really, why I need to leave.

To keep us all safe.

And why, in the meantime, we all need to come clean and share a few secrets.

A *few*. But definitely not all.

The charred scent of bacon and the sizzle of frying pancakes seeps out of the cozy *domus* kitchen. Which makes my tummy give an interested rumble despite my jitters. I'm not one of those romance heroines who can't eat when she's stressed. For me, it's pretty much the opposite. Some psycho wants me dead? Feed me.

I arrive on the scene to find the welcome sight of Lucius, tweed coat missing and shirt sleeves rolled up, standing before the stove with a spatula.

Which is really nice of him, because I was actually supposed to be on breakfast duty this morning before I overslept. I'll be sure to cover cleanup duty to compensate.

But I still can't shake the queasy horror of that awful moment when I thought he was dead.

"Early for once, Ms. Gemini," Lucius observes, flipping pancakes with panache. Which is unfair (I mean the observation, not the pancake flipping), because I've been late for our independent study exactly *once*, but whatever. I'm more unhappy that he's back to calling me Ms. Gemini.

"Yesterday in the belfry, I was Zara," I remind him softly, coming up behind him at the stove.

He can't keep me from doing this anymore, not after I thought he was dead. I need the comfort of his touch. I wrap my arms around his waist from behind, lean my cheek against the back of his shoulder, close my eyes, and breathe in the scent of predator. He's a lot warmer than I expect, like he's running a low-grade fever, all banked heat and wiry muscle. Under that starchy shirt, he's a deadly hunter.

I want to free his wild hair from that tidy tail and let his wolf out.

"Zara." In my arms, he sighs deeply, his whole Iron Curtain accent thicker and more guttural than usual. "Don't. He's difficult enough to control in your vicinity."

"Then maybe you need to stop trying so hard to control everyone and everything around you. And stop trying to push everyone away." I close my eyes and pull in another deep breath of wolf, which mingles nicely with the acrid scent of coffee.

He also smells, somehow, like Vasili. In fact, I'm catching a distinct whiff of the Goblin King's potent mating scent.

Which is intriguing as fuck.

Maybe Neo's right and we're all starting to smell like each other.

It comforts me to be close to him like this, the way I imagine it comforts the members of a wolf pack to be close to their alpha. I wish Lucius didn't feel like he has to work so hard to keep me… and all of us… at a distance.

"Maintaining the sort of control you're so determined to destroy is my responsibility as your headmaster," he reminds me grimly, "and one I dare not abdicate. The survival of this Academy hangs by a thread, Ms. Gemini. As our queen, you should care deeply about the survival of this institution. The faculty of Icarus Academy, and the powerful scions we train here, are all that prevent the arcane races from descending into another Dark Age. It's we, my queen, who preserve the heritage of witchcraft for our dying races."

Not long ago, I would've been pissed about being sandbagged by a lecture before I've had my morning coffee. Not to mention having to defend myself against another royal guilt trip. But clearly I've already stuck around too long, because this time I actually do feel guilty.

Lucius just explained in a nutshell why he does what he does. Why he feels he can't loosen his grip or step out from behind the lectern long enough to get close to any of us.

Why he feels he can't get close to *me*.

Right now, I can even appreciate how, from where Lucius is sitting, my whole just-in-it-for-myself rebel queen rebellion probably does seem selfish.

He stops flipping pancakes and goes still. Yet I take heart from the fact that he hasn't pushed me away.

"You're our queen-in-waiting," he murmurs (like I need reminding). "All I'm asking you to do while you wait is to give your people and your heritage a chance."

He's not being unreasonable, I know this, with the literal survival of the witching world hanging in the balance. Maybe, killer or no killer, I *have* been a little too quick to reject the whole queen concept. Besides, this entire situation is different now than when Damien and Cybelle were alive. Before, no one needed me queening it. I could live the way I wanted. Now, this is all so much bigger than me. The choices I make could affect the whole witching world.

I'm going to need to think about this a whole lot more before I make any decisions. But not now, because I can hear others tromping down the stairs, the solid thunk of Racetrack's combat boots mingling with Dez's low murmur.

For now, I have to tuck these thoughts away.

I lean my forehead against Lucius' neat ponytail and whisper, "I'll think about it, okay?"

"Just give us a chance, Zara," he whispers back. "A chance to survive. I implore you. I'm begging you."

For one moment, his hand drops to my thigh, which is pressed against the back of his. Warm knuckles graze the naked skin between my skirt and my stocking. A groan rumbles from his chest.

Just like that, I'm on fire for him. I like the sound of Lucius begging me. I like the sound of his groan. Conversely, I also like the sound of him issuing orders. I want him to back me into the counter and shove my skirt up and fuck me to a noisy climax. I moan and press into the back of him—

He clears his throat roughly, steps away from me, and reaches for a plate. "Would you mind fetching the maple syrup, Ms. Gemini?"

The insertion of maple syrup into that X-rated kitchen fantasy definitely makes my panties damp.

But I step back with a sigh and do what I'm told.

Like the good girl I'm not.

There's a brief reprieve from all these hormones while everyone files in and fills their plates at the stove and finds seats in the great room at the long table by the window. Beyond the glass, thickly falling snow blankets the narrow passage with its steep stairs. White drifts pile high against the faded cobalt wall and shutters of the abandoned villa across the way.

But Ronin ignites a brisk fire in the central hearth that makes the scene cozy.

Vasili's the last to arrive as usual, looking aloof and untouchable, like he's ready to walk down a runway in Milan with his sharply tailored black blazer and his signature smoky eye. His fashionable tie is a slash of crimson I'm already fantasizing about unraveling to drag him toward me in a consuming kiss.

And it's only when Neo shoots me an appalled but titillated glance that I realize I might be thinking about kissing Vasili a little too loudly.

Ronin studiously slathers butter on his pancakes, but he looks like he's hiding a grin.

"I went over the entire *domus* from top to bottom," Vasili says briefly, between sips of ink-black coffee. "There's no indication—beyond the wolf, obviously—that anyone who isn't *us* was ever here. Possibly the intruder came in through Lucius' window while he was out last night. All the doors were locked this morning."

"I, uh, got up for a glass of milk at one thirty," I say, with a cautious look at Neo. Because that's when I came home from my racy romp in the dive shop, and I don't particularly want Neo knowing I was off half the night with his archenemy plotting my escape from this island, and therefore from him. "There was nothing outside my door then."

Across the table, Vasili arches his Romanov eyebrow and silently mocks me for the lie.

Ronin's making impressive inroads into his stack of pancakes, but that doesn't stop him from murmuring in my head, *Thought you wanted us to spill the beans, love?*

And I do. Sort of. We need that if we want to get to the bottom of what's happening on this island before someone (like me) ends up dead.

But I'm worried about what spilling all my secrets will do to Neo, who knows almost none of them.

Ronin doesn't look happy with the outcome of my inner monologue, but he pauses in his pancake consumption long enough to say, "Didn't see a bloody thing when Neo and I pitched up at Zara's digs at two."

"Hmmmm," Vasili murmurs. "It seems our uninvited guest keeps fairly late hours. I did find an open window in the attic. A window that would normally be locked from the inside."

"The attic?" I didn't even know we had an attic. "What is this guy, a cat burglar?"

That's my gig, and I'm eager to scope out the scene—*after* my pancakes. Lucius' pancakes are light and fluffy and melt-in-your-mouth yummy, especially slathered in butter and syrup the way I'm engulfing them. I'm interested to see Vasili takes his with sour cream and cranberries, which is probably the Russian way to eat them.

"Or a Mogadon," Vasili says briefly, answering my question about the attic. "They could have levitated."

The only levitating Mogadon I know on this island is Vasili, and I'm suddenly distracted by the concept that someone in this house (like Vasili) could have done the unspeakable thing with that poor wolf, then left the window open to avert suspicion. God knows, the Goblin King seems completely capable of murder. And he's been more than clear about wanting me gone.

But then, wouldn't Vasili have wanted someone else to find the open window?

Shit. I really wish I could trust him.

His icy eyes veer to mine. "Oh, do be assured I'm hardly the only levitating anti-monarchist on this island who despises you, darling. Your amorous poodle can make you a list."

"Hey." Neo lowers his fork and frowns. "You can't talk like that to Zara."

That's typical Neo, rushing to my defense and completely ignoring that the person Vasili actually just insulted is Neo.

And I guess I know now where I stand with Vasili.

He just said he despises me.

Which means the Goblin King's still my enemy.

Suddenly my yummy pancake is a soggy mess in my mouth. I swallow my mushy mouthful and glare back at Vasili. "Never mind me. Stop swiping at Neo, you asshole. What are you, twelve?"

"Now, now, children, no fighting at the table." Racetrack leans across to steal a crispy strip of bacon from Ronin's plate over his indignant objections and pops it into her mouth. "Hey, Master Aries, we still having the Janus Dance tonight? Or will the Dean cancel it over the weather?"

That's Racetrack for you, crunching noisily through Ronin's bacon, seemingly unperturbed by the perennial shitstorm that swirls under this roof, yet capably deflecting the combatants before we all come to blows.

She doesn't seem all that conflict averse to me, but I'm sensing Dez doesn't like it when we fight, so Racetrack soothes the storm for her sake.

"It's an important tradition at this Academy, so I imagine the dance will go forward," Lucius murmurs. "Unless we lose power, of course, as we did during the last big blizzard—"

The old-fashioned ring of the landline rotary phone in the kitchen gives me a jump, because that contraption is ancient and I haven't heard it ring since I got here. Lucius touches his linen napkin tidily to his lips and gets up to answer. But I'm still focused on the last thing he said.

Great. I still have to go to that fucking dance with Vasili as his fucking date.

Clearly sharing the sentiment, Vasili eyes me over his coffee cup. His glacial gaze narrows dangerously. "Do tell, darling. Have you found a frock to wear?"

Of course, that rattlesnake's more worried about how I'll look on his arm tonight and whether I'll tarnish his trendy image than he is about the nasty threat just made against my life.

I barely resist the urge to flip him the bird.

"Neo had my suitcases sent from Singapore." Under the table, I give Neo's muscled thigh a grateful squeeze, which triggers his slow sexy grin. "I have some club clothes in there. If they're good enough for a Singapore nightclub, they're good enough for you."

"Dear God, are you insane?" Vasili lowers his cup and looks appalled. "The Janus Dance is a formal affair. You can't turn up on my arm looking like a manga character from a comic book."

"Oh, I'm sorry, did you think I was asking your permission? You don't get a vote on what I wear, Goblin King." This time I do flip him the bird. "How about you and I just nix this whole dating concept? Anyway, I'd rather go to the dance with Neo."

Vasili's pupils dilate and his nostrils flare, which for a cold-blooded reptile like him is the equivalent of a temper tantrum. "Oh, *that's* a lovely notion. You'll make me an obvious liar in front of Bucephalus Zerxes, who happens to be the warlock on this island who's most capable—aside from yours truly—of making anyone's life a living hell."

I'm in the middle of formulating a snarky takedown, but the thought of unleashing a vengeful Master Zerxes on anyone (even my snake of a housemate) does give me pause.

My hesitation gives Dez an opening. "No worries about the dress, cobber. I can loan you one of mine, yeah?"

Dez is a total sweetheart for offering, though her tastes run to girly pastels, which would make me with my hair look like an Easter egg. Besides, she's tall and slim, while I'm short and curvy.

I'm trying to formulate a graceful escape, but Vasili beats me to it. "That won't be necessary, Desdemona. Never fear, I'll arrange something suitable for the little queen."

Which sounds like he's planning to bash me over the head and hide my body in the attic.

I lob the thought at him, taking advantage of all that telepathy I'm practicing, and he gives me one of his irritating smirks. "My, my, we're paranoid. I meant something for you to *wear*, darling."

"Don't bother." I toss my linen napkin over my empty plate and glare at him. "I won't wear anything you give me."

His mouth crimps with annoyance.

Now it's Neo who steps in. "If the weather lets up, maybe the supply plane can land. This was supposed to be a surprise for you, babe, but guess what? All your stuff's coming. I closed out your lease in Egypt and had everything shipped."

On my other side, Ronin groans softly and raises a hand to cover his eyes.

As I absorb what Neo's just said, I can literally feel my face go pale.

"*All* my stuff?" I ask carefully.

"Yep," Neo says cheerfully. "I even managed to get your lease broken and your security deposit refunded from your rental house in Sharm."

He looks like he's expecting this to please me, but I feel sick to my stomach. Like all those pancakes I just scarfed down are in serious danger of making a violent reappearance. With one thoughtful gesture, Neo Mercury's just upset the whole apple cart and wiped out what little remained of my carefully arranged independent life.

Now, even if I do manage to get off this island, I'll have the clothes on my back and what little's in my vastly depleted bank account (which the Fabergé egg from that Singapore job was supposed to replenish) and that's it. My dive gear, my spare burgling kit, my books, clothes, all of it will be sitting here at Icarus.

Despite the complete disaster unfolding right in front of me, I realize Neo thought he was helping.

But he's just done it again, hasn't he?

"Babe?" Neo's eyebrows scrunch together over his anxious eyes. "Why do you feel like that? What have I just done?"

Right. He's reading me through our mate bond. The mate bond I stated repeatedly that I don't want, but which I seem to have acquired anyway. Now I focus on constructing that mental wall between us to keep him out. Which of course he senses.

His green eyes turn cloudy with hurt, and my chest clenches tight with guilt.

Damn it. Damn it. Damn it.

"Listen, baby," I say carefully, not really wanting to have this conversation with my whole cohort listening in and Lucius huddled muttering over the phone next door. "I know you want to help, I do, and it's sweet of you. But I really wish you'd checked with me first."

"But that would have spoiled the surprise." He's watching me just as carefully, since I won't let him in my head. "I don't get it. Why wouldn't you want your own stuff here with you?"

Vasili sighs and folds his napkin. I try to warn him off with my eyes, but he's unstoppable. "Because she isn't planning to *stay*, Einstein. She's planning to abdicate and leave. Incidentally, that's what your precious fated mate was off doing half the night. Since clearly you've been of no assistance whatsoever to her in this particular matter, your beloved was off with horrible me, plotting her death-defying escape."

I'm absolutely horrified and somehow shocked by this betrayal, though I honestly don't know why I ever trusted this terrible man to keep my secret in the first place. Of course, every word he's saying is one hundred percent true. But this is one secret I wasn't planning to spill.

Not like this. Not in a way that will hurt Neo.

Although really, there's no way I could have told Neo that wouldn't have hurt him. No way I could have told him I trusted Neo's enemy with something I couldn't entrust to Neo.

And now, given my own ambivalence, especially after this latest talk with Lucius, I'm no longer even one hundred percent convinced I'm leaving.

But that's a deeper secret I definitely need to keep buried, because if Vasili knows I'm thinking about staying, I'll have him *and* the queen killer to worry about.

Assuming they're not one and the same.

"I don't believe your lies," Neo says firmly to Vasili.

But I can feel my mate's uncertainty like a knife in my heart.

"Oh, honestly," Vasili huffs, "this revelation should hardly come as a shock. Our little queen hasn't exactly been reticent about her perspective on having been abducted and transported here in the first place. And if you don't believe me—a skepticism for which, admittedly, I can scarcely blame you—why don't you ask *her*?"

Neo's trusting face turns toward me. The pancakes in my tummy congeal to lead.

"Zara would never lie to me," Neo says stoutly. "Would you, babe?"

Under normal circumstances, I'm a good liar. It's a job requirement for a thief and a fugitive like me. Here, now, assailed by guilt and a sudden sense of shame, I find I can't even speak.

With unsteady fingers, I lift my cup to avoid meeting my mate's trusting gaze and take a careful sip of my rapidly cooling coffee.

Which is the closest I can come to admitting it's true.

Neo piles his silverware on his half-eaten breakfast and pushes his plate away. His big hands look unsteady too, but I'm too afraid to lower the wall between us to confirm what he's actually feeling.

"When were you going to tell me?" he asks softly. "Or were you just going to leave me a note and disappear?"

I feel like my world's crashing down around my ears.

Or maybe that's how Neo feels.

Either way, I feel horrible. Like I'm a total self-obsessed monster for leaving. And for lying. Even if I never lied outright, I never told him I'm going, I let him believe I'm staying, so it's a lie by omission.

I set down my cup and reach for Neo's hand, but he shifts out of my reach. His shoulders are stiff and he's staring straight ahead and he's hurt, he's *really* hurt, and it's all my fault.

"I-I was definitely going to tell you, Neo." My voice sounds thin and unconvincing, even to my own ears. "I just wasn't sure…"

I'm also not sure how to finish, and no one else looks ready to help me out of this hole I've dug to China. Vasili looks vicious (he's literally been a complete shit *all* morning), Ronin's avoiding my gaze, Racetrack's basically eating popcorn and watching the show, while Dez looks like she wants to envelop Neo in a sympathy hug.

I'm relieved when Lucius returns with a fresh mug of coffee, but his grim expression sucks all the air out of the room. He doesn't return to his abandoned pancakes, but prowls over to lurk near the window, where he sips his coffee and watches the street with a pensive expression. That storm's getting worse, and I'm not sure we'll be having class at all today, but that can't be all that's bothering him.

"Oh, bloody hell, now what?" Ronin mutters.

Lucius lowers his cup with a sigh. "That was the Dean on the phone. I'm afraid Mistress Agrippina hasn't recovered from her illness. In fact, her condition has considerably worsened. It's beginning to appear that perhaps we're not dealing with a bad case of foodborne illness at all, particularly since no one else appears to have fallen ill. And the Dean has decisively ruled out witchcraft."

"Well, hell, spit it out, Teach. What are we into then?" Racetrack demands, while the rest of us just stare at him. "Poison?"

"That does appear to be a distinct possibility." Lucius raises a hand to fend off our rush of questions. "As you're aware, this island's medical clinic is functional but rudimentary. We certainly lack a toxicology laboratory. Agrippina really ought to be flown to the mainland for treatment, but the plane can't take off in this weather. Meanwhile, the Dean is tending her welfare, which also means the Dean is guarding her safety. In short, there's very little we can do for Agrippina at the moment."

I'm frowning with concern for the frazzled-looking, grandmotherly headmistress of Villa Hadrian who taught my Genetics of Witchcraft class before she got sick. If this were Hogwarts, the Hadrians would be Hufflepuffs. And Aggie's like the Minerva McGonagall of Icarus. It's impossible to imagine anyone hating her.

"Who'd want to poison that sweet old lady?" I demand. "That doesn't make any sense."

"Maybe it's part of the pattern," Neo says slowly. Despite my worry over poor Aggie, I'm relieved to see him trying to get past my lack of trust in him—or at least back-burner it for later. "Aggie's a known royalist. She always has been. If that wolf was meant as a warning for Lucius as well as Zara, the killer could be getting ready to act against the royals and their strongest supporters at Icarus."

"Oh, well done, Einstein." Vasili lounges elegantly in his chair. "Do you truly think this is some sort of vast anti-monarchist conspiracy? If that were the case, wouldn't *I* know, since I seem to be the prime suspect for offing Cybelle?"

Lucius glances toward him with a frown. "You're hardly the prime suspect, Mr. Romanov. I fear that distinction belongs to Mr. Pendragon, given the victims' animosity toward his sister. But if I harbored any real suspicion regarding either of you, you may rest assured you wouldn't still be residing under this roof with all your residential privileges intact."

"Well, that's a relief." Vasili's poisonous gaze slews to me. "If someone's killing royals again, darling, that's another reason to expedite your abdication. Assuming your plans haven't changed?"

My skin tingles with danger. I can still hardly believe we're talking about my abdication so openly. And I don't dare betray a hint of ambivalence, since my apparent certainty might be all that's keeping me breathing with a warlock like Vasili in the house.

"No," I say flatly. Another lie to add to my ledger. "My plans haven't changed. I'm leaving."

Lucius turns toward me with betrayal written in every line. "So much for your promise to give the witching world a chance, Ms. Gemini. Are there perhaps any other pertinent secrets to which I as your headmaster should be made privy?"

"Oh, are we sharing *all* our secrets then, Lucius?" Vasili says silkily.

That's a loaded comment which makes Lucius look absolutely hunted. A look passes between them that would intrigue me mightily, if not for the fact that both Neo *and* Lucius are now disappointed in me.

Unexpectedly Ronin surges to his feet to loom over the table. "Maybe it's blooming time for that, mate. We're choking to death on the secrets in this house. Someone bumped off Cybelle and Damien, someone just poisoned Agrippina, and now that same someone's apparently got their sights set on Lucius *and* Zara. I, for one, am bloody ready for a bit of honesty. Just among us. To get to the bottom of this mess."

"Hear, hear," Racetrack murmurs. Dez nestles up against her side in silent concurrence.

This is what I wanted, of course, more of our secrets in the open.

But now that it's actually time to pull back the curtain, I'm suddenly not so sure.

"Very well then. Mr. Pendragon makes a compelling point. There are lives at risk. Including the life of our queen and my own student." Lucius pushes out a heavy breath, his sherry-colored stare meeting mine. His jaw hardens with steely resolve. "In that case, I believe it's my duty to begin. I suspect at this point you're all rather aware that I violated my own code of ethics, to say nothing of Academy expectations, when I inflicted a mating bite upon Mr. Pendragon."

Wow. My mouth pops open. I can hardly believe my reserved and intensely private prof is willing to share a secret that's like a mortal sin or something in his rulebook. Maybe it's a secret that could even get him fired. Fired from a job to which he's deeply committed.

And the fact that he's doing it to protect *me*?

A feeling I can't even put a name to unfolds and flutters in my heart.

Of course, my guys already knew this particular secret, so Lucius' big reveal is only news to Racetrack and Dez. And neither one of them even looks surprised.

Dez catches my eye and lifts her shoulders in a wry shrug. "I'm Valyrian, yeah? My gifts are telepathy and precognition. And I've been living under the same roof with these two since I got here. Kinda saw that one coming, didn't I?"

Which pretty much explains how Racetrack, who's adamantly Mogadon and doesn't have a telepathic bone in her whole body, knows as well.

"Afraid that particular secret turned out to be a bit of a non-event, love," Ronin murmurs, circling the table and crossing to Lucius' side.

Lucius still looks wary and skittish as fuck about being touched in front of his students, like he might actually bolt at any moment now the cat's out of the bag. He stiffens and lifts a hand in a subtle gesture to ward Ronin off.

But Ronin's a man on a mission. There's no warding him off. He slides an arm around Lucius' waist and tucks himself into Lucius' side.

For a second I'm afraid Lucius will push him away. Which will be devastating for Ronin. But I've clearly underestimated the power of the mating bond, because Lucius can't reject his mate when Ronin's right there needing him.

My prof sighs and softens and leans in to rub his face against Ronin's shoulder.

Which is the closest he can get right now to nuzzling Ronin's mating bite.

I sigh too, because it's so wonderful to see Lucius acknowledge their bond, to see him admit even briefly to needing anyone, and because Ronin deserves this acknowledgment that Lucius is asserting his claim.

And the sight of those two together in all their shared hotness—Ronin with his sleek raven ponytail and his black flame tattoos licking above his collar as he turns his face into Lucius' neck, Lucius looking tidy and professorial but positively feral with Ronin's mouth on his skin—is more than enough to light my fire.

Now that Lucius is actually admitting they're together, I really want to see Lucius bend Ronin over my big medieval bed and fuck him through his next heat. And now that their secret's out in the open (at least under this roof), I wonder if I might actually be that lucky.

Vasili's watching the two of them with a look hot enough to scorch anyone's skin, so I'm guessing I'm not the only person in this room who's entertaining that particular fantasy.

Ronin meets Vasili's smoldering stare with a slow smile. *Ready to spill one of ours, then, love?*

And, because I'm a telepath and my powers seem to be growing by the minute, I can listen in on their link.

"Oh fuck." Vasili sprawls carelessly and waves one hand in a languid gesture, but I can see the pulse fluttering hard and fast in his throat. "Go ahead then, darling, if you must."

Ronin's tiger eyes go lidded as he holds Vasili's insolent stare. "Vasili and I have been lovers for two years."

Neo blurts out a surprised sound. But no one can tear their eyes away from those two.

"And you don't ever have to worry about losing me. Because I've been bonkers in love with you," Ronin finishes softly, looking only at Vasili, "since the day I pitched up at Icarus and you knocked me on my arse with your fucking telekinesis."

I suck in my breath with a gasp. Somehow, with that one, he's managed to knock all of us off balance. Not about their being lovers… which, again, I'm sensing at least some of my housemates might have guessed… but with that declaration of love.

Racetrack's mouth is hanging open wide enough for sparrows to fly into.

Dez is hugging herself and looking happy, since she's apparently known this whole newsflash too for a while.

Neo's gaze swings between them. He's blank with shock and more than a little appalled.

But Vasili looks absolutely shattered. His face looks like someone's broken him. His cheeks flame with sudden color and his pupils blow so wide his eyes are all black.

And I realize with a pang it's because he doesn't believe anyone could ever actually love him.

Because no one ever actually has.

Unexpectedly my own eyes flood with tears.

"Ronin," he scrapes out, putting out a hand like he's warning the guy away.

"It's true, love." Ronin releases Lucius with a soft glance and goes straight to Vasili. He hunkers down before the Goblin King until their faces are level and rests his hands over Vasili's. "You don't have to say it back. But I've wanted to say it to you for so long."

Vasili's struggling, like really struggling to keep his mask on and his defenses up, and my heart aches to see him. He blinks rapidly, mouth opening and closing as if he'd like to speak but can't. His face turns toward me, and I try to convey silently that it's okay, he can trust us with this.

"I…" He turns back to Ronin, who's still kneeling before him, waiting patiently for Vasili to process what he's just heard. "I…"

It's all right, bad boy, I want to tell him. *It's safe for you to love him. It's safe for you to love all of us.*

And maybe I do tell him, because his gaze veers back toward me. His face fires with raw panic.

"I can't," he blurts, thrusting roughly to his feet. "I—just—*can't.*"

He pushes brutally past Ronin, knocking him off balance, and tears out of the room like his uniform's on fire. Ronin shoots to his feet, face stricken, but clearly doesn't know where to go or what to do.

And Lucius, who should really go comfort his own mate, looks too conflicted himself to take action.

Which leaves it up to me to rush over there and wrap myself around Ronin, which I do as fast as I can. He drags me into his arms with a gasp like he's drowning and I'm all that's keeping him afloat. I hug him as tight as I can and I stroke his sleek hair and I tell him silently it's okay, Vasili just needs time to process, and I think it's so freaking beautiful what Ronin told him.

"Wow. Just wow." Neo's strained voice brings my head up to find him.

He too has pushed to his feet, still clutching his napkin in one hand. Under his shock of purple hair, his face is white and his eyes are blazing. "Those two have been mortal enemies every day they've been under this roof. Every time they're in the same room it's like World War Three. Now it turns out they're actually lovers, and no one's even surprised? Except me. Why does everyone in this house seem to know everyone else's secrets except me?"

There are reasons, and Ronin starts explaining them, about Vasili being a private guy who doesn't feel comfortable showing his feelings, that it makes him feel exposed, something about his past, etc., but Neo's not listening.

Because what Neo's really asking is not why Vasili and Ronin didn't tell him, but why *I* didn't.

I'm Neo's fated mate. In his worldview, we're not supposed to have secrets.

The fact that we do clearly reinforces that I just don't trust him.

And he's devastated.

I give Ronin, who also clearly needs me right now, an apologetic squeeze and release him. "Now, hold on a minute for me, babe—"

"No," Neo says softly. "No. This time, I don't think I will."

He tosses his napkin on the table and walks out.

And even though he does it quietly, every soft footfall echoes like a shout in the empty chamber of my suddenly aching heart.

Chapter Thirty-Two

Zara

I'm late for my independent study with Lucius in the belfry.

I'm late because Vasili's been MIA since Ronin dropped the L word, and Neo's been avoiding me since he learned I lied, and I'm feeling wrecked by guilt and worried as fuck about all of them.

I'm also late because I skipped out of my Genetics of Witchcraft class (taught again by Master Zerxes given Agrippina's situation, and darn I'm so sorry I missed it) to test the dry suit down in the harbor. The timing worked out great, because Malcolm the great white shifter's been with the Schedule B's taking their Common Magics midterm with Lucius, so no Jaws in the water.

I also figure it's good to keep the gears turning and the mechanics of my escape plan in motion, even if I'm hesitating now about whether to actually escape.

At least going through the motions might help reassure Vasili that I'm abdicating. And therefore help keep me breathing. Even though I haven't so much as glimpsed Vasili since Ronin's emotional bombshell made the Goblin King bolt.

For what it's worth, that dry suit is aces. Held up beautifully during my brief immersion, and I even found a couple of topped-up nitrox tanks in the shop, so I'll have plenty of the good stuff to breathe down there if I do make the dive.

I just can't decide anymore if I should.

And not because it's dangerous. I'm a cat burglar and a casino czar's daughter. I grew up doing dangerous.

But the storm delays me getting back for my Double Witchcraft indie study. The wind's really starting to howl, and the snow's blowing sideways, and I almost get lost on my way back to the church.

Which is how I'm late again for Lucius. Even though in normal life—or whatever passes for normal in my life—I'm almost never late.

I scramble up the twisting stairs and burst into the belfry with an apology already forming on my lips. "So sorry to be late, Master Aries. I, uh, had to take care of something…"

The strong wind up here sucks the words right out of my mouth and blows them away across the snow-covered rooftops.

But that's not why I fall silent.

Lucius is standing on the low stone wall that guards the drop, legs spread wide, head tipped back, arms spread out to embrace the elements, the black folds of his caped greatcoat open and billowing in the breeze. The wind's unraveled his chestnut hair and it's blowing loose around his face.

He's basically one step away from plunging to a messy death on the cobblestone piazza far below. A danger that makes my heart pound. But he's so wild and so primitive and so exhilarated up there, every line of his body blazing with savage joy, that he lights me up like an electric current.

I freeze under the peaked roof in the open-sided bell chamber, the massive bells hanging still and silent beside me, and breathe, "Lucius."

Again the wind snatches the word away.

But this time, his wolf hears me.

His head whips around to find me, untamed hair flying free around his face, eyes flaming red, huge-ass fangs fully extended. His wolf's on the prowl and very close to the surface. Despite the cold and the snow gathering in his hair, his stern Vlad the Impaler features are flushed with heat.

"Zara," he rumbles, thick and guttural. His wolf lurks in his voice. "It's time to summon the lightning."

"Shit," I whisper.

I don't know how I know. My power's been surging and growing in weird unpredictable spikes ever since I got here. It's like being close to the four of them, these four warlocks, is setting me off somehow.

Maybe my Gemini DNA really does want me to claim them.

Because I don't know how else I'd suddenly feel so certain—like telepath certain—that the reason Lucius is flaming with heat and half-delirious in a snowstorm is because he's in heat.

Do purebred shifters even go into heat? Unless they're, you know, bitten?

And clearly I'm projecting again, because some of the crazy recedes from his eyes.

"We really must do something," he says through his fangs, "about your appalling ignorance of the arcane races. The *only* time a shifter goes into heat, Ms. Gemini, is when he's been bitten and bonded by a mate. After that, a shifter's heat is a monthly occurrence, following the cycle of the moon."

Well, okay. I guess that means he's been bitten. But Ronin's not a shifter and he doesn't bite. I could bite, maybe, I'm kind of a baby shifter, but I *didn't.* Then who in the fucking *hell*...?

As I gaze up at my teacher, my thoughts spin away. I'm completely flat-out mesmerized. He's still in there, my Lucius, standing one misstep away from death and giving me a fucking lecture. It's just he's sharing that space inside his head, like that space inside his body, with someone else.

With his wolf.

He stares down at me from the wall, wind licking his greatcoat like black flames, tie unknotted and shirt unbuttoned. Sweat glitters on his brow and the powerful contours of his chest. His sweat-slicked naked abs are so taut they make me feral. And underneath all that buttoned-tight propriety he's shedding with his clothes, there's a glimmer of antique gold on a chain, nestled in the hollow of his corded neck.

Sweet Jesus. He's actually wearing a crucifix. He's wearing a crucifix like Van Helsing.

Lust coils low and tight in my core and makes my pussy clench. I drag in a breath that's heavy and sweet with my own mating scent.

He hasn't even touched me, and I'm scenting.

His nostrils flare and his chest rumbles with a growl.

"Summon the lightning," he snarls, but it's his wolf, his wolf who's winning the war for dominance that's raging in his body. "Claim your power."

"Not like this." I don't even know who's talking, but the words are coming out of my mouth. And I've never felt so sure about anything in my entire life. "You want me doing what you need? Then I want you doing what *I* need. Get down here."

He flings back his head and bays with laughter, but that's not my cautious prof. That's his wolf howling.

And it's his wolf and his wolf's primitive instincts I need to lure.

Holding his flaming gaze, I unbutton my peacoat until it falls at my feet. I'm standing under the belfry roof, which shields me from the snow, while the massive bells hanging behind me block the worst of the wind. And there's so much heat pouring through my body that the cold doesn't even bother me.

His eyes burn hotter and his fangs punch lower. He drops from the wall to the flagstones with an animal's fluid grace and growls in that sandpaper voice.

"I'm yours to command, my queen."

My mating scent's pouring off me in waves, and we're both getting high on the pheromones. I unbutton my blazer and start working on the buttons of my blouse.

"Get over here," I say, low and husky. "And keep those fangs out. I want them."

I don't have time to glance at my dive watch, but he's under the roof with me in a hot two seconds. Looming over me, crowding me back against the thick stone pillar that braces the structure. I plant my back against the wall and stare up at him, heart hammering under my half-open shirt. His hot eyes follow the vee of exposed skin to the little pink bow that closes my virginal schoolgirl bra.

"Who bit you?" I whisper.

Because I don't know whether to thank that person or kick their ass.

Lucius is mine. They all are. Whether I leave or stay. With every day that passes on this island, I absorb that one essential truth deeper into every pore.

He braces a hand on the wall on either side to fence me in and leans close. "Who do you think?"

A powerful whiff of wolf rolls over me, spiced with a potent kick of Mogadon mating scent. It's a scent I know intimately, because it's all over Ronin.

Oh my freaking God.

"Vasili." Under my skirt, a surge of arousal makes me slick. Any minute, I'll have girl cream rolling down my thighs. If he doesn't start doing me, I might literally melt. "Did he fuck you?"

If he did and I missed it, I'm going to howl.

"No, thankfully, but he did get me off. Rather… explosively, I might add. Then he kissed me goodnight and sent me firmly off to bed. Would you believe I actually went?" In my teacher's voice, humor mingles with chagrin.

OMG. That's hot as fuck.

And some tiny stupid part of me can't help wondering if Vasili held back with Lucius so we could consummate this thing growing between us together.

All freaking five of us.

Triggered just by the thought of it, my skin is tingling and my power is rising. Lucius is trying to master his wolf, so he can reassert his usual control.

But I'm having none of that. Not now.

And you better believe I've never been happier in my life that today's floral lingerie comes with a front-closing bra. I hold his red stare and reach up to pop the clasp.

Liberated from captivity, my tits spring free, nipples already tight and tingling with anticipation. A growl rips from his throat and his fangs, if humanly possible, extend even more. He could yawn and rip my throat out, but that's not the need that's driving him.

So fast he makes me gasp, he pounces.

He swoops in to swipe his tongue down my neck. His fangs score my skin in a graze he probably doesn't intend. One sharp tip nicks my collarbone with a sting. A hot trickle of blood spills down my tit.

And that's all he needs to unchain the beast.

He drops to his knees before me in literal fucking worship. And I know that's what it is—worship—because he rasps, "My queen. Let me worship you."

Hell to the yeah. I'm definitely on board with being worshipped.

Then his powerful hands clench in my blouse, and there go those last three buttons I never managed to get to. With blazer and blouse both slipping off my shoulders, he grips my hips and drags me close and buries his face in my breasts.

I gasp and clutch his shoulders and brace for his bite.

But it's all lips and tongue he gives me now, ravaging my tits and suckling my nipples while short desperate cries rise out of me. My rings make me super sensitive—I've never been more sensitive—and I can feel every flick of his tongue on my rings and every hard pull of his hot mouth in my cunt like those spots are connected by a tripwire.

I clench my fists in his thick soft curls and tilt my head back and writhe under his touch. The gusset of my panties is soaked and my clit is swollen and aching for his touch.

"Merciful Christ," he mutters against my skin, the drag of his fangs making me crazy for his bite. "I swear your scent alone is enough to make any man drunk."

"Then imagine how good I'm going to taste," I groan. Beside me, the massive bells hum softly.

Because that was the lightning voice, just a wisp of it, a whisper of witchcraft buried in my deadly voice.

I go rigid in major alarm.

But he soothes me, warm hands sliding down my bare legs to coax my feet apart.

"Don't be afraid of your power," he rumbles. "You're the Gemini queen. That power is yours to claim. I'll always keep you safe."

"Yeah, well, it's not exactly *me* I'm worried about—"

The rasp of his whiskers against my thighs dries up all my words. God, yes, I am *so* ready for this. So ready for him.

I yield to the insistent press of his hands against my inner thighs and widen my stance for him. I've never actually come standing up like this—except yesterday in the gym, watching Ronin and Vasili go at it—but somehow, I don't think that's going to be a problem. I'm kicking out enough mating scent to make both of us high.

Underneath all that flowery sweetness lurks the dark musk of my slick.

His hands slide under my skirt and push the plaid aside. Which pretty much exposes the soaked scrap of my panties clinging to my hips and probably outlining my dripping slit. My clit feels so engorged with need it has to be the size of a cherry.

Clearly his wolf's not in the mood to be teased.

Two fingers hook in my gusset and drag the drenched scrap aside. For what feels like forever, he drinks in the sight of me, his breath rough and his chest heaving, while my cunt clenches hard under his stare. I smooth his unruly hair away from his face and he looks up at me with those fiery eyes, the mute adoration of the wolf at war with the tortured craving of the man.

He's trying to retract his fangs, but that's the last thing I want.

"Your tongue," I pant. "Do it. I need you to make me come."

"Your wish." His eyes hood and his face goes savage. "My command."

His hot wet tongue licks up my slit and laves my clit. The tips of his fangs score my tender folds, though he's being way too careful not to break my skin. My head falls back and a cry rips out of me that makes the bells hum. That low bronze note vibrates though my skull as he spreads me wide between his hands and fucks my cunt with his tongue and works my eager clit with a ruthless finger. My hips rock into his touch and his freaking teeth and my eyes fall shut and I angle my pelvis to get more of him, harder, deeper, *more.*

God, he's mine. This is what he's meant for. Meant to pin me to the wall, spread wide and wanton, with those powerful hands while I claw at the stone and sparks fly from my lethal touch and his tongue and fingers and teeth work their wicked magic.

He's growling against my pussy, which is making me *so* hot. And apparently this tongue fuck is just a warm up, because once I stop clawing the wall and start clutching his head and blatantly fucking his face, he switches things up and his ruthless tongue starts playing with my clit.

"Fuck, Lucius," I gasp. "Oh *fuck.*"

Which isn't super articulate, but he's so freaking good at this. He's so good at tonguing me that tingles shoot down my thighs and make my toes curl.

Especially when he eases a finger inside my aching channel. Slippery with need, I clamp around him in a freaking death grip and ride his hand hard.

In about fifteen seconds, he's going to ring my bell.

"That's what we want," he groans against my clit. "Want you to come all over our face."

Meaning him and that beast barely contained inside him. Which is sexy as fuck.

My breathless cries are rising, the lightning's in my voice, and thunder is growling and rumbling in the snowy skies. When he braces me against the wall and pulls one of my legs over his shoulder to open me wide and deepen the angle, then adds a second finger to the mix and pumps me, I bite my lower lip so hard I taste blood.

"Stop holding back," he growls. "Let everything go. I won't let you fall."

But it's only when his free hand smooths possessively over my ass and one finger slides down my crack to tease my back door that I lose it.

My first climax rips through me like a megaton warhead. My pussy locks around his thrusting fingers in my cunt so hard we'll need a crowbar to pry him out of me, but right now he's going nowhere. I fling my head back and shout to high heaven. The chemical reek of ozone drenches the air.

Then a blinding flash of lightning turns the world white.

My legs buckle under this blast wave of pleasure, but he holds me up until

I regain control. I'm still vibrating with the aftershock when he lowers my foot to the floor and surges to his feet. By now I'm so wet I can practically hear the suction when he pulls his fingers out of my pussy and engulfs them with his mouth.

Which I'm pretty sure is just about the hottest thing I've ever seen.

His eyes are wild and his face is brutal with need.

"There," I pant. "Lightning. Satisfied?"

He slides his fingers free and his voice drops two octaves. "Rest assured, Zara Gemini, I'm not even close to satisfied."

Eyes never leaving mine, he unbuckles his belt and opens his houndstooth trousers. "Now turn around for me. And take off those innocent schoolgirl panties before I tear them off."

Holy fucking shit.

Chapter Thirty-Three
Lucius

Zara's barely standing after the climax I just wrung out of her.

But she's never looked more desirable. Her face is flushed and her pigtails are floating, while her eyes are pools of periwinkle fire. Her shirt and blazer are slipping from her shoulders to expose her luscious breasts, those perfect pierced nipples furled tight and shining with my saliva.

These students of mine and their exotic piercings are very likely going to be the death of me. But, truly, what a way to go.

In this moment, my queen looks like a cross between a Penthouse pinup and a Roman goddess. It requires every last ounce of control I possess not to claim her with the mating bite she's clearly demanding.

And the reason for my monumental restraint is not merely because the last complication the fragile dynamic in our *domus* requires is yet another inhabitant rutting and mindless with mating heat. Given the acute shortage of faculty to staff this Academy, I might—just barely—escape the Dean's censure with a private reprimand and a formal letter in my personnel file for having bitten and bonded one student.

If I were to bite and bond another, much less abandon my duty entirely to join the queen's harem, there's no way to hide the truth. Who would trust me to teach their children after that? I'll certainly have lost all trust in myself. I'll leave myself no alternative but to resign on the spot, which means the most profound betrayal of a teacher's duty to my students and the races I've devoted my life to protect.

My restraint notwithstanding, although I adamantly refuse to bite Zara, my wolf absolutely insists that I fuck her. And my queen's made it entirely apparent that she too demands some tangible tribute of my devotion before she'll trust me the way I require her to trust me.

She needs to do more than blindly summon the lightning—an ability which was, after all, never in question.

What she needs most is to control it. For that to occur, she needs to stop fearing her power.

To conquer her fear, I need her to give me her trust.

Still, slinking behind all my noble reasoning like a predator, the despicable truth lurks. I want her. My wolf wants her. Here, now, we're finally going to possess her.

At least once.

In this moment, I'm not a tenured professor making rational choices.

I'm a wolf in heat.

I loom over her, my tongue saturated with the potent musk of her taste, my hands trembling with restraint as I unbutton my trousers, my wolf lunging inside my skin like he's rabid. I've kept him tightly in check, but he's lurking in my raspy voice.

"Panties off, Zara. Face the wall."

Some distant corner of my psyche that remains the sane and sober-minded headmaster barely holds me back from dragging her panties off myself as I've already threatened. Threat or no threat, throne or no throne, bond or no bond, there's a power disparity between us. Ethically, morally, the bare minimum I require is an affirmation that she wants this as much as I do.

She also needs to know I can make myself stop. I won't add coercion to my rapidly multiplying litany of sins.

Gaze never straying from mine, she reaches under her skirt and slides her panties down her thighs. Despite the encumbrance of her boots, she shimmies out of her lingerie with feline grace, which reminds me just what she was doing in Singapore the night we met.

Cat burglar indeed.

That's enough acquiescence for me and my wolf. Roughly I grip her waist and spin her to face the wall.

"Bend over," I snarl in her ear. "And hold on. I'm not going to be gentle."

Her head snaps toward me and her mouth claims mine, fangs and all, in a ravenous kiss.

Good, she whispers in my head. *Show me how much you want me.*

God in Heaven knows, showing her how much I want her isn't going to pose any difficulty.

I shove my trousers down with unseemly haste and grip my length in a rough fist. I give a few hard pumps to slow myself down while she spreads her hands against the wall and bends forward, head turned back to watch, face feral with hunger, ass tilted in the air under that obscenely short skirt.

And what an ass she has. Round and toned and suntanned except for the tiny white triangle of what must have been the world's most minuscule bikini.

Merciful Christ, how the sight of her inflames me.

"Hurry," she demands, and it's all I can manage to focus on what she needs rather than what she wants.

"Just a moment. We need a prophylactic." That's the very least of what she needs. I fumble in my greatcoat pocket, because I knew the instant I woke this morning that I'm going into heat, precisely as Vasili intended, and I didn't dare leave the *domus* unprepared. "I have a condom."

"Hmmm." Her lids drop over her glowing eyes and the corner of her full lips curls in a predatory smile. "Ronin says you've been celibate for, what, years?"

"Until this week, yes." I tear the package open with my teeth and unroll the prophylactic over my thick shaft and down my straining length.

"Then I wouldn't insist." At my blank stare, her smile deepens. "On the condom. Because I'm clean. And protected from getting pregnant. I don't have a clue why this is, but all I seem able to think about is fucking all four of you. In the bare."

I groan and grip the base of my cock, desperately bracing against a visual that nearly makes me climax in my own hand. In part, my reaction stems from the fact that she's talking about claiming all four of us—every male courtier she has—for her harem. In part, I'm reacting to the sexual invitation my queen has just issued, an invitation which comes quite close to a command. In part, I'm reacting to the fact that this—what she's feeling—is the mating instinct.

Despite her clearly stated intention to abdicate, every cell in my queen's luscious body is preparing her to ascend.

But this is the twenty-first century, and she isn't chattel to be claimed. I'm determined to protect her, even while my wolf's baying for me to fuck her raw.

"I'll never put your safety at risk." I crowd in behind her, spam her tiny waist in my hands, and nuzzle the back of her neck. "On that account, my queen, you may place your trust in me entirely."

"I do. I trust you, Lucius. Or I wouldn't be here." She shivers under my touch. "Now hurry up and fuck me."

Yes! My wolf tilts his muzzle to the sky and howls with triumph. *She's ours. Claim our queen.*

My lack of restraint may be sinful, but damn if my wolf isn't right.

I fit my engorged manhood to that soaked crevasse between her thighs, grip her hips to anchor her, and tunnel deep inside her in a single ruthless thrust.

Chapter Thirty-Four
Zara

The scrape of Lucius' fangs against the back of my neck almost spanks my monkey. I'm literally shivering with anticipation. Because I'm definitely rocking a vampire fetish. But it's the size and threat of him lurking behind me that has me pushing my ass back into his monster cock and squirming with impatience.

Until he grips my hips hard enough to bruise me and sheathes that thick shaft of his brutally deep inside. A cry rips from my lips and thunder crashes overhead.

Cheese on toast, this entire effing Academy is going to know I'm getting off. But I've got the hottest prof at the Academy bending me over and buried a good eight inches deep (at least) in my cunt.

So sue me. I love this.

My power's sizzling and sparking just under my skin like a live electric wire. Sparks crackle and fly between our joined bodies as he backs off and lunges back into me, so thick he's splitting me open. He snarls in my ear like a wild animal and I moan deep in my throat. The big bronze bells suspended beside us hum in tune with every moan.

I hope Lucius knows what he's doing with my lightning, because I haven't felt this out of control since that night in the Gemini casino. And they carted folks away from that one in body bags.

"You can—trust me," he grits in my ear, the words scraping out in time with his punishing thrusts. "My queen—Zara—you're so—damn—*tight*."

I gasp out a winded laugh. "That's because you're so damn *big*. Damn, Lucius, you're a beast—"

With a growl, he wraps one big hand around my throat to choke me. Which *really* shouldn't get me off. Really, it shouldn't. But all that strength and savagery he's exuding really turn me on, and I guess I really do trust him, because my slick pussy clamps hard around his cock and wrings out of him a hoarse shout.

I don't know where all that mannerly Old World restraint of his went, but

I'm thrilled to see it go. Now he's grunting in my ear and pounding into me like a battering ram, his breath hard and his pace relentless, and he's throttling me hard enough to assert dominance but not hard enough to actually choke me.

When I try to match his rhythm, his grip tightens to immobilize me.

"Don't move," he grits in my ear. "Or you'll trigger my wolf."

Okay then. Looks like I'm not going anywhere even if I wanted to. And, somehow, all this restraint makes me feel… safe?

He's basically pinning me in place and fucking himself into me and using my body like a sex toy to get himself off, and I don't think he could be any hotter. I drop my head and claw into the stone and absorb his punishing thrusts, the slap of flesh on flesh echoing through the belfry, the musk of wolf and Lucius and Vasili mixing with the mating scent that's coming off me in waves.

Oh fuck, Vasili. Just the thought of the Goblin King here with us, writhing against my front and painting my tummy and tits when he comes… or maybe, God, Vasili fucking Lucius while Lucius fucks me and controlling the pace for all three of us… yeah, that visual's going to launch me into orbit like the freaking space shuttle.

"Don't you dare come," Lucius mutters in my ear, his accent all thick and rumbly. "Not until you channel the lightning. That's a damned order, Ms. Gemini. Now turn your head this way."

Blind with need, I do what he wants and pry my eyelids open.

Across a span of snow-covered rooftops, the gray harbor spreads to the horizon. Barely visible through the snow lurks the dim outline of the rocky breakwater that guards the harbor. The slim pale finger of an ancient-looking lighthouse spears high into the pewter sky.

"See that lighthouse?" His fangs graze my ear, and I almost come around his cock right there. "It's been abandoned—for years. The power source burned out—while I was a student. I want you to—direct the lightning—there."

He's slowed his pace so he can deliver this little history lecture. But every hard pump of his hips is brutal. I'm going to fly apart into a zillion pieces under the impact. He's going to annihilate me.

But I'm going to claim him if it kills me.

With him fucking me like that, it's all I can manage to dredge up a sentence. "I, uh, don't think I can direct it like that."

"You can. I'll help you." He drags his fangs down my neck and makes me shiver. "Do it when you come."

"You told me not to come." Even though I'm teasing him, I'm tilting my head to give him access, baring the curve of my shoulder where I saw him bite Ronin. "I'll only do it on one condition."

His voice thickens to his wolf's guttural snarl. "Be very careful indeed what you ask for, Zara. He's close to escaping my control."

"You and your freaking control." My voice is deepening too, the lightning lurking deep inside and building all around us, summoned by the hum of my power. His pace is building, fueled by the telepathic link I'm forging between us, every slick sucking thrust more than audible as my pussy fists and ripples around his thick shaft. I'm groaning with every punishing thrust, and I'm definitely going to be sore after.

But he's going to be so worth it.

He's moaning my name and grinding his face into my shoulder and I know he needs this as much as I do, I *know* it.

And I know it's time.

It's *time*.

"Oh God, Lucius. Oh God. Oh God." My voice is spiraling and my climax is rushing toward me like a runaway freight train and my power is crackling through every pore. "I claim you. I fucking claim you. I claim you for my fucking harem. Now give me your fucking bite."

With a savage snarl, his fangs punch through my shoulder and sink deep in my flesh. It feels like his whole wolf is ripping into me.

I scream with raw anguish and primal triumph and lightning pours through me.

And even while my own blood's rolling down my shoulder to splatter the floor, the mating bond snaps tight around us in a whiplash of power.

My lightning's forking and sizzling through the sky, but he's with me, he's inside me, and together we're guiding all that awesome power. My deadly bolt sears across the sky and slams into the distant lighthouse. The whole structure glows blue, fingers of electricity zagging down its length. The deep toll of the church bell fills my head and echoes through my skull.

We did it.

We just freaking did it.

The two of us together.

He's the key, somehow, the key to controlling and channeling all this amperage that's running through my lethal Gemini blood.

And the lock of his jaws and the suck of his mouth against my shoulder don't make me feel menaced. He makes me feel safe.

Just like he's always promised.

The orgasm I've barely been holding at bay rips through every synapse in my body and breaks through every wall I've ever built around my heart to protect me from hurting anyone or being hurt myself. I clamp tight and hard around the vicious hammer of his monster cock. My climax ripples through me and I scream my triumph to the skies.

He lifts his head from my bite and announces our mating with a bestial roar. Our cries twine and mingle like our power just did. His cock kicks inside me, so I can feel the spurt of his come even through the thin latex between us.

Next time, we're losing the effing condom, because there will definitely be a next time and a next and a next. He's mine. I'm claiming him.

And I'm staying. I'm staying at the Icarus Academy to learn everything I need.

Everything I need to become the Gemini queen.

Chapter Thirty-Five
Zara

I have to admit it. This dress is freaking gorgeous.

It's a slanting one-shouldered style with an asymmetric hem that hits midway up my thigh on one side and just below my knee on the other. Cut from what looks like one solid swath of midnight silk, held together under one arm by a zigzag line of open turquoise lacing that manages to suggest a bolt of lightning and goes *all* the way down from my armpit to my hem.

Which pretty much means I can't wear panties. Or a bra. It's just me, my suntan, and the dress.

A dress that's totally me. Me as the queen I've secretly decided I'm going to be.

I freaking love this dress.

Not to mention, it skims over my freshly showered body and kisses my curves like a lover's hands.

This is a dress chosen by someone who knows exactly what's in my closet—both my size and my style—or else someone with a keen eye and an impeccable fashion sense.

Which pretty much means either Neo or Vasili.

Neither of whom showed up for Dez's yummy Pad Thai tonight. Looks like Vasili's still brooding over the whole Ronin revelation, while Ronin himself spent the entire delicious meal fretting and second-guessing himself for having spilled those particular beans in public.

While I spent the whole meal fretting and second-guessing myself over *not* spilling my own beans to Neo. My sunny-tempered mate's not usually the broody sort, and I'm starting to think I fucked up bigtime.

I should have trusted him.

To add to my worries, Lucius himself was a no-show. Which makes me wonder if maybe he's doing a little second-guessing himself about our thermonuclear sex fest in the belfry. At least he'll appreciate that the wide swath of fabric winding over my shoulder covers up the neat twin punctures he left when he bit me. He tongued me enough post-climax that his shifter saliva closed the wounds—all that affectionate post-bite tending he wanted to do after he bit Ronin, but couldn't.

Now there's a slow warmth building under my skin that tells me the mating heat's definitely coming. I'm already starting to feel frisky.

Suffice it to say, I came back from dinner distracted as fuck. Only to find this dress hanging primly in my open armoire, with the cutest pair of combat boots in the history of combat boots lined up underneath. Boots the exact shade of my teal hair, currently twisted in a sleek go-go girl ponytail high on my crown.

Maybe the outfit means Neo's ready to forgive me.

But, more likely, it's just the Goblin King living up to his half-threat, half-promise to dress me in a manner suitable to appear on his imperial arm in public.

Either way, I'm ready on time (of course), but I'm twitchy and jumpy as a novice thief breaking into her first bank (not that I'd ever do a thing like that). Darkness presses against my windows and I'm reduced to pacing my bedroom floor and watching the digits on my dive watch flash past.

That's what I'm doing when the sharp rap of knuckles on my door makes me jump.

There's no way Neo's ever knocked on a door like that in his life, so I know right away who's out there.

Now that it's finally showtime, my famous nerves of steel kick in. I take my time checking my makeup at my vanity, swiping on another layer of Betty Boop mascara and adding a fresh coat of bubble-gum lipstick to my pucker.

Another imperious *rat-a-tat* makes me grin. He's fuming out there on my doorstep, which he totally deserves for being such a shit to me this morning and to Ronin all freaking day.

I sashay over to the door and take my sweet time opening it, with my face arranged to project innocent surprise and a sassy remark all primed for that effing rattlesnake I've got for a prom date.

Too bad every single word flies out of my head the second I open up.

This happens because, one, it's not just Vasili standing outside my door. It's Vasili and freaking Neo, like, *together* (which never happens, as in literally never, given Neo's status as my fated mate and Vasili's hatred for all things royal). And, two, they both look so insanely gorgeous that I'm ready to cream my nonexistent panties right there.

Vasili's got that David Bowie rock star glam going full force in a sparkly electric blue frock coat with the collar popped over a swanky shirt, black breeches that hug his lean hips and sinewy thighs, and boots with heels that make his legs go on for miles. He's rocking MTV hair frosted so pale it's almost white, cat-eyes that glimmer like liquid mercury as they slide slowly over my body, and a glossy pink mouth set in his signature smirk.

And, smirk or no smirk, I want to drag him in close and kiss the lip gloss right off his sexy mouth and tongue his fangs until he moans.

He won't be smirking by the time I'm done with him. He'll be kissing me back the way he did last night.

His face is guarded because, after all, he is the Goblin King and it wouldn't do to look approachable. But there's a vulnerability lurking in his ice-blue eyes that tells me he's still broken inside.

Which just makes me want to kiss him more.

Until he untucks his forked tongue from behind his teeth and talks.

"At least you're on time, and the frock fits properly… more or less." He sneers. "A bit snug across the chest, isn't it? Let's get this farce over with."

Now I want to slap him. Same as always.

"Nice to see you too, asshole," I snipe back, all my stupid prom girl hopes of a magical night and a goodnight kiss fizzling out like a spent Fourth of July sparkler. "And you look lovely too, by the way, fuck you very much."

We'd probably just keep going like that, except Neo gets between us.

He looks like a magenta-haired John Travolta in *Saturday Night Fever* looming over me and filling my doorway in a trendy white tux over a jet black button-down that encases his wide chest and broad shoulders in a manner I thoroughly approve. His vivid hair's still grazing his shoulders and falling in his eyes, but he's wearing contacts instead of reading glasses tonight. His kryptonite-green eyes are wide as he drinks in every detail from my go-go girl ponytail to my cobalt-blue booties.

And literally one look at his kissable mouth is enough to start me scenting.

"Hey, babe," he says softly. "You always look incredible in everything you wear, but… wow. Just wow. And I'm totally saying that for both of us."

He shoots a reproachful look at Vasili and hands me a small flat box with a bow, which I accept automatically, almost brainless with relief and gratitude that my mate's talking to me again.

Then my brain gets stuck on what he just said.

"Wait a sec." I peer suspiciously past him at the Goblin King, who's checking his lip gloss in a little mirror and still (of course) sneering. But maybe I'm starting to see past that. "Are you, like, both taking me to the prom? Because last time I looked, the two of you hated each other."

"The Janus Dance is hardly a prom." Vasili snaps his compact closed and flashes me an irate look. "This isn't high school, darling. And, yes, we're both taking you. Assuming you intend to come at all."

Neo sighs over Vasili's waspish manners and gifts me one of his slow sexy smiles. "We agreed we'd try harder to get along, him and me, for your sake. We figure we need to do better at communicating, because there's a lot going on right now in this *domus* and we need to keep you safe. And he's asking you if you're ready, not telling you."

Neo's going to be so happy (I hope) when I tell him I'm staying.

The Goblin King, not so much. Him I'm not sure I can trust.

And I don't totally mind Vasili telling me what to do under certain circumstances (ahem), but now's not the time for that particular convo either. Or we'll be late for sure. Because I never had an actual prom in high school since I ran away so young, and now that I know I'm going to the dance with both of them, I'm actually looking forward to it.

"Okay, but I have something to say first." I give Neo my full attention and lay a gentle hand on his sleeve. "I owe you a major apology, baby. I never meant to lie to you or hurt you, and I flat out suck for doing it. I mean it—I literally suck."

"No you don't, Zara." This mate I really don't deserve blinks down at me. "You really don't. It took me a little while to figure this out, but you didn't know at first you could trust me, did you? Since you didn't actually know me? Now you know you can."

An overwhelming rush of relief pours through me and makes me feel all warm and floaty. Because knowing I hurt him has been killing me all day.

The last thing I ever want to do ever again is hurt him. Because he's… my fated mate.

"I am," he breathes, his voice thick with emotion, and wraps me tight in his arms. "I really am. And I'd go through a whole lot more than I went through today just to know you finally believe it."

"I believe it, okay? You're my fated mate. You are." I lean my forehead against his broad chest and whisper into his lapel, "Thank you for forgiving me, baby. But we're still going to talk more later. We need it." I lift my head and give both of them a stern look. "All freaking five of us."

"Deal," Neo says for both of them, smiling down at me. "Now open your present."

I've almost forgotten the little box I'm still holding. But I love presents and I don't get many of them, so I pop the lid with a happy sense of anticipation.

Coiled neatly in a nest of snowy tissue is a studded leather choker, suede-soft and dyed teal. And it's so frigging perfect for me that hot tears rush into my eyes and blur my world.

"It's not new," Neo says apologetically. "I bought it off Racetrack. But she hardly ever wore it, so I thought…"

"It's perfect, Neo. It's literally perfect." I rise on tiptoe and wind my arms around his neck like I've been aching to do all day. His big hands wrap around my waist in that possessive way I can't get enough of, and which I've missed desperately. I close my eyes and pull in a deep breath of his sage-and-juniper soap. "Thank you so much."

Sweet Jesus. I think I'm in love.

I'm in love with my fated mate.

He leans in and kisses me, a slow careful press of his warm full lips, a kiss that tastes cool and minty. Shivers rush over my bare skin and make my nipples tight. I part my lips a little and our tongues touch, a lick of fire in the drafty hallway, and we both moan.

The first flicker of mating heat uncoils like a sleeping dragon, low in my belly, and opens a slitted eye.

Holy shit. Just this kiss is making me sweat.

And I have to admit the bonfire is definitely being stoked by the hot weight of Vasili's smoldering stare tracking my every move. I open my eyes to look over Neo's shoulder and meet his silvery gaze.

And the raw heat burning in those feral eyes makes him positively predatory. Yeah, he likes what he's seeing.

He likes it a lot.

Come on, Goblin King, I whisper in his head. *You can be part of this. I dare you.*

"Hmmmm." He slinks up behind Neo and my heart starts racing. His sultry stare never leaving mine, he leans in and whispers in Neo's ear, "We're going to be late, First Boy."

His lips might actually brush the edge of Neo's ear, because my mate shivers in my arms and bites back a little moan.

"Nice." I break the kiss with a sigh and dab a smudge of my pink lipstick off Neo's mouth with my thumb. "Hold that thought for me, okay? And help me with this choker?"

"Sure thing." Neo rakes back his tumbled hair and fastens the choker gently around my neck. "Looks beautiful on you, babe. I'll be the luckiest guy at the dance tonight."

Then he offers me his arm. I slip mine through his with a soft smile. He makes me feel so special. Exactly the way every girl should feel on prom night.

Vasili pivots, speechless for once, and precedes us down the hall, lean hips swaying in his heeled boots. I've noticed he's carrying a little box too, but he didn't offer it to me, and I'm definitely not expecting anything else since he already got me the dress… somehow… despite the weather. A dress I actually like and would thank him for, if he'd stop being a brat for five minutes.

"You're welcome," he says without turning. And it almost sounds like he's smiling.

He slinks right past the staircase, straight to Ronin's closed door, and knocks.

Happy little butterflies start wheeling in my tummy, because I know what any overture from Vasili will mean to Ronin right now. And I can't help noticing the Goblin King sounds less imperious and more… supplicating, I guess… when he knocks this time.

Slowly Ronin opens the door. I swallow hard, because he's looking like sex on a stick in the leather pants and boots he wore in Singapore, paired with a black tuxedo jacket and a sleek button-down that I instantly want to peel off him with my teeth. He's showing plenty of ink and all that gorgeous blue-black hair is pouring loose down his back.

And he's packing. Those twin knives sheathed in his boots are definitely *not* formal attire. Which makes me think the top-ranked fighter at Icarus senses danger brewing.

But the raw expression haunting his face when his amber eyes lock on Vasili makes me ache.

Heat or no heat, Ronin needs comfort in the worst way.

"I'm a bastard and I don't deserve you," Vasili says simply, his voice low and raw. "But there's no conceivable way I can possibly do this… *any* of this… without you. And I don't want to, Ronin. I don't want to." He pulls in an unsteady breath. "Will you come with us tonight?"

I stare at Vasili's sparkly shoulders and stiff back in complete fucking shock. If I didn't know better, I'd think that was an actual apology.

Ronin blinks and his brittle face softens. His gaze drops to the box in Vasili's hands. Which Vasili is definitely offering.

"That an olive branch you've got in there?" Ronin murmurs at last. "Because you're not exactly known for that, are you?"

"If you like." I can hardly believe the Goblin King actually sounds hesitant. His voice goes so quiet I can barely hear him. "I'd like to say my heart's in this box, darling. But the truth is, I gave that to you years ago."

At last, Ronin's careful facade splinters. "I know that, love. I've known for a long time. But I'm not going to lie. Knowing you know it too makes me happy as fuck."

He wraps a hand around the back of Vasili's neck and drags him close. The Goblin King bends to meet him and their mouths collide in a scorching kiss.

Next to me, Neo hums happily and slides an arm around my waist. I lean into his warm solid body. Tension sparks between us at the contact. That mating heat I'm visualizing as a sleeping dragon rumbles and puffs out a wisp of flame.

Oh yeah. That's really gonna be something once my heat gets going.

But it's Ronin we're both fixated on now. Ronin who pulls back from the kiss slowly, Vasili's box in his grip. Hair spilling forward to hide his face, he lifts the lid. I crane to see around Vasili's obstructive body and glimpse the delicate spotted petals of a tiger lily.

Aaawwww. It's a boutonnière. Vasili's actually giving Ronin flowers.

I honestly didn't think the guy had it in him to be this sweet. Seriously, who knew?

"If I didn't know better," Ronin says softly, gaze still lowered to the flower, "I'd think you're asking me out. As in—on an actual date. In public. Where all your enemies can see you actually have a heart."

"That's what it is, if you'd like it to be. A date." Vasili takes a deliberate step sideways and angles his body to include me and Neo. His stare locks with mine, narrow with challenge. He looks like he's stepping off a cliff. "And if that's what the two of you would like."

I suck in a breath and my heart starts racing. "What are you asking us, Vasili?"

He doesn't miss a beat. "I'm asking if you have the appetite for a fucking date. A date with all fucking four of us."

I glance at Neo, who's blushing all over. And thanks to the mating bond between us, I've got a front row seat for how hot he's getting at the thought of all four of us together.

Wow.

If someone turns me on, I'm finally starting to figure out, that same someone's going to turn him on.

Because that's what it means to have a fated mate.

"Hell to the yeah." I snuggle into Neo's side and nail Vasili with a challenging look of my own. "I'm all over that. Assuming you mind your manners, Goblin King."

Vasili lowers his head to eye me under a fringe of frosted hair and a skillful application of eyeliner and purrs, "Now, darling, where's the fun in that?"

Energy sparks between us and heats my skin. My pulse trips and I can feel the ends of my ponytail float.

"What about Lucius?" I can't help asking. I know my teacher's not ready to go public with any of us. But he's part of this. It feels wrong to be doing this without him.

"He's on chaperone duty, along with the other faculty," Neo explains. "He's already at the commons. We'll see him over there. Actually, we'll see everyone over there. It's the social event of the season."

Well, all righty then.

Damn if the thought of tempting Lucius into a dark corner at the dance to tend my mating bite in secret hasn't just spiked my system a hundred kilojoules hotter.

Ronin tucks the tawny flower into his lapel, saunters past Vasili into the hall, and gives me a slow once-over with his tiger eyes that doesn't do a thing to counteract all that heat building in my body.

"And aren't you a proper sight?" he murmurs, low and luscious. "You wearing a blooming thing under that little dress, love?"

"Nope." I angle my body to show off the strip of exposed skin that runs all the way down my side. His eyes kindle and ignite.

"Mmmm." He wraps a hand around my waist and leans in to give me a slow savoring kiss. He smells like ambergris and wolf and Vasili, and he tastes like the peaty burn of scotch. Deep in my belly, the mating heat I'm imagining as a sleeping dragon uncurls her barbed tail and lifts her massive head.

"You smell a bit like Lucius," Ronin whispers against my mouth.

"Mmm-hmm." A smug smile curves my lips, and his topaz eyes fire with pleasure.

You rocking a mating bite under that sexy dress then, love?

Could be, I volley back, letting Neo listen in.

"Wow, seriously?" Neo whispers, his arm tightening around my waist.

Thankfully, he sounds awed rather than jealous. Once he realizes I'm going into heat, I'm guessing he'll be downright grateful to Lucius for biting me.

And I'm really starting to wonder if my baby shifter genes might give me enough bang to the bite to deliver a little mating nip for Neo.

"Well, look at you, Mr. Mercury." Still gripping me with a proprietary hand at my hip, Ronin turns to Neo. "You look tasty enough in that tux to lick like an ice cream cone."

Their mouths meet in a sweet kiss, and I sneak a peek at Vasili to see how he's taking all this. I'm even wondering if he just picked up my mental byplay with Ronin, since those two are linked. I'm wondering if knowing I plan to stick around and queen it's going to unleash Vasili's closet monster.

My warlock's hands are thrust deep in his frock coat pockets and he's definitely watching.

But he's got his walls up again.

Shit.

I can't read a thing in his shuttered face.

When he sees me looking, he deploys his infuriating eyebrow. "At least we'll be late enough to make a fashionable entrance. If we time it properly, we'll manage to disrupt the Dean's holiday toast, which is always interminable."

But he says it, for him, without malice.

"Looks like we're off to see the wizard. Or at least the witch." I loop one arm through Ronin's and one through Neo's and stick out my tongue at Vasili (which I know is childish, but he brings it out of me). "All freaking five of us."

Chapter Thirty-Six
Vasili

It seems entirely likely that I'm bespelled.

There's simply no other explanation for why I'm undertaking my notoriously grand entrance, at the premier social event of the academic year, in the company of the Gemini queen, her deplorable mate whom I've always volubly despised, and the secret lover I've spent years pretending to hate.

Not to mention I'm doing all this under the heated stare of my rival alpha, the perennially remote and untouchable headmaster I've inexplicably coerced into accepting my mating bite.

Then there's the fact that I've never before bitten anyone in my life, never even conceived of it, since I'm typically far more interested in hiding my loathsome fangs than drawing attention to them by burying them in someone's flesh. For one thing, I'm Mogadon, not shifter. For another, Lucius and I have been circling each other and snarling since the day I pitched up at Icarus, newly exiled by the darling family I haven't seen since, and totally devastated by their repudiation.

Now, thanks to my ungovernable actions and my unpremeditated bite, inflicted upon my rival on pure impulse while I was drunk and horny, I harbor the sneaking suspicion there might have been just enough shifter DNA in my saliva to send Lucius Aries into heat.

A heat with my name written all over it.

A development which would be—at the very least—a damnable complication.

Of course, I adore complications. Scorpios actually excel at them. Still waters run deep, darling, *et cetera*.

Bully for me then, because these days, thanks to the utterly mystifying set of choices I've made since the night Zara Gemini appeared and upended this entire Academy, my personal life has never been more complicated.

Thus, it's safe to conclude I'm bespelled.

Nonetheless, the show must go on. I'm Vasili Romanov, I'm the Scorpio scion, my enemies are watching, and I've an image to uphold. So I swank into the cavernous expanse of the student commons—bedecked with colored lights and tinsel by the overly enthusiastic student cheer club, good God, like someone's planted a bomb in a Christmas tree and lit the fuse—as though I fucking own the place.

With the Gemini queen of the witching world prominently displayed on my anti-monarchist arm.

Aside from offering her the privilege of appearing on that arm, I'm doing my considerable best to ignore our rebel queen.

However, she's always made that impossible.

With her showgirl curves encased in the couture cocktail gown I chose for her, eyes wide and lips parted as she drinks in the scene, lightning-blue hair swept into that ponytail I want to wrap around my fist and rebel queen attitude on full display, she looks like a punk-rock version of Marilyn Monroe. She has more curves than a cyclone, this girl does, and more balls than a Spanish bull. This is her Purgatory, she's standing beside her worst tormentor (that would be me), and there's a queen killer on the hunt for her head.

Yet she's defiant and determined and utterly fearless.

And the electrifying sight of her wearing the clothes I arranged for her is flipping every switch on my alpha male circuit board. If I get my way (and I typically do, darling), I'll soon be buying her entire royal wardrobe and styling her daily.

Admittedly, since that singular moment last night when I swiped my tongue through my own spunk and kissed her, since she kissed me back and sucked on my tongue like she wanted to ruin me, I've been a mental case.

I can barely manage to keep my psychic barriers airtight—because this queen *is* a wicked telepath, humming with untrained power—and my frisky hands to myself. The only way I've been able to maintain my distance (literally, the only way) is by provoking Zara so badly with my bratty antics that she's barely willing to suffer my proximity long enough to make our grand entrance. All too clearly, she can scarcely wait to be rid of me. Whereas I'm burning to drag her into my arms and brand my claim on that pouting Hollywood mouth before the entire astonished Academy with a scorching kiss.

Well, well, well. Just look who turns out to be fucking bisexual.

Apparently, that would be me.

Fuck.

At our side, Ronin and Neo make their own grand entrance. Both of them look impossibly luscious, Ronin's sleek black mane sliding down his back and his lithe body poured into those leather pants that cup his traffic-stopping ass precisely the way I'll shortly be doing myself, Neo's broad shoulders and corded thighs encased in that pristine tux I'm ready to peel off his beefcake body with my teeth.

My virginal housemate's blushing a bit under my heated attention, peering bashfully at me with his wide eyes under those soft curls, and clearly wondering just how far I'm planning to take this little *detente* between us.

Well, join the club, Mercury. I'm rather wondering that myself.

They saunter in with hands linked, Ronin and Neo, which also makes tonight their public debut as a couple. Already, the entire student body is agog. They suspect I'm playing one of my elaborate nasty tricks on the little queen. Now they're waiting for me to lower the boom so they can swarm in and devour her. The dog pack is likewise concluding Sir One and Done has made another casual conquest and added another tick, this one the hapless First Boy, to his impressive sexual tally. Neo, too, these dogs are slavering to disembowel.

Pity these junior witches and baby warlocks haven't any notion what's truly going down. This Gemini queen is claiming her harem.

If I'm not careful, she'll be claiming me.

But, God, I want that. I want that more than I want my parents' nonexistent love. I want to work *with* her, not against her, to secure the survival of the witching world.

Beyond all these Darwinian geopolitics, I simply want… *her*.

And none of these spotty prepubescents clustered in their Sunday best around the apse, where the Dean's droning on interminably about duty and honor and tradition, has the first fucking clue.

About any of this.

The four of us sashay straight into the lion's den, my heeled boots *rap-a-tap-tapping* nicely against the flagstones to draw the eye (which, naturally, I thrive upon doing). The underclassmen, like livestock in a Nativity play, stand about looking decorative and eye the four of us like we're the witching world's Messiah. My numerous boot lickers and sycophants practically genuflect, now they've gotten past the shock of seeing me pal around with the royals. While the royalists who've always despised me see their queen on my arm and yearn to sink their knives into my back.

I merely smirk at all the attention.

Having been violently rejected by my entire clan at barely sixteen for the so-called sin of my sexuality, I'm fairly impervious by now to social stigma.

At my side, Zara seems equally impervious. She's staring down the *hoi polloi* who've been hazing her all week in open challenge, lightning flashing in her gaze. Under my hand, my girl's literally humming with psychic voltage.

She's untouchable here, in this public setting, with the whole school still buzzing over the flashy pyrotechnics she unleashed earlier on the lighthouse.

(Blizzard or no blizzard, those were a bit hard to miss.) And I know precisely what it means that she's summoned her lightning. This queen is here to stay.

Unless the queen killer has his way.

Danger prickles down my spine and raises the hair down my nape, where my ruff would be if I could shift. Oh, he's here, quite near, whoever he is. Our queen killer. And he too knows Zara's come into her power.

She's no helpless Guinevere, Neo's no Arthur, and God knows I'm no Lancelot. But I am Vasili fucking Romanov. I slide a protective arm around my queen's waist and draw her tight against my side.

I'm claiming this queen.

I'm claiming her whether she wants me to claim her or not.

She's mine. I'm hers. And this entire Academy had better fucking get used to it.

She slides a wary glance my way, because she's a survivor and I'm a snake and she understandably believes she can never dare trust me. She's wondering if I'm about to slip one of my hidden knives between her ribs.

"I think that's close enough, Goblin King," she warns me, breath hitching.

"Oh, I beg to differ," I murmur.

Because I intend to get *much* closer.

Her pulse flutters in her throat and her fascinating breasts rise and fall under that snug little dress, but under my touch she's so combat-ready she's lethal. It occurs to me I'm precisely one martial arts maneuver away from being flipped ignominiously onto my aerobicized ass.

"Now behave, darling, *do*," I drawl. "You're supposed to be my date, and Zerxes is watching."

Her face shutters tight and her eyes flash purple. But she's far too clever to look toward the platform under the dome where Lucius and Zerxes stand flanking the snowy-haired Dean, who's tottering on her cane and saying something about healing energy for poor Agrippina, still down but apparently holding her own.

Well, good for Aggie. She's a scrappy old dame.

I've never been one for skulking in the rear, so I lead our little quartet through the massed and staring commoners to the forefront of the lot. This gives us VIP access for the show. Under the decorative arch the cheer club's erected to give the nod to Janus, the Roman god of doorways, Lucius looks yummy enough to devour whole up there in his vintage black tux, long and lean under slim-cut coat and buttoned vest, with a snowy white cravat knotted under his chin. He's stern and unsmiling, firmly grounded in his public persona, all that chestnut hair pulled back from his grim face and throttled in his usual ponytail.

But the way he's staring at Zara and me and Ronin, even innocent Neo— literally burning holes in our clothes with his hunting wolf eyes—tells me our headmaster's mating heat is raging nicely. This church is cold and drafty as a Russian train station, but Lucius is sweating in his tux, fists clenching and unclenching under his ruffled cuffs. And I can see from here that under his trousers, he's hard as tungsten.

I did that to him. With my bite.

Apparently, even latent shifter genes are potent. Because the very notion that I've mated him, that I've bonded my alpha, that I've persuaded *him* to submit to *my* bite, makes my entire body vibrate with a ferocious surge of possession and rapacious sexual purpose that's really rather astonishing in its intensity.

What Lucius needs most tonight is to be ridden long and hard and put away wet.

I certainly intend to oblige.

I'm no natural telepath, but we share a mating bond now, he and I, and color darkens Lucius' scything cheekbones. He locks onto my stare with his whiskey eyes and his wolf growls in my head.

You'd best behave yourself tonight, Mr. Romanov, and wait until I'm damned well ready for you and your antics, he says sternly. *I'm working tonight and I won't be distracted.*

Whatever you say, pet, I purr in response. *I do so enjoy a good hunt. But make no mistake. You will be mine tonight. Mine and hers. And we all damned well know it.*

To that, he doesn't say a word. His silent acquiescence to my little moment of domination makes all the blood rush straight to my cock.

Zara's buzzing with tension under my arm, and I realize she's riveted on the other man looming over our diminutive Dean.

Bucephalus Zerxes.

The headmaster of Villa Tiberius cleans up well enough. He always has. Tonight he's looking positively dapper, that powerful build encased in a black tux sharp enough to slice and a cobalt bow tie the exact shade of his eyes. The holiday lights burn in the pale sweep of his silver braid, but the light's unkind to the lines that bracket his ruthless mouth. His heated stare sears through Zara precisely the way he used to stare at Cybelle.

I happen to know Zerxes is one of the few Mogadon at this Academy, aside from myself, who can levitate. Which would normally make him a suspect in the slain wolf incident. However, there's the little matter that Zerxes doesn't actually want Zara dead. He's a royalist to the point of being a zealot.

Which means that, rather than wanting her dead, Zerxes wants Zara very much alive and breathing in his bed.

Which also happens to be where he very much wanted *me*, once upon a time, together with him and Cybelle and Damien. He wanted all three of us underneath him in Cybelle's revolting harem.

You can believe I was an extremely hard no to that proposition.

The doddering Dean finishes up (finally) with some holiday banalities and her annual toast, innocuously delivered with the innocent fizz of ginger ale. There's a smattering of polite applause from the *hoi polloi*, someone dims the lights and hits the music, and the Academy's premier social event finally achieves liftoff.

This first dance is traditionally a slow one. I turn toward Zara with anticipation sizzling through every synapse. After all, she is my date, and this is what dates *do*—

"Neo, baby." She twists deftly out of my arms and nestles up against Mercury. "Wanna dance?"

Of course, he wants to dance. He'd want to stand on his ridiculous purple head if that's what his precious mate wanted. He leads her happily into the open space under the mirrored ball and wraps his adoring arms around her.

Precisely as I'd meant to be doing myself.

Leaving me standing there marooned in space like a social outcast, watching my hated rival waltz away with *my* fucking date.

"What the hell was that?" I turn an indignant face toward Ronin, who's clearly trying (none too successfully) not to laugh.

Damn it.

"Guess you're stuck with me, love," he says casually. But I'm undeceived by all that casual. My lover's shoulders are stiff and he's shut me out of our link entirely. He thinks I'll shy away from dancing with him and shattering the carefully constructed fiction of our faux rivalry before my numerous enemies.

Even a day ago, I would have.

But I'm bespelled, remember? I can't be held responsible for my illogical and reckless actions.

And I'd rather cut out my own tongue than wound Ronin ever again by anything I say with it.

Oh, my sparkly frock coat is absolutely perfect for this moment. I sweep my love an elegant Renaissance bow, leg extended, booted toe pointed, and offer my princely hand with a flourish. "My dearest darling, do say that I can have this dance?"

A rush of pleased color heats his tawny skin. Still, he hesitates, because two years of engrained caution is a wickedly hard pattern to break. "You sure about this then? Really sure?"

I uncoil from my bow and hold his uncertain gaze. "Believe me, Ronin. I've never been more certain of anything in my entire life."

And it's true. When it comes to him and Zara and Lucius and even, I suppose, that purple-haired nincompoop, I've emphatically made my choice.

Ronin's silky lashes drop over his eyes. He prowls past me with his boot knives and his sinuous grace, laces a hand through mine, and leads me to the dance floor. But what matters even more than the familiar heat of his hand in mine?

He's lowered his walls and let me back in.

His heart is hammering under his tux just like mine. But he's trusting me not to bolt and make him an object of ridicule or, worse, pity.

Generally speaking, I'm not particularly known to be a man anyone can trust. But I grip my lover's hand firmly and do my damnedest to convey certainty and reassurance.

For both our sakes. Because I could do with a bit of reassurance myself. Exposing myself this way, showing where I'm vulnerable, revealing these secrets of my heart? It's foolish madness that places all of us in danger.

But, damn it, I've made my choice.

Under the mirrored ball, spangled lights play over the dim expanse. Scattered couples revolve slowly to the electric thunder of a power ballad. Neo and Zara are wrapped around each other like they're alone out here, her gorgeous face lifted to his, Neo's gaze heavy and fixed on her parted lips with a single-minded focus that's sexy as fuck.

I might have hated him since the day we met, but I begrudgingly admit (to myself) that he's not *entirely* unappealing. In fact, I realize with a tingle that I'm absolutely going to relish watching the First Boy fuck. I do wonder which of us is going to cause the earthquake when his climax triggers his gift.

Perhaps I'll prove equal to that challenge myself.

Ronin stops beside them and pivots to face me, his feral face firing with challenge. He's waiting for me to make my move.

Well, I've never been one to disappoint. I pull in a bracing breath, settle my hands on his waist, and ease my public enemy into my arms. His hands land on my hips, and *voila*!

There's one more little secret all exposed.

I'm taller than he is, especially when I'm wearing these heels, so he has to look up at me, which I don't mind a bit. My classmates' shocked murmurs trickle through the grinding beat, but I fall into my lover's golden gaze and I'm lost.

I pull in a lungful of dark ambergris fragrance and suddenly, violently, I want this dance over. I want Ronin and Zara and Lucius… and the other one too, I suppose, damn it… frolicking naked with me in Zara's medieval bed.

Hearing my thoughts, Ronin chuckles softly. "Joining the royal harem after all, are we?"

"Hmmm. I suppose I've surrendered to the inevitable." I make a petulant little moue of annoyance which I know won't deceive him, because he saw me with her last night. "Clearly our little rebel isn't going anywhere. She's claimed her power. If she's going to queen it after all, we might as well shape her reign. Perhaps we can even manage to halt the four races' inevitable decline. Or reverse it altogether—if she's capable of that. At the very least, she's a far cry from Cybelle."

Together we eye our dancing queen in her lightning-bolt dress and teal booties. Neo's nuzzling the side of her neck and her movie-star face is sultry with arousal, but her smoldering stare is riveted on the two of us—Ronin and me. Clearly she likes what she's seeing, and why wouldn't she? We make a striking pair.

I seize the moment to ease my boyfriend closer until we're cock to cock.

Her soft lips part and she whispers in my head, *Just how far are you willing to take this, Goblin King?*

I smirk in reply and wrap my hands around Ronin's ass. He moans low in his throat and entwines himself around me. My cock shoves against my breeches and he undulates against me like the damn minx he is. Suddenly we're both rock hard, our queen is watching and getting off on the sight of us while Neo sucks on her neck, and I'm done playing Prince Charming. I grind my aching cock into Ronin's in time with the tempo and wring out of him another groan. Louder this time.

"How's that heat of yours, darling?" I murmur into the fall of his silky hair.

"In bloody need of tending." His sharp teeth nip my ear in warning. I hiss in pain and pleasure. "But Lucius will be worse off than I am—this heat's damn near uncontrollable at the outset—so you'll need to tend him first. And you do realize he bit Zara, don't you?"

In point of fact, I hadn't, because I'm not a telepath and no one fucking told me. But that little tidbit certainly explains why Zara's roaming around smelling like Lucius and his wolf. And it even explains the lightning. She carries the DNA of all four races in her genetic code, and Kryll DNA like hers and Neo's channels the energy of other witches. If she and Lucius are mating… if she actually trusts him… our amorous headmaster could be precisely the key she needs to unlock the full force of that lethal Gemini witchcraft.

And, more to the point, control it.

"Sounds like we'll all be feeling frisky tonight," I whisper, kneading Ronin's ass and giving Zara a slow smile. She's going into heat herself, so she visibly shivers, and Neo's head turns to watch us. His eyes are heavy and he licks his lips with unconscious arousal. "Feel like giving those two a preview of coming attractions, darling?"

Ronin stops nibbling my ear long enough to swipe his hot tongue down my neck. "Something particular you've got in mind, love?"

"Hmmm. As a matter of fact, there is." I wrap my fist in Ronin's hair to immobilize him, drag his head back, and fuse our mouths together in a blazing kiss.

Chapter Thirty-Seven
Zara

Immolation is a rare Valyrian gift and the Geminis definitely don't have it, but I'm pretty sure I'm about to self-combust.

I've got Neo's buff body wrapped around me and his gentle teeth nibbling my neck and his sage-and-juniper soap filling my head, and I'm scenting hard enough to make the whole room horny. Not to mention I've got Vasili and Ronin moaning and writhing and dry-humping each other right next door in a way that's probably going to get us all suspended.

If not expelled. For public indecency.

Any other night, we'd already be clapped in detention for a show like that. But this is the Janus Dance, which is the ancient Roman New Year and a major party night for the whole witching world, and we're not the only ones on this dance floor getting down and dirty. Dez and Racetrack are wrapped up in each other too, and there's a little *ménage* action forming with three of the underclassmen from Villa Hadrian, which is actually kinda cute.

With the dim lights and the mirrored ball and the power ballad pulsing from the speakers, not to mention all the Mogadon scenting, sex is definitely in the air.

Looks like the chaperones will have their work cut out for them tonight.

And speaking of chaperones…

I drag my eyes away from Vasili and Ronin long enough to look for Lucius. I've been hyper-aware of him ever since he bit me, and I find him right away even though he's kind of lurking in the shadows near the refreshment table, probably monitoring to make sure nobody spikes the punch. Because alcohol's off-limits at school functions (according to my orientation packet) and the air's still fizzy with plain old ginger ale, which was the regulation tipple for the Dean's toast.

Still, Lucius doesn't seem overly interested in the punch bowl.

It's too dark to see much, but I can feel his predatory gaze locked on me from all the way across the room. The sleeping dragon of my mating heat's almost fully awake now, tail lashing in anticipation, but I can keep her leashed a little while longer.

Because tonight I intend to have all of them.

All four of my mates.

And that's a prize worth waiting for.

Heat pulses from my bite under the blaze of Lucius' stare. I slide my hands down Neo's corded back and grip his luscious ass. He lifts his head from nibbling on my neck and eyes me under his magenta curls.

Enjoying the show, Teach? I ask Lucius, letting Neo listen in too.

My fated mate looks a bit startled at suddenly sharing sexytimes with our teacher, but he's up for it, because I am. Neo's slow smile blossoms and he leans in to suck my lower lip into his mouth. I murmur approval into the warm suction of his kiss and squirm against the hardening jut of his cock shoving into my pelvis.

I'm roughly five seconds away from clapping all four of you in detention, Lucius growls in my head. *An immediate detention in my office in the crypt.*

A shiver of excitement chases down my spine and makes my skin heat. *That supposed to be a threat or a promise, Teach?*

It's a blasted warning. Even through the bond, Lucius sounds a bit ragged. *Now behave yourselves, damn it.*

For how long? I lick into Neo's mouth and project a playful pout.

My fated mate hums and hooks a hand under my thigh to wrap my leg around his hips. Now we're dry-humping too, and my inner dragon absolutely loves it.

Too goddamn long, Lucius rasps in my head. *Blood of Christ, Zara, be merciful.*

"Poor Master Aries." Neo chuckles against my lips and rests his forehead against mine. "The faculty are supposed to be on chaperone duty until midnight."

"Yeah, no. None of us are going to last that long." Especially now that Lucius himself has introduced the concept of a private detention in his office.

I plaster myself against Neo for balance and crane to peer over his shoulder. Vasili's flat out tongue-fucking Ronin's mouth and walking him slowly backward until Ronin's trapped against one of the stone pillars that march down the nave. Sweet Jesus, the Goblin King's actually kneading Ronin's dick through his pants.

This whole scene's about to get X-rated.

And you can bet we're drawing plenty of attention. Right now, half the Vasili wannabes that typically trail around after him look titillated, and the other half look confused, like they're trying to get with the program.

Yeah, people, they're together. As in, *together together*. Matter of fact, we're all together.

Starting tonight.

My naughty dragon rumbles a sexy suggestion, and suddenly I'm on fire with possibility. I glance toward the dark staircase that plunges down to the crypt. I've never been down there, because our independent study takes place in the belfry, but apparently that's where Lucius has his office.

In the crypt. Like a freaking vampire. God, I love it.

"Neo, baby," I whisper in his ear.

"Yeah, babe?"

"Why don't you sashay over there for me and help Vasili get Ronin all nice and ready? I want all five of us in Lucius' office in…" I glance at my dive watch "…less than five minutes max."

Neo's startled chuckle gusts over my bare shoulder. "Uh, in case you haven't noticed, Vasili's not a big fan of mine at the best of times. I'm really not sure he's going to appreciate me interrupting those two right now."

"Have you not seen the way he's been looking at you all night?" I trace his ear with my tongue and blow gently to make him shiver. "If you walk up behind him right now and nuzzle the back of his neck, you'll just about make him come in his pants."

"Wow, really?" My sweet innocent mate sounds dazed but intrigued by the prospect.

"Really, baby." I kiss the side of his neck. Cheese on toast, I love this big guy. "You have no freaking idea how sexy you are, do you? And I *really* want to see the two of you together."

"Five minutes, huh?" Neo kneads my bare thigh with his big hand. "What about Master Aries… I mean, uh, Lucius?"

"I'll take care of Lucius myself." Grazing his cheek with my lips, I disentangle gently from his hunkalicious body and smooth my short skirt down my thighs. "Five minutes tops to get the three of you down there all hard and ready for me. I'm timing you, First Boy."

That's all the performance incentive Neo needs. He rakes a hand through his hair, gives me a smoldering look, and navigates between couples and throuples to make his purposeful way across the dance floor. Someone's cranked on a fog machine and blue fog's billowing across the floor, dancers appearing and vanishing in the smoke.

Hot and sweating with arousal, I maneuver for a better view of my guys, then shimmy in place so I can watch when—

"There you are." A deep British baritone rumbles in my ear. "At last I find you alone, my queen. Have you been waiting for me?"

Hard hands close around my waist and spin me into a broad tuxedo-clad chest. Which is how I find myself squarely in the very last place I want to be tonight.

Alone on the dance floor with Bucephalus freaking Zerxes.

Chapter Thirty-Eight
Zara

I plant my hands on my substitute prof's chest to put some distance between us and swing my head way back to make eye contact. Because he's a whole lot bigger than I am.

And that's what you do with a predator.

"Thought you're supposed to be ladling punch for the freshmen," I say pointedly. Because he really ought to be on chaperone duty like Lucius, not getting his rocks off sneaking up on me like a creeper.

"Oh, I leave that sort of drudgery to Master Aries. After all, he rather excels at that sort of thing." He bares his teeth in a carnivorous smile and pulls me in *much* closer than any prof (except Lucius) has any business doing with any student.

Especially me.

I glance around for backup, but we're fogged in on the dance floor. Someone's really gone overboard on the atmospherics. Looks like I'm on my own.

Super.

Unless I call for help. Which has never been my style.

I've always fought my own battles.

This is awkward as fuck, but I clear my throat and wade gamely into this shitstorm like I'm wearing galoshes and a raincoat. "Here's the thing, Master Zerxes—"

"Why don't you call me Ceph? That's a privilege I extend to my intimates." His voice drops to a low rumble. He's scenting like hell, which in his case means all that Mogadon musk laced with a sharp abrasive pinch like cayenne that burns my nostrils.

Fuck.

That's his mating scent.

"Well, we're not exactly intimate." I hate to point out the obvious, but apparently it isn't so obvious. "You're my substitute prof, so that pretty much makes you Master Zerxes in my book—"

"I'll be Ceph in your harem." He drags my hips hard against his. Which gives me an up-close-and-personal with that massive freaking boner he's packing. "I'll be Ceph in your bed."

Fuck, fuck, fuck.

My mouth falls open. "Seriously? Are you for real? Because you're literally my teacher, and there are like ten *thousand* rules—"

"Oh, come now, Ms. Gemini," he purrs like a snow leopard, the kind with gore dripping from his fangs. "You're the rebel queen. We're hardly so zealous in our adherence to the Academy Codex, are we?" Still scenting like crazy, he looms over me. "I'll wager you're not nearly so formal with Lucius."

His oily tone leaves a queasy churn in my belly. Well, okay, you can call the Icarus equivalent of Severus Snape observant. Lucius is going into heat, so our headmaster's been eye-fucking Vasili and Ronin and me all night, with way less than his usual caution. Plus this middle-aged nightmare I'm dancing with is half Valyrian, and I haven't exactly been guarding my thoughts.

I remedy that right now by building that psychic wall between us. Ronin's been tutoring me during study hall, and I'm getting good at it. Good enough to keep Zerxes out.

The only problem is, with me still learning my witchcraft, I don't know how to keep just Zerxes out, without walling my guys out too.

Which means I really am on my own.

And I'm worried about what he thinks he knows about me and Lucius. I don't give a shit about me, but Lucius has his reputation to protect.

I tally up everything I know about this freak, which isn't all that much. He's a wicked telepath who can cast psi fire like Ronin, which is a trick I haven't learned to defend against yet. Plus he's half Mogadon, and I don't know what kind of witchcraft that genetic legacy adds to his bag of tricks.

Maybe he's telekinetic like Vasili. Which is something else I can't defend against.

He's a lot bigger than I am, but I've taken out guys that are bigger. It's not his physicality that worries me. It's his threat against Lucius… because that *was* definitely a threat… that makes me hella worried.

So instead of putting my prof on his ass and risking the consequences of his anger, I decide to be nice.

We'll do this the polite way.

"We're not talking about Lucius right now." I pull in a careful breath. "…Ceph."

That's apparently the right thing to say, because the cold threat burning in his laser-blue eyes warms to a sexual simmer. He rumbles with pleasure and rubs his face into my hair. He's fucking scenting me, which is going to piss Lucius and Vasili right off. I already want a shower.

"Oh, Zara," he breathes in my ear. "I've waited for you so long, my queen. You can't imagine how long."

"Um, not *that* long," I point out with a snort. "Cuz you were with Cybelle before me, right? That was, what, a few weeks ago?"

"Cybelle." His eyes turn raw and his voice splinters with grief. "Yes. I loved her. I was the alpha male in her quarrelsome harem. The one who kept the others away from each other's throats." A muscle ticks in his jaw. "But greatly though it pains me to say, my Cybelle was a weak queen. A selfish queen. A queen whose sole concern was for herself and her social standing and her monstrous little friends. Just like her mother Messalina."

His hands walk down my hips and settle right on my ass. "I've waited decades for a strong queen. A powerful queen. A queen who can summon lightning. A queen whose witchcraft is potent enough to save the witching world."

"With you to guide me?" I pry his hands off my ass, resettle them firmly at my waist where they belong (if he has to be touching me at all), and glance around warily. Where the heck is everyone? The fog's getting really thick, pea-soup thick, it's like the mists of Avalon or something, and I wonder if maybe Zerxes is wielding a little common magic to make it that way.

The music is throbbing from the speakers, I can't hear anything else, I'd have to scream to be heard myself, and I still don't like calling for help. I fight my own battles, remember?

"With me to love you," he whispers in my ear on an indrawn breath. "Your harem is magnificent, my queen. You've claimed this Academy's strongest warlock in Vasili, our fiercest fighter in Ronin, and our sharpest intellect in Mercury. Even the shifter I'll let you keep… if he'll bend for me." To my complete horror, his hot tongue traces my ear, and his breath roughens. "I'll even make it… enjoyable for him… so long as he doesn't fight me. How's that for generous? You'll find I can be an indulgent mate."

Yeah, no, I won't be finding anything like that anytime soon. A shudder of loathing squirms through me, which he totally fucking misinterprets. He moans and starts rubbing his body against me, which really turns my stomach.

"Okay, that's my personal space." I firmly reimpose the requisite inches of distance between us, but he doesn't make it easy. I wonder if Cybelle really liked having such a pushy alpha, or if she was just too afraid of him to say no. "Listen up, buddy—"

"Ceph," he reminds me. "With a harem as powerful as yours, you'll need a strong alpha like me to keep your subordinate males in line. I won't mind a bit, not with any of them." The image slinks from his brain and crawls against my boundaries, and yeah, it's pretty effing sexual. He hates Lucius, but he wants Vasili, and he certainly isn't opposed to Ronin and Neo.

Great. Now he thinks he's getting all of us in his bed.

He lowers his head to nuzzle my neck, right next to the wide swath of fabric that crosses my shoulder.

Now this whole thing is really getting out of hand.

"Ceph," I snap, using my queen voice to stop the kissing and get his attention. "My harem is full, I don't need any help handling them, you're totally not my type, you're touching me in a way I don't want to be touched, *and* you're standing between me and something I really wanna get back to. So, even though I shouldn't actually have to say this to my substitute teacher at a fucking school function, it's thanks but no thanks on the whole mating thing. Got it?"

But, no, of course he doesn't get it. He just keeps right on offending.

"Oh, I fully expect you to demand that I earn my place in your bed. That's your right as sovereign—" Lips pressed to my shoulder, he chokes off and goes rigid.

A frisson runs through him and my skin prickles in warning. Even before his gilded head jerks up to skewer me with a murderous glare.

"He gave you his fucking *mating bite*?" he barks, every word cracking like a whiplash.

What the actual fuck? Guess the psycho just smelled it on me. And now the guy's gone postal.

That's my cue to firmly detach his roaming hands from my unwilling body and exit stage left, but polite just doesn't work with this guy. He wrestles me closer and scowls down at me, and I scowl right back. My ponytail starts floating and my palms start tingling.

I've had it with this asshole.

"He did. He bit you. And now you're going into heat… for *him*." He actually hoists me off the ground so my arms are pinned at my sides and my boots are dangling two feet in the air—that's how freaking strong this guy is— and snarls the words through bared teeth like he's rabid. "*I'm* your alpha. I'm the father of the next queen. Not him! I swear on my soul I'm going to skin Lucius Aries alive and nail his pelt to my bedroom wall—"

"One sympathizes with the sentiment… or *did*, until rather recently." Vasili's bored drawl beside me has never been more welcome. "At the moment, however, my primary pique is reserved for *you*. Bucephalus Zerxes, I do believe you're attempting to poach my date."

Chapter Thirty-Nine
Zara

This moment right here? It's the moment I forgive Vasili Romanov for every single hateful horrid thing he's ever done to me since the day we met, even that time he tried to bully me into licking his boots.

Because the sight of the Scorpio scion gliding through the fog with his forked tongue dripping venom like the glittering serpent he is drags Bucephalus Zerxes' attention fully away from me for one critical moment.

And a moment's all I need.

No more Mr. Nice Girl.

While Zerxes holds me suspended in midair and glares blue murder at Vasili and snaps, "Did you know about this, Romanov? Did you know that mangy shifter—" I sweep up my booted foot and nail my bastard prof right in the balls.

Zerxes howls and drops me and I land on my feet because, hello, cat burglar. I hope I crushed his testicles to jelly, because that would settle things with Mr. Handsy pretty permanently.

But no such luck, I guess, because he's still on his feet, even if he's hunched over and groaning in agony. The second his head whips up and psi fire pulses in his eyes, I know I'm in major trouble.

"You spoiled little *witch*." He lunges for me.

And I don't even think.

A low hum fills my throat, I sweep my hands forward, and an electric jolt rolls out of me. That blinding crackle of purple light arcs across the space between us and knocks Zerxes sprawling on his ass. The chemical reek of ozone floods the air.

Well… *dayum*.

That wasn't the lightning (thank God) but it was definitely the lightning's little brother. Somehow, even acting on sheer impulse, I retained enough control—this time—not to fry the guy to a crisp.

My ponytail floats in a staticky rush of jubilation. I feel like screaming with sheer effing triumph.

Get it together, showgirl. This is definitely not the moment to pop the champagne and rent a limo to celebrate your newfound control over the lightning.

Zerxes is sprawled on the flagstones with wrath filling his face and, shit, his hands are starting to glow. He's revving up to let loose. And I don't have the first clue what to do about a pissed-off warlock wielding psi fire.

"Oh, darling, *really.*" Vasili prowls between us in his heeled boots and sparkly coat. "You simply don't know when to stay down, do you?"

He sighs and gestures with a negligent hand. Zerxes jerks into instant rigidity. He's immobilized, flat as a pinned frog in a high school biology lab, glowing hands stapled to the flagstones, face turning purple with wrath. I think it's weird that he doesn't say anything, until I realize he *can't* say anything.

Because Vasili's not letting him breathe.

My Goblin King is a vicious snake. But he's my snake.

I straighten my dress and tighten my ponytail, breathing heavily and appreciating the fuck out of my ability to do so.

That's the sitch when Ronin and Neo burst through the fog and find us.

"Whoa, babe, there you are! God, are you okay?" Neo beelines straight for me, but I give him a warning head shake and he gives me my space, because I can't drop my psychic wall just yet, and I don't want to look weak in front of Zerxes.

Neo's anxious eyes inventory every single inch of me, confirming for himself that I'm okay, before his gaze swings to Zerxes, whose face is now as purple as Neo's hair.

"Um, Vasili?" Neo knows better than to touch the Goblin King when he's wielding his lethal witchcraft, but my fated mate waves a hand for Vasili's attention. "You are gonna let the guy breathe again, right?"

"Oh, why, do I have to?" Vasili pouts maliciously. Of course, my pit viper's having the time of his life.

Ronin inventories the scene with a swift sharp look and barks a short laugh. He doesn't know exactly what just went down either, since I walled him out too, but he knows it wasn't good. His tiger eyes are dangerous and his laughter holds a vicious edge.

And, yeah, I love that these guys'll take someone out for me. That they'll do literal violence to defend me. I freaking love it.

After all, I haven't had that very often in my life. Instead, I've had a psycho mom and a casino czar dad and friends like Xiao and Cleo.

That's why I've always had to fight my own battles.

But I don't need to fight alone anymore.

And because these warlocks have my back, no one's exactly springing to poor Ceph's defense. Which leaves it up to me to say begrudgingly, "The guy's a creep, but that isn't a capital offense. Let him breathe, Goblin King."

"Give us just a moment more, darlings… and… *there*." Vasili sighs with satisfaction, and I see that Zerxes' eyes are closed. Another careless flourish of Vasili's glittering hand, and Zerxes' chest rises in a sudden full breath.

"You choked him unconscious?" I divide my appalled attention between the warlock on the floor to confirm he's actually breathing (he is) and the warlock standing over him negligently checking his makeup. "I just keep learning new reasons not to piss you off."

"Hmmm." His shiny compact's already open so he can primp properly, but Vasili's eyes are narrowed on me over the raised lid. "You can rest assured I would've discerned that piddling common magic fog spell of his *much* sooner if these two wicked mates of yours weren't such a terrible distraction."

I suck in a breath big enough to make my head spin and step right off the cliff. "They're your mates too, Vasili. Aren't they?"

His startled gaze jolts to Ronin, who winds one arm around Neo's waist and one around mine and nuzzles my cheek. Ronin's warm to the touch and his heat's building, which I realize the instant I lower my barrier and let them back in. But we're all fixated right now on the Goblin King.

Next, Vasili's pensive eyes shift to Neo, who (of course) blushes.

That blush of his makes me mighty eager to learn what all went down while I was peeling Bucephalus Zerxes' predatory hands off my petunia.

"Hmmm," Vasili murmurs, which I've figured out is his way of not answering questions he doesn't want to answer. With Zerxes out of it, the fog spell's dissipating fast, scattered dancers taking shape around us.

Vasili touches the small of my back to steer me away from the scene of the crime before we're discovered gathered like vultures over Zerxes' fallen form. Or, worse, before the guy wakes up.

Because that warlock's going to be mighty pissed.

"Before we realized we'd lost track of you, and divided our forces to find you," Vasili muses, "I do seem to recall Mercury saying something about a naughty little rendezvous in Lucius' office."

"And was he persuading you?" I twine an arm around Vasili's slim waist, which is taking a chance, but fuck, I want to touch him. That's when I realize he's wearing a freaking corset under that sparkly coat of his, and OMG, I nearly lose my freaking mind.

A breathy little moan slips out of me, and the Goblin King tucks me up against his side with a smug sidelong smirk. Yeah, he knows *exactly* what kind of damage he and his corset are doing to me.

Neo falls easily into step on my other side and loops his warm fingers through mine. "He, uh, wasn't exactly saying no."

"Nooooooo." Vasili draws the word out and reaches to snare Ronin's hand. "He certainly wasn't. It seems the two of you are horribly persuasive when you… work together… to persuade me."

Oh, hell to the yes.

"Only problem's the logistics, yeah?" Ronin leans past Vasili to give me a lazy grin. "Lucius' office is tiny and cold as fuck. Not like your nice warm bed, love."

"It is a nice warm bed, isn't it?" At first I wasn't sure getting Vasili and Neo into the same bed tonight (or any night) would be in the cards, like maybe there'd always be an F between those two M's in my harem, but it's definitely starting to look like these two particular males aren't opposed to touching. It's too bad to miss the crypt, of course, but I can always explore my vampire fetish with Lucius and his crypt later. And crypt or no crypt…

"Where is Lucius?" I frown. "We're not doing this without him."

"We're certainly not." Vasili pauses when someone screams behind us. That'll be some unsuspecting dancer tripping over Zerxes, who ought to be waking up pretty quick in all that commotion.

And it's probably for the best we're not hanging around the commons when he does.

There's no denying we made a bad enemy tonight. An enemy who's just added public humiliation to his tally of grievances. It'll be pretty obvi to the whole school he was overpowered by witchcraft, and I'm guessing the Scorpio scion's pretty much the only warlock at this Academy who could take him out.

Once he's awake and ambulatory, Bucephalus Zerxes will be spoiling for vengeance.

"Got a notion these festivities will wrap up early, along with Lucius' babysitting duties, what with all the ballyhoo," Ronin says with a dark grin at Vasili. "Fancy a romantic stroll by moonlight with that sexy alpha you just bonded, love?"

"Oh, very well, I'll play errand boy and fetch him home," Vasili purrs. "But don't get accustomed to that sort of thing. I'm not a valet. Now why don't the three of you run along to the *domus* and get yourselves… warmed up… for Lucius and me?"

That dragon in my belly lurches to her taloned feet with a roar of anticipation. Wow. My mating heat's definitely looming. And given the kind of heat I'm packing, getting the five of us warmed up is totally *not* going to be a problem.

In fact, it's all I can manage not to breathe fire.

Chapter Forty

Neo

With our whole cohort still at the dance, the *domus* is dark and quiet, and I'm really grateful for the respite. Losing my bond with Zara when Master Zerxes broke all the Academy rules and made his awful move on her was really upsetting. Zara's told us everything he said while he was feeling her up. Now I feel terrible that Ronin and Vasili and I were off messing around and left our mate vulnerable to a predator like that.

"You have to stop seeing it that way, baby," she says to me sweetly as the three of us pad up the stairs in our stocking feet, our snowy coats and boots left behind in the atrium.

Zara, Ronin, and I are headed toward her bedroom. Which is about to become our bedroom, since I don't intend to sleep anywhere else ever again in my whole life except right next to my beloved.

"I shouldn't have left you, babe." *And I'll never do it again,* I promise her silently.

This complicated mate of mine heaves a sigh. "Listen, Neo. I'm not some shrinking violet. I *asked* you to go over there and play with the guys, remember?"

"That's true," I say contritely. "But we shouldn't have lost track of you even for a second. You should always be our top priority."

"Why, because I'm queen?" My mate's snort tells me what she thinks of this proposition. "We're doing things differently around here when I, uh, ascend. We're not going to be like Cybelle's harem apparently was, with all the guys at each other's throats and Zerxes allegedly cracking the whip to keep them all in line, like orcs in a damn Tolkien film. In my harem, we're going to be *all* together. And we all matter, Neo. This queen and her consorts are one hundred percent equal."

I should probably object to that, but it's her call to make. I'll agree to anything that makes her happy.

"Not complaining a bit," Ronin murmurs, because we're all speaking softly, like we don't want to break this fragile spell and shatter what's about to happen between us. "But now we've got your basic psychic defenses shored up, love, we'd better bloody work on your technique. So you can protect yourself without shutting us out. None of us much fancied that."

"Bring it on," Zara says firmly. Her hair's been floating since she took Zerxes down. When she reaches for the doorknob to let us into her room, I mean our room, tiny violet sparks crackle and pop in the darkness. "I intend to be the most badass queen the witching world's ever seen."

And right there on her doorstep—*our* doorstep—I'm overcome with happiness.

We've all been tiptoeing around the complicated issue of Zara's future since she summoned her lightning, which was a really tectonic shift compared to what she was saying before, when she wanted to reject her power. We haven't addressed it yet because we've all been afraid to crowd her. Even though the witching world *really* needs her. But I know she'll tell us when she's ready.

And now she has.

"Babe, I'm so happy," I whisper.

The bedroom's cloaked in shadow, but there's so much moonlight streaming through the glass doors you can almost read in here. Tonight's not only a full moon, it's a supermoon, and that silvery orb floating in the sky is ginormous.

Ronin prowls over to crouch by the hearth and breathes the coals to life with a flicker of his fire gift. There's a skill to managing fire when you rely on it like we do, and we've all had to learn it, given the geriatric furnace. But no one summons fire like a Leo.

I can definitely feel his alertness, because he's a telepath and he has a link open for me. He's right on the edge of giving in to his own mating heat, though he's thinking it's more manageable today than it was yesterday, and maybe it's going to pass soon, at least until the moon waxes again (not that he needs to be in heat to be totally sexy to me).

Now he's thinking it's going to take all of us to break Zara's heat and we should focus all our energy on her tonight.

Needless to say, I'm totally on board with focusing on Zara.

But he's also determined to please me, so I can enjoy my first time. My first time with a guy, I mean, which I've been thinking about and obsessing about all day.

My first time with any guy. And especially with him, my secret crush. I still can't believe this is really happening.

My body floods with sudden heat.

Zara shuts the door softly behind us to keep out the cold. But she doesn't lock it, because Vasili and Master Aries are coming. She closes the distance between us with a smile and winds her arms around my waist.

"I know, baby." She rests her cheek against my chest and sighs. "Right now I'm pretty happy too. Even though we still have a ton of shit to deal with. That queen killer's still out there, and now Zerxes has a score to settle. I don't even know what my dad's gonna do when he finds out I'm queening it. Because he doesn't give a shit about the fate of the witching world. Like, will he call off the hit for my head, or will he just raise the bounty?"

"We'll deal with that lot tomorrow," Ronin says firmly. "Tonight's for us. For our queen and her mates."

He's got the fire kindled, and the warm light dances over the pretty rustic frescoes on Zara's wall and bathes her big canopy bed in shifting shadows.

I can barely even bring myself to look at her bed.

Our bed.

The bed where I'm going to worship my beloved. The bed where Ronin's already whispered every steamy detail of what he plans to do to me in there. The bed I guess I'll also be sharing with my history prof, which seems so scandalous I blush every time I think about it (but everything makes me blush). The bed I'll apparently even be sharing with my nemesis Vasili, who shivered and moaned deep in his throat so beautifully when I did what Zara wanted and kissed the back of his silky neck. But what if he—?

"You're doing it again," Ronin whispers in my ear, which makes me shiver myself.

"Doing what?" I whisper back. With Zara snuggled up to my front and Ronin hovering at my back, my dick takes instant notice. I know Zara can feel my heart pounding against her ear.

"You're thinking so hard we can blooming hear." His soft breath teases my hair. "Take a breath, Red."

Obediently I suck in a breath and do my best to think about something (anything) else. "Why do you call me Red? My hair's not red anymore. It's been purple for months now."

"Oh, I don't call you Red because of your hair." Ronin's hands land on my waist. "It's because of the way you blush. Go ahead and blush for me."

Right on cue, warmth sweeps up my neck and floods my face. Zara giggles and starts nuzzling my neck. Her mating heat's really close to overwhelming all of us. She's restless and squirmy and hot to the touch, and she's starting to sweat through her pretty dress. I was thinking she'd want to wait for Vasili and Master Aries, but now I don't think she's going to make it that long.

She isn't, Ronin murmurs in my head. *She needs to come hard as fuck for us tonight. And plenty more than once. Why don't you help our girl out?*

"Is that what you want, babe?" I ease my hands down her curvy hips to the hem of her dress. When my fingers graze her naked thighs, she gasps.

"I'm so hot I'm burning up," she says into my neck, grazing my skin with her sharp little teeth. Which makes *me* gasp. "You wanna help me out with that?"

I don't need to be asked twice. Carefully I peel her sexy dress up her hips and over her head. At my ear, Ronin's breath snags on a ragged hitch. Underneath that amazing dress, her tight sexy body is totally naked with not even a thong between us, just the studded teal collar I buckled around her neck earlier, which I plan to leave right where it is. Firelight gleams on her silver piercings and caresses the pouting fullness of her breasts and darkens her pretty nipples to ruddy pink. Shadows gather between her thighs.

The sight of my queen makes my mouth dry and my heart pound. Especially the way she's looking up at me, lips parted and eyes wide.

"Oh fuck," Ronin groans softly in my ear. "We're the luckiest bastards in the witching world tonight, aren't we, Red?"

"Uh huh." I'm not very articulate right now, but I can't resist cupping my love's gorgeous breasts, feeling their soft weight fill my palms, my thumbs grazing her nipples which harden to instant peaks at my touch.

"Oh God, Neo." She closes her eyes and sways under my touch. "This freaking heat… I can feel that *everywhere*."

"Fuck, the two of you are making me mental." Ronin's hands slide up my torso to tease the bow tie that's throttling my throat. "She gets off when you play with her rings. Want to give that a go?"

I'm more than happy to oblige, especially when her suntanned skin breaks out in goosebumps and she arches into my touch. Ronin tucks in close behind me, close enough that I can feel his hard dick nudge my bottom.

I nearly have a nuclear meltdown on the spot.

"You can be rougher than that with her," he rasps in my ear, deft fingers unraveling my tie. "A lot rougher. Trust me. She's going to want it rough to break her heat."

I give her rings a hard tug and twist her nipples, the way I've seen in some of the cruder porn I've studied. I'm a little worried about hurting her, but she lets out a nice throaty moan, grips my tuxedo lapels like she's going to attack me, and drags me into a desperate kiss.

She tastes like ginger ale and Zara, the sweet creamy taste of my beloved, and her mouth crashes against mine in hungry need. Her sweet body writhes against me and my dick shoves against my trousers. I've tried to be so patient, but I haven't stopped thinking for one second about how it feels to be buried inside her, and I want that again with her.

I want everything with her. I want everything with her so much.

I wrap my arms around her to steady her and knead her lush bottom with both hands, just loving it when she moans in my mouth and grinds against me. Ronin rocks against me from behind, and all I can think is that I'm wearing way too many clothes. I hope like heck I can get out of my tuxedo pants before I come inside them.

With a soft chuckle, Ronin slides his arms around me and swiftly unbuttons my shirt. "Let's get you naked then, love."

I let go of Zara barely long enough to fight my way out of my shirt and jacket. While I'm doing that, Ronin leans forward and Zara rises on tiptoe and their mouths collide, all lips and tongues and soft wet noises. I've never seen anything so hot in my life, and feeling the two of them writhe against my bare torso—Zara hot and sleek and naked in front of me, Ronin still fully dressed behind—wrings out of me a little whimper.

Yeah, you like this, don't you, baby? my mate whispers through our bond. Her nimble fingers unbuckle my belt and unzip my fly.

"So much," I gasp. "I'm trying to go slow, but I don't think I can…"

Then Ronin drags everything down my hips, including my briefs, and my face scorches with heat. Now I need to focus on getting my legs out of my pants before I fall on my face. I barely have time to manage that feat before Zara's hand wraps around my dick and starts jacking me.

I'm already slick with my own need, and a rough cry rips out of me.

"You're going to fuck me so hard with this tonight, aren't you?" She nips my lower lip, and all I can do is moan in earnest agreement.

When Ronin slides one finger down my spine to trace the crack between my buttocks, I don't know whether to shove my aching dick into Zara's stroking fist or push back into Ronin's teasing touch. I want both of them, all of them, everything all at once.

My beloved turns her sexy eyes toward Ronin. "You too, Adam. I want to see you naked in that bed."

Wow, that sounds amazing to me too. Zara's sultry laugh tells me she's heard that, because we're all really open to each other right now. She stops nibbling my lips and turns me around, but she keeps stroking my dick so I can watch Ronin strip down in record time and crawl sinuously onto her bed, where he lounges naked against her pillows like a pasha, all lidded eyes and streaming hair, his dragon tattoo spewing inky flames across his chest. When he wraps a hand around his hard pierced cock and gives himself a few lazy strokes, staring straight into my eyes the whole time while Zara matches his rhythm, I thrust into her fist.

God, oh God, I'm ready to spill in her hand while he watches.

"That's it," she whispers, kissing my shoulder. "You see how much he wants you, don't you?"

Words are a tall order for me right now, but somehow, I manage.

"I can feel both of you," I groan. "Better tell me where you want me, babe, before I make a mess."

"On the bed with Ronin." She stops jacking me and slaps my ass, which is almost enough to make me spill right there. "I can't wait to see him fuck you."

After that, I'm so turned on and so eager I can barely get across the room and climb into her tall bed without tripping over my own big feet, with him watching me the whole time. She scrambles up the little rolling staircase onto the bed behind me.

But I'm afraid to actually touch him, myself, or anyone until she—

"Go on," she whispers in my ear, all low and throaty. "He's waiting for you. I want you in the middle to start."

My heart's hammering so hard it feels ready to explode through my chest. So it helps that she's straight up telling me what she wants me to do. I can follow orders with no problem, especially when these two are the ones giving them.

I crawl over the pillowy softness of her duvet, the plump mattress sinking under my weight. My dick's so hard and swollen I'm afraid I'll come at the first touch. I can't take my eyes off Ronin… my unattainable secret crush for so long… and that thick shaft he's slowly stroking, the heavy silver ring lying against his ruddy crown.

I just wish I could stop blushing.

"Breathe, Red," he rasps, with a lazy smile that just makes me hotter. "Not going to bite you… *much*. I'll leave that bit to our alphas. Just going to get you out of your head so you can enjoy this. Come here."

This is for Zara, as much as it's for me. Even though the whole idea of being bitten by *our alphas* is sending me into another tailspin. I want all of this so bad I'm literally shaking.

Come here, Ronin coaxes in my head, releasing his cock and spreading his thighs to make room for me. *Going to make both of you feel so good.*

I suck in a breath and crawl between his thighs. He coils up and meets me halfway, hands cradling my face, his mouth meeting mine in a kiss so hot steam practically rises from our lips. He tastes like contraband scotch and Ronin, and his hands burn with mating heat. His tongue winds around mine and I love kissing him so much that I gather my courage and drag one hand up his thigh over the hard ridge of his shaft.

He arches into my touch with a deep moan. I accept that invitation to stroke every hot inch of him, his piercing bumping up against my eager hand.

"Mmm, that's so nice," Zara murmurs, her own hot hands sliding up the back of my thighs. I adore it when she praises me, so I widen for her and hope for more of everything, both the contact and the praise. Her silky fingers cup and fondle the swollen fullness of my balls. I squeeze my eyes closed and release Ronin to grip my own dick hard. Hard enough to stop the climax from boiling down my shaft and spilling all over Ronin.

"Here's what I want," she breathes, and implants a super explicit image in both our minds. She's getting so good at telepathy, our queen is. She's such a powerful witch and such a quick study, and her heat is riding her so hard.

That's how I end up lying flat on my back between Ronin's spread thighs, his legs twined over mine to spread me wide, pinning me against his hard dick jutting up against my bottom. So I'm spread and helpless and definitely eager when Zara crawls over both of us, dragging her luscious breasts slowly up my torso.

I struggle to get my hands on her hot little body. But Ronin has me pinned, his hands laced with mine, so all I can do is feel both of them.

"I've been thinking about this all night," she purrs, rubbing her breasts against my chest. "And I think you'll be much more relaxed after the first time we make you come."

If that's her plan, I'm completely on board.

She undulates back down my body and drags her tongue all the way down my dick in a slow hot lick. I try to arch into her, begging for so much more of that, but Ronin's legs keep me spread. She licks back up my shaft like a popsicle and rips a moan out of me. Then she starts circling my tip and flicking her tongue over my slit, lapping up the fluid that gathers there and licking her lips like she loves the taste of me.

Ronin rocks against me from behind, his own slippery shaft nestling between my buttocks. Not penetrating me, not yet, but I know that's going to be happening soon.

Between the two of them, I'm sweating and squirming and just about losing my mind. And that's before Zara envelops my dick in the hot wet suck of her divine mouth. Before her lips start sliding up and down my engorged length. She's kept her go-go girl ponytail, which gives Ronin and me a perfect view of her lush lips riding me, leaving me all shiny with her saliva and all that precum I'm generating.

It's actually embarrassing that I'm so wet and so eager for both of them.

No, don't be embarrassed, you're so sexy, baby, she praises me through our bond. *We love that you need this so much.*

With a groan, I drive my hips into her mouth and rock my bottom back into Ronin's shaft. But they still have me pinned, so I don't have to worry about what to do. All I can do is gasp and writhe against the coil of Ronin's body and watch Zara's head bob smoothly up and down my dick.

"Remember what I said I was going to do to you?" Ronin grates in my ear.

I rock against his cock and thrust into my love's captivating mouth. "Yeah… been thinking about it… all day…"

"Why don't you tell Zara?" His hot tongue licks my ear.

"Oh God," I moan, on fire at the thought of saying it out loud. But my mate hums encouragement and takes me in deeper, and the words just spill out of me. "You said you were going to… open my tight little hole… with your fingers."

Zara moans and starts fondling my balls. I'm rocking into her mouth and rubbing myself against his dick and getting more and more inflamed by the sound of my own words.

"Then what?" he grates in my ear. "Tell her."

"Then you were going to… tongue my hole… until I'm soaked and… desperate. Until I'm… begging you." God, I'm that way right now, without anything at all inside me, and the urgency of my need is spiraling. Especially when Zara deep-throats me and swallows me down, her throat tightening and rippling around me.

I writhe urgently in his grip and a harsh cry tears from my chest. "Oh God, babe, God—"

"Then what?" he growls. "Tell Zara what I'm going to do to you next. What you're going to let me do?"

"I'm going to tongue Zara's pussy until she comes while I—oh God, please, I can't say it—"

"While you what?" He's breathing hard and rocking into me and utterly relentless.

I can't, I can't say it, but she's deep-throating me again and he's thrusting against my crack, audibly slick with his own fluid, my climax is clenching my balls and boiling down my dick, and the words explode between my clenched teeth in a raw shout.

"While I—take your cock—in my ass."

The climax I've been fighting all night erupts with a roar, and I thrust with complete abandon into Zara's mouth and empty my load down her throat.

I come for what feels like hours, pinned and euphoric and writhing with pleasure between my mates.

When my climax finally passes, I'm spent and empty and completely relaxed.

Zara lifts her head and licks the taste of me from her smiling lips. Her eyes are glowing lavender in the firelight and her ponytail is floating and she's never looked more like the queen she is.

"You were so good, baby," she praises me, all husky with her own craving.

"Love you so much," I pant, though really, I'm falling in love with both of them so easily, and I don't mind both of them listening in while I think about it. I've never been the one keeping secrets in this relationship.

"No more secrets," she whispers. "I love you too, Neo."

She makes me so happy, they both do, and she gives me a minute to catch my breath. But I know they both need me, and I'm more than willing to give both of them everything they need.

"You're so sweet to us." Zara's hands slide down her own body, straight to the slick wet valley between her legs, which makes Ronin and me both groan. "Now get on your hands and knees for Ronin. He's going to make you all ready for him while you get me off."

Normally a sentence that loaded would have me obsessing in about ten different ways. But Ronin turns out to be one hundred percent right about the relaxing effect of an orgasm. All my worries about being the awkward virgin in this bed have just evaporated. Still, Ronin's coiled tight with his own need behind me, because somehow, he managed to stoke my climax without giving in to his own.

And clearly my cherished one needs me to make her come.

Lazily I roll up to my hands and knees, which they're now both happy to let me do.

"You're a good lad," Ronin praises me too, and I hum with happiness. "Ready for me now, aren't you?"

"Uh huh," I agree, lifting my face for Zara's kiss. She tastes musky with my essence, and she's hot and eager and desperate for my mouth.

Ronin rolls over, opens the nightstand drawer, and produces a slip of paper and a packet of lubricant. That sight would have sent me into a tailspin a little while ago, but right now my blissed-out brain is totally empty, and my hole gives a flutter of anticipation.

"Test results from today at the clinic," he says tersely, offering me the paper. "Like we talked about. I'm clean. So, well, if the two of you wanted to…"

"Skip the condom?" I offer helpfully. I don't even glance at the paper, because I know he's telling the truth. "That sounds so perfect. As long as Zara wants—"

"Oh, she definitely wants," Zara assures both of us.

"Then why don't you sit up against the pillows, babe?" I suggest to her. "Now it's your turn to come."

Chapter Forty-One
Vasili

Lucius and I don't exactly conduct a scintillating conversation on the wickedly cold hike back to the *domus*. He's entirely preoccupied with fretting over what could have happened to Zara with that first-class bastard Zerxes.

When he's not worried about that, he's fighting like blazes the mounting crisis of his mating heat and silently cursing me for inflicting it on him.

As for myself, I'm rather preoccupied with my own little obsessions. This dynamic between Lucius and me has shifted, and I'm feeling all the possessive, protective, chromosomal drive of an alpha shifter to tend my mate. I want to tongue his bite and care for him and fuck him until he falls absolutely to pieces under my cock. I blame the supermoon shedding its pale light all over the snowy streets for triggering all those restless, itchy shifter recessives I've apparently been suppressing all my life. Admittedly, they're quite the handful to manage.

I'm also craving Ronin, the way I always crave Ronin.

I'll admit I'm even curious to explore what might transpire between Mercury and me now that I'm not entirely despising his royalist guts.

Finally, I'm hot as fuck to bury myself deep inside Zara and ream her naughty little body until both of us lose our minds.

So Lucius and I are silent as we slip into the atrium and shed our outer wear and prowl through the chilly house to her bedroom. She's left the door unlocked for us, and I wait (uncharacteristically) for Lucius to precede me, because I'm deeply suspicious that he'll flee the scene entirely given half a chance.

My wolf shifter squares his shoulders and pulls in an audible breath before he pads inside. I sidle right in behind the poor darling and waste no time closing and locking the door, before he can even think of backing out. If I had a key, I'd pocket it.

He's not getting past me until I've thoroughly had my way with him.

Inside, I welcome the warmth of the crackling fire. Lucius is standing stock-still between me and the bed, so I can't see a damned thing. But the air is thick with the musk of semen and the creamy sweetness of a queen's mating scent, laced with the potent kick of Mogadon pheromones.

"Smells like you've started without us, darlings," I murmur approvingly, sliding up behind Lucius so I can see properly over his shoulder, while still thwarting his escape if my skittish new mate tries to bolt.

He's breathing fast and audibly, and I can certainly appreciate why.

Zara's lounging naked against the carved headboard of that spectacular bed of hers, head flung back, face languid with need while she moans and plays with her own nipples. Neo's buff body is likewise naked and well worth admiring, muscled back flexing and bulging shoulders rippling as he crouches with his vividly colored head buried between her spread thighs, his big hands cradling her knees to spread her wider.

And the *piece de resistance*? Why, that would be Ronin, kneeling naked behind Neo with three shiny fingers thrusting in and out of Neo's sculpted ass. Neo's breathing hard and his hole is swallowing Ronin's fingers with a greedy eagerness that gives my own cock a hard jolt.

My, my. It seems our Mr. Mercury truly does enjoy ass play. I file that handy little fact away where I won't lose it for later.

As for Ronin, my boyfriend's heat is clearly driving him. His gorgeous skin is gleaming with sweat and trembling with restraint. He's jacking himself with one hand while he stretches Neo's hole with the other, because he's such a talented boy. Indeed, I can see Ronin's perilously close to skipping the rest of his scheduled foreplay entirely and reaming our virginal First Boy until they all see stars.

I've been anticipating the need to seduce my skittish Lucius with the skill and persistence of a damn Romeo, but I haven't taken into account the impact of having Ronin and Zara both in heat. For every flicker of protective, possessive, fuck-you-until-you-pass-out alpha instinct I'm feeling toward Lucius, he's feeling the same toward those two.

In fact, he takes one long look at the three of them and starts peeling out of his vintage tux like this is an Olympic sprint and the starting gun's just gone off—coat, cravat, shirt all shucked and flying and hitting the floor in record time. He's got his belt ripped open and he's working on his trousers when I slide an arm around his waist to pin his back against my front and lower my mouth to the little half-healed punctures my fangs have left in his shoulder.

"Merciful God, Vasili, *yes*," he groans in a broken voice, his head listing sideways to give me access.

At least he's finally stopped calling me Mr. Romanov.

"Hmmmm," I murmur against his bite, laving the punctures with my tongue. When I pluck the tie from his hair, his soft curls tumble down around his shoulders. "Pet, you're so sexy like this I can barely stand it."

Zara's head lifts and her eyes open to find mine, but she's moaning steadily under what appears to be the inspired play of Neo's tongue, her breathless little whimpers rising in pitch, and she's far too close to her own climax to speak. Neo's utterly absorbed in getting her off, and even Ronin hardly spares us a heated glance, his amber eyes fixed on Neo's eager hole.

"About bloody time the two of you show up," my boyfriend mutters, slicking back his long hair. "What're the odds I can get both of you inside me for a proper DP to finally break this fucking heat?"

Now, there's an intriguing notion. Clearly Lucius is torn between the powerful but foreign instinct (as an alpha himself) to submit to my tending and the equally powerful drive to pounce on Ronin, but I appreciate that Ronin wants to finish Neo and Zara first. My boyfriend's going to have his hands full (to say nothing of his lovely tight hole) once Lucius and I have a go.

"Darling, I love how you're thinking," I purr. "And rest assured we do intend to give all three of you an extremely thorough railing… in due course. Lucius, pet, why don't you assist me out of this corset."

That certainly appears to be the magic word (you'd be surprised what the sight of me in a corset can do for a man), because my teacher turns on me with his face savage and his wolf snarling and drags me into a brutal kiss.

Chapter Forty-Two
Zara

The dragon of my mating heat is fully alert and pacing inside me, eyes flaming and tail lashing. Neo has my thighs spread wide and he's tonguing my swollen clit and I'm thrusting into his hot tongue while my aching pussy clenches and releases like a fist that needs to be filled.

Between my own desperate moans, I'm sneaking peeks at Ronin, who's alternately pumping his dick and stretching Neo's virgin hole to take his first cock. Neo's whimpering and fucking himself on Ronin's fingers and definitely looking ready to welcome the rest of him, but my dedicated mate circles and sucks my clit like a champion and spears into me while I writhe and cream all over his tongue.

I honestly didn't think I could get any hotter.

But seeing Vasili and Lucius loom over the bed, my shifter's rangy build already half naked, hair falling around his shoulders and eyes glowing red, while Vasili licks Lucius' bite and stares at me with his smoking eyes, I realize I was dead wrong.

I'm about to get much, much hotter.

Ronin dives in to apply his tongue to Neo's hole the way he's apparently promised Neo he would. My fated mate flings his head back with a tortured cry, his contorted face a perfect study of sexual ecstasy.

"Wow, the two of you… so freaking hot," I gasp.

They both stare at me with heated eyes. In fact, they're *all* staring at me with heated eyes. All four of my guys. Neo's magenta curls are falling over his face and he looks drunk with need, while Ronin's already licking his way up Neo's back and clearly lining up for the main event.

He's going to fuck Neo bare.

Lucius has Vasili peeled out of his sparkly coat and is growling and wrestling him out of his complicated corset—his elaborate, sexy-as-fuck satiny silver corset—by sheer brute force. Vasili's half laughing at Lucius' violent handling as he tries to assist. Finally, Lucius happens on the throwing knife

Vasili keeps strapped to his inner forearm and slices the corset laces clean though, ignoring Vasili's startled protest with a single-minded intensity I fully approve.

When I stop teasing my nipples and reach for my clit to finish myself off, all four sets of eyes snap toward me. Suddenly the tension in this room is thick enough to cut with one of Vasili's knives.

"Red, for fuck's sake," Ronin mutters, "will you please give our girl your big cock?"

Neo's more than hard after being thoroughly teased and tortured by all this foreplay. He willingly fits his cock against my soaked and aching channel. His blazing green eyes lock on mine. "I'll give her my whole soul to cut her teeth on."

He punctuates his sentence with an electrifying thrust.

My eyes roll back in my head as his thick cock surges into my dripping core and fills me to the brim. A hot spike of pleasure drives through me and I let out a resonant yell that makes sparks fly and a lightbulb burst in the bathroom.

Neo's unstoppable after that, driving deep into me with the hard hammering my mating heat demands, grunting with every powerful downstroke, smothering my desperate cries with his frantic kisses. He fucks the first orgasm out of me in fifteen seconds flat, though I'm way too far gone to check my dive watch.

I'm still shuddering and moaning with aftershocks when Ronin pins us both beneath him and works his way into Neo's well-stretched hole.

So I get to enjoy at my leisure the look of wonder that softens and transforms my fated mate's Clark Kent face as he loses his virginity all over again. I get a front-row seat for the mounting pleasure that obliterates him when Ronin sets out to ruin us both.

Ronin settles into a driving, relentless rhythm and leans over Neo to kiss me too, the two of them trading off with my mouth. I love that Ronin can taste Neo on my tongue and I can taste Neo (along with the sweetness of cherry-flavored lube) on Ronin's. I'm scenting hard enough to claim both of them… all of them… and at some point Vasili pushes a naked Lucius flat on the bed and sucks him off with that talented mouth of his, a suction that looks strong as a vacuum hose, hard enough that they probably hear Lucius bellowing all the way down at the commons when he erupts and empties every drop of his violent climax down the Goblin King's throat.

When Lucius lies spent and gasping, having survived the first peak of his heat, but with a whole lot more peaking (as I now know from experience) yet to come, Vasili finally slithers into bed himself. He's the only one of us still wearing anything, his rock star breeches half-unlaced and sliding down his lean hips, his lip gloss gone and his hair a tousled mess from the brutal way Lucius gripped his head and fucked his face when he came.

But I can't help wondering if the fact that the Goblin King's still half-dressed means he's still only half-committed to exploring this relationship with us.

And, specifically, only half-committed to me.

By now Ronin's chasing his own climax, and he's absolutely savage. The swollen moon shining through the glass doors is driving all three of us who are in heat, all three of us whom Lucius or Vasili has bitten, like we're being ridden by a demon with crop and spurs who's flogging all of us at a foaming gallop down the highway to Hell.

Neo and Vasili haven't been bitten (yet) and I'm amazed and impressed they're both keeping up with this punishing pace.

At this point, Ronin's fucking both of us—Neo and me. Every time Ronin slams into Neo's ass, snarling with every downstroke, Neo's cock hits my sweet spot. And I'm literally loving it. I'm about two pumps away from my next explosive climax, and I'm probably going to take down the entire electric grid when I shatter.

But this is a lot of pounding for a first timer to handle, and I'm getting a little worried about my fated mate.

Apparently there's a pretty strong bond forming among all five of us, because Vasili takes in the three of us with a single glance, then crawls over Lucius' spent but rapidly recovering body to wrap a fist in Ronin's hair and jerk his head around.

"Why don't you give Mercury a bit of a breather, darling?" Vasili purrs. "You're not the only one of us who wants to rail his perfect ass."

Then Vasili drags Ronin's mouth to his and shoves a brutal finger (without lube) in Ronin's hole. And our sexy Brit finally breaks his mating heat with a few last desperate pumps that have Neo spurting like Old Faithful in my pussy and the island's tectonic plates shuddering and groaning under the force of Neo's earthquake and me going off like Mt. Vesuvius all over Neo's well-serviced cock.

Which means Vasili's pretty much gotten all four of us to come on command in less than five minutes. That's going to make him cocky as fuck. After tonight, he's going to be insufferable.

And the Goblin King *still* hasn't taken off his fucking pants.

Ronin rolls off the two of us with a gasp and flops down limply alongside me, his tattooed skin dripping with sweat, like he'll never move again.

Vasili's smirking with satisfaction over the entire affair… until he sees something that makes his dangerous eyes narrow. He swipes a hand down Neo's crack and studies his long fingers, now dripping with Ronin's spunk.

"Well, well, well. No raincoat?" he muses, his poisonous gaze sliding over the three of us. "Now that's… interesting."

"I'm clean. Got tested," Ronin pants. "I'm all done… with my one-and-dones. And I'll fuck you bare too, love, no worries… soon as I catch my breath. I think you just broke my heat."

"Hmmm." Vasili licks his fingers clean with his pointed tongue. I can't read his face right now, and I'm hesitant to push this fledgling bond between us.

"That plan hardly seems appropriate." Lucius sits up with a frown. "Vasili should be tested as well if, well, we're all going to…"

"Vasili's been a one-horse cowboy since the day Ronin Pendragon enrolled at this Academy," Vasili says lightly. "Entirely monogamous, if you can believe that. We've always suited up because Ronin *wasn't*."

There's a lot happening in this bed right now (besides sex), but I'm still horny as fuck thanks to my heat, and Neo's pretty out of it. Still, my fated mate is worried about crushing me. He rolls sluggishly off me and comes face to face with a naked Lucius.

Confronted with his equally naked star pupil, Lucius looks suddenly alarmed and furtive. "Ah, Mr. Mercury…"

The Goblin King snorts and lifts his eloquent eyes toward heaven, which honestly doesn't help. But Neo really has had every single nerve fucked out of him. He smiles drowsily, says "Hello, Lucius," and leans in to give him the sweetest kiss.

When Neo eases back and flops down next to Ronin, it's actually Lucius who's blushing. And I totally can't wait for the two of them to find their way into this new relationship we're all exploring.

"Hmmm," Vasili says.

He's starting to look guarded, and I don't like that a bit.

I slide my hands down my well-ridden but still frisky body and say in my throatiest sex kitten whisper, "Hey, Goblin King. No one wears clothes in this bed tonight."

And you'd better fucking say something more than "hmmm" this time.

His lids drop over his eyes and his gaze takes its sweet time crawling over me. I'd probably feel self-conscious if I wasn't still so horny. Because I'm just a total mess, all flushed and tousled and damp and sticky, with Neo's come dripping out of me and Lucius' punctures throbbing gently at my shoulder and a love bite Ronin sucked into the side of my neck still stinging.

"A mess?" Vasili whispers on an indrawn breath. "No. Not at all. Zara, you're… glorious."

I launch toward him and he pounces on me and we meet in the middle, his pretty mouth fusing with mine like atoms colliding in a nuclear kiss. I shove my tongue into his mouth and lick his sharp little fangs and lap up the essence of Lucius mingled with Ronin in the silky heat of his kiss. He really loves that I'm so into his fangs, it disarms all that pissy Romanov attitude of his so beautifully, and he pushes me back on the mattress with a sudden roughness that makes me realize he's the only person in this bed who still hasn't come.

I roll us onto our sides like the equals we are and run my hands over his streamlined body. He's all sleek skin stretched over balletic muscle, and I quickly discover he's super sensitive around the pink nipples I've wanted to tongue since the first time I saw them. So I do, I flick my tongue across his nipples until they're tight and shiny with my spit while he moans, and when I bite them he hisses and swears at me.

But he still doesn't want me to stop.

His hands are learning the way I feel too. He's learning the way I shiver when he drags his sharp fingernails down my spine and the way I moan when he mouths my neck so I can feel his fangs and the way I keen for him when he slides one long finger down the crack of my ass.

"Hmmm," he purrs, his icy eyes going warm with mischief. "Darling, I can hardly believe no one in this bed tonight's taken advantage of *that*."

"Can't tap every ass in this whole blooming bed, love," Ronin murmurs. He's wrapped himself around Lucius now. Lucius is licking his bite with slow sizzling strokes that make me hotter with every swipe, and watching us with his wolfish eyes gleaming with secrets.

"I can't imagine why not," Vasili drawls.

A jumble of longing ties my insides in knots.

I've always been a back-door girl, and Vasili's obviously always been a back-door man. But I want Vasili to want all of me, the way I want all of him. And it isn't even reasonable what I want, since up until a day or two ago, he thought he was one hundred percent gay—

"I did," he groans, biting his way down my neck, which just about makes me climax for him right there. "I do. I still think I mostly am, darling. *Except for you.* I'm completely fucking in love with my fucking queen, who is most decidedly a woman, and I don't know what kind of label to put on this. It's you, it's me, it's all fucking five of us. I'm committed to all four of you."

He pauses, breathing hard, lying like Cleopatra's adder with his face pressed between my tits, and we all listen to the echo of his words.

He's in love with me.

If he isn't already in love with all of us, he's definitely headed in that direction.

And Vasili Romanov, the uncompromising anti-monarchist, has just accepted me as his queen.

I thread my fingers through his silver hair and cradle his head between my palms and whisper in the lightning voice. "You're mine to love. You're my snake. You're my alpha. You're the complete terror of the witching world and the worst nightmare of all my enemies. You're mine. You're mine. You're *mine*."

My window rattles with a peal of thunder. Vasili's head snaps up and he locks onto my eyes.

"Well, don't expect much in the way of technique, darling, because this is my first time cruising this particular highway," he murmurs. "But I do intend to make you mine in every single way I can conceive of. Starting with *this*."

Then he lunges in like the viper he is and sinks his deadly little fangs deep in my breast.

The stinging shock burns through me, even more intense than Lucius' bite. Lucius swears and Ronin struggles to restrain him and Neo sits straight up in alarm. Despite my own shock, I manage to send a pulse of reassurance to all of them through our bond.

Vasili's not attacking me. He's giving me his mating bite. Because my poisonous snake of a warlock isn't about to play second to anyone else's fiddle.

He wants me thoroughly and irrevocably mated to him as well as Lucius.

And that instant double wallop of mating heat makes my inner dragon absolutely feral. That golden monster inside me rears up on her back legs and roars and shoots a torrent of flame straight into the sky like a pretty Godzilla. Need claws through me and I writhe into Vasili and claw into his back.

"I fell in love with you—despite myself, Vasili Romanov," I gasp out loud, so he can't miss it. "Now you're mine, and I'm yours."

Vasili lifts his head and licks my blood off his lips with his serpent's tongue. Sly triumph lurks in his face.

But only I can feel the way he's trembling. This mate of mine will never be controlled through guile or violence.

The key to managing Vasili will always and only be love.

I hook my hands in those pants he's still fucking wearing and drag them down his hips. His pretty cock springs free, rigid and swollen with need, and smacks against his tight belly.

"I hope you're freaking ready for me, Goblin King," I snarl. "Because now you're going to fuck me until your dick falls off."

"That will be my absolute pleasure," he says silkily. "My queen."

Because he knows deep in his Mogadon DNA what I need most to hear.

"Say it again," I growl, pushing him on his back and straddling his hips. He's scenting for me and I'm scenting for him, we're both rubbing all over each other to stake our claim, and we're pumping out enough pheromones to make all five of us ready for another round.

"My queen." Pinned beneath me, Vasili rears up like a cobra and laps at my bleeding tit. Pleasure streaks through me and makes me savage. "My queen."

He's kneading my breasts and tonguing my bite and I wrap my hand around his perfect cock for the very first time and give him a few rough strokes that have him writhing and hissing between my legs and thrusting his shaft into my fist.

"Again," I demand, arching into his hands on my body.

"My queen." He seals his terrible mouth around my nipple and drags my ring between his fangs and tugs. Which makes me cry out and rock my soaking cunt into his cock. Because I'm an absolute slave to those fangs of his, and now he totally knows it.

"Zara, darling," he growls against my skin. "Stop teasing me to a demented frenzy and fuck me. Fuck me before you kill me."

I line him up against my pussy and sink down his cock, inch by inch, until he's buried balls deep inside me. His head falls back on the pillow, eyes wide with astonishment, pupils blown with pleasure, mouth falling open on a breathless gasp. I pin his shoulders to the mattress and undulate against all those hot tensile inches. Violet sparks spill from my fingers and race along his skin. Smoke rises from our bodies and nearly sets the bed alight.

Shit. The pleasure of having his cock inside me is so intense I'm losing control.

I'm going to hurt him if I don't stop.

But his hands lock around my hips and hold me in place while his pelvis snaps forward to thrust into me, finding a primal rhythm that has both of us crying out.

God, he's going to make me come for him so hard. And I'm going to kill all of us when I do—

Suddenly, behind me, a strong fierce presence looms. Hard hands trap my wrists and pin my hands behind my back.

"In case you've forgotten, Vasili isn't the only alpha in this harem," Lucius breathes into my ear. "I've got you, my queen. I'll keep you safe. I'm not going to let you fall."

The reassurance of his strength seeps through me. My hands stop sparking and Vasili's singed skin stops smoking. A shuddering sigh of relief spills out of me.

"But," Lucius growls, his wolf lurking in his guttural voice, "I am going to give you the tribute a twice-bitten queen deserves from her mates on the night of the supermoon."

He pushes me forward until I'm plastered against Vasili, tits crushed up against the Goblin King's chest, wrists still engulfed in one of Lucius' big hands and trapped at the small of my back. My shifter's other hand strokes down the crack of my ass and fingers the tender skin of my pucker.

I whimper and push into that teasing touch, my empty hole twitching and eager for him to fill me.

"Ronin, my dear one," he says thickly, his accent even more pronounced, "would you be kind enough to pass me the lubricant? Then perhaps the two of you will assist me with pleasing our queen."

Vasili and I moan in unison. I'm trapped and helpless between my two alphas in a way I normally wouldn't tolerate. But this is Lucius, and we all trust him. Ronin scrambles for the lube and Neo jumps up to arrange the pillows. At the same time, Vasili fucks lazily into me and angles my ass higher for Lucius.

Sweet Jesus. I'm about to get tag-teamed and reamed by both of them.

Chapter Forty-Three
Lucius

I've been telling myself repeatedly all night to be exceedingly careful and deliberate with her, my volatile young queen. I know better than any of her mates how powerful a mating heat can be, especially a mating heat during a supermoon.

Now that damnable, luscious brat of a Vasili has ensured she's been bitten twice.

I can feel Zara's raw power humming through her sex-drenched body like current arcing through a power cable. But it's entirely impossible to think coherently about anything beyond the tempting swell of her bottom lifted in the air and that sweet pink rosebud nestled in the pale triangle of her tan lines, that secret passage I have every intention of pillaging. Between the way she looks and the way she smells and the way my wolf feels clawing and snarling to get at our mate, I feel far more like a ravening Mongol raider than a mannerly history professor tonight.

Naturally, Vasili (being Vasili) hasn't bothered to wait for me. But he is biding his time, stoking her heat with short shallow strokes of his delectable cock inside her, his pretty face going soft with wonder whenever he thinks no one will notice.

I'm fully aware that he has every intention of fucking me through my own heat once he's finished with hers.

And I'm ruefully aware that, despite my own virginal status in that particular regard, I have every intention of letting him.

But what I need now is simpler and far more immediate. I need the intense anticipation of trapping my queen's wrists at the small of her back with one hand and drizzling a generous torrent of lubricant, thoughtfully warmed by a spurt of Ronin's fire gift, all over Zara's pretty pink hole with the other. I need the shudder of raw pleasure that licks through me when Ronin drizzles more into his own palm and slicks it down my aching length.

I've never even dreamed that I need my shy star pupil Neo, who delights and astounds me by leaning in to claim me with a slow sweet kiss.

The two of them are like ministering angels, Neo blushing rosy but eager with his bashful kisses, Ronin all too familiar with how best to work me, so rough he's almost careless, adding that twist at the end of every hard stroke that makes my wolf and me burn to pin both my male students to the mattress right now and not let either of them back up for a week.

But I'm not my wolf.

I'm in control.

I disentangle gently from their distracting ministrations to probe my queen's tender hole with my thumb. She voices a breathless little cry that shoots straight to my shaft and arches her back to push into my thumb, so eager she's fucking herself onto the digit with no coaxing on my part whatsoever.

She's clearly no stranger to any of this. No, she's impatient for this, for us, for me, and I'm buried in her tight passage to my second knuckle before I even have to stretch her.

"Bollocks, that's sexy as fuck," Ronin grates, watching her pretty rosebud swallow my thumb.

Neo rakes back his hair and leans in to watch with the same utter absorption he shows when he's poring over his textbooks, except that tonight he's not wearing his glasses.

"Wow," he breathes, sounding awestruck. "Is that how I look when I, um…"

"When you take my cock?" Ronin says, and Neo blushes to his hairline. "Yeah, Red, you're both bloody gorgeous."

Ronin pulls him into an open-mouthed kiss, which Neo happily snuggles into.

My chest swells with soft and tender sentiment. Dear God, they're my students, but they're all so easy for me to love. Even that scoundrel Vasili has been hovering protectively over me since the moment he bit me with a degree of devoted absorption I never dreamed he was capable of exhibiting. If he intends to keep on like this, I suppose I might as well surrender completely to my descent from grace and fall in love with him too.

"God, Lucius, don't tease me." Zara's getting rather desperate. When I withdraw my thumb, she whimpers. But she mewls with pleasure like a cat when I add two fingers and scissor them gently to stretch her.

"I'm telling you, she's ready for you," Ronin urges, barely getting the words out between Neo's increasingly eager kisses.

"Thank you, Mr. Pendragon. I didn't request an academic critique," I say a bit testily, because I'm in fairly acute heat myself, and I can barely manage to control it without having to entertain a running discourse on the matter.

"Dear pet," Vasili gasps between thrusts. "I do believe we've achieved—a sufficient degree of intimacy—to justify being on a first name—basis. For the love of God—will you please—get on with it?"

"Yet another peer reviewer joins the fray, Mr. Romanov," I say dryly, but it's obvious even to me that Zara's definitely ready for me.

"Hardly a peer reviewer," Vasili fires back. "Clearly, I'm the lead author."

"Cheese on toast," Zara pants, tugging impatiently at my grip on her wrists. "I'm not a scholarly manuscript. Just fuck me, Lucius."

That's obviously the heat talking, and I'm entirely amenable to servicing it, except for one last important detail. I withdraw my fingers from her strangling clutch that's going to feel so heavenly wrapped around my manhood and cast about with determination for—

"No. Fucking. Condom," my queen says savagely. "You've been celibate for years. I was tested in Singapore. We're all committing. Lucius Laszlo Aries, I need you to fuck me bare *right now*."

I don't have the first idea how she's managed to learn my middle name, but it's certainly effective. Without further ado, I fit the swollen head of my manhood to her slick rear passage, a feat made more complicated by the increasing intensity with which she and Vasili are coupling, and carefully press into her tight heat.

I mean to go slowly, still, because I feel responsible for all of them. But the instant she feels me probing her, she cries out and rocks herself onto my shaft. A hoarse groan rumbles out of me and my manhood throbs.

"Well, *finally*," Vasili drawls.

But I forgive him for his intolerable sarcasm because of the incredible way he feels inside her front passage, only a thin membrane separating my organ from his. He's my alpha, she's my queen, and I'm in desperate rut.

I grip Zara's sweet bottom in one sweating paw and thrust slowly into her. All three of us moan in unison.

"Oh, shit," she whimpers, but it's definitely a whimper of pleasure. "Shit, Lucius."

I ease out of her, but not very far. When I push back in, Vasili's eyes drill into me, stripped for once of malice or pretense or anything but raw pleasure.

"I can… *feel* that," he breathes. "My God, Lucius."

Thus am I forgiven by both my mates for my measured pace. My wolf is deeply gratified by this reception and excited to be this close to both of them, and my own reaction is scarcely more sophisticated.

This is especially the case once I release Zara's wrists and she starts to move between us like liquid lightning.

With every roll of her hips, my shaft rubs against Vasili's inside her, through the thin barrier between us. With every breath, her tight sweet hole strangles my manhood in a silken fist. With every thrust, I'm cupping a succulent breast or Vasili's licking her bite or Neo's leaning in to give me another shy kiss. Knowing that Ronin and Neo are watching and getting off again themselves, their breath growing hoarse and their hands and mouths all over each other, adds another level of erotic charge to this entire unprecedented experience.

I finally abandon the last of my restraint and surrender utterly to the hard driving pace my heat demands.

I grip my queen's hips and slam into her sexy ass, my eyes nailed to the inflammatory sight of my thick shaft, flushed purple with need, pistoning in and out of her shiny hole, wrenching cries from deep inside her that spiral higher with every brutal stroke. Vasili's got his lower lip clenched in his little fangs hard enough to draw a trickle of blood, his gilded brows furrowed, and every rough thrust of my alpha's shaft against mine inside my queen's slick passage makes me snarl like a savage dog.

Still, my wolf and I want both of them to climax before we do.

In the end, we climb that final peak together, and we fall together, my hands pinning Zara's overhead when her sparks fly, my mouth finding Vasili's in a desperate kiss, my wolf whining beneath my human skin, my release and Vasili's spilling in long endless spurts into her sucking heat to fill her while she writhes and sobs between us.

I know now beyond any doubt that I'm taking all four of them, and she's taking all four of us. It's inconceivable now that I'll ever let any of them go. This remains the case even though this forbidden choice will undoubtedly cost me my position. Ours is a union I'll kill to keep, even if it demands a sacrifice I'll forever grieve.

God only knows how I'm going to tell the Dean.

Chapter Forty-Four

Zara

The enormous moon is sinking behind the slanting eaves and my guys are deep asleep, all four of them, piled like sexy naked wolf pups in my big canopy bed. Vasili's sprawled protectively over Lucius and, I'm interested to see, over Neo. It's been fascinating to watch the two of them watch each other, and I don't think it's going to take very long before Vasili starts giving Neo what he's already giving everyone else in this bed.

But I've been so wrapped up in my mating heat that I haven't been able to focus on anything for very long.

Ronin's hot body is wrapped around me, his golden skin radiating plenty of banked Leo fire, though I'm pretty sure I broke his actual mating heat for good when he tied my wrists to my headboard and fucked me until I screamed and blew out the bulb in my desk lamp.

At the rate I'm going, this entire Academy will be reduced to stygian darkness by the end of the term.

Anyway, my guys have definitely earned their recovery sleep before we all go at it again, but I'm way too restless to sleep myself. I've had a boatload to process over the past few days, now including a lurking sense of imposter syndrome at the concept of being proclaimed queen of the witching world, given the still uncontrolled and largely unexplored extent of my witchcraft. Who knows if I can actually save the witching world? Maybe I won't live up to my star billing.

And now I have to pee.

I briefly consider holding it, because the fire's gone out and it's cold as fuck in my bedroom. But it's no use, I gotta go. Heaving a sigh, I disentangle carefully from Ronin's heavy limbs, because I really don't want to wake him. His first heat's taken a lot out of him. I'm glad when he rolls over and burrows into Neo with a heavy sigh without ever waking.

God knows we all need sleep to recuperate.

Groping through the dark, because there isn't much moonlight left, I shiver into my fur-lined Academy robe and slippers, then bolt into my bathroom with teeth chattering to take care of business. Which I also end up doing in the dark.

Turns out I've done more than blow out the big bathroom light. The nightlight's intact, but nothing happens when I hit the little switch.

That means I tripped the circuit breaker for the house again.

I better go down to the basement and flip the switch, or this whole house will be an icebox by sunup.

I fumble around my desk for the candle and matches I've started keeping, which we all use (very atmospherically) whenever the power goes out. I light a candlestick without much difficulty, unlock my bedroom door, and tiptoe into the hall—careful to close the door behind me to trap the fire's residual warmth.

The hallway overlooks the great room, but I can't see much down there. Even the hall is barely lit by the last moonlight seeping through the tall arched window at the end. Racetrack's door is open and it's dark inside, but Dez's door is closed. With those psychic senses I'm starting to hone, I sense the two of them in there, also down for the count.

As I pad past, a hearty snore seeps under that closed door that makes me grin.

They're not part of my harem, even though normally I don't mind having a girl or two in my bed. But they're not in my bed and they won't be, in part because Dez and Racetrack are monogamous, and in part because those two aren't my type. (I go for the sleek runway supermodel type like Cleo, and look how well that's working out.) But mainly, as much as I love seeing my guys totally fall for each other, I'm feeling way too possessive to share them with any other girl. And we all do share in my harem, everyone with everyone else, because that's the way I roll.

Still, Dez and Racetrack are mine in a different way. They're my courtiers, they're part of my court, and we'll work out together what all that means. They're maybe even… my friends. So I'm glad they're home safe and sound.

Cupping my candle against the breeze, I shuffle down to the main level, my slippers scuffing on the stairs. The cold deepens as I descend. By the time I reach the great room, I can see my breath frosting the frigid air. The power hasn't been out all that long, so someone must have left a window open down here. Which isn't so great for security, given the whole dead wolf incident.

I figure I'll get the power back on, turn on a few lights, then find the open window and close it.

I shuffle past the kitchen toward the basement stairs, which takes me past the front atrium. Here there's an actual breeze blowing and a shrill winter wind whistling through that raises goosebumps on my skin.

With an ugly jolt, I realize the front door's wide open.

The wood's old and swollen, so it doesn't close tight sometimes. Dez and Racetrack maybe left it open by mistake when they came home, because it doesn't seem like Lucius and Vasili would've been that careless. Either way, I'm suddenly not quite so comfy being downstairs in this big drafty house alone.

But that door needs closing ASAP.

Hunching into my bathrobe and thankful as fuck for the fur lining, I scurry through the atrium and wrestle the door closed. It's a two-handed job, which of course means my candle blows out in the process.

Still, I finish the job and slide the sturdy deadbolt securely in place.

Without the wind whistling, it's really silent in the house.

And pitch black in the atrium.

My heart bumps uneasily as I tiptoe through, past the darkened kitchen, into the great room. Here, there's enough light leaking through the courtyard windows that I can make out the looming shapes of the Renaissance couch and the settee with its high scrolling back and the central hearth. Red coals glow dimly in a pile of ash.

Seeing that homey glow makes me feel a little better. I want to relight my candle, so I head over, stir the coals with the poker, and get a little lick of flame going that pushes back against the darkness.

I've just replaced the poker in the rack when a floorboard creaks.

My heart gives a hard thump and I spin, even though it's probably just one of the girls coming down for a glass of milk, or one of the guys missing me. But, for some reason, I don't call out. I've been quiet as a flea since I found the door open, and I don't see any need to change that quite yet.

Instead, I reject the idea of lighting my candle and visually announcing *Zara's right here* to the whole house, and I edge away from the hearth where I'm silhouetted against the glow. I'm supposed to be going down to the basement for the fuse box, but the fluttery feeling in my chest and the squirmy sense of unease in my tummy make a very strong case against that plan. The door to the courtyard's the other way, where at least there will be more moonlight.

But what feels like the best option, all of a sudden, is just going back up to where the guys are, getting more candles, and maybe getting one of them to come down with me and check the house.

I've started creeping toward the upper stairs when another floorboard gives a labored groan. I freeze where I am and don't make a peep.

This time, I realize, the noise is coming from upstairs.

There's someone (or, you know, something, like maybe a monster?) *on* the stairs. It's between me and where everyone else is sleeping.

And that someone or something is coming down.

Now my eyes are adjusting to the dark, and that little lick of fire is helping some, because I can actually see movement. Whatever it is, it's big. *Way* bigger than one of the guys.

Big. Slow. Heavy.

It shuffles into the firelight, swaying on all fours, toenails clicking on the bare floor, the light picking out pale fur and shaggy bulk and a dark snout that swings unerringly toward me. The thing huffs out a breath and rises up… way up… on its hind legs to get a better look.

Ice water pours down my spine and sheets over my skin and shocks every nerve in my body into a clamor of violent life.

I'm staring at a polar bear. A fucking polar bear.

And it's *in* the fucking house.

I think I'm staring at Bjorn, the bear shifter on the custodial staff. In, like, his bear form.

I freeze where I stand like I'm that game warden in *Jurassic Park* before the tyrannosaur attack, but I don't think this is going to help, since I'm not actually dealing with a tyrannosaur.

Since I'm actually dealing with a shifter, I clear my throat and talk. "Uh, I'm guessing you're Bjorn? I'm Zara Gemini. New student."

The bear blinks at me. I have no idea how much human cognition Bjorn normally has in bear form, or in human form for that matter. To my knowledge, we've never actually met. Nor am I sure what the supermoon might be doing to him (because Lucius told me it fucks with shifters), but I'm not seeing much in the way of intellect in those little bear eyes.

I guess, to be on the safe side, I better treat him like an actual bear.

If I am dealing with an actual bear, I know I shouldn't run. Running triggers a bear attack, and the bear will be faster than I am.

This specific bear is between me and the guys, and between me and the front door, but he's not between me and the courtyard. If I can get out there… without running… I can lock the bear in, then maybe scale the trellis or at least call up to the guys for help.

In fact, I can call for the guys right now, using our bond.

Because I'm through trying to handle shit on my own. Especially serious, dangerous shit like a freaking polar bear.

I start edging carefully toward the courtyard door. The bear's snout swings to follow me, which is deeply alarming and makes me stop moving. Then the bear drops down to all fours again, which could be good or bad.

I give an experimental tug on the bond that connects me to my fated mate, my alphas, and Ronin who's the strongest telepath of the bunch. I'm still new at this, but all I can sense at the other end is a heavy, sluggish darkness.

That's probably because they're all asleep.

The bear huffs out a visible breath—visible because it's still freezing in the house. I edge another step toward the courtyard, while the bear watches me closely, and give another hard tug on my bond with the guys. I'm hoping to feel someone, or several someones, jerk awake, but I literally feel nothing.

Shit.

The bear sways slowly toward me, but he looks more curious than aggressive. I remember from childhood camping trips that sometimes you can scare off a bear, so I raise my robed arms over my head to make myself as large as possible and say sternly, "Go away, bear."

The bear lowers his head and eyes me.

As if, he seems to think.

"I mean it, bear." I raise my voice, hoping to reach someone upstairs, and keep tugging on the bond with my guys like I'm tugging on a rope. "Vamoose!"

Of course, since I've closed the front door, there's nowhere for him to vamoose to, but we'll deal with getting him out of the house later. For now, I'll settle for getting him out of the room.

The bear makes a woofing sound and lumbers decisively toward me. This is definitely not working.

"You're a bad bear!" I shout, possibly unfairly since he could just be curious and not aggressive, but I'm not giving this particular bear the benefit of the doubt. As I back slowly away, my hand bumps up against the rack of fire tools by the hearth.

I grab the poker and brandish it. "Bad bear!"

Bjorn doesn't seem to like the criticism, because he lowers his head and charges.

Terror thunders through me and hones my senses razor-sharp. I scramble back and yell and wield the poker like I mean business, but all of this is totally useless. I've got maybe three seconds tops before that bear's right on top of me.

A powerful instinct surges through my central nervous system. A sudden gust of energy lifts the hair from my shoulders and makes my robe billow. The lightning voice gathers in my throat, the useless poker falls from my fingers, and my tingling hands sweep up.

"Bjorn!" I roar at the charging bear in the lightning voice. *"Stop!"*

My voice unlocks a crack of thunder loud enough to rattle the windows and a flash of blinding ultraviolet light. The electrical discharge slams through me and pours from my hands in an explosion of purple sparks.

When my vision clears and the glowing spots stop dancing in my eyes, the bear is down, stunned and twitching, smoke rising from his fur.

Clearly I haven't killed him, which I'm kind of glad to see since there's actually a human in there. But I'm not wasting any time getting back upstairs either.

I give the twitching bear a wide berth and charge for the stairs.

I'm almost there when a robed figure floats gently from the second-floor hallway to settle before me, long silver hair whispering around broad shoulders. I scramble to a stop barely in time to avoid colliding with Bucephalus Zerxes.

"Sweet Jesus!" I yelp. "Is every warlock on this island in this fucking house?"

"Only the ones that matter." He's ditched his snazzy tux for the black robes slashed with sangoire that he teaches in. It's a fashion choice that has an ominous effect in the dark under these circumstances. Especially when he bares his white teeth in a silken smile. "Only the members of your harem."

"Oh, for fuck's sake," I exclaim in complete disgust. "This again?"

I'd normally go for more diplomacy, like I tried with him at the dance, for all the good that did. But my wilderness encounter just now took a lot out of me, and that bear's still moving his great big huge paws and looking like he might try sitting up.

And, bear or no bear, Bucephalus freaking Zerxes absolutely should *not* be in our house.

I actually prefer the bear to him.

I give the bond with my guys another hard tug, and God knows my peal of thunder was enough to wake the dead. But I'm still not getting anything back, because—

"Oh, you needn't bother calling your alphas, your fated mate, your courtiers, or anyone else who's currently occupying your bed," Zerxes purrs. "I've laid a common magic sleep spell over this entire house, yourself excepted, that will keep everyone well out of our way until dawn."

Well, fuck. At least that explains why no one's riding to the rescue.

A stillness settles over me. It's the quiet place I go to when I'm planning a heist, when I need to rely on my wits and my foresight and my intel to keep me alive. I angle my body so I can keep an eye on the bear. The warlock shifts with me, keeping his body between me and the stairs.

I search my prof's menacing frame for weapons and don't see any, but his witchcraft *is* his weapon, and there's nothing to see until he uses it. I study his face for clues to what he's thinking, but he's always been hard to read.

"Ah, you'd like to know what it is I'm thinking?" he breathes, which gives me a nasty jolt and reminds me to build my own psychic wall, which I hastily start doing. "All you ever need do when you desire something of me, my queen, is to ask."

"Okay, I'll bite." I go for bravado and plant my hands on my hips. "For starters, why the hell are you here?"

"Why, to see you, my queen." He gives me a secret smile, a private smile, the kind of smile a guy gives his lover. Which creeps me right out. "What else can I clarify for you?"

"Did you let that fucking bear in this house?" I eye the path to the front door, but I'm not really thinking about running.

Whatever this guy wants, I intend to deal with it right here.

"Unfortunately for all concerned, I did." His big shoulders lift in an apologetic shrug. "I trust you'll forgive me for wanting to witness firsthand a demonstration of your mighty power. Why didn't you simply slay the beast? You have that strength within you."

"Uh, because he's human, and I'm not a murderer?" Duh. Now for the question I really want answered. "What do you want from me?"

"Tsk tsk, Ms. Gemini." He purses his lips in playful reproach. "If you have to ask a question like that, you simply aren't paying attention. I want what I've always wanted. To be ruling alpha to a strong queen, to preserve the four races from global extinction, and to promulgate my powerful genetic legacy for the next generation. All of this to be achieved by siring. The next. Queen."

Looks like he hasn't lost his knack for oratory.

I fold my arms across my chest and hug my elbows. This whole concept of having mutual offspring with Bucephalus Zerxes revolts me, but I might as well suss out all I can while he's in this chatty mood.

"I don't think Master Aries is on board with your grand plan," I comment, because my headmaster seems like a sore spot for this guy.

"Hardly." His eyes flash an irate neon in the shifting firelight. "Indeed, Lucius has been rather tiresome in his approach to this entire affair. He's made my quest far more complicated and cumbersome than it needs to be. First he intervened with the Dean to secure the assignment of collecting you from Singapore, which I'd petitioned to undertake myself. Then he intervened once more to install you in his household rather than mine. He even rearranged your academic schedule to avoid placing you in my classes, but I addressed that little hiccup when I sidelined Agrippina."

"Sidelined her? Don't you mean you poisoned her?" This is bad, this is worse than I thought, if he's actually hurt a member of the faculty to get at me. "Dude, you can't just go around poisoning people. She's an old woman. You could have killed her."

"Oh, I suppose, but it would have been worth it." Light as a stalking panther, he glides toward me. "To get at you."

I shuffle back, definitely wishing I were wearing more than a robe and slippers, because this outfit isn't very menacing (at all). "Well, too bad it was all for nothing. I've already said there isn't a vacancy in my harem."

He pauses to tilt his head and study me. "Do you know, that's the same dismissal Cybelle once uttered, when I extended to her the same proposition? She wanted your worthless brother Damien as her alpha, but he would never have controlled her harem. In fact, I myself had to exert… considerable effort… to persuade her to accept me as her alpha."

Yeah, I just bet he did. Cybelle sounds like a total bitch, but I feel a flicker of sympathy for my predecessor now.

I tap my slippered foot on the floor and eye him. "How'd you do it then? Out of curiosity."

"Why, I merely threatened the thing she loved most, aside from herself." His purring voice hardens to ice. "I threatened her precious mother. What I know about the misdeeds of Messalina Aquarius, my former lover when we were both students at this Academy, would bring the house of Aquarius to its knees if those secrets were ever divulged. To protect her mother—and by extension, of course, herself—Cybelle welcomed me into her harem with open arms."

A fist of distaste punches me in the gut. He forced his way into his student's harem and her bed by blackmail and coercion. And guess what he thinks he's about to do to me?

"How'd that work out for you, Ceph?"

His fingers lift in a dismissive gesture. "Her harem was an entirely different sort than the one you're building. Cybelle demanded her mates' complete devotion at all times, even mine, even if she did originally accept me into her bed under duress. Her mates were forbidden from pleasing each other, even those who'd been together before, which led to considerable… friction… within the harem. I kept them all in line and ensured that it was I, and not they, who filled her womb when she was fertile."

"Whoa." Now this I haven't heard. "You saying Cybelle was pregnant?"

"She was," he says softly. "She hadn't been planning to give birth so young, but I saw no reason to wait. I cast a fertility spell that rendered her prophylaxis ineffective. Then I ensured the child she conceived would be mine."

I feel sick to my stomach, and my sympathy for the dead queen gets stronger. I hug my middle against that sick feeling and mutter, "She might have wanted some say in that, don't you think?"

"I truly believed that, once she conceived, she would welcome our child. How could she not?" He sighs. "But in this, admittedly, I miscalculated. She and your wretched brother schemed to abort our child to free themselves from me. I issued various warnings, arranged several little scares, hoping they'd turn to me to protect them from the threat. Instead, I overheard them plotting their escape from this Academy."

That sick feeling is creeping up my throat. Under my robe, my skin is icy. Because I'm starting to see way too clearly where all this is going.

I can't bring myself to ask what happened next, but no worries, this guy's on a roll.

"I confronted them, we quarreled, they fled, I acted," he finishes, like he's wrapping up a book report. "Your worthless brother I would have killed gladly, but her I never meant to harm. How could I, when harming her meant harming our child?"

"But you did harm her," I say carefully, my blood like ice in my veins. "Didn't you?"

"Her death was a lamentable accident." His cold eyes narrow. "His was not."

"Then you're the queen killer." It feels important for me to say it out loud.

An ardent royalist, which means no one's ever suspected him, hiding in plain sight.

I don't even care that he killed Damien, because anyone who killed my ogre of a brother did the whole world a favor. But I care desperately that Bucephalus Zerxes coerced a student under his care into a sexual relationship she didn't want, made her pregnant against her will, then terrorized and murdered her when she tried to escape.

And guess what he's planning to do to me?

My palms are tingling and my power is rising. I suck in a breath to summon the lightning.

"Oh, I don't think so, Ms. Gemini." He sweeps up one hand, fingers curled in a fist, and suddenly I can't move or speak. It's like I've been encased in concrete.

I've felt this awful immobility before. He's like Vasili, then, he's telekinetic. Another warlock with multiple Mogadon gifts.

Just my luck.

My heart hammers against my lungs, but he is at least still letting me breathe. He doesn't want me dead. He wants from me what he wanted from Cybelle.

This time, he's sure as shit not going to get it.

I give the hardest mental tug I've ever given in my life to my bond with the guys. Imagine a tug-of-war contest between two rival teams, feet slipping in the mud, muscles straining, rows of hands locked around a rope thick as a power cable. *That's* how hard I'm pulling on the guys.

I can't feel anything at the other end, but I can still think. Which means there's plenty, actually, that I can still do.

For starters, I can play for time.

We're both telepaths, so I can still talk too.

So what's your big plan, Ceph? What comes next for you and me?

"Oh, largely the same course of action I intended for Cybelle," he murmurs, prowling around the great room to study my immobilized form from all angles. "If you don't accept me willingly, I'll destroy Lucius and his sterling reputation and his academic career. Then I'll ruin your precious Neo and that political career he and his father in the Arcane Senate are dreaming of, because I've plenty of political dirt on the Mercurys. It will require very little fodder from me for the Romanovs to disinherit their queer son once and for all, and I've something very special indeed planned for Ronin and the Pendragons that will make what happened to his sister Gwendolyn look like a school picnic."

My mind's racing a mile a minute, but I keep hauling and dragging at my bond with the guys. The problem is, my barrier's up to keep Zerxes out, so I can't tell if it's working.

Once I get out of this mess, I'm going to need a *lot* more training on how to use my witchcraft.

How exactly is this whole thing supposed to work? I open a porthole in my barricade just wide enough to fire another barrage of questions at the jerk. *You just join my harem, but we keep it all secret?*

He slashes a hand in negation. "I make it a point of pride to learn from my mistakes. No more covert alliances carried out beneath the Dean's hooked nose. Instead, you'll withdraw from this Academy and marry me tomorrow in a public and entirely legal ceremony on the mainland. Ours is a marriage we'll consummate promptly… and quite frequently."

Oh, right. Like *that's* happening. This guy must be certifiable if he thinks I'll go for that.

But apparently he does think it, because the crazy keeps right on coming.

"I've a cornucopia of spells and potions to encourage your fertility… and your docility. Once you bear the requisite heir and a spare of my lineage, I'll allow you to build your harem, but this time *I'll* choose your mates. I intend you to have an abundant harem, my queen, but anyone who fucks you will accept me in your bed as well. They'll require my permission, which is how I'll keep them all in line."

All of them, huh? My throat is so dry I can barely swallow, and my gut is heaving. *Out of curiosity, just how many guys feature in this X-rated harem fantasy of yours?*

"I've selected more than a dozen," he murmurs, "all powerful warlocks from my cohort at Villa Tiberius, past and present. They're hoping for heirs of their own, of course, but they'll require my consent for that honor, and only the most loyal will receive it. Malcolm the great white shifter is eager to be among the first, but I think we'll start with Bjorn here."

The nutcase pivots to face the bear, who's now sitting up and looking groggy. "That's what I promised to entice him here tonight—an early opportunity to sample the wares, as it were. He has a lamentable fetish for fucking in his shifted form, which I assured him a dutiful queen like yourself will be prepared to indulge."

At this point, I'm beyond disgust. Spells or no spells, potions or no potions, he can't keep me immobilized forever. As soon as he lets up, I'm going to go Thor son of Odin on his telekinetic ass. I'm going to summing my lightning and hammer him into the next century.

So what happens now, Ceph? You and Bjorn here planning to tag-team me on the great room floor?

"Oh, hardly. Bjorn will have to wait his turn, and even I must be patient a little longer. The skies are now clear, and I've ensured your so-called mates will sleep until dawn. We'll depart for the airfield now, I'll deactivate the island wards, and we'll be well aloft by the time they wake."

I'm curious to see how he thinks he's going to move me, because I'm definitely not going willingly. But he goes for the straightforward approach, scoops my immobilized body into his arms, and strides swiftly for the front door. Maybe he thinks it's romantic, carrying me across the threshold and all.

We'll see how romantic he finds it when I summon the fucking lightning.

The bear rolls to his feet with a chuffing snort and heads straight for us. I don't think Mr. Bear's on board with the whole "wait his turn" program, since this freak show apparently promised him pussy now. My head's hanging over the top of Zerxes' psychotic arm, which is awkward as hell, but it gives me a good view of the bear attack I'm about to experience. At least it'll distract this whack job, and then—

The bear's six feet away and closing in a rush when a torrent of golden fire streams between us. It slams into the bear's furry chest and the big guy lets loose a roar loud enough to knock pictures off the wall. Zerxes falters, and for one blessed second the cement-like vise around my body loosens.

My fist shoots up with the full force of my rage behind it and slams into the warlock's jaw. His head flies back, silver hair swirling around him.

Then he drops me.

I hit the floor hard, already rolling away, bracing myself with my arms while my leg sweeps around. It's critical to keep the psycho preoccupied, or he'll have me immobilized again before I can blink.

Startled as he is, Zerxes manages to leap back and avoid the takedown. While he's doing it, he evades a fresh torrent of fire that sears across the space between us, dropping fiery gobbets of magma on the floor. It's sloppy fire, poorly aimed, and it totally misses him. I keep rolling right to my feet and sprint out of the kill zone.

The bear's writhing on the ground to smother the flames singeing his furry chest. Zerxes has small fires smoldering in his robes from those flying gobbets of magma that he extinguishes with a hissed word.

Because it's psi fire, of course, it's Ronin's psi fire. And that's a gift Zerxes shares. I race for the stairs which Ronin's trying to race down.

But Ronin isn't his usual feral self. The best fighter at Icarus is shaky and staggering, literally reeling down the stairs, barefoot with pants sliding down around his hips like he's shit-faced drunk. But what he really is?

He's three-quarters asleep.

He's fighting that sleep spell to ride to my rescue. But his legs slide out from under him, and he tumbles hard all the way to the bottom.

I'm too far away to catch him or do anything but yell for help as I race toward him.

But Ceph Zerxes gets there first. He scoops up my beautiful fallen mate, who's lying limp and boneless with long hair draped over his face, and drags Ronin up against his body. From somewhere in his robes, he produces a hunting knife and presses it hard to Ronin's exposed throat.

I freeze in place, still way too far away to help. At least Ronin's still alive, because he's heaving for breath and trying to get his rubbery legs under him, but he's not moving much for obvious reasons. He actually looks like he might fall back asleep right there in Zerxes' arms, like an enchanted Sleeping Beauty, any second.

"Let him go!" I shout, because shouting might help with keeping Ronin awake and maybe waking up some others. "I'll go with you, okay? Just let him go."

"Actually, I believe I'll take both of you, at least as far as the airfield." Zerxes grins companionably at me and drags Ronin backward toward the atrium. "Clearly Mr. Pendragon has his uses, since you're so terribly concerned for his fate. Come along, my queen."

The bastard knows I actually will follow him rather than let him drag Ronin out of sight and do God knows what with him. There's also the fact that the bear has managed to extinguish himself and is staggering to his feet looking pissed as fuck, and I'm not interested in getting any closer to him either.

"Don' do it," Ronin says thickly, struggling to keep his eyes open. "Zara… take care of m'self…"

"I don't think so, Adam." I edge after Zerxes to keep that psycho calm. "Just give him an inch of breathing room with that knife, okay, Ceph? He's barely staying on his feet."

"In truth, I'm amazed he's ambulatory at all," Zerxes murmurs. "You must have formed a considerable bond with these mates of yours in this fleeting time. A bond far stronger than I anticipated, I'll confess. But this development too can prove advantageous. Come along quietly and there will be no need for violence."

Somehow I seriously doubt it. But a flicker of movement catches my eye.

There's someone else lurking in the darkness of the upstairs hall. And assuming whoever's up there is as out of it as Ronin, they're going to need all the help they can get.

"Hold on a sec, Ceph," I say pleadingly, holding the warlock's stare, fiercely resisting the impulse even to look toward the stairs. "I'll absolutely come with you. I'll even marry you, okay? I will. I'm sorta, um, intrigued by you actually. I just need you to answer one last question for me. So I know I can really trust you."

"Zara, ro…" Ronin mumbles, still sagging into Zerxes' punishing grip, but finally managing to get his legs under him as the warlock drags him along at a good clip.

"Come on, Ceph. It's really important." I make my voice as soft as I can. "You're going to be my alpha, and I need to know I can trust you. Please?"

Zerxes doesn't look particularly persuaded, but he does stop for a second. "This had better be an exceedingly quick question, my queen. My patience is scarcely infinite—"

He chokes in mid-sentence, and his face goes rigid. In fact, his entire frame goes absolutely rigid. It's the rigidity of telekinesis, and suddenly I realize who's lurking on the landing.

It's my snake.

Vasili lurches into view, wearing his long filmy shirt and not much else, swaying on his feet and gripping the banister, his long legs groping down step by careful step. He too is barely awake, and I think his grip on Zerxes is pretty precarious. He couldn't even cast until his target stopped moving.

Ronin seizes his moment to wiggle out of the warlock's grip, but he falls to hands and knees right away. I rush over to drag him clear, in case Vasili loses his grip. But we're both still standing way too close, Ronin sagging and heavy in my arms, when Vasili misses his own step and slides down the last few stairs to land on his ass at the bottom.

Which definitely shatters both his concentration and his spell.

Zerxes straightens and raises his knife with a smile. "And to think, you imagined you'd actually elude me. Now, my queen, unless you truly do want me to slit both their throats—"

He coughs suddenly and raises a hand to his own throat. A trickle of dark blood slips between his lips and rolls down his chin. His gaze locks with mine and his brow furrows. Then he drops heavily to one knee, elbow propped on one thigh, and bows his head. That's when I see the hilt of Vasili's throwing knife jutting from the back of his neck.

At the base of the stairs, Vasili lowers his throwing arm and sags against the banister.

Not to be forgotten in all this fun, Bjorn the polar bear charges.

For Vasili.

Who looks like he might actually fall back asleep before the bear mauls him.

"Bear!" I roar and dive for the shifter, sparks spraying from my fingers. But he's not close enough for the uncertain lightning, the little lightning, that I'm still casting more by instinct than intent.

And the shifter's closing in on Vasili.

Until a massive freaking timber wolf comes boiling and snarling down the stairs and leaps straight for the bear's throat. The two shifters collide and roll across the floor, wolf growling, bear roaring, me screaming and dragging Vasili clear. I try to keep an eye on Zerxes too, but his head's hanging low, blood dripping from his mouth, and he doesn't look like he's going anywhere.

Lucius gets his jaws locked in Bjorn's throat, but the bear's ripping at him with those massive claws and opening gory slashes down my shifter's sides, and it's not looking good for Lucius.

They burst through the glass doors in a splintering crash and tumble into the courtyard.

The lightning voice is rising in my chest, summoning the great wallop of power that calls down the real lightning from the sky. I've never had to be so accurate with an actual bolt of lightning, but there's no way of getting close enough for anything else. I shove Vasili in the couch's general vicinity and charge after the shifters, slippers crunching through a sea of shattered glass.

As I burst into the frigid courtyard, that mighty cry builds in my throat.

Outside, the bear has a writhing Lucius pinned on his back in the snow, growling, mauling, lunging for his throat. I thrust both arms skyward, fling back my head, and howl for the lightning.

A gale-force wind hammers into me. A jagged bolt of ultraviolet fire forks down from heaven and slams into the courtyard with an earth-shattering crash. The shock of impact knocks me off my feet and hurls me backward through the air.

The whole world turns white.

I slam ass-first into a snowbank with bone-rattling force. Stars explode across my vision and my ears start to ring.

Slowly, my vision clears. I claw up to sit in the cold wet snow, head spinning, eardrums screaming, the whole world blurry and far away. Ronin's swaying in the shattered doorway, clinging to the lintel to stay on his feet, his face transfixed.

In the snow, the bear lies smoking, a charred and blackened hulk.

And my wolf—my beautiful wolf—is scrambling unsteadily to his feet. Bloodied and scraped and savaged.

But alive.

I did it. I saved Lucius. I summoned the lightning and I fucking controlled it.

I'm still too dazed to feel much of anything. I think maybe I might be going into shock, but there's no time for that. Lucius' wolf limps over to me and drags his hot wet tongue across my numb befuddled face. I grope with my shaking hands to stroke his thick soft ruff and look deep into his whiskey-colored eyes. Gently he laps at my tears, because it seems I am crying. Then he nudges me with his big muzzle and trots off, rising on his hind legs to slather Ronin's face with affectionate kisses that nearly knock the guy over.

Suddenly, the wolf whines and darts into the house.

I struggle to my feet and weave after him as fast as I can with my ears still ringing and my balance hinky. Ronin tries to steady me, his mouth moving in words I can't hear, but he's still barely ambulatory himself.

I cling to his half-naked body for a sec, then pull him after me into the house.

In the great room, Vasili's sprawled half over the Renaissance couch where I shoved him to get him clear of the bear. Lucius' wolf is nosing him and licking his face in long eager swipes between jaw-splitting yawns that suggest the wolf too is headed straight for dreamland.

But the Goblin King is fast asleep.

On the great room floor, Zerxes is still breathing, slumped and swaying on his knees, ribbons of dark blood running down his chin and soaking the robe to his chest as he gropes feebly at the knife jutting from the back of his neck. His own knife lies abandoned at his feet.

A few small fires are burning in the carpet before the hearth. I shuffle unsteadily over to stomp them out with my soaked and freezing slippers. Through the ringing in my ears, I'm trying to decide whether to call 911 on the antiquated landline and wondering if anyone on this island will even pick up if I do, when my sweet baby Neo staggers down the stairs buck naked, grabs the fallen poker like a baseball bat, winds up like a star hitter on opening day, and slams the poker with brutal force into the side of Zerxes' head.

Chapter Forty-Five
Zara

There's definitely something to be said for living in a house that's equipped with a renovated Roman bath. Sure, the electrical wiring in this joint is geriatric and the antique Edwardian-era furnace is gradually giving up the ghost.

But I swear this bath makes up for it.

Right now, I'm floating naked under the skylight in five feet of steaming green water, lit up from underneath because I've finally managed to get the power back up after all the pyrotechnics last night, in the big central pool that reeks of sulfur and minerals. Overhead, a brilliant sky peeks through piles of melting snow on the leaded glass roof. Sunlight mingles with the green aquatic glow down here in a shimmering haze of light. That light makes the faded frescoes of naked mermaids and sea monsters frolicking and foaming on the walls look like they're floating.

According to my dive watch, it's late afternoon. But there's no class because it's Saturday. The guys are supposed to have the *thermae* all day today per the house schedule, but they're more than willing to share with me, their queen.

They're sweet like that.

In fact, a naked Neo has my feet trapped in his big hands right now to deliver a languid foot massage as he floats across the way. And the steady knead of his thumbs against my arches is making me moan.

A naked Ronin sprawls behind me with his legs spread to accommodate me between them, his pierced cock tucked against my back, his palms digging into the knotted muscles in my shoulders. Which is making me moan even louder.

Not that it's a moaning contest or anything, but these two mates of mine are both really good at doing this.

I frown at the flashing digits on my dive watch. "Shouldn't they be back by now? They went to see the Dean, like, *hours* ago."

"The Dean likes to do things properly, babe." Neo grins at me under a damp fringe of curls. "She's probably doing the whole tea ceremony for them. Master Aries—uh, I mean Lucius—is trying to resign so he can officially join your harem. It's a major event. She isn't going to want to rush."

I eye him through the billowing steam. This long hot soak has definitely relaxed me, but the sight of my fated mate's bulging shoulders flexing under all that silky pale skin has me burning to sink my teeth into him.

Thoughtfully I run my tongue over those teeth. My incisors actually do feel sharper than usual, what with all those pheromones from being bitten (twice!) triggering every recessive shifter chromosome in my Gemini DNA. Maybe these canines of mine are even getting sharp enough to puncture skin.

Maybe.

And no one's bitten Neo.

Yet.

"Chin up, love." Ronin leans in to nuzzle my ear. "No one's popped up to drag us all off in handcuffs. Even though the inspector from the Arcane Senate landed hours ago. Don't think anyone's going to miss Bjorn much—he was pretty much a loner, yeah?—and Master Zerxes even less. He terrorized his entire fucking cohort."

Despite the steamy water that encases me, a ribbon of ice snakes down my spine and coils in my belly. I'm thinking it'll definitely be a while before I get past what happened with Bjorn and Zerxes.

Just the thought of being dragged to the mainland for some sort of official investigation into their deaths makes my shoulders clench right back up again.

"Obviously what happened was self-defense." I slip my feet out of Neo's sinfully indulgent clutches, hunch forward on my little submerged shelf, and hug my knees. "They literally broke into the house and were trying to kidnap both of us, Ronin. But honestly speaking? I just killed a man with my fucking lightning. It's all I can manage not to head for the hills."

"Yeah, you've been on the run a bit too long." Ronin's fingers dig into my knotted shoulders to loosen me back up. "Don't think you've got the first clue how far the witching world will go to protect our queen. Freshman or no, you own this Academy."

If only.

I hug my knees tighter. "It sure doesn't feel that way to me, Adam."

Gently Neo retrieves my feet and resumes his seductive kneading. "Told you my dad has the family lawyers working it. Dad's pretty motivated, considering I'm actually the one who swung that poker. It was pure self-defense, in both cases, like you said."

Calmly my fated mate raises my foot to his luscious lips and engulfs my big toe in the warm suction of his mouth, which feels so heavenly my eyes drift shut. Still, I have to make a conscious effort to be patient and let this whole scenario play out. I have to trust Lucius and Vasili to placate the inspector and the Mercury hired guns to do their lawyering.

Yeah, that's right. I've actually agreed to let the guys handle the aftermath of everything that went down last night.

But that doesn't mean it's easy.

A tendril of awareness coils tight around me and snaps my gaze toward the door. I'm hyper-aware of Vasili since he fucking bit me, and he's coming down the hall right now at a pretty good clip. I sit up straight and would absolutely stand to face my fate, except Ronin's still wrapped around me, and Neo's still nibbling on my toes.

Vasili lets himself into the *thermae*, and I'm honestly impressed to see him. He's dressed to the nines in a narrow pin-striped purple suit that he totally owns, and he's wearing quite a bit less gaudy bling than usual, which for him passes as conservative. He looks like a rock star with a court date. Under his moussed-up silver layers, his sexy-pretty face is pensive until he sees the three of us lounging naked in the bath.

Then his smoky eyes turn predatory.

I retrieve my feet again from Neo and scramble up. "Where the hell's Lucius?"

"Well, the Dean didn't eat him and grind his bones like the witch in a fairy tale, if that's what's fretting you. Nor has he been clapped in irons and hauled off to jail." Vasili undulates across the mosaic floor, hips swaying, loosening his violet tie with a languid tug. "Don't even think of getting out, darlings. I'll come to you."

We all like the sound of that, even Neo, who's pretending not to watch as the Goblin King deftly unbuttons his shirt to reveal the sleek chest and rippled abs I tongued every single inch of last night.

The golden dragon of my mating heat uncurls in my belly with a rumble of interest. I can almost feel steam puff from her nostrils when she noses me from the inside, like she wants to spread her wings and take flight.

"Don't try to distract me," I warn both of them, my dragon and Vasili. Because I can't always be fucking. And I can already see I'm going to need to establish some boundaries, or Vasili will be running this whole harem. "I want Lucius and I want answers. Where is he? What did the inspector say?"

"No need to crack your bullwhip just yet." The Goblin King's heated gaze roams over me, standing there naked with water lapping my hips, while he slithers out of his shirt and jacket to reveal more of that sinuous ballet star's body we're all so hot for. "My, we're terribly impatient today, aren't we?"

"You haven't seen me impatient, bad boy, so don't fuck with me. And I'm entitled, because you've both been gone for *hours* while I…"

I lose my train of thought and my power of speech, because my snake of an alpha has just eased down his zipper to reveal a peek at the black lace lingerie stretched tight over the mouthwatering bulge of his cock.

"Whoa," I whisper.

Over the bubble of water rising from the hot spring underneath us, Ronin gives a hard swallow.

Vasili shows a sliver of a smile. "See something that interests you, darlings?"

What I can see is that he's in the mood for mischief. Which typically means someone's about to start bleeding.

Well, I can play that game.

"Hmmm." I wade leisurely across the pool to Neo, who eyes my approach with interest. I straddle my fated mate's seated form and lower myself onto his lap. Fully on board with this little tease, he grins up at me, wraps his arms around me, and cups my ass in his big hands with an approving murmur.

And his cock definitely sits up and takes notice.

But his wide green eyes drift back to Vasili as the Goblin King peels out of his pants, retains his sexy lingerie so we can peel him out of it ourselves, and slides into the pool like a water moccasin.

Suddenly the scent of sex and pheromones is thick in the steamy air.

Oh, wait. That would be me scenting.

"Don't even think about coming over here until you answer my question," I instruct Vasili. Then I lean in to give Neo a slow hot kiss, our tongues meeting in a scorching lick.

Last night while I patched up Lucius after his bear encounter, then patrolled the halls protecting my guys while they slept off the remnants of Zerxes' spell, I was pretty worried about Neo. But I have to admit in the light of day that my mate doesn't seem to be suffering much remorse over swinging that poker (not that he should, but maybe the inspector won't see it that way?)

I'm more worried right now about Lucius losing his job and me getting sent to the witching world equivalent of Azkaban Prison for frying Bjorn with my lightning.

Completely ignoring my edict, Vasili comes snaking up behind me. His electric mouth nuzzles the bite on my shoulder, which is actually Lucius' bite. They've both started tending each other's bites on Ronin and me, which I think is cute as hell.

You'd never take Vasili for the nurturing kind, but maybe he just needed someone to nurture.

Still, I refuse to be distracted. "I mean it, Goblin King. You better start talking and fast."

"Now, now, Ms. Gemini." His commanding hands wrap around my hips, which also brings him into contact with Neo. "You really ought to treat me with more respect. As the newly hired professor of Mogadon Magics, my stature at this Academy demands it."

I squeak in surprise (I may have mentioned that Vasili has the knack of wringing undignified noises out of me?) and try to turn, but he crowds in behind me to keep me right where I am on Neo's lap. And since my snake's completely naked except for a soaked scrap of black lace stretched over his burgeoning erection, he's a fairly significant distraction.

This development explains why he dressed up to see the Dean (although, being Vasili, he's always dressed up).

He went for a job interview.

And it isn't Lucius' job the Dean apparently just gave him either. Vasili just picked up Zerxes' former gig.

"Hey." Neo's mouth pops open with indignation. "You can't join the faculty yet. That's against the rules. You haven't even graduated."

"Well, aren't you clever, First Boy?" Vasili purrs, his fingers threading through Neo's around my hips. "It's a provisional appointment until I graduate this spring. I've intended for some time to join this faculty, and there just so happens to be an immediate vacancy. And now that I've answered at least one of your questions, darling, I do believe I've earned a congratulatory kiss."

Now he's talking to me, but I'm not about to waste this opportunity while I've got the two of them this close and actually touching.

"You two first," I breathe, and Neo blushes to his hairline.

"Tut tut," Vasili murmurs, sounding reproachful. "I'm afraid it's against the rules for Mr. Mercury to kiss the faculty."

Mutiny sparks in Neo's eyes. "It would have to be a provisional kiss. Since you're not irrevocably *on* the faculty—"

Vasili laughs, wraps one hand around the back of Neo's neck, and drags him close. Their mouths are only an inch apart when Vasili abruptly stops. His surge of discomfort roils the mating bond between us.

I instantly get what he's worried about.

Neo stiffens up too, not understanding what's happening and wondering what he screwed up this time, until I whisper reassurance through our bond. *He thinks you won't like his fangs, baby. He's sensitive as fuck about them.*

"Wow, really?" Neo breathes, his wary face going all soft. "I've actually, uh, been wondering what it would take to persuade one of you to bite me. Because I'm practically the only one who hasn't been… you know…"

"Bitten? Somehow I feel certain that can be arranged," Vasili says, far more mildly than he typically says anything.

When their lips bump together, it's a tentative touch, a gentle negotiation, a careful slide of mouth meeting mouth. Vasili's still hanging back and worrying about his fangs, but my sweet Neo leans into him and nudges his mouth open with all the innocent hunger that always turns my crank. Vasili moans low in his throat and tightens his grip on his former enemy.

In fact, I'm pretty sure we'll all be biting Neo if my fated mate keeps this up.

"Now there's a sight I never thought I'd see," Lucius murmurs.

My breath rushes out in relief and my eyes eat him up.

Our headmaster is standing just inside the door looking all buttoned up and proper in his professorial tweed and houndstooth with his chestnut hair tied back. All he's missing is his oxblood briefcase. I'm still learning to read him, though I can sense his wolf frisking happily at the sight of me and wanting to be let out so he can play with my dragon.

At least he's not in handcuffs.

Or paw cuffs.

"There you are, love. It's about blooming time." Ronin levers out of the pool in a lithe scramble. Naked and dripping, he prowls across the *thermae* to grab Lucius by the tie and pulls him into a hard kiss.

A few days ago, Lucius would have resisted, out of some misplaced sense of decorum. Now he wraps a rough arm around Ronin's waist, shoves a possessive hand into the man-bun thing Ronin's done with his hair, dislodges the whole arrangement, and claims our mate with a thorough kiss.

"Mmmm." I sigh and squirm happily on Neo's lap, his hard cock sliding between my slick folds, one thrust away from penetration.

Bathtub sex is one of my favorite kinds of sex, and I like where this is going.

Silently sharing my sentiment, Ronin starts unbuttoning Lucius and coaxing him toward the pool, which is a nice prelude to totally undoing him. "Didn't fire you, did she, Lucius?"

"Entirely to my surprise, she didn't." Lucius' rapidly heating gaze locks on mine. "I tendered my letter of resignation so I can join our queen's harem with a clear conscience, but the Dean refused to accept my letter. Since our queen's place is emphatically here at this Academy until she masters her rapidly growing powers—and since my place is at your side and in your bed, my queen—it seems the Dean's opted to make a virtue out of a necessity."

"That's bloody large of her," Ronin snorts, pushing Lucius' coat and shirt off his shoulders, "since she's got no one else to teach History of Witchcraft, you're bloody brilliant in the classroom, and she's not about to go and make Vasili headmaster of this house. Even she's not that mental."

"I'm really not sure I shouldn't be offended," Vasili muses, hands sliding up my ribs to cradle my tits and toy with my piercings. I turn my face into his shoulder to nibble his sleek neck and arch into his grip with a murmur of encouragement.

Lucius' voice deepens and his accent thickens, because he clearly likes what he's seeing. "It seems the Dean is far less troubled by my various sins than I've been myself. We've agreed I'll finish out the term on probation, then we'll have the entire summer once everyone else goes home for the holidays to continue Zara's studies. The Dean claims she'll decide later whether to keep me on permanently, but she's not known for indecision. In all likelihood, I'll be allowed to remain in my post, notwithstanding my indiscretions, though I fully expect an excoriating letter in my personnel file. I consider that a price well worth paying."

"Thank fuck," Ronin mutters, rough with relief, and definitely speaking for all of us. "You and that Catholic guilt. You're nothing like Zerxes and the Dean bloody knows it. Told you that you were giving yourself a fucking complex for nothing, didn't I?"

"I believe you may have mentioned that, dear one," Lucius says wryly.

By now Ronin's gotten Lucius out of the rest of his clothes, and I'm really glad to see the damage that bear's claws and teeth left on my shifter's rangy body is mostly gone. Purebred shifters like Lucius heal *really* fast if they survive an attack long enough to shift, according to those textbooks I've finally started studying in earnest.

Looks like those textbooks weren't lying.

Watching Lucius hoist Ronin into his powerful arms and descend the stairs into the pool with our mate wrapped around him, I'm overwhelmed by how lucky I am to have them.

All four of them.

We still have plenty of issues to work through, the most pressing being that inspector who's come to conduct the inquest and fly Zerxes and Bjorn back to the mainland. Speaking of which…

I slither around in Neo's arms to tuck my back against his front and loop my arms around Vasili's slim waist. "Out of curiosity, is either one of you ever planning to tell me what the inspector said? Or do I just wait for him to show up here and arrest us?"

"He's flying back to the mainland with the remains as we speak." Lucius wades toward us with Ronin still wrapped around him. "He's launched an inquest, of course, but the Dean's discouraged the inspector from undertaking a witch hunt, and this fellow doesn't seem overly interested in burning witches at the stake. All Academy personnel sign a liability waiver when we join the staff, given the… perilous nature of our duties. And neither Bjorn nor Zerxes had much in the way of friends or family to press charges."

"That's really sad," I sigh, and I mean it, but it sounds like I've got a stay of execution. At least for now. The worst of the nervous knot in my chest loosens its grip. Looks like it'll be a while before we know for sure.

At least now, today, we're free.

That's all I've ever wanted.

Vasili distracts me by leaning in to tongue his mating bite on my tit. I'm healing up nicely with both of them to tend me, but that hit of biochemicals and the accompanying mating ritual are still really soothing. I let out a happy sigh that makes Neo hum in my ear.

"Not to mention," Vasili says casually between slow sizzling licks, "your wealthy father's generous charitable contribution… to the Arcane Foundation. The inspector's a founding member… made a point of mentioning his gratitude. Seems your father… made that sizable donation… in your name."

What he's saying makes zero sense, so I figure he's fucking with me. That's getting harder for him to do given our mating bond. But I still wind my hands in Vasili's hair to stop his distracting licking and look to Lucius for validation.

My shifter's reached my side. Now he leans in to graze my mouth with his warm lips. "Every word this brat is saying is true, for once. Rest assured we'll never lie to you, my queen."

"What the actual fuck?" I demand, because this still doesn't compute. "That can't be right. Mick Gemini's never donated a cent to charity in his life. He's a casino rat. And he's been gunning for my head since the day I flipped him the bird and split."

"Seems our Mickey's a political beast," Vasili murmurs, "with an admirable survival instinct. Your glorious return's making headlines across the witching world, darling. I do believe your father may just have concluded it's more advantageous to lean into his connection with our future queen than to continue his murderous vendetta."

The hell if I even know what to say to this. It's not like I'll be running to kiss and make up with that lowlife who calls himself my dad anytime soon, and probably never.

"No one's saying you have to invite him to the wedding, love." Ronin wiggles out of Lucius' arms to wrap himself around all of us, bridging the gap so instead of three and two, we're all five entwined. This sullen bully who started out in Singapore hating me has turned out to be a total snuggler.

And I freaking love him for it.

In fact, I'm totally in love with all of them.

Still, that definitely doesn't mean…

"Who said anything about a wedding?" I counter. But my pulse is tripping and my heart is hammering, because I don't even like the thought of having to choose just one of them to walk down the hypothetical aisle with, at some future date.

Ronin's nuzzling Vasili's neck, but he stops long enough to give me a narrow look. "Bollocks, it's criminal how blooming little you know about your own legacy. No one needs you to choose. You're the queen."

Not that I'm anywhere near ready to have this little convo, and I may never be ready to talk picket fences and white dresses.

But I can't seem to let it drop either.

"Meaning…?" I'm looking at Ronin when I ask.

But it's Neo behind me who murmurs in my ear. "It's witching world law, babe, because you're the queen. If and when you decide to tie the knot, you're allowed to take all of us. Legally as well as, you know, sexually."

I'm not exactly picking a date and sending out invites, but my inner dragon's still pretty pumped by the whole idea. She's rising on her hind legs, beating her golden wings inside the shell of my skin, and screaming with primal triumph.

Sure, I'm in double heat and all, but the strength and clarity of all these inner dragon visuals are really starting to make me wonder.

Because these days, I have to admit, I'm feeling kinda shifty.

The five of us are parked next to the glass wall that separates the pool from the rain shower. I swipe a hand across the steamy glass to clear a space and check out my reflection.

I've piled my hair up in a knot like Ronin's to keep my color-treated locks away from the sulfur, but a few damp curls tumble down around my face, all flushed with warmth and mating heat.

In the glass, my eyes stare back at me.

And holy freaking *shit*. They're my own eyes—but not. Because even as I watch, they're *changing*. Instead of the basic turquoise blue I've had my whole life, my irises brighten till they're golden and glowing. Then my pupils lengthen to oblong slits that dilate while I watch.

Those are shifter eyes for sure. But they're not wolf eyes or snake eyes, like the guys who bit me.

Nope. Nothing so normal.

Cheese on toast, I know exactly what kind of eyes I'm staring at. Because I've watched enough Tolkien movie marathons to recognize what I'll apparently be shifting into sometime soon. And those freaky fucking peepers staring back at me aren't elf eyes or orc eyes or hobbit eyes.

They're dragon eyes.

THE END

Want to read more dark paranormal academy reverse harem books like this one?

Check out these steamy books by my author friends,
all set in wildly different witchy worlds!

Read more witch academy RH books:
https://books.bookfunnel.com/rhdarkpnracademy

Want to read more intense and sexy out-of-this-world why-choose adventure
starring the four witching races and a whole new harem?
Check out my MMMF Astral Heat Romance Series! Complete on Kindle
Unlimited and in print.

*For exclusive access to more of my scorching paranormal and sci fi poly
romance, plus monthly freebies, giveaways, and updates from my nomadic
travels, sign up for my newsletter.*
https://www.lauranavarrescifi.com/

THANK YOU

Hey, lovelies! How'd you like this story? *Gemini Queen* is the first academy book I've ever written, and I meant it to be a standalone tie-in to my Astral Heat why-choose series. But!! Zara and her guys really grabbed hold of their story and ran with it like the rebels they are. Vasili did what he wanted from start to finish, Lucius and Neo both surprised me in ways I never anticipated, and Ronin carried forward the time-honored tradition of having an Adam Driver-inspired hero in every single one of my harems.

I gave these guys a happily-ever-after, but I'm thinking I could go on with more if you liked what you just read. I'm kinda looking forward to exploring that Vasili & Neo enemies-to-lovers dynamic, that Lucius & Vasili double-alpha dynamic, Zara's journey as a dragon shifter and her reign as queen, what happens with the witching world, and whether Zara's really done with Xiao and Cleo, or whether there might be more to their story?

Will you drop me a line and let me know what you think? Your opinion really matters to me! In fact, your opinion will be pretty central to what I write next. You can **contact me through my website here: https://lauranavarrescifi. com/contact/**

Wanna help me out by sharing your thoughts on Zara, Vasili, Lucius, Ronin & Neo with other readers? You don't have to write a lot. Even a few words helps! Reviews persuade readers like you to give writers like me a chance. **Here's the link to post a review for *Gemini Queen* on Amazon: https://www.amazon. com/dp/B09V1PQRPB/**

Acknowledgments

I would never have written *Gemini Queen* if not for Traci Lovelot! My fellow fantasy RH author invited me to join her plus 20 other gals releasing dark paranormal academy RH reads back-to-back through summer 2022. She and all the lovelies in our group taught me so much about publishing and marketing in what's still a new genre for me after a career writing traditional romance for mainstream publishers.

I couldn't have finished this project or launched my indie career without the wisdom, support, encouragement, and experience of my writing guru and mentor Angela James, who was also my former editor at Harlequin. Her insights and feedback on this story were invaluable, and her author community From Written To Recommended (FW2R) has been an essential support and anchor for my indie journey. Her Before You Hit Send (BYHS) self-editing course ran at exactly the right time to give me the help I needed with *Gemini Queen*! I heartily recommend her, her courses, and her author community.

I'm deeply grateful for my wonderful beta readers Taylor Ross and Kara Donovan, whose early encouragement and insights were so critical in fine-tuning this story. None of my stories would have their pristine appearance without my formatter, uploader, and hand-holder Judi Fennell at Formatting4U. Kim Killion designs my gorgeous covers, and Rochelle Parry of Megabite Design is the IT goddess who makes my website sing and keeps my Mailchimp functional. And I could never pull off a book launch without my awesome ARC review team, the Astral Angels. Your incredible encouragement and help spreading the word make a massive difference!

Finally, and most fundamentally, I just wouldn't be me without the absolute rock-solid and unfaltering support, perception, generosity, wisdom, and love of my alpha reader, proofreader, business partner and CEO of Ascendant Press, best friend, and happily-ever-after karmic mate Steven. He's the first reader and the last for everything I write before it goes to print. I'm the luckiest girl in the galaxy to have him as my co-pilot in this starship of life!

Keep scrolling down for a sexy sneak peek at INTERSTELLAR ANGEL, Book 1 of the MMMF Astral Heat Romance Series!

INTERSTELLAR ANGEL
By Laura Navarre

Prologue
The Felon

He was sentenced to die in the fighting pit at dawn for butchering the Third Indomitable of the Mogadon Empire in his tyrannical and sociopathic sleep. But the Mogadon prison guards wanted to work Zorin over before he kicked the bucket. Same way they'd worked him over the last three nights running.

Well, that was A-okay with Zorin.

Matter of fact, he was counting on it.

While he stood waiting for the shindig to start, magnetoelectric cuffs shackled his muscled arms overhead, clamped his booted feet to the floor, and left his naked torso exposed to the biting temps in the Mogadon slammer. He definitely wouldn't have minded sporting more than leather pants and space boots on his ugly carcass while old Tiberius went to work with the boning knife.

But Zorin could roll with what he had going.

Sweating under the nuclear-powered fluorescents in the interrogation *cella*, Tiberius swaggered up to Zorin with a scowl on his fleshy mug. His two sidekicks skulked by the exit. True to habit, Boots and Pyro would only risk coming in close to get their jollies after the blood loss softened Zorin up.

Even chained to the wall, the deadly combo of his massive size and his brutal reputation still gave Zorin plenty of intimidation factor.

"Ready for a little fun, Theodophilus?" Tiberius slid his knife gently along Zorin's jaw. "You're gonna bite the big one in twelve clicks—just in time to make the interstellar broadcast. But we got plenty of time to play before Dex Draven meets you in the pit and puts you six cubits under."

While the lunker brandished his shank, Zorin snuck a peek at the timepiece strapped to the guy's wrist.

Two ticks to showtime.

Zorin hawked to clear out the blood still leaking down his throat from his

349

nose. Which he hoped to hell wasn't busted again. "You wanna be careful with that one-armed scissor, Tibs. Pretty sure Dex's counting on killing me himself."

"You think I'm scared of that punk Draven?" Tiberius sneered, looking back at his buddies for validation. "That pretty-boy stunt pilot don't have his dad's moxie, even if you did just bump off his old man. Comets! Bet Dex'll thank me for softening you up."

Tick.

"One way to find out," Zorin said softly. A bear-baiting he'd probably regret, but he wanted the guy in close.

Tibs took the bait and closed on him with a snarl.

Attaboy, Tibs. Mosey on over.

The first cut burned through Zorin like a laser—a searing score carved down his naked side. He gasped as a line of white agony sizzled through his system. Liquid heat spilled down his skin and the meaty tang of fresh blood hit the back of his throat. The world blurred and darkened.

Tock.

The stone beneath his boots shuddered under the sonic *boom* of impact. That'd be the cyber bomb. Hitting the reactor bloc smack on schedule. Knocking out the defensive energon shield that bubbled the Mogadon capital. And plunging the whole city—including this funhouse down here—into blackness.

Knew I could count on my boys.

Tingling with an adrenaline rush of aggression, Zorin felt the metallic snick of the maglock release. The cuffs around his wrists and ankles sprang open and he got clear of the rack.

A tick later the backup generator lumbered to life. The ruddy wash of emergency lighting switched on. Giving him an up-close-and-personal of Tiberius's shocked and staring face. Their eyes met and locked.

One corner of Zorin's mouth lifted in a grin.

"Howdy, Tibs."

The guy's sweating face convulsed in sudden terror. "Look alive! He's *loose*—"

From barely a cubit away, the boning knife came at him. Then Zorin's doubled fists, powered by the full force of his body and three days of pent-up rage, hammered down on the guy's noggin. The sharp *pop* of Tibs's neck cracked through the generator's asthmatic wheeze like a snapped wishbone. His torturer dropped at Zorin's feet.

Dead as a sack of moon rocks.

A primitive surge of bloodlust roared through Zorin's brain. The gamy musk of wolf and steel flooded the air, triggered by a heady spurt of Mogadon pheromones. Weakened by three days' torture with no grub to sustain him and blood still spilling down his side, Zorin's big body swayed on his feet. His adrenal glands were going haywire.

Jumpin' Jupiter. I'm weak as a pup—

A howl of rage brought Zorin's head snapping up. Just in time to see good old Pyro barreling at him with the flamethrower. A thermobaric weapon the Quorum had outlawed ages ago all across the galaxy, but Pyro kept the contraband relic squirreled away down here in the playroom.

And here comes the nozzle…

Zorin hunkered down and just charged the guy. He hit him at a dead run and knocked him sprawling. The nozzle of the flamethrower flew wide, spraying an inferno of blue fire across the *cella*. He landed on Pyro's sinewy frame like Vulcan's mythic hammer. Pyro writhed beneath him, ferret-sharp teeth bared and snapping in the bloody light.

Fighting like the dickens to bring that flamethrower around—still spewing fire—for another pass.

Zorin got both hands around Pyro's greasy head and slammed his skull into the floor with brutal force. The guy's weaselly face went blank and his eyes glassed over.

Permanently.

The flamethrower slipped from his grip and went dark.

Breathing heavily, Zorin rolled off him and wrestled the thermobaric out of the man's slack hand.

"Belay that, you space junk!" a shrill voice cried. "Or I'll put you down like a rabid dog. I swear to gods I will!"

Zorin's eyes flashed up to find his old pal Boots hunkered by the door with his shadow all distorted in the horror-flick half-light.

And his blaster leveled at Zorin's chest.

Zorin froze right where he crouched, one hand gripping the flamethrower, one knee braced against the floor. A steady drip from his gaping gash spattered Pyro's limp carcass.

Aw, shoot.

"Here's the deal," Zorin rasped, locked on the youngster's wild-eyed stare. "You can pull the trigger on that thing if you want. But you better make damn sure you take me down—cuz you're only gonna get one shot. You shoot and it's anything less than a kill shot? Then it's barbecue time. And once you're seared medium rare, if you ask me nicely? I'm gonna snap your neck like I did with Tibs and put you outta your misery."

"I got the drop on you." Holy helium, the kid's voice was shaking. "I got the drop on the First Indomitable! If I pull the trigger, I'll be First Indomitable myself."

Zorin kept his own voice nice and easy. "Pretty sure Dex wants that gig himself. Besides, you ain't exactly a crack shot, are ya, Boots? Or your centurion wouldn't have you pulling guard duty down here in the armpit of the Empire, would he? Keep your head screwed on straight and you can still walk away from this hootenanny."

Think it through, you big dummy. I can see your hands shake all the way over here.

Deaf and clueless to his silent urging, Boots straightened his scrawny shoulders and looked dazzled by the prospect. "I can be First Indomitable. Have the whole Mogadon army and the Mogadon fleet and the nukes and the novicide—the whole Empire at my command. Mine! I'll be the youngest First Indomitable in history."

Neptune's knickers, he's talking himself into it.

"Better be sure," Zorin said softly, his big body tensing to attack.

The silence was shattered by the soft *whomp* of an incoming missile. The slam of impact—no farther off than a Mogadon mile—made both of them stagger. A clamor of distant shouts echoed down the hall, thin and scattered under the whooping wail of the battle claxon.

Boots lowered his blaster in confusion. "What the seven bloody *hells*—?"

"That'll be the sound of Dex's dad getting the galactic war the old psycho was jonesing for when he kicked the bucket. The sound of the Valyrian fleet attacking this popsicle stand." Zorin clambered carefully to his feet and swallowed a groan as his side gave a wicked stab of protest. "Since my boys took out the main reactor, the dome's been down."

"The dome's *down*? But—we got the whole Valyrian fleet parked just off Parthon!"

"Yep." Zorin eased an arm against the oozing gash down his side in a bid to slow the bleeding. He needed a med kit like blazes. "And with the dome down, the Empire doesn't have squat to deflect those psi-powered weapons away from the city. Intel says the Precursor herself—strongest telepath in the whole damn galaxy—she's in orbit on the Valyrian flagship. And she's pretty ticked about that biowar Dex's dad just unleashed on her whole flipping race."

"The Precursor!" Boots gasped, in a tone usually reserved for Swarm cannibals or a spacepox outbreak.

Zorin tried to stay focused on the convo, but the blood loss was making him woozy. The blinking blaze of the hazard lights and the whooping wail of the battle siren weren't helping any.

Dimly he registered the heavy thud of running feet, the welcome sound of Boots losing his head and taking to his heels, clumsy in those titanium-toed clodhoppers of his. A factoid Zorin knew because he had the bruises on his aching ribs and back from those boots to prove it.

Hearing his footfalls fade, Zorin let the tension ease from his battered body.

Then he got his head together and staggered over to the guard cubby where his captors kept the med kit and the Mogadon whiskey. Squinting to focus his blurred vision, he slathered on a clotting agent and slapped the glossy square of a polymer bandage over the bloody gash.

Mars, he was gonna need nanostitches again, wasn't he? Old Doc Cicero was gonna chew him out bigtime—assuming they even made it to the *Relentless* like they'd all decided when they threw together this half-assed plan.

Grimacing, Zorin jabbed an antimicrobial booster into his deltoid.

Then he schlepped back to the *cella*, wrestled off Tibs's black uniform jacket with its double row of steel buttons, and eased his arms into the sleeves. Zorin's shoulders were too damn big and his chest way too wide for a standard jacket, so the thing gaped open all the way down his front. And he already knew there was no way he was getting his big feet into standard-issue army boots. His own clunky space boots would have to do the trick.

But maybe if he got lucky, with the reactor down and the Valyrians attacking and this whole humdinger of a planet-wide crisis unfolding around him, he'd pass the once-over test.

Zorin tossed back a burning slug of Mogadon whiskey—a hit of thirty-curie fortitude that seared his sinuses and shot straight to his head—then made tracks for the rendezvous point. Where his boys and Julius, the cyber samurai behind the downed reactor, would hopefully still be waiting to rearm his sorry ass.

Cuz he might be out of the slammer, but he still needed to get the heck off Mogadon before the Precursor's attack mobilized the whole planet into furious retaliation.

And he needed to be a parsec away in deep space before Dex Draven figured out his dad's killer was MIA and had eluded the ruthless reckoning of Mogadon justice.

#

"Here's what I want." Dex Draven fired the staccato barrage of directives at a goggle-eyed prefect as he wrestled the fuel nozzle from the belly of his nuclear-armed Zephyr. "I want four wings of fighters under my command prepared to launch into exospheric orbit ASAP to protect the city. And I want every engineer in the Empire flown hotfoot to the power plant to bring that reactor back online. We *need* to get that dome up."

Around him, the cavernous expanse of the Mogadon capital's spaceport echoed with the drum of running feet on tarmac, curt voices shouting commands, the rumble of fuel trucks racing to feed Dex's wing of armed Zephyrs—flown by those men under his direct command he'd managed to mobilize since the first missile strike.

Beyond the immediate impact of his personal efforts, the claxon's wavering wail would muster every able-bodied soldier in the city to battle stations.

And if that prefect he was bossing like an illegal galley slave retained any wits at all amid the exigencies of the current crisis, he'd surely stop to question why newly minted Wing Commander Decimus Draven—who'd only just celebrated his twentieth birthday—was issuing orders that should rightfully be issued only by Second Indomitable Septimus, resident boozing blowhard and commander of the Mogadon civil defense force.

Or, failing that, by Dex's father.

If only Dex's father weren't already dead.

"B-but, Commander—" The youngster flinched as an incoming missile screamed past overhead. "Shouldn't I, uh—"

"Good lad." Dex forestalled the objection by thrusting the fuel hose into the prefect's unsteady hands and giving his adolescent shoulders a bracing shake. "I knew I could rely on you entirely. Make it happen."

Dex focused on unlocking the docking cable that tethered his fighter to the tarmac. But he was heartened to hear the prefect's booted feet beat a swift tattoo as he raced to carry out Dex's commands with gratifying alacrity.

No doubt his formidable father would've cuffed the poor kid to instill blind obedience. But Dex had opted early on not to emulate the extremes of his father's brutal command style.

Greatly to the old war dog's displeasure.

That displeasure had fueled their most bitter battles. Battles exceeded in intensity only by that final, furious, no-pulled-punches blowout the night Third Indomitable Maximus Draven accused his own son of craven cowardice.

The infamous night his father unleashed his genetically targeted bioweapon against the entire Valyrian race.

The high-pitched scream of dying thrusters dragged Dex's narrowed gaze from his preflight checklist to the crimson heavens, where the sleek silver ovule of a Valyrian cruiser spiraled across the sunset sky, the purple pulse of its psi-powered cannons pounding away pointlessly at empty air. A classic indication of his father's biological novicide—his *Valyrensis novicida*—eating away at the command crew's brains.

The streamlined spacecraft twisted into a death spiral that culminated in a holocaust of heliotrope fire in the Mogadon mountains, etched stark against the bloody sky. Dex's heart contracted with a wrenching spasm of grief.

Are you on that ship, Ben Nero? Or on the flagship, the Precursor's ship, the ship raining megaton warheads of psi-powered death on the southern cities, the ship I'll have to shoot out of the sky whether you're aboard or not?

His boyhood friend. His oathsworn brother. His closest ally in the youth ashram, where they'd been packed off in that laughably futile bid to build interracial tolerance.

Or did my father kill you weeks ago when he unleashed his novicide on the Valyrian homeworld?

Ben Nero with his psychic gifts and his flamboyant charm and his effortless ability to inspire indulgent affection in everyone he'd ever met. Ben Nero with his violet eyes and his silken hair and his secret smile that promised forbidden favors which Dex, with his emphatically masculine Mogadon DNA, had never known how to ask for.

Nor even how to name.

Between his bottled-up anguish over Ben Nero's unknown fate and his smothered guilt over the grief for his tyrannical father he should have felt but didn't, Dex's head was a space wreck.

He prayed it wouldn't fatally affect his judgment in battle.

Firmly banishing the past from the present, Dex slanted his head to fire his next barrage at the comm unit strapped to his wrist.

"Alpha wing, I want you in the air. Beta, Delta, be ready to launch on my command. Epsilon wing, I want you on standby in the stratosphere playing active defense against any Valyrian vessel that slips past our assault on the flagship. All wings, give me atomic torpedoes in the tubes with safety tethers engaged until we clear the thermosphere."

He'd just swung several rungs higher up the chain of command than his current rank merited. But he knew that Beta and Epsilon would follow him, with their own commanders offworld running scout patrols off Parthon. And the wing commander of Delta had always been diplomatically deferential to Max Draven's favorite son.

Planting a resolute boot on the Zephyr's boarding ladder while he assumed his flight helmet, Dex sliced an assessing glance across the tarmac to gauge his wing's readiness. Good pilots to a man, they'd be in orbit in less than ten ticks.

He was lowering the helmet over his head when a knot of activity surrounding a Sirocco scout shuttle caught his eye.

A knot of activity with a distinctly furtive air.

Suddenly Dex's battle sense was tingling.

By rights he ought to report the anomaly to spaceport security and get himself aloft. But someone had just cyber-bombed the main reactor and wiped out the dome. And intel whispered it was an inside job.

A Mogadon job.

For no logical reason, Dex found himself quietly lowering his helmet to the tarmac, checking the blaster holstered at his hip, and slipping across the flight deck toward the concealment of a blocky maintenance drone. Overhead, the first steely streaks of outbound Zephyrs, silent but for the hiss of displaced air, sliced across the darkening sky.

Dex himself needed badly to be among them. But there wasn't a pilot in the Empire he couldn't outfly. He'd catch up with his wing before they reached the exosphere.

The bulky concealment of the maintenance drone, tagged out and off grid for the night shift, rose before him. He eased his head cautiously around the battered neptunium casing to scope out the oddly furtive scene near the shuttle.

A scene that failed utterly to compute.

At a glance, the scrum of dreadlocked disreputables of all genders loitering about the Sirocco in their battle-scarred fighting leathers and space boots looked like dead ringers for Syndax pirates. Except for the irrefutable fact that the Syndax were emphatically outlaws—bloody nuisances to the Pax Mogadon—and expressly unwelcome on any civilized world.

But what truly confounded Dex were the three men in Mogadon uniforms racing the scout ship through its preflight checklist.

Men he knew.

Men he trusted.

Men who were, in fact, the First Indomitable's very own indispensable right-hand men.

Make that ex-First Indomitable, Dex corrected grimly. Fighting back the blistering surge of aching loss and furious incomprehension and anguished betrayal that short-circuited his system every blasted time he allowed himself to contemplate his father's friend. His father's murderer. Not to mention his own trusted mentor, his boyhood hero and the man Dex himself would be obliged to slaughter in the fighting pit come sunup.

And if these particular men with their particular loyalties were stealthily launching a getaway ship twelve clicks before the leader they revered was sentenced to meet Mogadon justice—just after some traitorous insider had sabotaged the reactor and torpedoed the dome—those factors could only possibly comprise one unavoidable truth.

Damnation.

Dex's battle sense was bloody *screaming*—

Even before he felt the unmistakable mass of a powerful body looming over him from behind. A cascade of warm breath spilled into his ear.

"Howdy, Dex," a familiar voice whispered. "Do me a solid and shimmy around real slow. I don't wanna have to hurt you."

Heart thudding like a Mogadon war drum, Dex eased into a slow pivot. Which indeed brought him eyeball to eyeball with his nemesis.

His teacher. His friend. His idol. His enemy.

"Zorin," he scraped out, feeling as though he were choking.

"Take it easy, kid." Looming larger than life a good cubit plus over Dex, the ex-First Indomitable of the Mogadon Empire stood deceptively at ease with booted legs spread.

Holding a blaster leveled squarely at Dex's chest.

Dex's eyes skated over the sinewed thighs encased in fighting leathers, the powerful abs and chest framed in an open uniform jacket that had to be at least three sizes too small, and finally the craggy features and square jaw and aqua-blue eyes of his father's killer. Crowned with an unruly thatch of sandy hair sprinkled with silver—hair the legendary First Indomitable had always worn a whisker too long and too unruly for regulation.

One corner of Zorin's full-lipped mouth lifted in a grin.

And Dex Draven, favorite son of the Third Indomitable, youngest wing commander in Empire history and relentlessly heterosexual Mogadon male to the last chromosome of his DNA, felt the same confused rush of tongue-tied, tingling heat he'd always felt every blooming time his boyhood idol smiled.

Blast. I thought I'd outgrown this dangerous nonsense. He's my father's killer, for Neptune's sake.

Dex dragged his wits together. "What the devil are you doing out of your cell?"

"Spoken like a true tyrant," Zorin said, blaster fixed firmly in place. "You're growing up to be more like Max every day. Just a chip off the old block."

"I suppose that means you'll want to butcher me in my bed as well. And I'm properly addressed as *commander*."

"Keep your voice down, *Commander*." Zorin's eyes flashed silver with caution as a phalanx of uniformed legions trotted past. He angled his big body so his blaster stayed hidden. "I don't wanna kill you—either in your bed or out of it. Which is why I'm splitting before our scheduled go-round in the fighting pit."

"You're escaping," Dex said bitterly. "And it's immaterial to you that you've exposed this planet to the full wrath of the Precursor and the vengeful Valyrian fleet."

"They're a dying race. Your dad saw to that." Zorin's massive chest heaved in a sigh. "I guess you'll finish the job he started. But I won't be hanging around to watch."

"Because you're a coward as well as a traitor?" Dex lashed out, voice dripping with contempt.

"Come on, kid. How many times have we fought together, back to back, hip-deep in the shit? I'm no coward and you know it."

A hundred memories seared through him. Memories of battles fought and triumphs shared. Under the weight of those treacherous memories, Dex's hard-won poise fractured like ice under a chainsaw.

His voice splintered, edges sharp enough to draw blood.

"Then why won't you face me in battle? Why won't you allow me at least the chance to—to avenge his honor and mine? Knowing if you win—knowing if you kill me—knowing it's over and done under Mogadon law and you'll keep your rank and your freedom. Even knowing you're my equal in combat."

"Wouldn't be a fair fight. Sure, you're smart and strong and fast on your feet in a fracas. I trained you myself, didn't I? Five years from now, maybe, when you got a little more meat on you? Then we'll be equals."

"Then you've no reason under the sun not to fight!" Dex pulled in a frustrated breath and, to his utter alarm, felt his eyes burn with thoroughly unmanly tears. "I simply can't—can't understand why…"

"Comets, Dex. Don't do that." Looking helpless, Zorin lowered the blaster and eased a step closer. "Don't cry, for the love of Juno. I can stand anything from you but tears."

Dex scowled fiercely to force back this unseemly weakness he flatly refused to tolerate. "Then you tell me *why*. I *deserve* to know why."

"Stars, kid. You don't wanna know why. You really, really don't." Zorin heaved a heavy sigh and braced one muscled arm against the drone beside Dex's head. His eyes darkened to navy and a shiver slid down Dex's spine. Suddenly, for no earthly reason, his heart was pounding and his entire body was tingling.

"Tell me why," Dex whispered stubbornly. His voice gone deep and husky for reasons he still couldn't fathom.

"You really want me to say it, do ya? After keeping my big mouth shut all this time? Well, hell with it," Zorin muttered. "Remember you asked for this."

And just leaned in and kissed him.

That singular moment was so extraordinary, so astonishing, so wildly unexpected that Dex stood as though frozen in carbonite and just let him do it. He gripped the man's waist to… push him away of course, that went without saying, and forcefully…

But the unprecedented feel of hot sleek skin rippling over miles of solid muscle right under his hands sucked every molecule of oxygen from his lungs.

Dex voiced a startled syllable of what was surely protest. Which gave the other man all the opportunity he needed to groan in response and deepen the kiss. One big hand engulfed the back of Dex's head to ease him closer. The slick heat of tongue meeting tongue shot through him like a stimulant, spiked with the peaty burn of Mogadon whiskey.

Filling the air between them, the predatory musk of Mogadon mating scent rose dark and potent.

Dex clutched him harder… in protest, this was *protest*… and their hips crashed together. Desire blasted through every determined barrier he'd built around his heart with the force of fifty Gs of thrust. Desire for *him*.

Zorin.

The hero he'd worshipped with a boy's innocence.

The soldier he'd craved with a man's passion.

An inferno of craving simultaneously stoked and smothered by years of desperate denial, suspended halfway between gratitude and despair when his shameful longing for what no red-blooded Mogadon male should ever want from another man stayed firmly unrequited. He'd finally managed to convince himself it was a boy's crush on a teacher he lionized.

A crush he'd outgrown years ago.

Until now.

Throbbing with passion and blind with need, Dex grappled to haul the man closer. Gods on the mountain, how he *needed*—

The *whoom* of a distant explosion jarred him to his senses. Dex summoned a superhuman effort and wrenched violently free, dragging the oxygen his lungs were starving to breathe past lips tingling with heat. Yet for some blasted reason, he still felt powerless to speak or move while Zorin leaned his forehead against Dex's and panted.

"Well, that's pretty much why," Zorin said wryly, shattering the spellbound silence. "Any questions?"

Far too late, Dex found his tongue. "What in the seven bloody *hells* was that? Are you trying to get us both *killed*?"

"It's okay, kid." Zorin heaved a sigh. "Your dad's not calling the shots on military morals around here anymore, is he?"

Rendered speechless with stupefaction, Dex could only stammer.

And pray with frantic fervor that no one had seen that catastrophe of a kiss.

He should be bloody outraged and offended as blazes. He *was* outraged and offended as blazes, damn it. In the army, male-male couplings were capital offenses. With his own late father the Empire's most rigorous enforcer.

Even a kiss like that could get them both crucified.

That bastard was mocking him, that's precisely what this was. His father's killer was eluding Mogadon justice. Now his father's killer was mocking him. Mocking this childish, unmanly, un-Mogadon infatuation it seemed Dex hadn't managed to hide and still hadn't—quite—outgrown.

Rage bloomed in his head. A rage born of withering shame. A rage directed equally against Zorin and himself.

"Zorin, dude, will you stop horsing around with that space cadet." Without warning, a dreadlocked head poked around the maintenance drone. "Precursor's entered orbit with guns blazing. And *Relentless*—she's all fired up in the troposphere and ready to rumble. Either your boyfriend's part of the package, or you gotta say sayonara."

Humiliation scorched the back of Dex's neck. His scandalized outrage at being called any man's *boyfriend*, as though he were some bloody catamite, was eclipsed only by the shock of sudden comprehension as the full brazen outline of his former hero's escape plan zoomed into focus.

"You're stealing the *Relentless*?" Dex's appalled gaze swung from the tattooed Syndax back to Zorin. "She's a damn retired Tornado-class battleship. She'll never clear orbit. She's scheduled for the scrap heap!"

Zorin waved off the Syndax and lifted one shoulder in a rueful shrug. "Yeah, well, so am I. Listen, Dex—I gotta skedaddle."

"Like bloody hell you are," Dex said furiously. "I'm taking you to spaceport security straightaway—"

The blow he never saw coming, a crisp clip from the butt of Zorin's blaster, collided with his temple and knocked him sprawling. He fought to get his wobbly legs under him, the spaceport swirling with light and sound. Zorin's powerful arms eased him gently to the tarmac.

"Sorry about that, Dex. Afraid you're gonna have a real thumper of a headache. Try to forgive me for all this someday, will ya?" Dimly, the wretch's voice reached him through a telescoping tunnel of darkness.

Dex struggled to articulate the merest whisper of the incandescent fury that consumed him. "Never forgive… *never*…"

"Yeah, I pretty much figured." Zorin's resigned sigh chased him down into blackness. "See you around, kid."

As Zorin's big-shouldered frame receded in his kaleidoscoped vision, Dex wrestled desperately to hold the swirling oblivion at bay.

#

Zorin was hauling tail up the Sirocco's boarding ramp, while wings of Zephyrs streaked past overhead and psi-powered missiles rained down around him like parade confetti, when the shrill whine of a blaster made him duck and curse.

A blue burst of laser fire ripped over his head to burn a hole in the shuttle's blast shields.

He hunkered down and powered up the ramp, sneaking a peek over his shoulder as he bolted. He caught a single skewed glimpse of a formidable figure in uniform black, blazing with tawny hair and rows of gleaming buttons, clutching the maintenance drone for balance and unsteadily raising a blaster.

Zorin was two ticks from shelter when the next burst caught his shoulder and spun him around, gasping under the searing burn of impact.

By sheer stubborn luck he managed to fall into the cockpit rather than off the ramp onto the tarmac. While the world went blurry and soft around him, friendly arms hauled him to safety and retracted the ramp. The engine throbbed beneath him and the floor tilted gently as the Sirocco lifted off.

And for the next eight years, while the ex-First Indomitable of the Mogadon Empire achieved lasting notoriety in the outer colonies as the scourge of the galaxy, head honcho of that galactic menace, the Syndax horde, Zorin would wonder if his former student—a crack marksman and compulsive perfectionist at every pastime to which he ever applied himself—had been trying not to kill him.

Or if he'd really meant to see Zorin dead.

Wanna read the rest of this MMMF steamy Star Wars adventure?
Interstellar Angel is available now in KU and print!
Read INTERSTELLAR ANGEL now!

Other Laura Navarre Adventures Now Available from Ascendant Press:
Anticipated Angel: An Astral Heat MM New Adult Novella Prequel
Interstellar Angel: An Astral Heat Romance #1
Renegade Angel: An Astral Heat Romance #2
Atomic Angel: An Astral Heat Romance #3

Or binge the complete series with The Astral Heat Romance Box Set

About The Author

Amazon category bestselling author Laura Navarre (she/her) is the sexy psychic why-choose romance author for smart and fearless readers like you! She offers intense and steamy out-of-this world adventure with powerful heroines who don't have to choose, passionate prose that packs a punch, and enough male/male heat to set your spacesuit on fire.

A long time ago in a galaxy far away, Laura wrote dark fantasy romance for Harlequin, while her sinister twin Nikki Navarre wrote sexy spy romance. Now, with fourteen sexy stories released worldwide, this Washington, DC-based nomad writes erotic paranormal and sci fi action romance featuring bi heroes, badass heroines, and truckloads of poly heat.

Laura is a cat lover, globetrotter, wine addict, PhD student, and president of Ascendant Press. When she isn't conjuring witchy worlds, she's a diplomat with a professional background in weapons of mass destruction and an MFA in writing popular fiction. She's a 2009 Golden Heart finalist, two-time winner of the Golden Pen, winner of the Pacific Northwest Writers Association romance award and many RWA awards. She's also relentlessly obsessive, alarmingly efficient, and a recovering perfectionist. She's deeply suspicious of the Oxford comma, but she's never met an em dash she doesn't love.

Stalk Laura across the galaxy like a space pirate you're sworn to shoot from the skies! Her adventures across the witching world are trackable by witches, warlocks, humans, and aliens alike at:
http://www.LauraNavarreSciFi.com
https://www.facebook.com/LauraNavarreAuthor
https://www.tiktok.com/@LauraNavarreAuthor
https://amzn.to/3FrX5t7
https://www.bookbub.com/authors/laura-navarre
http://www.goodreads.com/LauraNavarre